WILDEST FOREVER

LOVELOCK BAY
BOOK THREE

ASHLEE ROSE

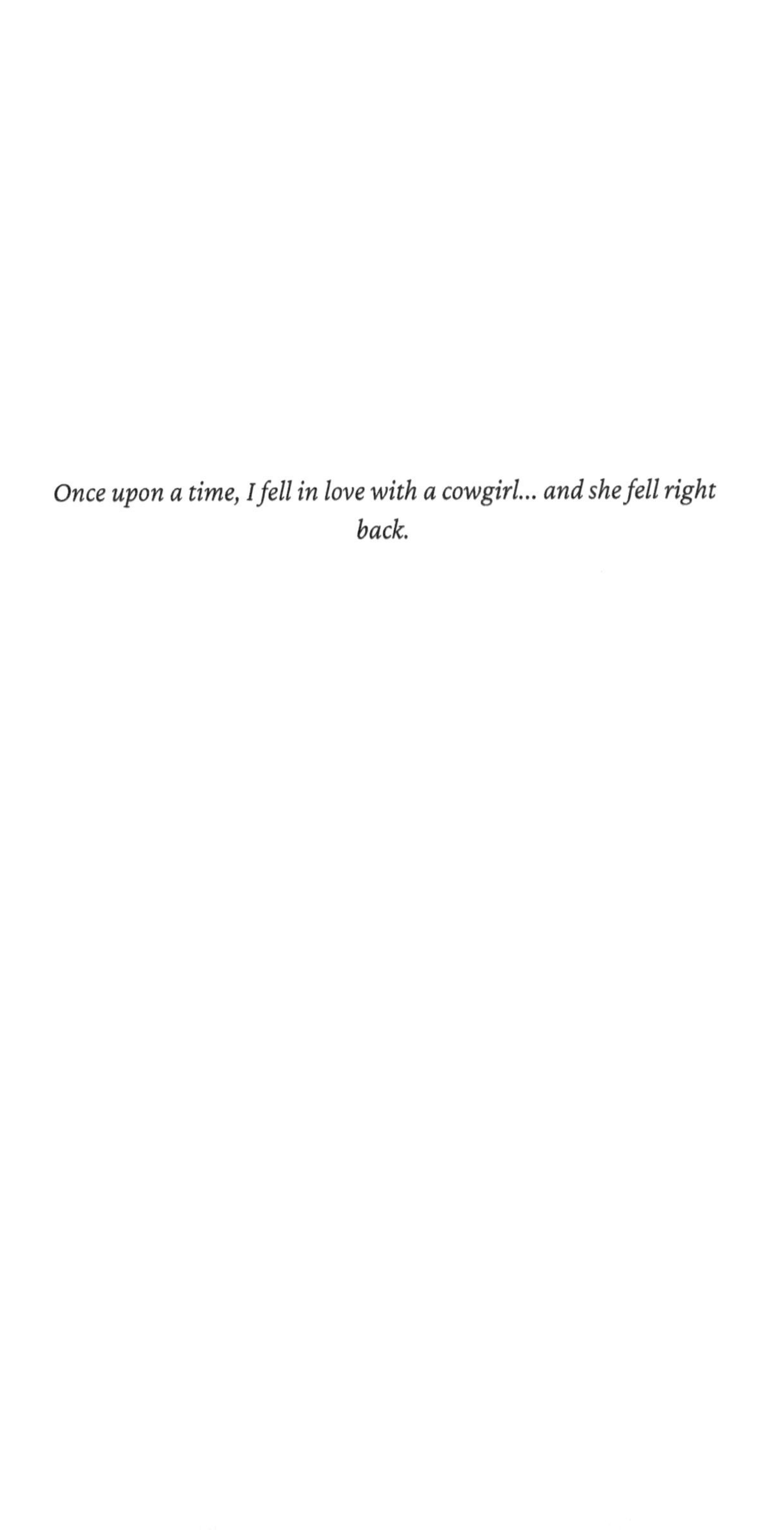

Once upon a time, I fell in love with a cowgirl... and she fell right back.

TRIGGER WARNING

Trigger Warning:

Terminal Illness
Death caused by terminal illness

OTHER BOOKS BY ASHLEE ROSE

STANDALONES

Unwanted

Promise Me

Savage Love

Tortured Hero

Something Worth Stealing

Dear Heart, You Screwed Me

Signed, Sealed, Baby

DUET

Way Back When Duet

NOVELLAS

Rekindle Us

Your Dirty Little Secret

A Savage Reunion

RISQUÉ READS

Seeking Hallow

Craving Hex

Seducing Willow

Wanting Knox

Pursuing Hartley

Tempting Klaus

Valentine Belle

ILLICIT LOVE SERIES

The Resentment

The Loathing

The Betrayal

The Revenge

LOVELOCK BAY SERIES

Wildest Love

Wildest Dreams

SINFUL READS

Sinful Brothers

Sinful Affair

Sinful Doctor

Sinful Enemies

Sinful Nanny

Sinful Temptation

All available on Amazon Kindle Unlimited

Only suitable for 18+ due to nature of the books.

PLAYLIST

Dirt Cheap - Cody Johnson
Indigo - Sam Barber, Avery Anna
You look like you love me - Ella Langley, Riley Green
Beneath Oak Trees - Dylan Gossett
C'mon Cowgirl - Cody Johnson
Wreckage - Nate Smith
Cowgirls - Morgan Wallen, ERNEST
Straight and Narrow - Sam Barber
Save You a Seat - Alex Warren
No Horse To Rise - Luke Grimes
Don't Mind If I Do - Riley Green, Ella Langley
Love Somebody - Morgan Wallen
Slow Dance In A Parking Lot - Jordan Davis
Life With You - Kelsey Hart
Country Boy's Dream Girl - Ella Langley
In Your Love - Tyler Childers
Fall Into Me - Forest Blakk
The Fall - Cody Johnson

You can grab the playlist HERE, or through the QR code <3

PROLOGUE
PACEY

We incorporated the wedding with the cow branding. Call us crazy, but us Riveras like to be different. We branded the calves in the morning, lunched, danced and then just as the sun was about to set, we watched Aspen and Riggs get married.

The soft country voice of Dixie rolls over the field, her fingers working her guitar as she sings Riggs and Aspen's first dance *Invisible String - Taylor Swift*.

Tripp is dancing with my mom and Lainey, Conrad is dancing with Sunny, and Austin is dancing with his mom.

Me? I am sitting alone on a bale of hay whilst nursing a whiskey.

I know I'll get my happily ever after, but for now, I have too much to do to save my ranch, to save all the ranches.

I haven't wanted to stress Riggs and Tripp out with the news that I have heard, but the sale of land is moving forward, along with the second biggest ranch, Cottonwheel Ranch, just outside of Lovelock Bay.

I have a meeting with Mr Wheeler at the beginning of

next week and I am hoping we can work together to finally squash these suits once and for all, because it seems this runs much deeper than just Clay and his lot.

We have a much bigger problem.

Shaking my head from side to side, I drain the rest of my glass and push myself to my feet. Slightly missing my footing, a hand reaches mine.

"Careful there, Sheriff," and my eyes connect with hers.

Dirty blonde hair hidden under a cowgirl hat.

Beautiful green eyes.

And a smile to drag you into her soul.

"I don't think we've met," she holds her hand out for me to shake, "I am Morgan Wheeler."

"Pacey Rivera..." and just as our hands clasp, the ground begins to tremor before a loud bang echoes around the ranch followed by screams.

"I don't think we caused that," her eyes widen, and I whistle, calling the cowboys and Marty. Rushing towards the stables, I grab my horse, Morgan hot on my tail as she grabs one of my boys' horses and I kick him on, following the still echoing bang and it doesn't take me long to find out what caused it.

"Shit," I groan as I look at the old back entrance of the gold mine that runs under the ranch blown, smoke coming through the ground.

"What's happened?" she whispers, just as Marty and the boys catch us up. I look at them before my eyes find hers, and I honestly could lose myself in them.

"They've started a war," I tilt my head, before opening the rein to my horse and kicking him down the field towards Riggs and Tripp.

And I know this is going to be the biggest fight of our

lives. The breeze dances around me as I gallop towards the party when my dad's words echo around my head.

Live by the ranch, die by the ranch.

CHAPTER ONE
PACEY

My heavy feet move through the wildflowers that are in full bloom, my fingertips brushing against the delicate flowers. My chest aches slightly as I move closer to the large, oak tree that stands tall at the bottom of the field. Inhaling sharply, tears burn behind my eyes as I glance down at the wooden cross that is dug into the soft dirt beneath me, a gold plaque polished on the front.

Jorge Rivera

My exhale shudders as I curl my fingers around the top of the cross, my heart a little heavier now as I drop my head, my hat falling to my feet and I don't bend to pick it up.

"I miss you dad," I whisper into the wind that dances through the branches of the oak tree and I know he is here, he is always here with us. "Things aren't quite the same, and I am terrified that the war on the land has only really just begun." I mutter my thoughts out loud, softly.

Letting my eyes close for a moment, I inhale heavily when I feel a grip on my shoulder, a soft squeeze has my eyes lifting, casting behind me and my heart settles deep inside my chest when I see Buck standing there.

"Son," the quietness of his voice causes my skin to erupt in goosebumps and I can't even hold back the tears as the raspiness of his voice hits me right between the shoulder blades, winding me in an instant.

I turn, seeking him out and I don't care that I am a thirty-year old man, I throw myself into his body as the tears soak through his sky blue checkered shirt. His arms envelope me, holding me tight.

No words are said.

He just lets me sob into his chest, comforting me like I am a little boy who needs his dad.

But that was just it.

I did need my dad.

He wasn't here.

My chest rattles as I suck in a breath before I feel it cave in, the unbearable ache presenting itself.

"It's okay, it's okay," he soothes me, his head bowing and I feel his nose on the top of my head as he inhales heavily.

I have no idea how long I stand in his embrace, but it felt like time had stopped still.

It was only me and him.

The sound of a branch cracking underneath a boot has me lifting my head and looking over Buck's shoulder to see three men standing in suits, head tilted as they take in the scene in front of them.

I move back, sniffling as I do, quickly picking up my cowboy hat and place it back on my head as I try and hide my red rimmed eyes.

"What do we owe the pleasure," Buck spins, hands in the front of his dirty denim jeans as he steps forward, head tilting to the side and he sizes up the three guys in front of him.

"Here to talk about taking this land off you."

And Buck lets out a throaty laugh.

"Then we have nothing to talk about," he gives a soft nod as I step up behind him, but he holds his arm out, silently telling me to stay where I am.

"Come on, you surely don't want to run all of this land at your age," the tallest one looks down at Buck before giving his two suited friends a toss of the head and a laugh.

"It's *my* land," I find myself saying, tilting my head higher, thumbs hooked into my belt and the low afternoon sun reflects off my sheriff badge.

His eyes fall to it then settle back on mine.

"Okay, let us take it off you then," his lips twitch as his fingers flex around the handle of his briefcase and I shake my head.

"I can't do that I'm afraid," I go to step forward, but Buck stops me again.

"What does this land have over you apart from a few cows, horses and a wooden house?"

I suck in a breath, rage burning beneath my skin and Buck drops his head for a moment before lifting it and glancing at the rolling hills.

"What does this land have over us?" I repeat the words and I clench my fist by my side.

"Yeah?" the one beside the main guy looks at me, and I see the softness that flashes across his eyes.

Buck lets out a shaky breath before speaking. "This land isn't *just* land. It's so much more than that. It's where my daughter grew up, it's where my son grew up and still lives, working on this land every day, it's where my family are, my friends, my blood..." Buck trails off and this time he lets me stand beside him, my shoulders rolled back and my chest pressed a little further out. "It's where we make a living. Sure, it's tough at times with the harsh winters and the constant rising costs of living, but we make it work. We have to. This is not just land, it's a choice, it's a home, it's our life." Buck continues and his eyes slice across all three of them.

"My best friend, who's land you are standing on, he is buried under the oak tree, he is part of the soil, part of this land, this is *home*. This is his. His body is buried with the place he loved the most, so in answer to your question, what does land have over us..." Buck turns to look at me, "it has everything over us. We live and breathe this land."

I nod, stepping forward.

"As my father imprinted onto us, *live by the ranch, die by the ranch.*"

Silence breezes around us for just a moment.

"You can't hold onto it forever," the main guy says.

"We will hold onto it for as long as we can. When I'm gone, I'll be buried next to my friend, along with my wife and his, but our kids will live on, our grandkids will run these fields, and when they're old enough they will also run this land, and so on, so forth..." Buck inhales heavily.

"So I suggest you go back to whatever hole you came out of and fuck off our land, because at the moment you are trespassing and we have every right to remove you from our land with any means necessary..." and I open up my bodywarmer to show my pistol that sits tucked in my rib holster.

"And with the law here by my side... well, we can hide you and make you disappear just like that," Buck clicks his fingers and we watch as he swallows, his throat bobbing and his two friends begin to move back.

"Tell whoever sent you we're not selling. We already have enough to deal with, we don't need three jumped up assholes trying to push us into selling land. Land that has been in our family for years, it's our heritage... try all the land owners, they will all tell you the same thing."

The main guy steps forward whilst the other two shrink back.

"This isn't over old man," and he stands toe to toe with Buck.

Buck chuckles, his shoulder lifting up and down, his fingers brushing back and forth over his lips.

"I don't take threats lightly," Buck replies, his voice low so only me and the suit can hear.

"This isn't a threat," suit grits his teeth.

"Oh, it is," Buck nods, his lips curling into a soft smile.

"We could have done this amicably, but it seems that isn't an option so we will move onto phase two," suit flares his nostrils before looking over his shoulder as he hears footsteps approaching.

Relief swarms me at the sight of my brothers walking towards us.

Riggs and Tripp.

Riggs tall, stocky, broad shoulders.

Tripp a slimmer build to Riggs, a little shorter too.

Riggs' cowboy hat lifted slightly, Tripp's brown hair blowing softly in the summer breeze.

My lips twitch into a smirk, and I watch Buck's shoulders visibly relax.

"Gentleman," Riggs' loud voice echoes around the empty fields and I have no idea why he is addressing them as gentleman. They're vermin.

The taller suit turns to look over his shoulder and I

watch as his eyes scope over my two brothers, Tripp's eyes are locked on mine and I give him a gentle nod.

"Who are you?" he shoots his question to Riggs and he chuckles, his shoulders vibrating as he does.

"The owner of this land."

I feel my stomach twist.

Because it's the truth.

He is the man of the house.

The land is technically Riggs'.

It was always going to be like that.

"Is that so?" suit eyes me and Buck over his shoulder before they're back on Riggs.

"Yup," his hands fold into the front of his worn jeans, his eyes narrowing on the suit in front of him.

"We want the land," the suit says it how it is, shooting straight for Riggs' throat, but he just whistles through his teeth before turning his head and looking at the rolling green hills.

"Yeah," he says on a sigh, his brown eyes connecting with the suit, "that won't happen."

"No?"

"No." Riggs' softer side has been tucked away as the low growl of a rumble drifts across.

"Like I said to the guys behind me," he pauses for a moment and glares at his two silent friends. "We will get our hands on this land."

Riggs laughs again but this time shakes his head from side to side as one of his hands slips from the pocket of his jeans and pulls on his beard.

"Okay," he rolls his lips, amusement dancing through his eyes and Tripp steps forward, his eyes moving between me and Riggs.

"There is only so long you can hold onto this, the plans are already in motion for what we are doing with it."

"I know the Governor who would have to sign off the plans, I really am not worried," Riggs glares at the suit, his gaze narrowing.

"Okay," suit nods then whistles, and his two lap dogs follow him as he knocks into Riggs' shoulder and scoffs a laugh as he does. I see the way Riggs' shoulders rise, his nostrils flare and his fingers bend into his fist.

"Calm it," I hear the way Tripp says softly to Riggs knowing that he is about three seconds from exploding and ripping the suits limb from limb and burying them at the bottom of the field.

Hot ragged breaths flare from his nose, and I find myself drifting towards my big brother.

"You good?" I ask, my eyes pinned to the back of the three suits that begin their way across the field.

"I will be as soon as these fuckers are off our land," my eyes cast up to him, his shoulders slowly dropping as the seconds pass.

"They're never going to stop," Buck says as he approaches us and I watch as Riggs finally tears his eyes away from the suits and lets them settle on his father-in-law.

"I don't give a fuck, there is no way in hell I am letting them get this land..." he pauses before casting his gaze to where our father lay buried in the ground. "It'll never fucking happen," he growls, "live by the ranch, die by the ranch," and with that he gives a heavy nod and trudges back down the fields and towards the house.

Buck places his hand on my shoulder and gives it another squeeze before he follows my brother down the field, and I sigh heavily.

"You okay?" Tripp nudges into me and I nod.

"Well... I think so," I lift my cowboy hat and run my hand through my long, dark blond hair before placing it back on my head.

"What's on your mind?"

"Everything," I admit and that ache is back in my chest and I fucking hate it.

"It's been a tough couple of years," he breathes out and I nod.

"It really has, when is life going to stop fucking us?"

"I don't think it ever will brother..." he trails off and throws his arm around my shoulders as we begin to walk back towards the house, "we just need to ride the storm; we're experts at this now." He chuckles softly and I swallow down the lump that has lodged itself in my throat.

I have no idea how to ride the storm.

But I'll try anyway.

CHAPTER TWO

Sitting in Randy's, the small saloon just on the outskirts of Lovelock Bay, my chest feels tight, my shoulders heavy.

The suits riled me up this morning, I'm not one to come to this side of town, I liked The Boot, but since that is nothing but ash on the floor, well, it's either here or my Sheriff's office. I needed noise. I needed the sound of the antique jukebox as it played John Pardy through the crackling speakers. The floor was sawdust, the bar teak wood with a solid countertop in cherry red. The room smelt of stale beer and leftover bonfire smoke.

Kind of liked it.

Marty sinks onto the stool next to me, shortly followed by Riggs and Tripp and I secretly hope Austin walks through the door, but he doesn't.

He is struggling, and as much as we try and get him out of the house, he is still very much grieving the loss of Harlow.

We all are, she left a gaping hole in all of our lives, but to Austin, her death was cataclysmic.

I swear the ground shifted beneath our feet when she left the earthly plane.

But she is being looked after by dad, and that makes the bitter pill a little easier to swallow.

"What a day," Tripp groans as he gets the attention of the barman and orders another round of whiskey over ice.

My chest rattles as I suck in a heavy breath.

"Mm," I just about muster as I drain the rest of my glass and slam it down onto the bar.

"Don't let them get to you," Riggs' deep voice breezes across me and I find myself turning my face to look at him, my breath catching at the back of my throat.

"But they get under my skin."

"That's the whole point," he smirks as he lifts his cowboy hat from his head and places it on the bar before thanking the barman with a nod of his head as he places the whiskeys in front of him.

I lift my own hat off my head and mirror my older brother's move, placing it on the bar before he slides the glass of whiskey into my hand.

"What if they get the land?" I mutter quietly so only Riggs can hear me. He looks at me, his brown eyes softening.

"They won't," his tone is a little assertive, his head lowering but his eyes burning into mine. "I promise you Pacey, they will not get this land."

I swallow down the bile that threatens to rise.

"Okay," I smile at him, but it doesn't meet my eyes. It's more out of forced habit then genuine.

"Okay," he smiles back and sits tall in his stool before he turns his attention to Tripp and Marty and I just sit and listen to their conversations whilst being lost in my own head.

My eyes skate down to his hand, the gold band wrapped around his finger, and I feel my heart pump a little harder in my chest.

I am so glad that he and Aspen ended up together, it was always him, she would have always chosen him.

I'm not mad that she wanted him over me.

But it cut me a little, especially with what happened all those years ago.

I drove her out of Lovelock Bay and that evening still haunts me.

I spilled secrets that weren't mine to spill, yet I did it because I was vicious.

I had her.

I wanted her.

But she wanted him.

Unrequited love was always the worst.

I loved her with all I had.

It was never reciprocated.

Hated that.

It burned in my bones.

Then I drove her out of Lovelock Bay only for her to return ten years later and turn everyone's worlds upside down.

But it seems everyone is spinning back on their axis, except me.

I don't think I will ever feel the same again.

Sighing, I bring my glass to my lips and take a large mouthful, wincing as the burn coats my throat.

A whistle has my head snapping up as I see Marty nudging Tripp, giving him a *fuck, look at her* look. Tripp takes his word for it, as he and Riggs don't even bat an eyelid. They're talking amongst themselves.

Furrowing my brows, I turn to look in that direction and that's when I see her.

Sunshine blonde hair, tanned skin, sea green eyes that remind me of the ocean and freckles dotted across her nose. She is slim, petite and wearing tight high waisted jeans, a sage green crew neck tee and tanned cowboy boots.

Fuck.

I swallow down my heart that has lodged itself in my throat before it's back down inside my chest and banging against my rib cage.

It's her.

The cowgirl that showed up on the day of Riggs and Aspen's wedding.

The one who took my breath away.

But after that day she disappeared.

Never to be seen again.

Until now.

Her eyes dust across the room before they land on mine, and I give her a soft head tilt, my lips twitching before I pull my eyes and turn forward, taking a sip of my whiskey.

The heel of her boots skate across the floor and I know she is walking towards me, but I don't give her the satisfaction of facing her.

"It's you," her soft voice floats across me and I roll my lips.

"It's you," I mirror her words and try to fight the tug at the corner of my lips as a smirk tries to present itself.

"Finished saving the ranch?" she teases, and I scoff a laugh as I shake my head from side to side.

"Not quite," and I focus on the bottles of whiskey that are lined up behind the bar.

"I'm sure you'll do it, Superman," my smirk defeats me

and only then do I turn to look at her, her fingers teasing the rim of my cowboy hat. "Unless you want some help?" and her teeth are bared as she widens her grin.

"I fear you'll be my kryptonite," I sigh, my eyes sweeping over her again and I watch as her head tilts slightly, eyes narrowing on me.

"Guess we'll never know," she laughs softly before swiping my hat from the bar and placing it on her head and I groan internally.

"You shouldn't have done that," I whisper, and I can hear the commotion from Riggs and Tripp behind me, Marty cussing because she isn't giving him an inch of attention.

"Why's that *cowboy*?"

"You know what they say," I curl my brow as I twist my body to face her now, playfulness flitting across my hazel eyes.

"I don't," she leans a little closer, letting her eyes fall to my lips and it takes everything in me to not lean into her. She's brazen.

"You wear that hat..."

"I ride the cowboy?" her cheeks dust pink at the words that leave her lips and I shake my head, laughing as my fingers tap against the whiskey glass.

"You belong to me, you become *mine*, Sunflower... is that what you want?"

and her grin widens.

"To be the Sheriff's girl?" she steps back, scoping me out as she looks me up and down.

My jeans dirty, tee a little grubby and my long hair swept off my face, messy and knotty after being tucked under my hat for most of the day.

"Yeah?" I tease her, knowing full well my heart isn't capable of loving another again.

The first girl wrecked me.

I'm not sure I have it in me to fall again.

"I've had worse offers," she winks at me before she lifts the hat from her head and places it on mine, "but not today cowboy, not ready to be wifed up yet," she blows me a kiss before turning her back on me and walking away, her hips swaying and I find myself staring at her peachy ass as she does.

"Fuck," I groan, rubbing my palm across my thigh and turn to look at the guys.

"Got a little crush, Pacey?" Riggs teases, a rumble of a laugh passing his lips as he drains his glass and I flip him off.

"Like fuck," I grunt, finishing my whiskey then stepping off the stool. "I'm off," I nod as I begin to walk away, and I hear the sound of footsteps closing in behind me.

"You good?" Tripp's voice wraps around me as I tug on the door, walking into the warm air before I turn and look at him.

"I will be," I smile, nodding my head before I step towards the truck. I needed my bed.

Tomorrow was a new day.

DRIVING the truck down the long and winding driveway of Cottonwheel Ranch, Blossom Cove, my heart drums in my chest. Mr Wheeler contacted me a couple of weeks ago requesting a meeting to try and stop the suits from pursuing the sale of their land, but it's not looking good.

I tried to get Tripp and Riggs to join me, but Mr Wheeler denied their help.

Apparently, he only wanted me which then makes me unsettled. Glancing out the window at the rolling green fields, I can see the tipped mountains in the distance that sit on our land.

We're close, but a town along.

After the warning explosion in our derelict mine, things started moving pretty fast.

I have arranged for a team to go into the mines and see if they can find the diamond that is apparently buried down there—the one my grandfather found and hid for safe keeping—only problem was, he hid it so well no one has found it.

It's not the land that they want.

It's what lays under the land.

What runs under our home.

Buying the rest of the land around us just makes sense, it won't be long, and our picturesque town will be filled with new homes and shopping centres making it a bigger tourist attraction than what it already was.

We were okay though, we were tucked away and didn't seem to draw any attention until Clay and his family made themselves known and that's when everything began to crumble down around us.

Pushing the truck into park, I inhale heavily then reach for my hat and place it on my head before I slip out and make my way up to their house.

A small panelled farmhouse tucked between maple trees. The step creaks beneath my boot and my brows furrow. Stepping forward, I lift my hand to knock but I don't get a chance to when I see an older man with graying thick hair and large, round glasses smiling at me.

"Pacey?" and I give him a firm nod just as he pushes his large hand out towards me, I clap it into his palm, and he gives me a firm handshake.

"Mr Wheeler?" I smile and he steps back, inviting me into his home. Crossing the threshold, I hold my breath for a second. No idea why.

I am feeling a little apprehensive, but I can't work out why.

"Tea?" he asks as he walks towards a large kitchen and I feel like I have been transported back in time.

The kitchen units are worn, slightly yellow tinge to them, the lino floor tiles are starting to peel at the corners and the walls could really do with a lick of paint to freshen the room up.

Glancing down at my boot when I hear the floor peel away from the sole, my lip curls and I try and hide the disgust on my face because I don't want to be that person.

I'm not like that.

Everyone is fighting a battle that you know nothing about.

Some are big, some are small, and I have no right to judge anyone.

"Please," I answer his question as he pops a kettle on his open topped stove before igniting the gas.

I drag one of the wooden chairs across the floor and sit down at the worn table, my eyes watching him, his hands trembling as he reaches for the tea bags, popping them into the mugs and then spins to look at me, eyes burning into my soul.

"Camomile, okay?" he asks.

I nod.

More of a coffee man myself but I am being polite.

"How are you finding being sheriff?" he asks as his

fingers curl around the edge of the chipped veneer work surface, his breaths rattling as he inhales and exhales.

"It's been okay, a little quiet at the moment but I am not complaining," I snort a soft laugh and sit further back in my seat.

"Have you managed to find out who set the explosion off in the mine?" his eyes not moving from mine and I just shake my head in response. "Make sure you check on the ones that are closest to you... it's not always the ones who you think it would be," and I give a nod, I know I can trust everyone around me. I have no worries about that.

"Will do," I murmur just as the kettle begins to whistle and that has him turning around, his shaky hands lifting it and pouring it over the teabag.

A clamber of a bang echoes as he places it back on the stove then picks up the teaspoon and stirs the teabag before straining it and dumping it on the work-surface. He picks one of the mugs up and I can see it slipping from his hands so I dart up, walking across the small space and scooping it from him, thanking him as I do. I then reach for his own as I walk back towards the table and place it down but then search for a coaster, mindful that it'll burn a ring into the untreated table.

"Don't worry about that, I'll just sand it out," and now it makes sense on why the table looks so worn.

He sands any imperfection out of it.

I watch with intent as he sits down slowly, grunting as he does.

His eyes narrow on me before they drop to the mug then back to me.

I smile softly, curling my fingers around the handle and bring the mug to my lips, blowing softly before I take a small mouthful and give him an approving nod.

"So," I say softly as I place the cup back on the table, "what do you need me for?" there is no point beating around the bush.

I watch as he inhales heavily, the crackle of his chest evident.

He looks over my shoulder to make sure the coast is clear before his eyes land on mine.

"I'm dying," he says those two words so matter of fact. I mean, I am not sure how you're meant to tell someone that you're dying, but I never imagined it to be like that.

There was no emotion to his voice.

It was cold. Hard. Like stainless steel touching my skin and it caused a shiver to dance up and down my spine.

"I'm sorry to hear that," because what am I meant to say when he tells me he is dying.

"Don't be, glad to be out of this hell hole if I am honest," he grunts as he takes his own mouthful of tea then turns his lips down in disgust. "This tastes awful."

I take another mouthful and lift a shoulder, "I think it's okay." I mean I have had better, but I am not about to tell a dying man that.

"This place is only going to get worse," he scowls as he places his mug back down.

"Blossom Cove?"

He shakes his head. "All of it, son, it's all fucked and I dread it for the generations to come."

I nod.

Because what he is saying is not a complete lie, but I don't want to deter from the conversation, I want to know what he wants.

There is a reason that he called me here.

"What did you need me for?" I ask him the question

again and wait for him to answer me this time with an actual answer.

"I need you to do something for me."

I nod, rolling my lips as I twist my mug around trying to keep my hands busy.

Nervousness blooms in my chest and it's making me antsy. My stomach is knotting and coiling and nausea threatens to ripple through.

I'm no good at being nervous.

Hate it.

I end up blurting shit out that I really don't need to, and I have caused some major issues because of my anxiety but I'm not about to rip that band aid off.

I wait for him to continue, his breaths growing ragged.

"This is all I have," he holds his hand out, palm side up as he moves it around the room.

I nod again.

"I need it kept safe, need you to get these suits off my fucking back. They're like damn backpacks and it doesn't matter how much I shrug those bastards off, they tighten around my shoulders."

"I can do that," I smile, "I am fighting them for my land too so one more ranch won't hurt," and his eyes flit away before they're back on me.

"Then there is the matter of my Morgan," and I swallow down the lump that has presented itself in my throat.

"Morgan?" and I know who she is.

The pretty blonde cowgirl that rode into Rivera Ranch like a princess.

She has plagued my thoughts for a while but not for reasons you may think.

"Yes," he sucks in a deeper breath.

"What about her?" my tone is curt, but I don't mean for it to be.

I'm tired.

"I need you to look after her too," he leans across the table so I match him, leaning into the middle, elbows resting on the surface.

"Okay, so watch the house, watch Morgan," I nod, making a mental note.

"It's not just looking after her Sheriff Rivera," his throat bobs and I see the tears line his bottom lid and my heart twists in my chest.

"No?" I breathe, brows raising in my head as I gaze at him now, too scared to lift them from his empty, blue eyes.

"I need you to take her hand... keep her safe... give her your name so they can't come after her, the house deeds will go to you too... Can you do that for me Rivera? Can you give this dying man his last wish?"

And I feel like I have been sucker punched straight in the gut, the air being snatched from my lungs.

His eyes burn into mine and I see the glisten of a tear coating his cheek.

"Please," he begs, the crack in his voice breaking my own damn heart. "Can you do that for me, Sheriff Rivera?"

I have no idea what the fuck I was thinking, but I nod, swallowing down my own tears that are threatening.

"Yes sir, I can do that."

"Can do what?" I hear the front door shut before her voice floats around the spacious hallway, drifting into the kitchen where me and her grandfather are sitting.

I stay facing forward, not quite ready to look at her as I gaze at the man who has just laid down my future.

"Pacey is going to help me out, help me keep this place safe... and you," his hands are trembling as he pushes from the seat, the sound of the wooden legs scraping across the floor and I watch cautiously, making sure he doesn't fall.

Not sure why all of a sudden I am feeling protective of him.

"Oh," her voice pitches slightly higher, the sound of her boots dusting across the worn-out floor make my ears prick and only when she has walked past me do I lift my head to look at her.

But her sights aren't on me.

They're on her grandfather who reaches his hand out and holds onto hers, tightening his grip.

My eyes scope over the back of her.

Long, wavy blonde hair, high waisted Levi jeans that are tucked into tan cowboy boots and an off-white tee that is tucked into the waistband of her jeans.

"What is he going to do to help you out?" I see as she lets her eyes skate over her shoulder, looking me up and down before she is back focused on the man in front of her.

He glances at me momentarily before his blue eyes settle on his granddaughter.

"What have you done?" and I can hear the sharpness in her tone as she drops his hand then spins with her hands on her hips as she turns to face me, head tilted to the side. "Is anyone going to tell me what's going on?" she glares at me, her boot stamping on the floor.

I sigh heavily, rubbing my hands together as I eye Mr Wheeler.

"You're getting married," he just rolls it off the tongue like it's nothing.

Her eyes widen as she glares me down as if it was my idea.

"Sorry?" her brow raises before she turns around and now puts her dagger eyes on the old man in front of her.

"I've made a decision," he nods.

"Pops..." and I can hear the panic that claws in her throat.

"It's done." He nods and then sits himself down back at the table and reaches for the now cold camomile tea and takes a mouthful, his lips turning down and he shakes his head and pushes the mug into the center of the table.

"Please..." her voice cracks but her grandfather doesn't even look at her. Just stares at me, drinking his cup of tea.

I sigh and take that as my cue to leave.

"I'll speak to my lawyer tomorrow and get the contract drafted up ready for you to sign," he speaks directly to me.

I nod, giving her one last look before I walk out of the door and climb into my truck.

Once I am sat in there, I stare at the house in front of me and let the last twenty minutes of information sink in.

Scrubbing my face, what the hell was I going to say to my mom?

I had only ever loved one woman, unfortunately, she never loved me back.

And now she is my sister-in-law.

I knew she loved Riggs. Always loved him and I knew it would never be more than what it was.

Friendship.

But if that's all I could have, then I would take it with both hands.

Starting the engine, I put the truck into reverse before swinging it into the turning point and boot it down the long, winding drive like a bat out of hell.

Times like this I would have gone to The Boot, but I couldn't do that, so I head for my office in the lazy town of Lovelock Bay and sink a glass of whiskey to calm my nerves.

I had agreed to marry a girl so her grandfather knew she would be safe, so he knew his ranch would live on, his legacy somehow.

But the fear soon crept in, swallowed by anxiety.

What if I had made a huge mistake?

What if I couldn't keep her safe?

What if I lost it all?

What if...

CHAPTER THREE
MORGAN

I paced up and down the hallway, I had no idea what to do.

I could run? Pack my bags and start fresh, but let's be honest, it would break my grandfather's heart.

He has arranged for me to marry a Rivera.

It could be worse, I mean, it could *always* be worse.

He wasn't bad looking, but the family had a reputation... and not a good one.

They've been so wrapped up in the land scandal and murders for a while and now my hand was being given to him.

The sheriff of Lovelock Bay.

"Morgan," I hear the sound of my pops' voice, and my heart shatters inside my chest, the aching makes it cave in on itself and I find myself catching my breath as I stop, turning to face him.

I let my eyes roam over his tired face. Wrinkled, pale skin and dull eyes. Hated it. Hated that the only man who ever loved me and I have loved back is getting old.

"I am doing this for you," his voice trembles and I know his words are meant to make me feel better, but they don't.

"I can manage by myself," I snap at him and look out of the window at the low sun and the rolling green hills that wrap around the bottom of the mountains and I sigh.

"What about the horses? The heifers? What about all of this?" I stammer.

"Sheriff Rivera will take care of it all, you don't need to worry."

I laugh. "Oh good, so because you said I don't need to worry… I shouldn't worry!?" and my stomach knots almost instantly as the words leave my lips.

"Morgan," his tone is gravelly, and I shake my head from side to side.

"Just tell me why…" and my voice cracks just as a knock on the front door pulls my attention but I ignore it and focus on my pops.

I know it's just Dusty, my fellow cowboy.

"Tell me," and that's when I see his eyes shift before he focuses on me and I see the tears that threaten to fall and my heart can't take it, it throbs inside my chest, the ache presenting itself.

"I'm dying, Morgan."

And his words slice through me like a knife, splitting me in two but before I can even try and soothe the pain, the air from my lungs is knocked from me and I find myself gasping for breath, begging for air and I feel like I am suffocating whilst the knife is lodged and twisted deep within my windpipe.

"It's okay," he moves closer to me and I see the trail of tears that stain his cheeks and I feel like my whole world has been turned upside down with three words.

I'm dying, Morgan.

"It's not okay," I choke, my eyes brimming with my own tears. "I have lost everyone, you're my whole world pops." He continues moving closer to me, his hand cupping my cheek.

"I know my sweet girl, but these are the facts... hence why I am trying to get all of this into motion. You won't be able to do this on your own."

My bottom lip trembles, chin wobbling and I blink and that's when the tears spill.

"Don't leave me," I throw myself into him as he wraps his arms around me.

"I'll hold on for as long as I can," and I hear the way his voice cracks.

"I'm twenty-three pops, I've already had so much loss in my life, I can't lose you too..."

He just holds me as my tears soak through his shirt. I wasn't lying.

He was my whole world.

And now my whole world was about to implode into nothing but dust.

<hr>

THE EVENING SOON CREEPS AROUND. I am laying on my bed, eyes pinned to the ceiling and I have no idea what to do, but the truth was, I couldn't do anything.

I had to honor his wishes.

He was doing this for me. For the ranch. To save us from the suits.

But I was worried that it was too little too late.

A handsome, suited and booted guy turned up three months ago selling my pops the dream, he ate it up.

Why wouldn't he?

He needed to pay for his treatment somehow.

I knew he was ill.

Just never knew *how* ill he was.

My intake of breath shudders from all the tears I have cried, and I know I have dried myself out.

Turning on my side, I look at my ajar bedroom door.

The house is silent and in darkness apart from the glow of the bathroom light.

I didn't want to live here without pops, but I knew I had no choice.

He was leaving me.

I was going to run the ranch with Dusty and Pacey.

I had no idea if Pacey even wanted to run a ranch when he not only had his own ranch to run but he was also sheriff for the whole of Lovelock Bay, why would he want to help us out too?

No idea what my pops promised him, no idea if he paid him money to take my hand, but the deal was set.

Paperwork was to be sent over tomorrow, the ranch being put into mine and Pacey's name.

Better than just mine apparently.

It would be safer with the Rivera name dotted on the line.

Sighing, I roll back over so my eyes are pinned to the ceiling.

It could be worse.

I could have been married off to Dusty if he didn't already have a wife.

My nose crinkles.

Not that there is anything wrong with Dusty, but he isn't my type.

Pacey on the other hand.

Feel like he is a sunshine boy, a good boy, the kind that

still opens doors and kisses you on the forehead. The kind that would still give you butterflies ten years on.

I always thought I would meet someone and fall in love slowly, letting everything seep beneath the surface.

But that wouldn't happen.

A quickie marriage before my pops takes his last dying breath.

My mind drifts back to Randy's, the night I saw him sitting with his brothers, nursing a whiskey.

The brazenness of me as I walked towards the bar, my eyes were set on him from the moment I walked into that room.

I met him a few months back, we were invited to Riggs and Aspen's wedding.

Didn't know them, but my pops was invited. Kind of keeping peace between the neighbours and all that.

I rocked up, spotted Pacey from a mile off.

Something about him drew me in. He seemed haunted and I always seemed to gravitate towards the boys who had been through stuff.

Not sure why. I don't even have experience, kind of liked the flirting then backed away.

Maybe because my life hasn't been perfect and I find myself gravitating to the ones who are in similar situations to me.

He seemed like a loner.

Like he has been hurt before and maybe it was because I thought I could fix him. I liked the challenge, and he seemed like he would keep me occupied for a while.

Tapping my fingers on my stomach I ponder what my life may be like in the next coming months.

As long as he made me happy and kept me safe, this would be fine.

Once the initial threat is done, we could get a quickie annulment and be on our way with our lives.

Pops' ranch would be safe and so would Rivera Ranch, plus having the sheriff in my pocket didn't seem like a bad thing.

Inhaling heavily, my chest rattled.

It was all going to work out the way it was supposed to.

I believed in all of that.

Everything happens for a reason. Your path is laid out in front of you... but sometimes you have to take the dirt track or hit a few speed bumps along the way.

This is all this was.

A speed bump.

A minor inconvenience.

Swinging my legs off the bed, I nodded to the empty room and padded towards the bathroom.

It was late but I needed to wash the day off me, then hopefully, sleep would come before I was up at four, starting my day.

I wake, groggy as hell and my eyes feel like they have grit in them. I dropped off about one, woke at three.

I thought I always had a plan, and honestly, I was never sure a husband was in that plan.

I wasn't even sure that I wanted kids.

Just wanted to keep the ranch running enough that I could keep a roof over mine and my pops' head, as well as keep Dusty on and not turn him out of work.

He was only young, well, a bit older than me maybe but still. He had a young family and the last thing I wanted to do was to take food off his table. Turning the faucet on, the old pipes banging through the house as I cup my hands under where the water spurts out before splashing my face.

I had no idea if it was going to wake me up, but I needed

something and I wasn't even sure coffee was going to hit the spot that it needed to. I was grouchy and I was ready for the sun to set behind the mountains so I could soak my tired body into the tub and try and relax my muscles.

But I knew that wasn't going to happen. The day was going to be full on. We had the vet, and the farrier, Conrad coming along with some buyers to potentially take a few of the calves.

Hated getting rid of them, but knew it had to be done.

We were haemorrhaging money and even with a Rivera linking us together, I still don't think I would be able to keep us afloat.

They had money, they were one of the richest ranches this side of Montana, but since Jorge died, well, I have no idea what kind of state it is in now.

Turning the tap off, I curl my fingers around the edge of the off-white sink and look at myself in the small mirror.

My eyes were hollow, my once sparkling greens were dull and lifeless and my skin looked pale.

I needed to get my shit together.

Let's rationalize this.

No, I didn't want to marry Pacey Rivera.

No, I didn't want to have to be reliant on a man.

No, I didn't want my pops to die.

But those were the facts.

He was dying.

I was going to be left alone.

In this broken-down farmhouse and a pretty poor excuse of a ranch, but it was all we had.

All I had.

This is where I grew up. It's all I knew, and as much as I hated what was about to happen, it was my job to make sure I kept the ranch going. I would not let this break down.

I would not let the suits come in and take everything from me.

This was my home.

It was my legacy.

I wasn't about to screw it all up now because of my pride.

The only man I truly loved was dying.

He was doing this for me.

His last gift before he leaves me forever.

I watch as my throat bobs, swallowing past the lump, the thickness evident and I swear if I had food in my stomach I would have thrown it up by now.

Running my toothbrush around my teeth, I clean them then scrub my face with my cleanser before wiping it from my skin with a damp cloth then patting it dry.

With one last heavy sigh, I nod to myself and walk into my bedroom, dragging my jeans up my legs and buttoning them, I pull a loose tee over my head before sitting on the edge of my bed and rooting through my bottom drawer where my socks are. Slipping on a pair of cream socks with pretty sunflowers on, I smile at the nickname Pacey muttered a few weeks back.

I knew it was just a coincidence, but still, it kind of made my heart glow a little.

Slipping my feet into my old but comfortable cowgirl boots, I push up and grab my matching tanned cowboy hat. Pulling a brush through my long blonde hair, I tug at the knots before placing my cowgirl hat on my dressing table. Pulling on the small drawer, I pick out my concealer, mascara and lip balm.

Swiping it under my eyes, and dotting it over a couple of spots, I blend it in with my fingertip before coating my lashes in three strokes of mascara. Applying the soft lip balm to my full, dry lips, I rub them together and slip it into my back pocket. Tousling my fingers in the root of my blonde hair, I decide I need a bit of color to my cheeks, so I add some cream pink blush and blend it up my cheek bones.

Sure, I work my fingers to the bone on the ranch and get dirt under my nails, but it still doesn't stop me from wanting to put my make up on and look nice.

I was a girly girl.

Pink was my color.

Rom-coms were my jam.

Taylor Swift was my music of choice.

I liked ice coffees, losing myself in happily ever afters in the form of romance books and I adored getting flowers.

I wasn't a materialistic girl, but I liked the smaller things.

A little piece of jewellery that reminded someone of me when they saw it, any type of flower—but sunflowers were my favorite—a cupcake, an apple from an orchard or even a little penned note with the words '*I love you*' tucked onto my pillow for me to see when I wake.

I was a simple girl.

Grabbing my hat, I pop it on my head and pull on my door. The creak making me freeze. I knew the door creaked, yet I still do it most mornings. I didn't want to wake pops up but once I was out on the landing, I saw the orange glow of the light from the kitchen and I knew he was already up, no doubt a pot of hot coffee already brewed and my favorite cereal out on the side.

Moving down the stairs slowly, I stepped off the bottom one and plastered a fake smile on my face as I moved around the door frame and saw him sitting at the small, worn, untreated wooden table reading yesterday's newspaper.

I never knew why he did it, just knew he always had.

"Morning," I walk towards him, leaning down and placing a kiss on the top of his thick, gray hair just as he tilts his head back, a warm, infectious smile on his face, dimples pressed into his full cheeks and my heart throbs in my chest.

"Morning sweetheart," his voice is raspy as I look at his near empty coffee cup and swipe it from the table before I place it on the counter top and reach for my own mug off the branch stand and place it beside his.

Glancing over my shoulder, he is back to reading his paper.

Sighing, I press onto my tip toes and reach for the old ice cream tub that houses his pills and vitamins and line them up on the side. Walking towards the fridge, I grab a large blood-orange and place it on a chopping board and slice a knife through it before putting it on a plate and dusting it with a small shimmer of brown sugar. Pacing back towards the fridge, I grab the fresh orange juice and top up a small glass and walk over to where he sits, placing my hand on his shoulder as I place the glass in front of him.

He gives me that look.

The one he does every morning when he is down here with me.

The one where he silently begs me not to wait on him and administer his meds.

But it's always been this way.

It's always just been me and him.

My pops has always had heart issues, but five years ago he was diagnosed with a terminal illness and well, things haven't been the same since.

These small, little mundane things that I do for him seem more important now, seem to have more meaning than they once did.

Because I have no idea if this will be the last morning, I prepare his fruit, his small glass of orange juice or to sort his pills into size order before giving them to him to take.

Everything means a little more than before and again that makes my heart ache deep in my chest.

I place a kiss on the top of his head as I turn and reach for his fruit and his tablets, and like always, I place his plate down first then line his tablets up and I have no idea why, but I always watch as he takes every single one, swallowing it down with his juice.

I know he isn't going to not take them, but it makes something settle inside of me knowing that I have witnessed him taking them.

"Good job," I praise like always then dust across the floor to fill up our coffee mugs but not before adding creamer and a scoop of sugar in mine.

Pops takes his black and bitter.

I take mine white and sweet.

Once I know he has everything he needs, I reach for my fruit loops and cover them with milk before I perch myself on the wooden chair.

He sits with his back to the kitchen; I sit at his right side.

It's always been that way.

I ask how he slept; he gives me a grunt and then we sit in silence whilst we eat.

Clearing the table, I brown his wholemeal toast and slice a banana as I re-plate it up and place it in front of him.

"I'll see you tonight, okay?"

He nods.

"Come back for twelve though, I need you to sign the paperwork," and I watch as he rolls his lips into a thin line, a grimace apparent over his face and I push a fake smile onto my own lips.

"Okay," I tuck my chair under the table then curl my fingers around the top of it. "Any request for lunch?"

He sits back in his chair, folding his newspaper and placing it beside his toast.

"Would you mind popping to Sunny's and grabbing me a bowl of soup and a seeded roll?" and I wink at him.

"Of course I can."

"You're my angel," his words make my chest tighten and I drop my head for a moment, so he doesn't see the tears that are threatening to fall.

"I'll see you at twelve," I squeeze out before I turn on my heel and walk away.

This is going to be the hardest goodbye I am ever going to make.

Stepping onto the porch, I take a deep breath and push down the sadness that threatens to ruin my day.

I will not cry anymore.

I move forward before curling my hands around the wobbly fence post and look out at the land in front of me. It's not much but it's ours.

The snow tipped mountains in the distance look a lot prettier today and I'm not sure if it's because I am only really noticing just how perfect everything is here.

Letting my head fall, I squeeze my eyes shut and my heart begins to race.

This is all I have known. It's always only been me and pops.

My mom abandoned me on this very porch when I was a few months old.

She has never once returned. Not even made a phone call.

She chose her habit over me.

But yet, my pops never says anything bad about her. Still talks about her as if she is his whole world.

I know she's not.

I'm his world.

But she was still his daughter.

I tried reaching out to her a few times via emails and letters but never heard anything back, and my dad? No idea where he was or who he was. My pops tells me it was some deadbeat she got with when she fell into her new lifestyle, but I block all of that out.

Pops was my family. Only him.

But now... well... it was only going to be me.

CHAPTER FOUR
PACEY

I was up early; sleep hadn't come easily. My mind was wracked with the what ifs and what could possibly go wrong. It also didn't help that the paperwork was arriving today. I wanted to make Gerry Wheeler happy, I didn't want him to have to worry about Morgan or Cottonwheel Ranch when he had so much more to focus on.

I had no idea what our timeline was, but I knew he wanted to move quickly.

I had debated telling my ma, but then I didn't want to put any more strain on her. She puts on this big show that she is okay, plastering a fake smile on a not so brave face, but I knew deep down that she was barely holding on.

Riggs and Aspen lived on Crooked Creek; Dixie, Tripp and Lainey were still at home but wanted to move out soon. Ma kept telling them they didn't have to, but with her only having a few months until she drops I don't think they want to burden ma with a toddler *and* a newborn.

Scrubbing my face, I push to my feet and drag my heavy legs to the bathroom, closing the door behind me before I am under the shower and trying to wash the tiredness from my soul.

It didn't work.

I am still groggy as hell and my shoulders hurt from how tense they are.

I wrap a towel around my waist start to pace across the hall when Dixie walks from their bedroom, long brown hair messy, Lainey clung to her hip and she gives me a small smile before a yawn presents itself.

"Morning Pacey," her voice slightly muffled as she walks towards the stairs, and I find myself tightening my towel around my waist.

"Morning," I grunt as I keep my head down and make a move for my room, closing the door behind me.

Sighing, I pace to my closet and drag out a gray tee and dirty denim jeans. I felt like today was going to be one of those days. I needed to go into the office, but I also needed to get this paperwork signed and work out what my next move was.

Morgan isn't going to want to move in here, so I am going to no doubt be moving across the town line and into Blossom Cove.

Ma isn't going to like it, which pushes me to think I need to tell her what has happened, or I could get Gerry and drive him over so he can tell her himself.

Might make the news a little easier to swallow.

Pushing my hand through my hair and away from my face, I puff air through my bottom lip and glance over at my bed.

Single bed, pushed up against a large window, carpeted floors and a few baseball team photos on the wall.

Never really found my thing as a kid. Most kids have hobbies, but not us Rivera boys. We were put on the ranch to work as soon as we could; our childhood wasn't an easy one.

We were loved, but it wasn't sunshine and rainbows.

My dad was a tough man, God rest his soul. He always treated Riggs a little different though. Was stricter with him, made him do a lot more than me and Tripp. But I suppose he was getting him ready to take over the ranch one day, and well, that day has come.

Riggs is running the ranch, making all the decisions. His latest one was a whole new bunch of cowboys. I personally didn't think we needed anymore, but he seemed to think we did. He made Marty Livestock Commissioner instead of his right-hand man—again, a choice I possibly wouldn't have made, but what did I know? I was only his kid brother.

Getting myself dressed, I brush my teeth before reaching for my hat that sits on the back of my door, placing it on my head as I move towards the kitchen. Tripp is sitting feeding Lainey, Dixie is brewing a fresh pot of coffee and my mom is sitting, elbows resting on the table as she watches her son and her grandbaby quietly.

"Morning," my boots move across the tiled floor and ma's head pops up, her eyes settling on me.

She is dressed in all black. She tells me she won't wear anything else, and the only time we should put her in color is when we're placing her in the ground next to my father.

I give her a soft smile as I place a kiss on the top of her head and my heart twists in my chest.

"You doing okay?" Tripp lifts his eyes to me, narrowing his gaze slightly before they're back on Lainey.

She is babbling away, pinching the buttered toast from his hand and shoving it into her mouth, her eyes wide and playful as she kicks her legs in her highchair.

"Yeah fine," my tone is sharp as I walk over towards Dixie and reach for a mug, placing it next to the ones already lined up. "Ma, you about today?" Her eyes find mine and I can see the worry that dances through them momentarily.

"Yeah, is everything okay?" I hate that I have made her panic, that's not what I wanted.

I give her a nod, "Just need to ask your advice on something." The sound of the front door closing has us all turning and looking, Riggs strides forward, cheeks red, sweat beaded on his forehead.

"Am I in time for coffee?" he glances at the clock on the wall then back to the full kitchen.

"Just in time," Dixie smiles at him as she grabs another mug down from the cupboard and I watch as she fills his first.

"Errr..." Tripp says the words we're all thinking, "why does he get his first?" Tripp spins to look at Dixie and she gives him a playful smirk, her hand rounding under her neat bump. She is dressed in a long, white, cotton nightdress, sitting just above her ankles with frilly straps.

"Because he is out working and has been since..." she looks at the time, "four hours ago, so yes, he gets his coffee first," she turns her back on us as she grabs his mug and walks it over to him, pushing it into his hand.

"I knew I liked her for a reason," Riggs winks before dragging out a chair and slumping himself into it, his large, callous, dirty hand resting on our Ma's as he gives her a sympathetic smile.

My eyes pull when Dixie places Tripp's coffee down and then passes me mine.

He rubs his hand over her bump and she smiles with adoring eyes at him.

"Not long to go now," Riggs smiles and I can see the pain that masks his face. I know how desperate he and Aspen are for a baby, and I hate the way my stomach coils every time I think of her. Hate that still, somewhere deep inside of me is this resentfulness, but I have no idea why.

I don't even want her.

Sure, I may have loved her all those years ago, but not anymore, yet I am still harbouring something and I can't put my finger on what it is.

"Nope," Dixie smiles and Ma looks at her daughter-in-law, then to Lainey.

"I can't wait to be a nana again," she says all glassy eyed, her voice quiet.

Tripp just gives her a look before Lainey is causing a commotion, clearly fed up as she pushes the plate on the floor and stretches her arms out for Ma.

She laps it up. Standing up and swooping Lainey from her highchair before cuddling her into her chest, placing a kiss on the top of her head then whizzing her off into the living room.

My eyes follow her over my shoulder before I am back facing forward and that's when all sets of eyes are on me.

"What?" I snap, brows furrowed, digging into my skin.

"Something is going on," Riggs tilts his head towards me and I shake my head.

"Nope, nothing is going on," I swallow down the nerves, coating my dry mouth with bitter black coffee that only dries it out even more.

"Then why do you need to speak to Ma?" Tripp calls me out and I throw him a dagger glare.

"Ohhhh, something must be going down then if you've said you need to speak to mom," Riggs lets out a breathy laugh and my back is up in an instant.

"Nothing is going down, I just need her advice," and Dixie's eyes light up as she leans across the table.

"Is it a girl? Is there girl trouble... or is it more of a crush?" I face palm myself; this is not happening at eight a.m. on a Tuesday morning. "I can help if it is, I know a few good chat up lines," she wiggles her brows which gets Tripp's attention, turning his head so quick I fear he has given himself whiplash.

"I don't need any help, I just want to talk to my mom about something that doesn't concern anyone apart from me, okay?" my tone is curt as I push up from the table and toss my mug into the sink, the hot liquid pouring out and I instantly feel bad. Tipping my head back, I exhale heavily before I turn around and meet their gazes. "When I can say something, I will, but at the minute, I have so much shit going on in my head I can only focus on one thing at a time."

They say nothing, they're all just staring.

"Okay, cool, I'll catch you all later..." I begin walking forward towards the archway that leads into the hallway. "And get back to work you two... lazy fuckers," I grumble a laugh as I walk out the door and down to my truck.

I needed to play catch up at work, I had piles of paperwork on my desk. This job is more paperwork than action, but after everything went down last year, well, I am kind of grateful for the paperwork. I don't think I had it in me to look into anything other than a few loose ended cases.

The odd missing pet.

Drug deals on land.

Theft of livestock.

What with Riggs re-appointing Marty, Austin had became Livestock Agent. I didn't think he was ready but

Riggs, Buck and the Governor agreed that it would do him good.

Marty was ready for a little more and had asked for Livestock Commissioner. Marty has kind of got a bit big for his boots, but again, not my place. Riggs made that decision, and I am a supportive kid brother.

Turning the key, the truck kicks in and I loop it out of the drive before I am riding to town. Parking in the parking lot of the Sheriff's office, I lock my truck then walk along the tree lined sidewalk and push into Sunny's.

The little bell rings above my head and she pops up from behind the counter.

"Morning Pacey, you okay?" she asks me as I glance at the fresh pastries and baked goods that are stacked up in the chiller counter.

"Morning Sunny, I'm all dandy thank you," my eyes lift to her. Short brown hair, kind, blue eyes, pretty face.

"Good to hear, how's your mom?" she asks, head tilted and I see the sadness that strikes across her face.

"She's getting there, just taking each day as it comes," I give a soft nod before I am looking at the board. Not wanting to be rude, but each time someone asks me how my mom is, I am taken back to that hospital room, back to where my dad lay lifeless, where my mom sobbed over his body... that's the last memory I have of him.

And I fucking hate it.

"Good," I hear the sound of her key fob unlocking her till, "what can I get you?" she asks.

"I'll have a white coffee, pumpkin bagel with cream cheese and a lemon muffin please."

"To go?"

"To go," my eyes settle on her. As much as I would love

to sit in here and watch the world go by, I had so much to sort out.

"Not a problem, I'll get started on that now for you," she says as I reach into my back pocket and slip out some notes before placing it on the counter, then slipping out a few more and sliding them through the tip jar.

"Thanks Pace," her cheeks turn pink as she grabs a paper cup and gets started on my coffee. I wait patiently, but I'm not waiting long when she holds out the steaming cup and hands me a paper bag. "I popped a couple of treats in there for your mom too," she smiles innocently at me and my heart constricts in my chest.

I find her attractive, but not enough to want to pursue, not that it matters anymore because soon I'll be a married man... all to help out a neighbor.

Giving her a soft nod as I take the bag from her grasp, I turn on my heel and make my way back down to my office. Reaching for my keys in my front pocket, I hook my finger around the keyring then slip them in the door, letting myself in.

My office is not big, but it's ample for me.

I normally have someone else work here, Avery, but after everything went down, I sent him off for leave until I needed him back.

So going forward, it was just me, myself and I.

Not that I minded, I was left alone.

It only causes a problem if I have someone held in the cells over night, but that's a rarity.

Kicking out the wheel of my office chair, I slump down into it and place the brown paper bag and coffee on the desk before I switch my computer on and wait for the machine to kick in.

Sitting back, I cross my feet at my ankles, fingers locked

together and in my lap, as I stare out the large window, the town quiet for now, but give it an hour or two and everyone will be about their day.

The chime from the monitor has me focused on that and I settle myself down to work, losing myself in a couple of hours of admin work and to be honest, I needed this today. I needed the distraction, if only for the morning.

Locking up behind me, I walk towards the truck and place the brown paper bag with the goodies for mom on the passenger seat. My phone connects to the Bluetooth and I pop it into the cradle as I dial my mom's number.

She answers on the first ring.

"Hey ma, I'm on my way home now, all okay?" I ask as I reverse out of my space and pull onto the quiet roads of Lovelock Bay.

"Yes, all is fine, I'll put the kettle on," and I can hear the smile that taints her lips.

"Perfect, see you soon," I cut her off as the radio begins to play soothing country music, the voice of *Lainey Wilson* filling the car, my fingers tapping on the steering wheel to the soft beat.

The drive is short and it's not long before the tires are crunching down the long and winding drive of our ranch. I see Riggs and Tripp talking to Conrad as I pull into the space in front of the garages and cut the engine.

Stepping down, I grab the bag and slam my driver's door.

"Lunch?" Riggs calls out and I flip him off.

"For ma!" I shout back and push a wide smile on my face then climb the steps onto the porch, the step creaking beneath my boot and I make a mental note to fix it this weekend.

Twisting the handle, I step into the house and the smell of a freshly baked pie fills my nose and my stomach grumbles.

"Ma!" I call out, kicking off my boots before I toss my hat on the side table.

"In here," she replies from the kitchen, and I duck my head around and see her sitting at the table with two cups of tea.

"Hey," I smile softly as I place the bag on the table, and she looks at me. "I went to Sunny's for breakfast this morning, she put some treats in there for you," my head tilts slightly as I narrow my gaze on her.

"Oh, thank you," she says, rolling her lips and peeking at the contents that sit inside the bag. "That's very kind of her, please tell her thank you."

Dragging a chair out, I sit down next to her and reach for my cup of tea.

"Work okay?" she asked, wrapping her fingers around the mug and bringing it to her lips.

"Yeah, just working through paperwork, never ending," I roll my eyes, and she gives me a ghost of a smile. "Being Sheriff is not how I imagined it when I was a kid, chasing down bad guys with my pistol and a patch work pony," and that causes her a laugh, her face lifting to look at me.

"You should know by now my sunshine boy, that life isn't like the ones we dreamed up as children," and I nod, swallowing the thickness down.

"I know," I whisper as she pulls out a chocolate muffin, swiping her finger through the frosting before popping it into her mouth.

"Tasty," she grins at me then places it back down on the table.

I try to speak but slam my mouth shut.

"What is it Pacey?" her voice is quiet as she slips her hand over to mine, placing it over the top and brushing her thumb back and forth.

I sigh before there is a knock at the door.

"One moment," I slip my hand from under hers then push back, moving towards the door and opening it. Gerry is standing there. Battered cowboy hat on his head, off white shirt and beige slacked pants.

"Come in Gerry," I step aside and wait for him to make his way in before I close the door behind him then lead him to the kitchen.

My ma's head lifts, her eyes volleying between me and Gerry and I can see the hundred questions that are whizzing through her head.

"Gerry, this is my Ma, Orla," I look at him then turn to my mom. "Ma, this is Gerry," I smile at her, her brows furrowed.

"Nice to meet you Gerry," she goes to stand but Gerry holds his hand up, insisting she stays in her seat.

I pull his chair out and he falls into it, a heavy sigh leaving him as he does.

"You good?" I ask, giving him a curt smile as I take my own seat, and he gives me a nod before dumping a bag on the table.

"Care to explain?" My ma's eyes are on me, and I swallow.

"I do, but I think Gerry might be best to explain it, so you understand it a little bit better maybe?" my heart is banging in my chest.

Gerry shuffles before looking over his glasses at my mom then back down to the table.

"Firstly, I would like to offer my condolences on the passing of Jorge," his voice cracks, "he was a major part of this town... and of Blossom Cove."

My mom just nods, giving him a tight smile.

"Secondly, my reason for being here..." he pauses as his trembling hands fumble with the bag as he pulls out a large pile of paperwork then drops it on the table with a loud thud. My mom jumps slightly, her eyes on the paper but they're not on it long before her eyes find mine.

"What is this?" she whispers and I'm not sure if she is scared or disappointed.

"It's a contract, and deeds..." Gerry clears his throat.

"Contract? Deeds... Pacey... no, you haven't," and her eyes widen, and she breaks my damn fucking heart that she would even think that.

"No, no, mom, no," I shake my head and scoop her hand into mine, pressing the back of it against my lips.

"It's the deeds for *my* ranch," and my mom's hollow eyes sink to Gerry. "I need Pacey to be on them... I also need him to take my granddaughter's hand in marriage."

Now her attention is back on me.

"Marriage?" she whispers.

"Yes ma, marriage."

"I'm dying Orla," he grumbles, his eyes glassing slightly and he is destroying me. "Morgan has no one else, the suits have already squeezed in on my land and I am one signature away from letting them have it all, but now, it's going to be on her. She can't do it by herself... there is no way in hell I would leave her to do it alone. Well, I knew Pacey would be a man of his word... plus, your reputable name and I know your eldest boy is dealing with the suits as well... I need this ranch to survive, not for me, but for her and it will only survive if Pacey will take her hand. He has agreed to it, but he wanted me to tell you *why*."

He pauses for a moment, pushing the deeds towards her along with the contract.

"Read it, tell me if there is anything you want changed."

But Ma's eyes are settled on mine.

"And you're okay with this?" she blinks at me, "This is what you want?"

I pause for a moment, ignoring the way my blood pumps around my body, the way it bangs in my ear like a drum.

"I am," I nod, "it is."

She slips back into her seat and drops her head for a moment.

"I don't need to read the contract or the deeds, I trust that you have *my* son's best interests at heart."

Gerry bows his head and gives her a nod.

"Then I suppose I better go and buy a new hat," she pushes back from the table. "If you'll excuse me," and my heart implodes in my chest.

She isn't happy about this, far from it.

But it's done.

Gerry passes me a pen and I sign on the dotted line on both documents and my stomach flips at the sight of her name next to mine.

"You'll never know how much this means to me Rivera," he just about manages before his head is in his hands and he's crying.

My chest caves in and I find myself placing my hand on his back, palm down between his shoulder blades as his body trembles through the tears.

CHAPTER FIVE
MORGAN

Standing at the bottom of the makeshift aisle with a few seats scattered either side, I cast my eyes over the large tree trunks placed as an edging, dressed in foliage and topped with pretty wildflowers. Battery powered fairy lights are entwined through and a matching set wrapped around a metal framed arch.

This is not what I had once pictured when I dreamt of getting married, but as I got older, the dream of a marriage soon diminished into nothing.

I never wanted kids.

Never wanted a marriage.

Yet here I am, about to walk down the aisle for my pops' last dying wish.

Talk about guilt tripped, jeez.

I glance over at him, his cheeks all rosy, thick gray hair combed over on a side parting, and he has never looked more handsome than he does now, and damn, I can see the pride shining out of him like rays of sunshine.

Inhaling heavily, I glance down at where I would

normally see my tanned cowboy boots before my eyes lock on the man who I am set to marry.

Ivory sheer bows tie over each of my shoulders, the dress fits down to my waist, then moulding into a soft tulle skirt that flows down to the ground. My blonde hair is half up, half down and finished with a pretty diamanté clip, the rest is down in soft curls that tease the skin on my open back.

"You ready sweet girl?" my pops asks me, his chin lifting as he stands a little taller and inhales deeply.

"Ready as I'll ever be," I whisper just as soft sounds of *In Your Love – Tyler Childers* begins to fill the meadow of our ranch and that's when the Rivera family stand. Dusty and his family are the only ones on our side.

They are all we have.

My heart twists in my chest as I take my first step, slowly walking to seal my fate.

Pacey isn't hard on the eyes, in fact, he is real easy.

He has never had a serious relationship from what I have heard. The town sheriff and golden boy of Lovelock Bay… but is he really the ray of sunshine everyone thinks he is?

He stands tall, shoulders rolled back and dressed in an off white suit with a white shirt and matching bow tie. Hair tousled back, stubble shadows his jaw and chin with a hint of thicker stubble coating his upper lip.

I wanted formal with a hint of rustic; he was happy to agree with whatever just to get me down the aisle before my grandad left this earthly plane.

His eyes swept over me and never did I think that three months after meeting him at his brother's wedding, would I be walking down the aisle to marry him.

Difference was, there were no feelings attached to this marriage.

It was a business deal.

There was no time limit though, this was it.

I mean, sure we could get divorced once my pops passes over but at the same time, Pacey would still be on the deeds.

I needed him. I needed him to help me keep this land, to keep this ranch.

Blood sweat and tears went into this, and I would never forgive myself if I let someone take it from me.

From us.

We planned to bury my pops down the bottom of the meadow, tucking him under the large apple tree that he planted with my grandmother Marjorie when they first moved here. I don't remember her though. She died when I was four so when I say it's been just us two, it really has.

Just the two of us.

Now I had to not only learn what it was like to live without him, but in fact have him replaced by someone new.

He would never fill the gaping wound my pops would leave, but he could help try and pull me back together again, even if for a short while.

We begin to walk, and I let my eyes focus on Pacey.

His dark blond hair looks like it has slightly golden tips in the light, it's pushed away from his face and his whiskey eyes are locked with mine.

High cheek bones, strong jaw, full cupid bow lips.

Hot.

He was.

I felt attracted to him the first time I met him at Riggs

and Aspen's wedding, then again when I saw him a couple of weeks back at Randy's.

There was something about that man that made me gravitate towards him, but I had to remember why we were doing this.

I have no idea on his type, no idea if he even finds me attractive, but still, we were diving into the depths of the ocean headfirst with no life ring.

Just me and him.

Floating and trying to make our way back to shore.

My pops lifts my hand to his mouth as he kisses it delicately before his lips are on my cheek and I ignore the silent tear that rolls down where his lips just were.

"I love you, Morgan," he whispers then places my hand into Pacey's but he doesn't let go straight away. "You promise me, Rivera…" my pops pauses, "you promise you're going to look after her," and I watch as Pacey nods, his face not wavering, there wasn't a moment of hesitation that left that man.

"Don't let me down," my pops chokes as he finally lets me go and I move to stand in front of my husband-to-be.

"You look beautiful," he whispers, and I give him a coy smile.

I know he is just saying it because he feels like he has to say it, but it still felt nice hearing those words.

I have never been called beautiful before.

Never even been kissed.

My throat bobs.

"Thank you," I manage to croak just as the officiator begins speaking.

"Dearly beloved, we're gathered here today to witness the marriage between Pacey Jorge Rivera and Morgan

Palma Wheeler..." and the rest I block out until those famous words leave his mouth.

"You may now kiss the bride," and I freeze, my eyes widening slightly and Pacey senses it in an instant.

He leans in and kisses me softly on the cheek before his fingers lace with mine as we turn and face forward. Dusty is clapping and whistling through his teeth, but the Rivera lot? All faces like thunder, except from Orla.

She is smiling, her cheeks damp from tears but I am unsure whether they're happy or sad or maybe a mix of both.

Sucking in a deep breath, I squeeze Pacey's hand as he leads me back down the aisle and into the converted barn where tables are set out back under the rotten wooded frame, fairy lights wrapped around with the matching foliage and flowers entwined down the middle. He stops just as we break through the back and turns to look at me, his hand cupping my face, so I have no other choice but to face him.

"You okay?" he asks, the cool metal of his gold wedding band on my flushed cheek.

"I think so," I whisper, because if I speak too loud he will hear the crack in my voice, he will hear that I am lying and that's not the best way to start a marriage.

"We've got this, a few more hours to get through and life will go back to how we know it."

I let out a soft laugh as I look out across our land, the dusting of stars twinkling between the mountains.

"I don't think life will ever return to how we knew it."

THE EVENING SOON SETTLES IN, the air is warm and sweet, the

fireflies are hovering and blend with the fairy lights and light chatter floats over the rustic wooden table.

"Do you think your family are angry?" I find myself asking as I sip on the glass of champagne.

He looks at me then casts his eyes down to where his family sit.

"No," his answer is short and to the point.

"They didn't look happy when we walked down the aisle," and a soft chuckle vibrates as he shuffles and leans back against the chair, his arm hanging over the back of my chair, his fingertips brushing over the bare skin of my shoulder.

"Would you be happy if your child was in this situation?" he swings his head to look at me, a strand of his hair hanging down onto his forehead and I find myself focusing on that and wanting to push it away from his eyes.

"I wouldn't be in this situation because I don't want children," my voice flat as the truths seep from me.

"No?" he looks at me, brows furrowed before he smooths them out.

"No," I glance down at the table and see my pops in conversation with Riggs.

"Is that a hard, no?" Pacey asks me and piques my interest. Turning my head to look at him, my eyes bounce between his whiskey ambers.

"Yes, why?" there is an air of sarcasm attached to my tongue when I answer him.

"I want kids," he shrugs his shoulders up and I just stare at him.

"Off to a good start then," I roll my eyes, shaking my head as I reach for my champagne flute and drain it.

"Seems that way," his fingers stop trailing over my

skin and before I can even respond he pushes from the table and sulks over to where his mom sits. He lowers himself in the chair, elbows on the table as he begins talking quietly and I am desperate to know what he is saying.

He must think that this will last, but I don't think we will be in it for the long run. I think it'll run its course and we'll both walk away when we know the ranch is safe.

I'm not alone long when a pretty honey blonde haired girl sits next to me, her hair short and wavy, hazel eyes dancing with mine and she wears a pretty dusty pink chiffon dress and cowgirl boots.

"Hi," she says sweetly, "I'm Aspen."

"Aspen," I repeat her name as if testing it out on my tongue.

"I'm married to Riggs," she nods at the tall, burly guy at the head of the table, thick beard, broad shoulders and his eyes dance with hers.

"I was at your wedding," I half laugh and look for the champagne bottle that is floating around the table.

"Oh, yes, of course you were," she thinks for a moment as she laughs softly. "Sorry, it was a long day, plus, I was a little tipsy," she leans into me and whispers the last bit.

"Wish I could say the same," my eyes follow the bottle and before I can even grab it, Aspen has a fresh bottle in her hand and she is popping the cork before filling my glass to the brim and I lick my lips.

"Thank you," I nod as I take a large mouthful, the bubbles hitting the spot.

"So, let's address the elephant in the room shall we," she laughs as she fills her own glass and clinks it against mine.

"What's that?"

"How are you feeling with all of this? It must have been a shock."

I nod, rolling my lips. "It was a shock, but I need to remember the bigger picture," I sigh as I look down at my pops who is laughing with Tripp and Riggs and my heart warms slightly.

"Is this thing..." she pauses, "between both of you, is it gonna turn into more than a business transaction?"

I shrug a shoulder up as I look down at my new husband.

"No, I don't think so," I say blasé, because it is the truth. As much as that would be a wonderful ending to our story, I just can't see it panning out that way at all. We want different things.

I think it will stay as it is, a deal between a dying man and a proud one.

He wants to help, swoop in and save the day and my pops gave him the equipment to do it.

"That's a shame," she sighs, her head tilting as she looks at him. "He is a good kid," she nods before her eyes trace mine.

"I'm sure he is," I return her nod with a soft smile. "Has he ever had a girlfriend?" and she shakes her head.

"Not that we have known and we're all a pretty close-knit group."

"Huh," I say a little intrigued but then doubt settles into my stomach at why he hasn't.

"It's a him thing more than anything else, he's a hopeless romantic that one." She sighs, as if memories flash through her eyes. "Wears his heart on his sleeve, desperate to find *his* girl."

I lick my lips as I avert my gaze to my husband, his whiskey eyes on me and my heart jolts in my chest.

"Well, I've ruined that now haven't I," I admit and reluctantly drop my eyes to my fingers that are curled around the stem of my champagne flute, a delicate gold ring wrapped around my finger and my chest is heavy.

"You might be the dream girl he has been wishing for since he was eighteen."

I scrunch my nose.

"I doubt that very much, I'm more of a burden to him than a dream girl," I laugh softly and drain the rest of my glass.

We're not alone for long, when a pretty brown-haired girl with a small bump takes her seat opposite.

"I'm Dixie," she pushes her hand across the table for me to take and I do, shaking them before I withdraw mine. "So, what a surprise this was," her gaze drifts to Aspen before her blue eyes are on mine.

"Tell me about it," I swallow down the dryness that coats my throat.

"I mean, you have got lucky with this family," she smiles softly, her hand rounding the underside of her bump, her lips pressing into a smile as she looks down at the life she is growing.

"Have I?" I find myself asking which gets her head snapping up fast.

"Yeah, you have," and I don't miss the harshness of her tone.

"Dix..." Aspen says softly, shaking her head in a disapproving manner. "I think what my sister-in-law is trying to say," she turns herself to fully face me, "you have got lucky with this bunch," she gestures her hand down the table lined with Riveras. "You will never find a more loyal, hardworking, loving family. Sure, they've had their moments," she winks at me, "but everything they do is for *their* family, and well, Morgan, whether you like it or not, you're part of this now. I know this is not what either of you wanted, trust me, but this is the cards you have been dealt. So, you can either go with the flow and go all in or put up resistance making both your lives miserable for however long this goes on for," she rolls her lips before settling back in her chair and twisting back around.

I let her words play over on loop.

"Exactly what I said," Dixie rolls her eyes but I can see the playful hint of a smile on her lips.

"Exactly," Aspen nudges into me and I let out a soft laugh.

"Just don't put your walls up, let him in... get to know each other, just ride out the storm because I promise by the end of it, you'll be real glad that you did."

A lump presents itself and I find myself trying to swallow constantly to budge it.

I nod, ignoring the way the tears tease at the back of my eyes.

"Trust me, he is a good boy."

Dixie hums in agreement.

"Now, no tears on the wedding day," she wraps her arm around my shoulder and pulls me in close which only makes the tears fall harder.

I've never had this. Never had someone looking out for me.

But now I had a whole family it seems, and I was terrified.

"May I..." Pacey's raspy voice pulls me from my thoughts, and I feel the way Aspen's arm slowly slips from my shoulders, her face lifting as she looks at him and gives him a warm smile.

Aspen steps up and nods for Dixie to follow before

Pacey is sitting down next to me, his body on an angle, him twisted to face me. Legs apart, elbows resting on his thighs and hands dropped between them.

Silence crackles between us, the soft chatter amongst family fading into the background.

"You doing okay?" he asks me and I give a half smile, tilting my head as I shrug my shoulder into my cheek. "Same," he admits, a hint of a laugh passing his lips.

"Are we crazy?" I whisper, finally letting myself sink into those whiskey amber eyes.

"Yeah?" he puffs his cheeks out.

The silence is back and I watch as he pushes his hand around the back of his head.

"I mean, I would have finished that sentence with *what a story to tell the grandkids* but..." and he gives me a slow wink.

I find myself laughing at him, nodding as tears threaten to spill once more.

"This will be okay, Morgan," his large hand drifts up and cups my cheek and I find myself leaning into him. "We will be okay, maybe this is what we both needed hey? Maybe this was always God's plan," and I find myself nodding again as a tear rolls down my cheek, but he is there catching it with the pad of his thumb before he brings it to his lip and kisses it.

"Now... may I have this dance?" he asks as *life with you - Kelsey Hart* begins to play through the small speakers dotted around a makeshift dance floor.

"You may," I whisper as he stands, holding his hand out for me to take which I do, gladly.

Leading me to the open space, his ringed hand slips around my lower back, pulling me close as his other hand clasps mine as we slow dance, and for a moment it's just us, the stars, the moon and the mountains.

But that doesn't last long, Riggs and Aspen, Dixie and Tripp, Dusty and Marsha, a few other couples stand up and when I glance at the table, I see Orla and my pops sitting there and I don't know why but it breaks my heart.

Pacey spins me around slowly before I am pressed closer to him and that's when I see that my pops is leading Orla towards the dance floor, his hand in hers, one on her hip as they dance.

"That's the first time I have seen a genuine smile on her face," Pacey whispers and my eyes drag to his, lips parted.

"I'm glad he managed to do that."

"Me too," he lowers his head, his eyes dropping to my lips and panic sets in as I slip my hand from his and let it meet the other one that is resting on the breast of his suit jacket and push back. It got too intimate and I'm not ready for anything like that.

"Excuse me," I nod as I turn and walk into our home and lock myself in the restroom.

Once the door is closed, I push my back to it and close my eyes, heart drumming against my skin.

I just needed a moment alone.

It's been a lot, and I am desperate for today to be over and to go back to how my life was before, but uneasiness settles in my chest, it'll never be how it was.

CHAPTER SIX
PACEY

itting in the large kitchen of my family home, my head is throbbing.

"You okay?" my mom's voice floats through me as she sits next to me, her hand pressed to my cheek as I look at her.

"Yeah ma, I'm fine," and she gives me a sad smile.

"How about you? Are you okay?" my hand over hers as I bring it down and cup it tightly.

"I'm fine, my sunshine boy."

"Good."

"What are your plans for today?" she asks as she slips her hand from under mine and makes her way to the stove to boil the kettle.

"Packing up my room I suppose," my breath catches at the back of my throat, and I have no idea why but this hurts more than I thought it would.

"I'm going to miss you," she turns to look at me before she reaches for the mugs and I swallow down the lump.

"I'll only be across the town line ma," I stand and walk

across to her and wrap my arms around her shoulders as I rest my chin between her neck and shoulder.

"I know," her hand reaches up as she rests it on my cheek, patting it slightly in reassurance.

"You still have me," Tripp's voice pulls me away from my mom and a boyish grin spreads across my face.

"Yeah, but you're not her favorite," I wink and Tripp scowls at me. "Just telling the truth," I shrug as I pinch some fresh toast from the middle of the breakfast bar and smother it in honey before I take a bite, still grinning ear to ear.

"None of you are my favorites," she says a little louder as the kettle begins to whistle and that's when we hear the front door slam and the sound of heavy boots thudding across the tiles.

"Don't lie to them ma, you know that I'm your favorite," Riggs grumbles and now me and Tripp both roll our eyes.

"I'm not lying," she turns to face all three of us, her eyes trailing between each and every one of us.

"I think you are," Riggs runs his hand over his beard.

She sighs, hands on her hips and she is so over our shit.

"You are all my special boys," she comes in with the classic line and we all roll our eyes.

"It's okay ma, you don't have to admit it whilst they're here," I step forward before thumbing behind me, "but I know I am your favorite." I stop, placing a kiss on her cheek before I am moving forward and grabbing the kettle from the stove as I pour the boiling water into the cup, making us all a cup of tea.

"Where's Dix?" I ask, looking over my shoulder.

"Nursing Lainey, but she will have a coffee," Tripp nods

at me before I glide over and turn the switch on for the coffee machine and wait for it to boil.

Swiping my cup from the side, I bring it to my lips and blow softly.

"How's married life?" Riggs chuckles as he takes his own mug, trudging dirty footprints through the kitchen.

"Going great," sarcasm drips from my tone and I roll my eyes in an over exaggerated manner.

He chuckles a little louder.

"I'm moving over there today, I have no idea what it is going to be like... feel a little weird about it."

"I would be worried if you didn't feel weird about it," Tripp says as he places a cup under the coffee spout, the hot brown liquid trickling out.

"What if this is all it'll be? Living together but not being together...how long should I ride it out for before I call it quits?"

"I suppose once the old man pops it, then you're a free man right?" Riggs says and that gets a clip around the back of his head from Ma.

"What?" he groans, rubbing his head but laughing.

"Don't say stuff like that, you took vows, you made an oath... you know how it works," she furrows her brows at him and his smile drops.

"Yeah, but their marriage isn't actually a marriage," Riggs tries to back pedal but fails.

"Pacey, did you sign in front of witnesses?"

"Yes ma'am," a smile pulls at the corner of my mouth.

"Then he's married," she shakes her head as she busies herself.

"And that's why I'm the favorite," I wink at Riggs, patting him on the chest as I move past him.

"Fuck you," he says but I see his shoulders lift and fall as he laughs softly.

As much as I wanted to stand around and talk shit with them, I had my life to box up.

I wasn't sure how this was going to work. Gerry was still very much alive and kicking, but we agreed that I would move in the day after the wedding, and well, here we are.

I would live there and be respectful, but when the time comes, I'll start working on the house. It was in desperate need of some tender loving care, and I don't want it to fall apart around us.

It wasn't a small job, I would be busy working on it for a good few months, but between family, work and everything in between I have no idea how I would fit it all in.

I didn't really want to take leave from my job, but again if I needed to I would.

I loved Tripp with every fibre of myself, but when he handed the reins over to me, I internally cursed at him. I loved being Livestock Agent, but after getting shot and everything that went down with Kelcie and The Attaways, well, he thought it was best we all got a fresh start. I agreed and took the badge because he wanted me to, but honestly —and I have never spoke this out loud—it's been a burden since.

I can't seem to get my foot in the door and I honestly sometimes think that someone else would be better suited for the job.

Pushing the door on my childhood room, my heart stutters in my chest. I've spent every night in here and yet, right now, it feels so raw.

Checkered blue comforter and matching pillow, thick carpets that have tread evident from where I walk the same line over and over. Teak wooden drawers with matching doors that lead into a closet where my clothes hang.

A window seat overlooking the front of the house, a cream pillow resting on top.

Sad that I used to sit there and watch Aspen run down the fence line, the small lights illuminating as she passed them, guiding her home.

Shaking the past out of me, I move to the closet and start dumping out my clothes onto my bed and that's where I stay for most of the day, boxing up stuff and loading up the back of my truck.

My mom comes in occasionally to help, Dixie too.

Tripp is out on the ranch so it's just the three of us and Lainey.

I didn't know how I felt about this next chapter in my life, but excitement bubbled deep inside of me.

I felt I had a purpose now.

I wasn't just the baby Rivera brother who was trying desperately to follow in his older brothers footsteps.

This was my chance to become my own person, and Morgan Wheeler was going to be the one to do that.

I hoped.

Closing the back of the truck, I dusted my hands off and looked over at my family's ranch, the sun lowering slightly between the peaks of the mountains and I spot Riggs and Tripp in the distance as they ride back down. I needed to get my horse over to Cottonwheel but I'll sort that in the next few days.

My mom creeps up behind me, the sound of her feet crunching over the shingle has me looking down, a soft smile gracing my lips as she stands next to me.

"You ready for this?" she asks as she leans into me, my arm lifting so she rests her head on the side of my ribs.

"Not one bit," I admit, my exhale shaky.

"It'll be okay, you will get on perfectly with Morgan, I really do believe that," and I look down at her, but she doesn't look up at me, she is watching her two sons gallop on down the field to meet us.

"Yeah?" I mumble as my own sights drift to my brothers.

"Yeah," and her voice doesn't even tremble.

"I hope so ma," I whisper just as Riggs slows down in front of me, tinted glasses on, a smirk on his face.

"You all packed up?" he eyes the truck, and I give a steady nod.

"Do you need help getting it over?"

"Nope, think I've got it," and I lift my arm from my mom and step aside.

"Do you want me to bring Chase over?" he asks as he looks at the stables and I shake my head.

"I'll collect him tomorrow maybe, can't leave him here with you two, he'll get chubby and never be worked." I scoff a laugh and Tripp chuckles beside Riggs.

"Of course we would work him, probably more than you will over at Cottonwheel."

"Hey, he will work wonders over there," I smirk and fish my keys out of my pocket.

"Never thought I would see the day when our kid brother was leaving the nest."

That's when all eyes move to my mom; she's sniffling.

My heart throbs inside my chest.

"Ma," I rasp as I close the gap between us, wrapping my arms around her as she silently sobs into my chest.

"I am so proud of you for stepping up like this... but at the same time," and she can't even finish her sentence before she is sobbing into my tee.

"I know, I know," I whisper, my hand stroking the back of her head and I gaze my eyes up to Riggs and Tripp. Riggs gives Tripp a nod as he swings his leg over the back of Travis and hops down just as I roll my mom into Tripp's arms.

"I just feel like if none of this would have happened... then you wouldn't have to move out," she lifts her head from Tripp's chest and her glassy green eyes are on me.

"I know ma, but look, you still have Tripp home, and Dixie and Lainey."

A ghost of a smile graces her lips.

"I know he isn't the favorite, but I will be home every Sunday for dinner, I will pop in all the time, plus, it's not going to be forever is it," I soften my gaze on her as I tilt my head to look at her. I feel awful for leaving her, but I have to do this. She understands that, I know she does, but it still doesn't make this any easier.

One day it'll just be her rattling around in this big old house, but I am hoping Dixie doesn't want to move back into her childhood home and they choose to stay here, then when Ma is reunited with dad again, they can keep our legacy going, or if they don't, I'm sure I'll be back, single and childless.

"Are you okay?" I ask as I look at my mom, Tripp still holding onto her.

"Yes," she smiles at me and steps away from Tripp's grasp, glancing over at Riggs before she closes the gap between us. "Don't forget who you are Pacey, shoot for the stars and don't settle for anything less okay?" her hand is on my cheek. "Do what you have to do, but don't lose yourself whilst you're trying to help someone else," and I nod, giving her a smile.

"I promise I won't ma," leaning forward, I place a kiss in the center of her forehead.

"Love you, my sunshine boy."

"Love you right back," I mutter before I am pulling her into my arms, enveloping her in my grasp and in that moment, I didn't want to leave.

"He is definitely the favorite," Riggs grumbles and I smile, laughing softly as I flip them off behind her back.

"They're right," she whispers before lifting her head from my chest as she looks at me, "but don't tell them that," a soft laugh escapes her as she winks.

And I know she is playing, but I kind of needed that in this moment.

Driving out of Rivera Ranch felt odd. I knew I wasn't leaving for good, I knew that deep in the crevices of my soul, but it still felt like a goodbye.

I glance back in the rearview mirror and see my mom, Riggs and Tripp all standing in the dusty driveway watching me drive away.

Swallowing down the lump, my eyes cast to the large oak tree where my dad lay and I bring my fingertips to my lips and kiss them before my fingers are locked back around my steering wheel as I drive out of Lovelock Bay and into Blossom Cove.

My story was only just beginning.

CHAPTER SEVEN
MORGAN

Sitting at the top of the field, I glance over our home, our land, and a shiver dances up my spine.

The thought of this being taken away from me physically hurts.

I know why my pops has done what he has done, but it somehow tastes a little bitter.

I knew from a young age I never wanted to marry and I sure as hell didn't want kids. But as part of a promise to him, I agreed to marry Pacey Rivera.

The sun is sitting high in the sky, the late morning peeking between the mountains and I know it's the calm before the storm.

The storm being Pacey Rivera.

My mind drifts back to life before my pops was ill. He was all I knew.

It's always been me and him.

Taught me everything I know.

I was always his little cowgirl. I knew I wanted to work on the ranch from a young age. I was always in such awe watching how he worked, he never stopped but he also never neglected me in anyway. He was there for every supper, every drop off, every pickup and every school event. He drove me to prom and collected me at ten p.m. sharp.

He was the mom and dad I never had.

He learned how to sew, and do my hair, he even used to shop for make up with me because I never knew anything. I never forget waking up in the middle of the night and he was reading up on what to expect with a teen girl my age.

He gave me everything and more.

And as much as I don't want this next stage in my life, I knew I had to do it.

I owed it to him after all he has done for me.

Turning the rein on my horse, I open her up and canter down towards the house.

Slowing Barley to a slow trot, I gaze across the field when I see the blacked out Sheriff's truck pulling into the driveway and my heart drums in my chest.

I knew he was moving in today, but I don't think it had properly settled in.

I had no idea on what to expect, we would be living with each other as strangers but tied legally together as husband and wife.

Apprehension pricks at the base of my neck and nerves swarm in my belly as I tighten the rein and kick my mare on, picking up into a canter as her hooves hit the hard ground. I lean forward, my hands up her neck, the warm summer's breeze tangling in my hair. He was always going to beat me to the house, but I gave it a good go.

Slowing my gray palomino quarter horse, I halt as I look down at him, his eyes brightening when he meets my gaze and I give him a hint of a smile.

"Well, hello wife," he teases, sun in his eyes, skin crinkling at the side as he places his hand over his eyes trying to shield it. White tee wrapped around his toned torso, light denim jeans and a backwards cap.

"Hello," my tone is curt, and I twist my lips to try and hide the smirk that wants to present itself.

"Busy?" he tries to make small talk.

"Always," my hands rest on the pommel of the saddle, reins loose as Barley drops her head. Pacey's hand is out immediately, her pink nose burying in his hand as she sniffs him out before nudging her way to nuzzle into his chest. His hand runs down her nose as he steps to the side so she can see him.

"She's pretty," his eyes lift from Barley and are back on mine.

"She is," I nod, my lips twisting into a smile.

"Do you want to show me where to unpack? Don't want to just go wandering around your home looking for a room."

"Sure," I lean forward and swing my leg over Barley's back, both feet hitting the floor as I scoop her reins into my hands and lead her towards the water feeder, tying her up loosely.

"Do you need a hand out on the ranch?" he offers as I walk towards the porch, the step creaking.

"Mind that," I say just as he steps on and his step falters.

"I'll get that fixed," he looks below his feet at the now snapped wood.

I ignore him, pushing the latch of the handle down and move into the house, holding the door for Pacey to follow.

He doesn't deserve to look as good as he does.

His eyes scope the boxed hallway as he lets the door close softly into its frame.

"Where's your grandad?"

I look at the time then back at Pacey.

"Napping most likely," I lower my voice as I look in the direction of the living room before I begin climbing the stairs and I hear the sound of his foot on the bottom one as he follows me.

Turning up the small hallway on the stairs, I continue forward.

"This is your room," I roll my lips as I twist the old round doorknob and push into it with force as it opens. "Door's a bit stiff, the old wooden frames swell in the heat," I shrug my shoulders up before stepping into the room.

I wish I could calm the nerves in my stomach and the way my heart races in my chest.

Anxiety pricks at the base of my neck, and I really do hope that this is smooth sailing because I have no idea how to deal with him.

This is all new to me.

But instead of letting him into my heart, I throw my walls up and guard it off.

PACEY

I take one look in the room and my lip curls in distaste.

The bed is covered in a thick, cotton dust sheet, the walls chipped and marked. My eyes scope around the boxed bedroom slowly and I sigh.

Mold creeps into the corners, the windows nailed shut. The hardwood floors in desperate need of treatment, the room has a musty smell to it, and I can't stop my expression.

"Did you not think to sort the room before I moved in?"

I try and make a joke of the situation, but I also wanted to make a point.

"I've been busy," she shrugs a shoulder as she steps into the room and rips the dust cover from the bed and I watch the dust particles floating through the air.

"Look," I step in, placing my hand on hers then moving it towards the dust sheet as I tug it from her grasp—with a little more force than I intended—then ball it up in my hands. "This is not an ideal situation, and I can tell that you're clearly pissed about all of this, but let it be known, I'm not best pleased about it either, but it is what it is. We both agreed to make a dying man happy, so please, can we just drop the childish, bratty behavior and get along for the sake of your grandad?" my tone is curt and it has her staring at me all wide-eyed, lips popped open at my words.

"I don't want this anymore than you, trust me, but here we are. I've showed up, I'm willing to play the damn part but I can't play it alone, so have your five minutes of self-wallowing or throw yourself a pity party then get over it," my eyes volley between hers and my heart is banging in my chest.

"Suck it up, *Sunflower.*"

She says nothing, just storms out of the room and it's not long before I hear the sound of the front door being slammed.

"Childish," I shake my head, scoffing as I do then throw the sheet across the room in a slight temper.

She got under my skin, and I let her.

Would have been easier to just bite my tongue, but I will not live here if she is going to make it insufferable.

It's not just her life that has been turned upside down, mine has as well.

Walking across the room to the large window, I inspect it before furrowing my brows at the nails.

"Was a terrible draft in here," I hear Gerry's voice float through the room, and I exhale sharply as I turn to look at him. "I had no way of fixing it, so just nailed it shut," he leans against the door frame, his chest rising and falling a little faster, his eyes burning into mine. I can hear the crackle as he inhales sharply, his nostrils flaring slightly.

"Am I going to find a lot of this?" I thumb behind me and my shoulders vibrate in soft laughter.

"I could lie but..." he smirks at me then glances over his shoulder, "don't mind Morgan... she is hot headed, she'll come around and once she does, you'll be smitten."

I drop my eyes and kick the toe of my boot into the hardwood floor.

"Sir, I'm just here to fulfil a promise, that's all," and when I look back at him, he has this charming, boyish grin slipped on his lips.

"Few things to know around here..." he trails off as he pushes from the door frame and begins walking into the room I am standing in. "Supper is at dusk, breakfast is at dawn,"

I nod.

Six p.m. and six a.m. give or take, depending on winter and summer.

"Morgan likes to cook, but she will give out chore lists." I keep my lips tight and let him talk. "Fridays, she likes to go to Randy's, Sunday is family day. Doesn't matter what we do, we spend it together."

His eyes break from mine as he brings his hand to his mouth and rubs it across his face. "I would like to keep all of this the same whilst we can."

I know what he is insinuating, but I don't say anything.

"She could do with a hand on the ranch even though she will point blank refuse help."

"I can help where I can, but I also have days where I'll be gone with the work being Sheriff brings."

He bobs his head in a knowing nod.

"I understand you're not going to be here all the time but just read the room. Morgan is pretty good in showing you when she needs someone, she will never ask but her emotions and body language will tell you everything you need to know."

"Okay," I mutter, placing my hands on my hips as I look around the room that is to be mine for the next however long.

"I know it's run down, but a bit of paint and some odd jobs and it'll be good as new," and I scoff a laugh.

"It'll be fine, it's just a room to get my head down at night," I glance at the bed and I really did want to get a new bed set, I have no idea how long this has been sitting here for and who has slept in it.

"If you're thinking of changing anything..." Gerry continues like he can read my mind, "that's fine by me, just don't chuck any of it away," he steps back and I mutter in agreement.

"I'm going to find Morgan," he says, turning and gripping onto the doorframe as he steps over the threshold and back into the hallway. Dropping my head, I kind of feel like I have bitten off more than I can chew. But like always, I'll bury my head and just get on with it.

"Oh, and Rivera," Gerry's hoarse voice has me lifting my head.

"Don't give up on her, she's a good girl... I promise she will be the sunshine on your darkest days."

A genuine smile pulls at my lips.

"I hope so," I say softly before he disappears, and I am left alone in my room.

Sighing, I make a mental note of what I needed to get done, but first things first was getting the bedding off.

Stripping the sheets and cover, I drop it to the floor then tackle the pillowcases.

The mattress is pristine, and I wonder if anyone has actually slept in here.

Bending, I fold the sheets and pillowcases and stack them neatly on the side unit on the end wall.

Moving out of the room, I take the stairs and I'm straight out the door as I begin to unload the boxes.

Morgan is nowhere to be seen and Gerry is sitting in the living room, the radio on softly as *Dolly Parton's* voice fills the small space.

After six trips up and down the stairs, all the boxes are unloaded, and I am back out the door but not before telling Gerry where I was going.

Climbing into my truck, I call my ma and fill her in about the last few hours and I didn't want to tell her but I am already missing her and worrying if this was a huge mistake.

I had no idea just what I had got myself into but no backing down now.

I glance at the gold band wrapped around my finger and my chest aches.

I was married.

I had a wife.

And yet, I had never felt more alone than I did now.

Pulling into the parking lot, I slam the door shut and make my way into the department store and grab a cart on my way in.

Moving straight for the home section, I toss bedding,

pillows and a new comforter in. I browse through the lamps before deciding on a light gray one with a white shade. Reaching for a couple of pictures, I slip them in the cart then finish it off with a small gray rug.

I needed something to cover the hardwood floor until I had some time to sand it and treat it.

The house was beautiful, set on land with amazing views, but it had fallen into disrepair and if I could do one thing in this marriage, I would fix her house up like it was brand new.

The wrap around porch needed work, it was rotten and I swear it'll fall before I get a chance to fix it. The porch deck is also in need of love, the steps cracked beneath my feet earlier and I know I need to make that a priority.

Paying the cashier, I move to the truck and load it up before I am pulling into the hardware store.

I grab what I need and just as the afternoon creeps in, I am pulling down the long and winding driveway.

Pushing the car into park, I grab the bits for my room first and walk straight upstairs but not before giving Gerry a quick glance as I pass and he holds his hand up.

I am petrified that I am going to find him dead.

I didn't need that.

Dumping it on the ground, I would get to work on that soon. I dropped my new bedding back to my mom's to wash and dry whilst I made a start on the mold wash in the corner of the room, then hooked out the nails of the windows.

Testing it out, it was a quick fix.

After an overhaul and new handles, the wooden framed windows were opening and closing as if they were brand new.

The soft hint of bleach filled the room so I opted for

leaving the window slightly ajar to get some of the fresh air in.

Glancing at the time, it was just past four.

I needed to get a shift on before supper.

Moving back to the truck, I glance at Gerry who is now sitting at the small wooden table, Morgan has her back to me as she preps the food but I don't let her see me.

I am out that door like a flash and pulling the back of my truck down as I lay the new wood on the ground just before the steps.

Lifting my cap from my sweaty head, I push my damp, blond hair away from my face then twist my cap so it's backwards as I begin tearing the wood from the steps and shaking my head at the way it's bowed through the rot.

I made a mental note to get the house checked over because I am anxious that the wooden shack that stands won't be standing for much longer.

Tossing the old planks behind me, a thud echoing as I measure the new steps then make my way to Gerry's old work-shed to see if he had what I needed.

Probably should have checked if he had a chop saw, if not, I'll be sawing it over my leg and hoping I don't cut through my jeans.

Unbolting the rusty lock, I drag the dropped heavy wooden doors across the shingle and dust my hands off when I look at his work space.

I had no idea what Gerry did before he got ill, but it must have been some kind of craftsmanship.

I step a little further in and my eyes bounce around the room like a kid at Christmas sneaking down to see all the presents piled up.

Spotting some metal legs under a sheet, I think I have found what I am looking for. Lifting it and turning my head away so I don't inhale a lungful of dust, I smile when I see the saw.

"Bingo," I say softly as I begin to drag it along the floor and closer to the door so I can get the light. I did check to see if any lights were connected but didn't seem that way.

Dragging the wire over to the socket by the entrance, I pray that it works otherwise I am going to have to run it from the house.

I wait a moment as I slip it on then turn and switch on the chop saw and relief swarms me when the saw kicks in then turn it off again as I march over to get the wood. Looking up at the house, I step over the gap and onto the porch as I hunt down a pencil, wood under my arm.

"Gerry," I say as I look at him, staying in the hallway.

"Son?" he says and my heart twists.

"Where can I find a pencil?" and before he can even answer, Morgan, my wife, turns and drags a drawer open before pinching a pencil and walking over to me, holding it out for me to take, but not before her pretty greens sweep over my body then land on my eyes.

My lips twitch into a smile but she turns away, cheeks pink at being caught.

"Thank you, wife," I say a little louder and I watch as Gerry laughs. Slipping it behind my ear, I move back outside and re-measure the step, this time marking it where I needed to cut with the pencil then placing it back where it was as I walk across to the chop-saw, flicking it on and sawing it to length.

I don't even need to look up to know that she is standing at the kitchen window watching me.

I wouldn't want to give her the satisfaction of letting her know that I know.

Petty yes.

But she riled me up.

Switching the saw off, I pace back to the front of the house, kneeling on the dusty floor beneath me as I lay the first step in, nailing it in place before I measure the boxing in and repeating until they were done.

Standing up, I dust my hands off and place my hands on my hips as I admire my work. Sure, it needed to be stained and treated, but the whole deck needed it so may as well do it in one job.

I see her tanned boots before I hear her.

"Supper is ready," she announces before turning her back on me and disappearing into the house.

Pushing my tongue into my cheek, I shake my head as I look towards the mountains and feel the annoyance flick against my skin.

I inhale heavily, puffing my cheeks before exhaling as I climb the new steps, smiling when they don't shift and step into the house, kicking off my boots.

I go to walk into the kitchen, but Morgan shakes her head before leading me towards a room at the back of the house, a four seater dining table sits in the middle of the room, all set for dinner.

"I'm just going to clean up," my voice echoes around the room as I make my way back down the hallway and duck inside the small bathroom, washing my hands before splashing my face with cool water. Shaking them off, I look at myself in the mirror. I really did need a shave, but I was kind of digging the stubble and honestly, I might keep it... plus my upper lip would soon be housing a moustache.

Drying my hands on the small hand towel, I pull the cord light and slip from the now dark bathroom and pace down towards the dinner table.

I see Gerry is sitting head of the table, Morgan to his

right so I take the seat to his left. Dragging the chair out, I sit and before I can even take my hat off, she is walking behind me, flipping it off my head and I give myself a minute before I react.

"No hats at the table," she snipes as she returns to the room with a casserole dish and places it in the center of the table.

"I would have removed my hat, but my ass had just met the seat..."

"Then take it off before," she glares at me as she walks out the room again and I ball my fist, my eyes following her and I see Gerry raise his brows before rolling his eyes.

Next the green beans go down before she is out of the room again.

"Is there an escape clause in this contract, like fourteen days to change your mind kind of thing," and that gets Gerry laughing loudly as she bangs the dish of mashed potatoes down.

"Unfortunately, not," he rubs his lips together.

"I was brought up in a family with strict manners." I say in a levelled tone. "No hats at the table, *cowboy* hats hung on the back of your door when you were finished work, boots off and on the mat, wash up for dinner, table set, and glasses filled..." my eyes skate across the table to see the three glasses empty, "and then we say grace. Take this as a threat or a warning, don't ever treat me like that again." My voice is sharp, and I watch as her face falls.

"Like I said earlier," I drag the napkin from my plate and lay it over my lap, "neither of us want this clearly, but we made a promise... and I intend on keeping my end of that promise," I drop my head for a moment before my hands are palm up on the table. "Grace?"

She doesn't mutter a word as her hand sits in mine, her

other in Gerry's and I close my hand around the both of them.

"That was delicious," I wipe my mouth with my napkin then place it on the plate. "Thank you, Morgan," I softly bob my head in her direction, and she meets it with her own.

"Thank you for fixing the step," Gerry says as he shuffles in his seat.

"Not a problem," I smile at him and Morgan just sits there staring at me and I swear if looks could kill I would be laying flatlined on the table.

"Morgan," Gerry snaps and her eyes drag to her granddad's.

"Yes?" her arms cross in front of her chest causing a small cleavage and my stomach knots.

I should not be looking at her like this.

"I think you owe Rivera a thank you," he lets his chin fall as his brows furrow in his forehead and she swings her face back in my direction.

"Thank you," and there is not an inch of sincerity in her tone.

"You're welcome, *Sunflower.*" I watch the way her eyes soften at the name I used a month ago at Randy's.

Silence falls over the table, so I take that as my cue to leave.

"Excuse me," I mutter softly as I push back on my chair before standing and reaching for the empty dishes.

I can see she wants to say something, but she pouts her lips as I leave the room and place the dishes in the sink.

I return and grab the serving dishes and place them on the work top. Turning, I see her standing there, leant up against the door frame.

"I'll wash that up when I come back down, I need a shower," I flash her a toothy grin, "then I've got to swing over my mom's if you want to come with?" I offer but she shakes her head before turning her back on me and disappearing. "Suit yourself," I say to the empty room before I am climbing the stairs, peeling my tee from my body as I step into my room and grumble when I see the boxes still sitting there along with the new bits I brought.

Scrubbing my face with my left hand, the coolness of the metal band on my skin has me sighing.

It's only seven, a few hours in here and it'll be good as new.

Unbuttoning my jeans, I grab my towel and toiletries bag from one of the boxes and take myself to the bathroom. Lifting my hand, I knock on the closed door before I twist the knob and let myself in, locking it behind me.

Removing the towel that is already sitting on the towel rail, I hang mine over it and place my hand on the rail, it's lukewarm. Folding the other towel up and placing it on the shelf, I unload my bag and grab what I need.

Not that the room was cold, but nothing beats a warm towel after a shower.

Pushing my jeans down, I discard them along with my boxers before twisting the stiff shower, a loud bang echoes around the small room as the water kicks in.

Holding my hand under the water, it takes about five minutes for the water to warm and when it has, I step under and groan as the hard water hits my skin.

Lathering myself up, I clean myself before washing my hair. Letting my head tip back, I give myself a minute more before I step out and am back faced with the angry blonde-haired woman I married.

She is trying to throw down her dominance.

Bit like when a dog pees up a tree, marking his territory.

I'm the tree, covered in dog pee.

Shutting the water off, it bangs again and I pull back the wet shower curtain as I reach for my towel, wrapping it around my body.

Brushing my teeth, I bend for my dirty clothes before spitting in the sink and placing my brush back in my bag.

That would be a tomorrow job.

I'm not back to work until Monday so I have another full day of sorting out the house that I am terrified is going to fall down around us, but I need to have faith.

It's lasted this long.

Twisting the handle, I pad out into the hallway, feet still wet as I move down the hardwood floor and towards my bedroom when I see her standing at the top of the stairs, eyes trailing up and down my wet torso.

I wasn't overly toned, but I had definition. Arms were more of a statement than my torso. I watch as her eyes graze down to my bullet wound, they narrow slightly before she looks at my face, her hand slipping into the back of her jeans and I know she is desperate to ask but doesn't want to.

"I was shot," I say as if it is no big deal, but in reality, it was a fucking huge deal.

Still wake up some nights screaming.

Her eyes widen.

"Yeah." I nod then begin to walk past her and I don't look back.

I could have been an asshole and not uttered a word.

But I was brought up better than that.

Slamming my bedroom door, I get myself ready before I am back in my truck and driving towards my mom's.

Warmth radiates around my body as I step into the bright, large, hallway and I seek my mom out instantly.

She is sitting in my dad's chair in the lounge, knitting a blanket. A pastel rainbow length of woven wool is stretched out in front of her and I know how desperate she has been to get it finished before baby Rivera arrives.

"Hey Ma," I smile at her, leaning in and giving her a kiss.

"Hey sunshine boy," she smiles wide as I take my seat opposite her and I fall into easy conversation, telling her all about my day.

CHAPTER EIGHT
MORGAN

Leaning against the doorframe of his bedroom, I scope the room out. He has already fixed the window, they're both open slightly and the once musty room now smells fresher.

The bed is stripped and bare, boxes still littered over the floor.

My chest aches a little and I find myself flattening my palm across my heart and through the thin material of my cotton tee.

We made this room up years ago. I asked my pops if we could make a room for my mom, you know, just in case she ever came back.

He knew she would never return, but me, a child, dreamt of the day she wrapped her arms around me and promised to never leave me again.

But of course, she never came.

The harsh reality sunk in finally and I knew it would always be me and him.

It wasn't a problem. He was the best mom, dad, granddad and grandma all rolled into one. He was there for every damn thing and I will never not be grateful to him. I never went without; he worked his fingers to the bone until he fell ill.

I hated that he was leaving me, but I knew that it was out of my control.

Sighing heavily, I feel his hand on my shoulder, and I turn to look at him.

"You need to stop biting his head off," he gives me a small smirk, but I know that he is only smirking to soften his scolding.

I know he is right.

But I am bitter.

And I am allowed to be.

By gaining Pacey, I'm losing my pops.

And I wasn't ready for that.

"He isn't a bad kid, there is no way I would have chosen him if he was," his grip on my shoulder tightens. "Don't ruin this before it has even started Morgan, I know this isn't what you wanted; it's not what I wanted, but this is the hand we have been dealt and whilst I can still make choices that I feel are best for you and this ranch, then I will make them. Rivera was the right call. He will fix this ranch up like it is his own, he will work hard, and he will support and care for you." I lower my head so he can't see the tears that prick in my green eyes.

"If you're really that unhappy, once I am gone and the ranch is out of trouble, then divorce him. Just don't take him off the deeds. I don't trust anyone but you and him, I can't have the risk of someone swooping in and taking my legacy away."

I roll my head up as my eyes volley between his and I suck in a breath.

"We will work together, I may not always see eye to eye

with him, but I'll try and not be so harsh..." I pause when I hear the sound of the creek on the bottom step before I see his head pop up as he climbs the stairs.

"That's my girl," he places a kiss on my cheek before turning his back and patting Pacey on the chest as he passes him then disappearing into his room, closing the door behind him.

I allow myself to look at him, skating my eyes up and down his body.

I wish I didn't find him attractive, it really would help with this whole situation, but of course he has to look like he has been hand carved by God himself.

He stops in front of me and my stomach knots when his whiskey eyes burn into mine.

"How was your mom?" I ask, eyes dropping to the linen laundry bag that his fist is clinging to.

"Good, knitting," he lifts his chin, his voice raspy. He goes to step around me after an agonising minute of silence, but I step in front of him.

"Look," I drop my gaze for a moment before my sights are back on him. "I know I am a lot, I have not been very welcoming to you..." I knot my fingers in front of me and see the way his lips twist into a half smile. "But this is all new to me, I kind of feel a little out of sorts with it all... and well, you're you... I'm me. At Randy's that random Friday night I was feeling brave, I remembered you from the wedding, and well, I had a little fun being flirty. Never thought I would see you again and then a few weeks later you're in my kitchen and I am being told that we're to be married." I take a breather, swallowing down the dryness in my throat. "And here we are, married, living in a house together and I'm sure it's not just me who can feel the tension that brews between us... and I am worried that this is how we're going to live our life out. Worried that I am stopping you from finding your one true love," and the rest of my words get stuck at the back of my throat after the words that slipped past my lips.

"You're not," his voice is flat as he answers me, "trust me, there is no one out there for me."

I have no idea why, but it feels like he has just plunged a knife straight into my heart, and just when I finally catch my breath, he twists it up, slicing it open and watching as I bleed out in front of him.

"Cool, that's all I was worried about," and tears mist my eyes, but I stand tall, my voice quiet as I roll my shoulders back.

"Cool," he mimics my words, and I can feel the cold tone of his voice blanket me in a shiver.

He steps passed me again and this time I let him; I close my eyes and hold my breath until I hear the sound of the bedroom door close behind me, I jump slightly even though I knew it was coming. I give myself a minute or two before I head for my own room, slamming the door.

I needed to wash this mood off me, needed to sink into the deep copper tub and let the hot water wash all my stress away.

We're not going to co-exist without problems, but I was hoping our relationship would have been a bit warmer than it was. Then again what did I expect when I have treated him the way I have.

I have been immature.

He is living in my home, with my pops, with *our* rules and I am expecting him to be okay with it.

I have turned his life upside down.

He has had to leave his home, his family, his rules... to live with me.

My mind is in overdrive and by the time I sink myself in the bath I have given myself a tension headache.

Letting my shoulders dip beneath the hot water, my fingers press against my temples as I try and rub the ache away but it doesn't shift, just lowers to my neck, my shoulders... the tension growing the more I think about my situation.

I have been such a child about this whole thing because I didn't like the reason.

The reason is out of my control.

My pops is dying.

He has found someone to care for me, and maybe even love me.

Not that I think he wants love from the way he just shut me down, but, there is a chance.

But I needed to focus on the ranch and us not losing it.

That was our main job.

Keep the money coming in.

Keep the ranch in safe hands.

Pacey Rivera had an army he could use if needed.

I had me and Dusty.

We were small fry compared to Rivera Ranch, but still, this was our home, our livelihood and there was no way I was going down without a fight.

They may have offered stupid money for this bit of land, but there was no way in hell I was handing it over. They got my pops at a vulnerable time when his hospital bills were at an all time high, but I will not let him or them take away his legacy.

I would stand beside Pacey Rivera, my husband, and fight this war.

This may have not been the way I had envisioned my life going, but this is the hand we have been dealt.

I could either continue acting the way I am or stand shoulder to shoulder with him and keep the promise we both made to my pops and I know in that moment that I would always choose the latter.

Dressed in light cotton pyjama pants and a cropped tee, my hair is dry and tied into a messy bun on the top of my head. I open my bedroom door and glance down the hallway but it's deafly silent.

It's past midnight, I had debated going into Pacey's room to make sure he was okay but I didn't, I stayed right where I was until now.

I should just go to bed and sleep the day off, but before I can tell my mind what to do, we're walking down the narrow hallway and towards where his room is.

Stilling outside, I see the door is a jar. Pushing slightly and praying it doesn't creak, I find an empty room.

But the boxes are all gone, the bed is remade in new bedding, a lamp sits in the corner on his bedside unit and a new rug covers a small amount of the hardwood floor. A candle is flickering away on the low window ledge, a cosy aroma filling the room and I cannot believe how much he has done to this room in such a short amount of time. I cast my eyes to the corner where the black mold presented itself and I see that it has faded slightly, and I feel instantly bad that I put him in this room in the first place. I would have been better putting him in my room and me taking the sofa for a few nights until it was sorted.

But, I was a bitch and let him move into it anyway.

I knew he was coming. I could have sorted it but I was being a brat, throwing my toys out the stroller in a sulk.

Guilt twists in my stomach and my thumb and finger finds my delicate wedding band as I twist it around my finger.

Stepping back, I pull the door two and turn on my heel as I make my way downstairs. I have no idea if he has washed the dishes, but if I was him, I wouldn't have out of spite. Because that's what I am like.

I am petty.

Walking down the stairs quietly, the kitchen is dimmed and I know he is in there.

Stepping off the bottom stair, I walk into the small kitchen to see him standing at the sink, in a tee and pyjama pants, washing the dishes.

Leaning against the doorframe, hands linked in front of me as I watch him silently for just a moment.

"I would have done them," I eventually say quietly, and he looks over his shoulder at me, his messy blond hair tufty and unkept.

"It's fine, you cooked, I clean..." he trails his eyes forward and off me. "That's the rules in *my* house," and I don't miss the sharpness to his words.

Stepping closer into the kitchen, I drag one of the wooden chairs out and sit myself down, crossing one leg over the other as I sit and watch him.

"Thank you for fixing the step," I mumble, just trying to make any form of conversation.

"Not a problem, it needed fixing so I fixed it," and I know he is acting this way because of me. Sighing, I tilt my head to the side.

"Well, thank you anyway," I try again, my voice a little lighter.

I watch as the back of his head bobs and I know I have properly fucked up.

"Can you dry?" he throws the dish towel over his shoulder, and I push up to my feet as I make my way to meet him.

Turning my head to the left as I look up at him all wide eyed and feeling guilty as hell, I take the towel from his shoulder and begin to dry up the dishes he has washed.

We don't talk.

Just stand in silence.

Once we're done, I move towards the stairs and I hear the sound of him tapping the kitchen light off and he is behind me, following me up the stairs.

Reaching the top, I go right, he goes left.

We both stand, eyes locked with each other, and I wait for him to speak.

But he says nothing.

Just turns his head away from me and walks into his bedroom, closing the door softly behind him and once I know he is behind it, I go into my own room and disappear.

Eyes pinned to the ceiling, I have no idea how long I am laying there before my eyes finally flutter shut and I am plunged into a deep sleep.

My alarm screams and it takes me a moment to realize it's coming from my alarm clock. Slamming my hand down on the button, I cover my head with my duvet and groan.

I was not ready to face the day.

Rolling over, I sigh as I see the sun peeking through the curtains.

And then it dawns on me, it's Sunday and I have no idea why my alarm is even set.

Dragging my duvet back over my head, I force my eyes shut and try and fall back to sleep but it is no use.

I have spent an hour tossing and turning and finally decide to call it a day. Sitting up, I stretch and then toss the covers from me as my feet touch the thick carpet beneath me, toes scrunching as I glance over my shoulder and see the sun still shining.

Summer in Montana is my favorite, but it doesn't last as long as I needed it to.

The winters are harsh and long.

The days seem darker than light, and the work feels ten times harder.

Pushing from the bed, I make my way to the bathroom to splash my face and brush my teeth before I make my way downstairs.

It's quiet and I know I am the only one awake so I make a start on the laundry before I put a fresh pot of coffee on and keep it warm.

Opening the fridge, I raid it to find something to make a nice breakfast for Pacey and pops. Placing all I need from the fridge on the worksurface, I move to the small pantry cupboard that sits over the back of the kitchen and sigh when I see the egg house empty.

Closing the door softly, I walk across into the small hallway and open the closet and grab my trench coat, wrapping it around my slender body as I unlock the front door and the crisp morning air fills my lungs.

Wrapping the coat around me a little more, I close the door behind me and duck out. The skies are pink, the trees softly dancing in the summer breeze. The air smells sweet, the sound of the narrow stream that runs behind the ranch trickling. Dusty will already be with the horses, the heifers are over the hill and we have two cowboys sitting up top overnight watching them, while Dusty takes the day shift.

The sound of my rubber boots crunch over the loose stones as I make my way to the coop, glancing over the rolling green hills and see a couple of the geldings out and grazing.

We really wanted to get Bonnie—our piebald cob— foaled this year, but I just can't see it happening, unless

Pacey can make it work, plus it's cash we don't really have spare. I know you have to put in to get back but the pot is running on empty and we can just about keep our heads above water with the ranch.

Business has dropped and I have no idea where the hell we are going to go from here.

We used to be a cotton mill ranch, but my pops pulled away from that once my grandma died and went to the cattle auction. Came home with eight... that eight is now thirty.

But it's continuous.

Buying, breeding, selling.

The want for meat is dwindling in these parts of towns and we haven't made it out of Montana yet, it doesn't help that we have the Riveras in the next town along, they always have first refusal of any sales, if they don't want it, they pass it along to us.

This is why my pops has paired me and Pacey together. Not only for the ranch, but for the connections that Pacey has.

Livestock Agent turned Sheriff; he also holds a well-known name. Everyone knows the Riveras.

The good, the bad, the ugly.

It didn't matter.

They were still who you wanted on your side.

If we were going to war like my pops thinks, then he has chose a good army to take us into the depths of it.

Slipping open the lock on the pen, I lift it up and see my hens sitting all cozy.

"Hey girls."

Roost, the rooster shakes his feathered wings before stretching his neck and strutting himself out of the coop and I know he is about to do his morning call.

He shouldn't even be in here. He is normally in the little coop with the hens that I want to have chicks, but the little shit does what he wants.

He rules all.

Slipping my hand beneath them, I check for eggs and then peep the box that hasn't been collected in a couple of days and fill my wicker basket up before slipping out the coop and closing the small gate.

I wish I could have them more free roaming, but what with the foxes and wolves, I can't deal with the heartbreak of waking up and seeing them mauled.

They're not cooped up, they have more than enough and probably don't even feel like they're shut away, but I know they're locked away and guilt eats at me.

Right on cue, just as the sun peeks over the mountains and comes into full glory, Roost's morning call echoes around the ranch and I smile.

I have never wanted to leave Blossom Cove, the city life has never appealed to me.

I'm a homely girl.

Like the feel of the grass beneath my bare feet, the sunrise each morning and the clear nights skies, stargazing and the family feel you get around the town.

Everyone knows everyone.

You never feel alone.

You could move here as an outsider and everyone would make you feel welcome.

Unless you've done something to make them hate you, then that's a different story.

We're all close knit.

We know everything about everyone.

We may not be in Lovelock Bay's town, but we're on the outskirts and share it. Sure, we have a narrow strip which has the odd shops scattered, but it's nothing special.

But it's home.

Pushing in the door, I close it behind me and place the basket on the high, round table that sits just inside the small hallway before I shrug my coat off, hanging it up then lose the boots, tucking them back inside the closet on the shoe rack.

Walking back into the kitchen, I smile. There is nothing that caused it, but maybe having the fresh air and seeing the sunrise was the reason.

Placing four eggs on the side, I pop the rest in the pantry and hang the basket up on the hook that sits on the back of the door.

Glancing at the time, it's just past seven and I feel like I have been awake hours.

Turning the radio on, I twist the volume dial so you can just about hear it when the sound of *Riley Green - don't mind if I do* plays and I sing softly along.

Plating up pancakes, bacon, eggs, toast and fruit, I lay it all out on the work surface before I fill a jug with fresh orange juice.

"Morning," his voice has me spinning around, eyes a little wide as I scope him out.

It's not fair for someone to look that hot.

All the god damn time.

"Morning," I smile, walking the plates over to the small round table, I place them down then grab the cutlery.

"You're in a good mood," his voice is slow and full of rasp.

"Slept well," I shrug a shoulder up as I reach up for the mugs and I feel his eyes burning into my back. "Pops up yet?" I look at him, head tilting and he shakes his head from side to side.

"Not yet, heard him snoring," he walks over to the food that is plated up then places his hand on the top of my head, rubbing his hand back and forth and messing my hair.

"Hey," I scowl, pushing into his side and he chuckles. "Let me go check on pops, don't really want to eat without him," I say, eyeing my husband as he slips a piece of bacon into his mouth and bites it.

"Oops," he smirks at me over his shoulder as I walk out the room and go to wake my granddad.

Softly knocking on the door, I walk in and smile as his eyes find mine.

"Morning pops you okay?" I walk over and pull back the curtains.

"Feel a little off today," he grumbles as he tosses the covers back and swings his legs with a groan.

"Want me to call the doctor?" my brows furrow as I help him to his feet, my eyes scanning over his face. He looks a little gray. Placing my hand against his forehead he is burning up. "Why don't you stay in bed? I'll get you breakfast brought up and I'll call Doctor Carlos."

He nods, as I lower him back down and tuck him in.

"I'll get your meds," I place a kiss on his forehead and make my way downstairs.

Pacey's eyes follow me and I am muttering incoherent words.

"All okay?" he asks as he stands, hands in the pockets of his pyjama pants.

"Pops isn't feeling well, I'm going to take him some breakfast up then call the doctor," I don't look at him, I am too busy setting out his tablets.

"Need me to do anything?"

I want to say no, but I need to learn to use him for help.

"Could you cut a large blood-orange in half and sprinkle it with brown sugar?" my voice is soft. "Then fill a glass of tap water?"

He doesn't reply.

Just does as I ask.

He is in the fridge and slicing the blood orange before he plates it up then fills the glass up. Before I can even ask, he is getting the lap tray out and places it on the work surface.

"Thank you," I whisper as I lay the plates down and place a hot cup of coffee on it. I go to lift it but Pacey shakes his head from side to side.

"I'll take it, you get his meds," he gives me a sympathetic smile and I don't know why, but it makes my chest ache.

He waits for me to walk out of the kitchen before I climb the stairs, him following as I walk into my pops' room, plastering a fake smile across my lips as I tilt my head, looking at him then placing his meds on the bedside table with his water. He thanks me with a soft nod as Pacey tiptoes behind with his tray of food. I step aside as Pacey places it down and he gives Pacey a small smile.

"Take your meds pops," I say as I sit on the edge of the bed. I know he wouldn't not take them, but I always feel better when I have seen him swallow them.

His trembling hand skates across as he reaches for his water then scoops the tablets up, tossing them back in one mouthful as he swallows them down with the water.

His playful manner doesn't go unnoticed as he sticks his tongue out before lifting it so I can see that he has in fact taken his meds.

"Thank you," I mutter, then place my hand over his and the coldness of his skin shocks me.

"Doctor will be here soon," Pacey slips in and I smile at him before turning my attention back to my pops.

"Eat your blood orange first, then eat the rest if you feel up to it. I'll be back soon," I say as I stand then lean over and give him a kiss on the forehead, his feverish skin warming my lips and my heart twists.

"No problem sweetheart," he rumbles, and I feel Pacey's hand rest on my lower back as I stand up and I want to break down in front of him, but I don't. I keep as positive as I can that he will break the fever and he will be back to himself after a full belly and a good sleep.

"Come," Pacey whispers, ushering me out of the room and then slips the door two behind me.

"I'm worried," my words dance on a whisper as we make our way downstairs, Pacey close to me and I know he can pick up on my mood.

"It'll be okay," and I know he is trying his best to reassure me, but my heart still skips a beat or two.

Walking back into the kitchen, a heavy sigh has my shoulders sagging at the now spoiled food on the side.

Pacey keeps moving, grabbing his plate from the table as he does and begins scooping the food onto his plate.

"Don't eat that, it's cold."

"You cooked it, I'll eat it... always," his eyes meet mine over my shoulder and I can't stop the small smile that tugs at the corners.

Turning, he walks back to the table and he gives me a soft wink and my heart swells in my chest at the small bit of sweetness he has shown me.

Sitting at the table, I watch as he bites a bit of bacon, his eyes closing slightly as he hums in appreciation.

My lips twist and I know he is probably doing it just to be kind.

Moving over to the work top, I plate my own food up and take my seat next to him.

My appetite has gone, pushing my food around my plate but I do manage a few small bites.

We sit in silence as we eat and I am very aware that this food is dry and cold but Pacey eats the whole plate then goes back for seconds.

Pushing his plate away, he taps his stomach softly and puffs his cheeks out.

"That was," he makes a circle with his finger and thumb as if to say perfection.

"You're being kind," I shake my head as I push my own plate away.

"I'm not," he grumbles as his eyes narrow on mine for a moment. "It was really good," he nods then looks behind him, silently debating whether to go for another serving.

"Thanks for calling Dr Carlos," I mutter as I look towards the kitchen window and sigh, I didn't want to say the words out loud, but I knew his time was running out and it broke my heart that there was nothing I could do.

"Always, you should know I'll always be here for you..." he trails off, "whether you want me here or not."

I can't look at him.

My eyes burn and I try to blink away the tears that are threatening.

"I am so worried," my bottom lip trembles and I hate that I am going to cry in front of him.

"I know you are," his hand skates across the table and hovers over mine, his thumb brushing back and forth and that's when I look at him, tears edging on my bottom lid.

Before I could even respond, the front doorbell chimes

through the hallway and I slip my hand from under his and I swipe my tear away.

Pushing from the table, I pace to the hallway and swing the front door open and I give Dr Carlos a soft smile.

Dark hair, tanned skin, brown eyes. Mid-forties.

"Morgan," he gives me a small nod, a grimace on his face.

I step aside and let him in, he removes his black cowboy hat and places it on the hook outside the closet where we hang our coats and store our shoes.

"What's the problem?" Carlos asks just as Pacey moves around the door frame. Carlos' eyes flick to him, his jaw tightening before he focuses on me.

"He looks a bit gray, said he didn't feel too good. He has a fever, hands are cold." I sigh, letting my head turn and looking up the stairs to where my pops is. "He has had his meds, we left him with breakfast whilst we ate ours."

Carlos nods, his fingers flexing around his black leather doctor bag.

"May I?" he asks, his eyes lifting from mine and trailing the stairs.

I give a nod and turn on my heel, walking up the stairs as he follows me, Pacey close behind.

"Have you got a houseguest?" he asks me as he follows me up the stairs.

"I'm her husband," I hear the way Pacey's voice rumbles, it's low and slow.

"Oh," Carlos' response has me smirking.

He is a good-looking man.

Older yes, but devilishly handsome.

Pacey is a little more rugged, rough around the edges but a pretty boy.

Carlos was clean cut, hair always swept back and

styled, dressed impeccably. I'd always had a bit of a crush on him.

But totally wouldn't go there.

"I didn't realize you had a husband," Carlos says as we reach the top of the stairs.

"We've only been married a short while," I wait for him to walk next to me and my cheeks turn pink.

Pacey steps up behind me and curls his hand around my hip, pulling me into him and I know this is all for show.

If I was a betting woman, I would say he was jealous.

Carlos' eyes cast down to his little public display of affection and clears his throat.

Stepping away from my husband, I give the ajar door a knock and then step into the room, my pops turning to look at us, his lips pressing into a smile.

"Ah, doc, good to see you," he says as Carlos walks past me and moves over to the bed, sitting on the edge as he looks at him.

"We will leave you to it," I say quietly, and Carlos gives me a soft nod as his eyes meet mine over his shoulder. I step back and Pacey follows as I close the door. "I know that look," I whisper as I pace up and down the landing.

"What look?" Pacey glares at the closed door then his sights are back on me.

"The look Carlos gave me; it's bad news..." I nibble my non-existent nails as I continue moving.

"Hey, hey," Pacey says as he cups my face in his hand and slowly my fingers drop from my lips as my eyes burn into his. "He is with the best person... you've got to try and keep positive... can you do that for me?" his eyes volley between mine as he waits for me and all I can do is nod, over and over. "Good girl," he whispers before dropping my face and I go back to pacing, and he just leans against the stair rail as we wait for Carlos to re-appear.

I freeze when I hear the door handle twist and I am next to Pacey in a second as Carlos steps out of the room, closing the door behind him quietly before he lifts his head to look at me.

He doesn't even need to say the words.

His eyes tell me everything.

"How long?" I whisper, because saying the words out loud are too terrifying.

"A couple of weeks..." he trails off before his hand is on my shoulder, "I'm so sorry Morgan."

Running my tongue over my bottom lip, my eyes fill with unshed tears, and I can't stop them falling, even if I wanted to.

"I will be back tonight; I can give him meds to make him comfortable. I can get nurses in too, twenty-four hours a day to help you both out..." he pauses as he drops his hand from my shoulder and looks at Pacey. "It's going to be a lot for you to deal with Morgan, I really do suggest you accept the help."

I can't respond. I am completely numb to the words that have just left his mouth.

"Thanks doc, we'll be in touch once we have had a chance to talk." he clasps Carlos' hand before he leads him to the front door.

I am still frozen on the spot.

My legs felt anchored to the floor, my heart thumping hard in my chest. My mind was whizzing with a thousand questions, but I just couldn't voice them, I just couldn't get them out to ask Carlos what was wrong.

Pacey's fingers curl around my wrist, slowly pulling my

hand from my face as he looks at me, head dipped and tilted slightly.

"Baby," his voice is quiet and sounds as if it is in the distance. I blink a few times, and finally, I manage to look at him.

His lips twitch into a smile and before I can even fall apart, he pulls me into his body, my head on his chest as I sob silently into his tee, soaking it through.

He says nothing.

Just wraps his arms around me and holds me whilst I cry.

Sure, crying isn't going to cure my pops.

But it feels damn good to let it all out.

CHAPTER NINE
PACEY

My own heart aches at seeing Gerry looking as poorly as he does. I follow Morgan out the room, a heavy sigh escaping her.

"I know that look," she whispers as she steps onto the landing. I close the door behind myself and meet her in the middle of the landing.

"What look?" I ask, twisting my head to look back at the door.

"The look Carlos gave me; it's bad news..." her voice trails off, fingers against her lips as she nibbles on her already short nails.

"Hey, hey," My voice is rushed as I close the small gap between us, cupping her face into my hands as I tilt her head back so she has no other option but to look at me, trying to reassure her. "He is with the best person... you've got to try and keep positive... can you do that for me?" my eyes bounce between her beautiful blues, and she nods over and over again and I don't miss the blanket of unshed tears that threaten to fall.

"Good girl," I whisper before I drop her face and I lean

against the stair rail as she resumes her pacing of the landing as we wait for news.

Given the situation, I won't voice my concerns over the doctor, but it's quite clear that he may have a little crush, or vice versa. He didn't seem to like the fact we were married and I know, I know, I played into it a little too much as I curled my hand around her hip and pulled her against me, but I just wanted him to know that she was mine.

My head lifts when I hear the door handle twist and she is by my side in an instant, her fingers back near her mouth. He closes the door quietly behind him before he even looks at us.

Nothing is said.

His eyes are on Morgan and Morgan only.

But whatever is going on, she seems to know exactly what is going on.

"How long?" she just about manages to squeeze out.

"A couple of weeks..." he trails off before his hand is on her shoulder and jealousy bites at my skin, "I'm so sorry, Morgan," but as soon as those words leave his mouth, my heart throbs inside my chest in an unbearable ache.

Skating my eyes to my wife, I watch as she runs her tongue over her full bottom lip, her beautiful green eyes fill with unshed tears and I am desperate to swipe them away with my thumb pad.

Carlos shuffles on the spot, his eyes not lifting from hers as he begins to speak. "I will be back tonight, I can give him meds to make him comfortable. I can get nurses in too, twenty-four hours a day to help you both out..." he pauses as he drops his hand from her shoulder and looks at me with a knowing look, a quick raise of the brow and I know he is more telling her than asking.

"It's going to be a lot for you to deal with Morgan, I really do suggest you accept the help."

She says nothing, just keeps her eyes on him and I'm not sure if its the shock or she just doesn't know what else to say to him. Carlos steps aside and levels himself to me.

"Thanks doc, we'll be in touch once we have had a chance to talk." I clasp my hand in his and give it a firm shake before I turn and lead him down the stairs.

"Try and get her to accept the help," Carlos says as he plucks his hat from the back of the door and places it on his head before he is picking his bag up again.

"I will," I nod, running my hand around the back of my neck and rubbing slightly.

Carlos sighs, and I can see the sadness in his eyes. "How bad is it?" I say quietly, mindful that she is just above us.

"He has an infection, he has had it a while and what with everything else going on in his body..." he pauses. "When I saw him a month ago, he was riddled... we knew it would be three months if that, but I prepared him for the worst and gave him a month," and I swallow down the lump that has housed itself in my throat, nodding as I take in his words.

"He is ready to go, think he may have been holding on to make sure she was going to be looked after," and he gives me a lopsided smile.

A smile slips on my lips momentarily.

"I'll wait for your call, I can have the nurses here for supper time."

"Thanks," I mumble, reaching behind him and twisting the door handle, pulling it open as I wait for him to leave.

He gives me a heavy nod before he steps across the threshold, and I shut the door quietly behind him.

Dropping my head, my chest aches.

My own grief bubbles at the surface and I know she is going to have to go through this all herself.

I may be here by her side, but I can't take any of this pain away and it guts me to my core.

Inhaling sharply, I stand tall and climb the stairs to find her but when I reach the top, she hasn't moved.

She is still standing there.

Anchored to the spot.

Fingers pressed against her lips, but this time she isn't biting on her nails.

Her glassy eyes are pinned to her granddad's bedroom door, and I know she is seconds from letting the tears fall.

Stepping in front of her, I hear the inhale of her trembling breath. I reach up, curling my fingers around her wrist and slowly pull her hand away, my head tilts to the side, dipping it slightly and that's when she finally looks at me.

"Baby," I whisper to the quiet room and that's all it took. I pull her into my body, her head on my chest and I wrap my arms around her trembling body as she sobs, her tears soaking through my tee but I don't care.

I just hold her until she is done.

My lips press to the top of her head as I close my own eyes, pushing down my own grief as I let her cry.

Once she had calmed down, I walked her into her grandad's room and then slipped out silently so she could spend time with him.

I took myself downstairs and put away breakfast, then cleaned the dishes before drying and putting everything back. Sure, it took me a while to find out where everything went, but I got there in the end.

Moving upstairs, I walk into my room and make my bed up before reaching for fresh clothes. I needed a shower.

Padding across to the main bathroom, I close the door behind me and turn the faucet on for the shower before I hear the bang in the pipes. Placing my hand under the water, I wait for it to warm up before I peel my clothes from me and dump them in a pile on the floor then stepping into the shower tray as I wash the morning off me.

I needed to prepare myself for what was about to come. She was going to be distraught and heartbroken, and I had no idea how to comfort her. If she is anything like how I was, she will push everyone away and of course, she only has me and Dusty.

I needed to get her familiar with my family, needed to introduce her to Sunny and Conrad so she always had someone to turn to if she ever needed it.

Even if she pushed me away to the point of hating me, I would still be here for her.

Because that's what I promised.

I promised her grandad that I would look after her and their ranch.

Scrubbing my skin and then my hair, I rinse the suds off before turning the shower off and wrapping the towel around me. Drying myself, I dress and brush my teeth before I hang my towel up to dry and make my way back to my room.

Gerry's door is still shut and I am assuming that she is still in there.

I didn't want to disturb.

Glancing at the time, it was nearing midday.

I had some laundry to take over to mom's and I needed to catch up with Austin.

Pacing the small hallway, I debated going up there to let her know that I was leaving. I really didn't want to just disappear and her wonder where I had gone.

Stopping when I stand at the bottom of the stairs, my eyes drift up when I hear the sound of floorboards creaking above me. I hold my breath for a moment, then finally make my way up them as I search for her.

Gerry's door is now ajar and hers is wide open.

"Morgan?" I call out as I step to the entrance of her room and I see her sitting on her bed, all docile, fingers locked in front of her, eyes cast down.

I lean against the door frame as I look at her.

She looks so small.

"I'm going to pop up to the ranch, did you want to come for a drive?" I ask and her head lifts, red rimmed eyes bouncing between mine and I am waiting for her to decline my invitation, but she doesn't.

"Can you give me ten minutes to shower? Then if it's okay, I would really like to come with you," her bottom lip trembles.

"Of course," I smile at her, "I'll speak to Dusty, tell him to stay close to your grandad."

She nods, pushing from the bed as she slips into her own bathroom that is adjoined to her room.

Glancing towards Gerry's room, I walk over quietly as I poke my head around and make sure he is still breathing.

"Rivera," he rasps and I step into the room, hands rubbing together as I close the gap between the both of us.

I sit on the edge of the bed, and his breathing is rattled.

"She knew this day was coming," he says as his glassy eyes drift to the door.

"I know," I say softly because what else am I meant to say to him, "but it doesn't make it any easier," I slip in just as his sights are on me.

He sighs heavily.

"I am going to try and get her to let Carlos get some nurses in, help her out…"

He smirks.

"Good luck," he winks at me, and I chuckle lightly.

"I don't want her to burn herself out, what with the ranch, keeping on top of chores…" my own eyes move to the door. "I will help out where I can but she is a proud lady… she doesn't want to be seen as being helpless."

"Exactly that," his hand reaches for mine as he places it on my wrist, "just give her time, and you're going to have to make the call with Carlos and the nurses because she won't like that… but once they're here, once she sees how quick I am going to deteriorate…"

"Gerry," I say softly, shaking my head. "She would rather be with you in your last days. I agree on the nurses, but, she won't just step away."

He grumbles.

"I'm going to take her up to the ranch, she is going to need family around her over the next few weeks, I don't want her to feel any more isolated than what she is feeling now so I will arrange to get Dusty to sit with you whilst we're gone."

He nods, eyes casting to the door.

"You promise you'll look after her?" he doesn't look at me and my breath catches in the back of my throat as his fingers tighten around my wrist.

"Always."

"You're not going to run away when it gets tough are you?" his brows raise as he rolls his head around to face me.

Shaking my head, "No sir."

"She is going to need you more than ever and trust me,

you'll be the worst person to her, she'll push you away but just don't give up on her."

I say nothing. Just listen.

These thoughts have already crossed my mind so I know exactly where he is going with this.

"I need to know that you're in this for the long run, that this is going to be your home now... with her, until death do you part..."

"I swear it," I clasp his hand in mine and give it a gentle squeeze. "You have my word and my signature in ink, we made a deal."

He nods, tears forming in his eyes.

"As my father used to say..." and my own voice cracks, "live by the ranch, die by the ranch."

DRIVING DOWN THE DUSTY ROAD, it's not long before we're pulling into Rivera Ranch. Morgan has been quiet, just staring out the window.

Anxiety pricks at the base of my neck as I slow the truck down and park it in front of the garages.

Her soft green eyes cast out the windshield before they're on mine.

"You okay?" I ask, desperate to place my hand on her thigh but I know I shouldn't.

I don't think this will ever be more than a business transaction, but the want to feel her skin beneath my fingers is only going to grow.

She nods before pulling on the handle of her door and jumping out.

I follow, walking around the back of the truck and grabbing the linen laundry bag out of the back seats.

"You do know you can wash that at home?" her brow raises as her eyes fall to the bag then back on mine.

"I know... but..." I shrug a shoulder up and cast my eyes over her.

Bell bottom jeans over her boots, lemon tee that sits cropped, teasing her tanned skin on her torso. Sunshine hair in loose waves, sunglasses pushed onto her head.

"Come," I nod my head in the direction of the house as we walk past Tripp and Riggs' trucks.

I had no idea the whole family would be here.

She stalls as she gets to the front door and I do what feels natural. I slip my hand inside hers and push the door handle down with my elbow as I lead her through into the hallway.

"Ma!" I call out, dumping the laundry bag at my feet. Riggs walks down the hallway, lips twitching as his dark eyes scope over Morgan than shift to me.

"Hello, little brother," he smirks as Aspen bounds down behind him and pushes past to wrap Morgan into a hug.

"He finally brought you home," she smiles before letting Morgan out of her grasp, her eyes drifting up to Riggs as he wraps his hand around her body and pulls her close.

"Just to do laundry," I mumble as Riggs nods back towards the living room and we follow down, Morgan's hand still in mine and I realize this is the first time that she has been inside the house.

Her fingers unlock from mine as we walk into the room, my mom sitting cuddling Lainey, Tripp sitting on the armchair, Dixie is nowhere to be seen.

"Hello sunshine boy," she smiles at me before her eyes drift to Morgan. "Hello darling," her smile only widens and my heart swells inside my chest. "I would get up and give you both a kiss, but I am nap trapped," she laughs softly as she looks down at Lainey who is laying on her chest, my mom's hand softly stroking the back of her head.

"It's okay ma," I say as I walk into the room and Morgan follows to sit on the sofa, Aspen sitting next to her. "I'll go put the kettle on shall I?" I say to the room and my mom nods.

"Lunch will be done soon if you both wanted to stay."

I glance at Morgan, but she doesn't look at me.

I turn and make my way to the kitchen and fill the kettle up before placing it on the stove.

The sound of heavy boots creeping behind me has me turning around.

Riggs stands, arms crossed against his chest.

"You doing okay?" he asks, eyes burning into mine.

"Yeah," I nod, scrubbing my face, "it's been a bit of a morning; been told that Gerry only has a couple of weeks left..." I trail off and I see Riggs' mouth pop open before he closes it again.

"Shit," he sighs, dropping his arms from his chest just as he rests his hand on the back of the barstool.

"Yeah," my voice low, "thought I would bring her here for a little while, just to get her out the house. I need her to know that she has a support network around her for when she needs it. It's only ever been her and Gerry, and now... well, it's just going to be me and her. We don't even know each other and yet I have got to be there, ready to support her when she falls." Tipping my head back, my eyes pin to the ceiling, "It's a lot of weight on my already heavy shoulders," I admit, and before I can even let my head fall forward, Riggs' hand is on my shoulder giving me a reassuring squeeze.

"We're all here, we will all be here to support her when

she is ready," and just hearing those words makes me feel a little better.

"I feel like I am in well over my head," I admit, letting my head roll forward as the soft sound of whistling begins to echo around the kitchen.

"You're not, you just need a chance to find your feet. A lot has gone on over the last year. Dad, the mines, the suits..." he trails off. "It's a lot, but it's even more now you have Morgan and Cottonwheel ranch to factor in as well."

I nod silently, my fingers curling around the cupboard and reaching for some mugs then placing them on the countertop.

Riggs' hand slips off my shoulder when I hear the sound of soft footsteps approaching, looking over my shoulder, I see Morgan entering the kitchen.

She looks so innocent.

Eyes are glittery, bottom lip dragged behind her teeth.

"Shout if you need help, I don't want one," Riggs mutters before he nods softly at Morgan then slips out of the kitchen.

Letting out a deep, slow, exhale, I turn back around and pop tea bags into four mugs.

One for mom, one for Morgan, one for Tripp and one for Aspen. I had no idea where Dixie was, but she would sure as hell tell me if she wanted one.

Morgan is beside me in three small steps, she spins, and the edge of the worktop presses against her back, her arms folded across her chest.

"You okay?"

But I know she isn't. Her mind is elsewhere.

Probably with her granddad.

She looks up at me, but I focus on pouring the hot water over the tea bags and stirring gently.

"Just feel a little out of sorts," she admits, her eyes lifting from mine before they're on the archway of the kitchen.

"That's understandable," I mutter softly before adding honey into mom's chamomile tea.

"I'm scared to go home," she whispers and this time I do look at her, and fuck I hate seeing the unshed tears that threaten to fall.

I sigh, holding my hand out for her to take.

She is hesitant, her eyes dropping to my open palm and as soon as her skin is on mine, I pull her towards me, her chest to mine, head tipped back as her stunning greens bounce between mine.

"What's scaring you?" I whisper, locking my fingers around her lower back, holding her against me.

"What if I go home and he has died," her throat bobs as she swallows, and I try and stay positive.

You would never walk into that. I want to promise her, but that would be one promise I couldn't keep. There will always be someone with him, but it still doesn't stop it from happening.

"Hopefully we can both sit next to him, hold his hand until he has passed over peacefully," I try and keep my voice steady, but this is all bringing back my own hurt. I wasn't ready to lose my dad. But he was taken away from me because he chose to be the hero.

I will never blame Dixie for his death. I do hold blame, but it's more on myself. I should have run in and saved her.

"That would be nice," she stammers over her hushed words, a tear slipping down her cheek and my lips turn down as I watch it drip off her chin and into her tee.

"Please don't cry," and I know it's easy for me to say

that, but at the same time I hated that she was sad and there was nothing I could do about it.

"I really am trying," she half laughs as another tear runs and this time, I catch it with my thumb and press it to my lips, kissing it away.

"Anything else on your mind?" I ask, but she shakes her head from side to side. "Okay," I smile as she steps out of my grasp. Clearing my throat, I grab my mom's and Tripp's tea, Morgan grabs Aspen's and her own as she follows me back into the lounge.

"Here we go ma," I say softly as I place the mug on the coaster then hand Tripp his who is now sitting on the arm of the chair, Dixie sitting next to him, her hands under her bump.

Morgan passes a cup silently to Aspen who thanks her, then she sits on the sofa and I sit next to her, our knees touching, my hands locked in my lap.

"How you feeling Dix?" I ask, my eyes drifting to her.

"Not too bad, getting a little uncomfortable now," she sighs as her head rolls back and onto the back cushion of the sofa.

"Not much longer to go, Dreamcatcher," Tripp says softly, scooping her hand into his as he brings it to his lips and places a kiss on the back of it.

She looks at him, smiling.

"I can't wait for a new baby niece or nephew," Aspen beams as she takes a mouthful of her tea, her eyes flitting to Riggs momentarily.

"I think it's a boy," I say a little too confident, nodding and my mom agrees.

"Nah, I think we've got another little princess on our hands," Dixie looks down at her bump, her small hand running back and forth over it.

"I am just praying they come out healthy, whatever the gender," Tripp smiles, bringing his own tea to his lips.

Lainey stirs, a soft cry passing her lips but that soon stops as mom pats her toosh softly, soothing her.

"Here, let me take her," Dixie pulls herself from the chair and waddles across the floor to where Lainey is fidgeting on my mom's lap.

"Hey sweet girl," Dixie whispers, scooping Lainey into her arms, resting her on her bump as Lainey rubs the sleep out of her eyes, a little groggy as she places her head on her momma's chest, her fingers pinching at the thin gold necklace that sits around Dixie's neck.

"When will it be our turn," Aspen whispers to Riggs who stands beside her, his arm curling around her waist.

"Soon Wildflower, so soon," and I don't miss the sadness that etches across his face for just a moment as his lips press against the top of her head.

"Do you want kids, Morgan?" Aspen sighs as she looks at my wife, Morgan's eyes widen as she begins to rub her palm against her thigh, her mouth parting then closing.

"You don't need to answer that," my mom eyes down Aspen as she shrinks back into Riggs momentarily.

I know the answer.

Kids were never in her plan.

But then again, neither was I.

I always knew I wanted kids, wanted the big family.

But I could maybe make peace with the fact of not having any if that's what she wanted.

Morgan drops her head for a moment and eyes her mug of tea.

"I am just trying to focus on each day as it comes at the moment," she looks up at Aspen and smiles sweetly at her.

"How's Aust? I wanna shoot over to see him after," I aim my question at Aspen, trying to change the subject.

"Yeah he is okay, good days and bad… today's a good day," she rolls her lips and I know Aspen well enough to know that my mom's comment has made her feel bad.

"Perfect, I wanna catch up with him anyway so will pop in after I am done here," I smile. "Ma," I say just as she stands up from the chair, giving herself a moment to stretch out after being nap trapped for far too long.

Dixie has walked from the room to sort Lainey so it's only me, Morgan, Tripp, Aspen and Riggs.

"Yeah?" she reaches for her cup and takes a mouthful, a little hum of appreciation escaping her lips as she swallows.

"I brought some laundry home," and I hear Morgan tut beside me. "What?" I laugh softly and she rolls her eyes in an over exaggerated manner.

"I have told him to do his laundry back home, but nope…" she side-eyes me then raises her brows at my mom.

My mom twists her lips and fights the smile.

"He is particular," she winks at me, "but you're thirty Pacey, you should be doing your own laundry." She steps in front of me and places her hand on her cheek. "Momma can't keep doing it for you," she winks then walks out of the room and Riggs falls into the seat our mom has just left, Aspen following and lowering herself onto his lap.

"Have you decided whether you're going to do your book tour or not next year?" I ask and Morgan looks at me before drifting her eyes to Aspen.

"Book tour?" she crinkles her brow.

"Yeah, Aspen writes romance books," I smile at my wife, eyes soft before I am back on my brother and Aspen.

"Wow, I never knew... where can I buy one? I would love to read it," Morgan shifts to the edge of her seat as she waits for Aspen to talk.

"You don't have to buy one," she tilts her head, her lips pressed into a permanent smile. "I'll pop one to your ranch later on today, I have loads at home that I bought for my tour this year but..." she trails off and Riggs wraps his arm around her, pulling her close to him.

"I know, baby," he rasps as he places a kiss on her cheek, and I hate that I feel some kind of resentment towards them.

The feelings I had for Aspen have well and truly been buried, but in certain moments, an echo of them resurfaces, and I find myself wondering what could have been, but I know we would have never worked.

She was destined to be with Riggs.

They were written in the stars.

I just needed to lick my wounds and get over it.

I deserved to be loved, but I made peace with knowing that it may not come for me.

I am brought back to the room by Lainey climbing up my legs and I smile down at her. Wide blue eyes, curly brown hair. She's babbling away.

"Hey princess Lainey," I whisper, scooping her up onto my lap as she grabs my bottom lip.

Dixie smiles as she stands a little back from where I am sat, Tripp now standing at the back of the sofa.

"Are we close to walking yet?" my voice is muffled as she tugs on my lip.

"So close," Tripp beams at his daughter over my shoulder.

"Dada!" she squeals as she lets go of me then slaps her little hands on my face.

"Ow," I laugh and Lainey stops suddenly as she looks at Morgan, her smile slowly slipping into a frown, but as soon as Morgan leans in and smiles, Lainey goes back to beaming her toothy grin. She crawls onto Morgan's lap, her little hands tucked in front of her as she just stares.

"Hey little lady," Morgan says quietly and the whole room falls silent.

Lainey coos at her, her smile only widening and my heart slows for just a moment.

"You ready?" I ask after what feels like hours, I could watch her all day, but I have stuff I need to get on with and watching my wife and my niece was not on that list.

Pushing up from the sofa, Morgan looks at Dixie and scoops Lainey under the arms before standing and passing her to her mom.

"Thank you for letting me hold her," she smiles then says goodbye to Dixie before she waves bye to Riggs and Aspen.

"Bye hun," Aspen beams, waving back before she ducks her head down and says bye to Tripp as she passes.

Walking into the kitchen, she is close behind me as I see my mom going through my laundry bag.

"Ma," I say softly as she stands up and looks at me.

"You've been gone a day Pacey Rivera, how the hell is there so much?" and I smirk.

"Did you pack dirty washing?" her hands are on her hips as she taps her foot to the floor.

My cheeks turn pink.

"Pacey!" Morgan squeals as she shoves her hand into the top of my arm and I laugh softly.

"I will never understand you," Mom huffs, pulling more laundry out the bag.

"Mrs Rivera," Morgan begins, "I will teach your son how to use the washing machine."

"Orla, please," my ma beams at Morgan.

"What time shall I pick this up?" and I get a thunderous glare from Morgan.

"What?" I half laugh, and her eyes widen.

"She's not a laundromat!" Morgan clips me around the back of the head, and I laugh.

"Ow," I rub out the sting.

"Orla, pack it back up, I'll do it," and my mom shakes her head.

"No sweet girl, I'll do it today, Pacey can grow up and learn to do his own laundry tomorrow," she winks, and I roll my eyes.

"You shouldn't be bringing laundry home to your mom," she whispers as she knocks her shoulder into mine.

"I know, but..." I shrug my shoulder up as I pace over to my mom, placing a soft kiss on her cheek as she leans into me.

"Collect it tomorrow after work," she says softly before I turn and smirk at Morgan, but she just crosses her arm in front of her and shakes her head softly.

"Ready?" I ask, winking at my wife before she rolls her eyes.

"Bye Orla," she waves, and my mom closes the gap between the both of them before she pulls her into an embrace, holding her tightly and my chest hurts.

Once my mom breaks away, Morgan gives her a soft smile before she is walking past me. I give my mom one last look and she blows me a kiss. Following behind Morgan, I close the door behind me and climb into the truck.

If we were coming back here, I would walk down the fields and climb the fence like we did as kids, but knowing that we're going back to Cottonwheel Ranch, well, it seems a bit pointless.

Turning the key, the truck rumbles as she closes the door behind her.

"You don't mind coming to Austin's with me do you?" I ask, looking at her before I pop the truck into reverse.

She just nods, her fingers picking the skin around her nail.

"Sure?" I raise a brow as I run my hand through my thick blond hair. She nods again.

"Okay."

Turning the car around, I move out the long and winding driveway of Rivera Ranch and within minutes I am pulling into the orange dusty road of Maple Farm. I look at the idyllic house in the distance, maple trees line the road and my heart pumps in my chest.

We spent many of our childhood days here. More so Riggs than me.

But Riggs' childhood was different to the one me and Tripp remember.

His was hard.

Ours was a little easier.

Riggs was always going to be made to work the ranch, made to stay in Lovelock Bay.

That's what happened with prom night.

Dad was so concerned that Riggs would ruin his business with Buck that he wouldn't let Riggs near her.

Work was too important.

So, he broke her heart.

Stood her up, but little did she know at the time it was all part of the plan on my dad's part. I was told to put on a suit and lead her to prom knowing that Riggs was watching from the shadows.

It was no secret that I crushed hard on Aspen, always had. She was the same age as me, but her eyes always found Riggs.

Sad thing was, I noticed everything about her yet she noticed nothing about me.

Why would she when she loved him?

"You okay?" Morgan's voice slips over me like silk and my thoughts settle down for a moment or two.

"Yeah, just thinking," I admit as I pull into the parking spot just right of the stables.

"About?" she continues to pick.

"Our childhood," I smile across the car at her, "we spent a lot of time here as kids, kind of grew up here I suppose," I shrug a shoulder up.

Pointing down the fence line, I sit back a little further in my chair.

"You see those small little lights that are cable tied to the fence posts," and I glance at her as she nods, "well Riggs put them in for Aspen, so when she ran down the fence line towards ours, or if she was coming home, she would have a trail of lights guiding her door to door," I smile a little wider.

"Scared of the dark?" she asked and I sigh a little heavier then turned to look at her once more.

"Yeah, hated it," I nibble the inside of my bottom lip as my arms rest over the steering wheel, shoulders up a little.

"Bless her," her lips twist.

Silence fills the truck cab for a moment before I slip out and she follows me, her feet hitting the gravelled floor.

She walks cautiously beside me, her hands tucked into the ass pocket of her jeans. Climbing the steps, I knock on the door but am not waiting long until Blue answers the door, the little terror that is Butch yapping at her feet.

"Pacey," her eyes soften as she steps out onto the decked porch and wraps her arms around me, pulling me into an embrace as she kisses me on the cheek.

"Blue," my voice is warm as I hug her back and it's not long before she is pushing me away and letting her eyes scope over Morgan.

"It's nice to see you again," she smiles then cups Morgan's face in her hands, tilting her head to the side.

"You too," Morgan replies softly as I step past and make my way to the kitchen.

Buck is sitting with his newspaper before his eyes lift over and he places it down.

"There's our boy," he stands from the table and strolls across to me, closing the gap in four strides then wraps his arms around my shoulders, patting me in between the shoulder blades.

My lips pull into a wide smirk as he holds onto me for a bit longer before he pushes away from me.

"How have you been?" his hand is on my cheek and I see the way his dark eyes settle on mine.

"Taking each day as it comes," I admit when I hear the sound of boots clicking across the floor.

"That's all you can do son," his smile fades, "we're all wrapped up in grief, but some days are easier than others," his eyes lift to the doorway and I'm not sure if it's Morgan or Austin.

"There she is..." Buck taps my cheek softly with his hand, then moves aside to greet Morgan and I sigh blissfully, turning slowly as he pulls her into an embrace before giving her a kiss on the cheek. "Good to see you again," his voice is quiet, and she gives him a small smile. "How's your pops? I haven't seen him in a while," and my heart twists deep inside my chest.

"He is not good," she rolls her lips before her tongue darts out and wets it.

"I'm sorry to hear that, if you need anything..." he trails off for a moment and eyes Blue, she gives a grimace of a smile. "We're here for you, you're family now," he pulls her in for a hug again.

"Where's Austin?" I ask as I push my hands into the front of my jeans, my wedding band catching on the hem of the pocket.

"Office." Buck nods his head down towards the back of the house and I give a heavy nod. Blue inhales heavily just as I approach her.

"He doing okay?" and she just shrugs her shoulder up. I nod again then turn my attention to Morgan.

"Can you just give me a bit..." and I don't have a chance to carry on, she is pressing her finger to my lips and giving me a nod.

"I'll make you a coffee, love," Blue says as she walks towards the coffee machine and finds a pod and I give my wife one last smile before making my way towards the back of the house to find Austin.

I can hear the sound of his fingers dancing across the keyboard and I pop my head around the door and give him a whistle. His head pops up over the computer screen and his eyes glisten.

"There he is," I smirk as I step into the room and around to where he is sitting. He pushes to his feet and pulls me into the tightest hug, his face burying between my head and shoulder.

His body begins to shudder in my arms and the pain in my chest radiates through to my shoulders and back.

I say nothing.

Just hold him tight against my body and let him sob into my tee.

He obviously needed this and I wasn't going to be the one to take it away from him.

So I just stood silently until he was ready to talk.

I have no idea how long it has been, but he finally pushes away from me and palms at his tear-stained cheeks.

"You okay man?" I ask as he steps away and sits back in his chair and he gives me a nod. "Sure?" I don't want to press too much but at the same time I want him to know he can talk to me whenever he needs to.

"Yeah, Harlow was just on my mind today," he admits, locking his fingers into his lap.

He is dressed in a black tee, light washed jeans, dirty boots and his cap twisted backwards.

"That's understandable," I nod, rolling my lips into a thin line.

"Some days are just harder than others, you know…" and I nod my head, I know that feeling all too well.

"I just miss her," and he pulls his glassy eyes from mine and focuses on his computer screen.

"We all do bud," it's true. She may have been a menace between Aspen and Riggs but she was part of us. Always had been.

Silence creeps around the room and I shuffle on my feet.

"How's work?" I ask, looking at his badge sitting on the desk.

"Busy." he sighs, "had a load of cattle go missing two ranches up," I watch as he shakes his head from side to side. "I don't get how they can just be taken," he looks at me and I shrug my shoulder.

"Happens, so close to the border here, what's to stop them taking them straight across?"

He taps his fingers on his stomach.

"Suppose it makes sense," he spins his chair around, "how about you? How's things with you?" he asks, but his eyes are now fixed on the screen.

"So So," I admit, "not really sure what I want at the minute, there is so much going on at home and with Morgan and her pops that..."

"Keep forgetting you're married," his eyes find mine and I don't miss the slither of sadness that fills them just for a moment.

"Me too man," I laugh, rubbing my hand around the back of my head.

"How is it?"

"How's what?"

"Married life?" and I twist my lips.

"Bit hard to say, we don't know each other, it's one of those... I did it because her granddad asked me too, but I'm also kind of enjoying it if that makes sense?"

"Yeah it does," he nods.

"But it's all so new, so fresh... I have no idea what I am doing. We're just at the tip of the iceberg, there is so much that is going to be going down in the next few weeks that I am just trying to mentally prepare myself for it."

"Can imagine it was a bit of a shock to the system."

"Yeah," I laugh softly.

"I never thought you would settle down," he twists back to look at me and my brow raises.

"Nah?"

"Nope, you were so hung up on Aspen, I honestly never thought you would have moved on."

I laugh a little, but my stomach knots.

"Look, me and Aspen..." I pause and he holds his hand up.

"I don't need to know the details, I swear I am still scarred from the night in the Boot where you confessed everything."

I roll my eyes.

"I wasn't going into details, all I was going to say was, me and Aspen, we were friends... but then things happened the way they did. It was never going to be me, we all knew that, I just didn't want to admit it. But I kind of wrote myself off for finding love. Once you've been on the receiving end of unrequited love, then well, you kind of don't want to put yourself through that again. She hurt me."

I pause for a moment and inhale heavily.

"You hurt her too man," Austin grits his teeth, lips turning down.

"I know."

"You drove her away..." and I can see the annoying smirk that is teasing the corner of his lips.

"Wasn't just me... Riggs played a part in that."

"We all did in a way I suppose..." Austin trails off and looks at the photo of Harlow that sits on his desk. "God, we were so young and naïve when all that happened. We were terrors growing up, we were so flippant with our choices..."

"Yes we were," I sigh, leaning against the wall and crossing my arms across my chest.

"If you could go back in time, would you do it again?"

I blink at him, brows knitted.

"Do what again?"

"Take Aspen to prom... cross the bro code line."

My breath rattles in my chest.

"Honestly?" I ask, pushing off the wall.

"Honestly," he nods, feet now kicked up on the desk, hands in his lap.

"Yeah, I would."

Because maybe in another life, we would have got our shot.

Just maybe.

CHAPTER TEN
MORGAN

Sitting in the kitchen with Blue and Buck, I thought it would have been awkward, but they made me feel at home. They made conversation and the time that Pacey was down the hall talking to Austin felt like seconds had passed.

My ears prick when I hear the sound of footsteps approaching, turning to look over my shoulder I see Pacey and Austin.

"Hey," Pacey steps forwards and places a hand on my shoulder.

"Hey," my hand automatically finds his and I freeze momentarily before I slip it away.

"Hey Morgs," Austin says as he reaches for a glass then grabs some cold drink from the fridge, opening the bottle and dumping the contents of it into his glass.

"Morgs," Pacey crinkles his nose as he looks at his friend and I can't help the smile that crosses my lips.

"Yeah, what's wrong with that?" he asks as he slowly looks over his shoulder at me, then his eyes lift to Pacey's.

"Her name is Morgan."

"Right?" his tongue is in his cheek.

"So call her Morgan," and I nibble my bottom lip.

Austin rolls his eyes in an over exaggerated manner.

"Fine, hey *Morgan*."

"Better, thank you," Pacey nods then drags a chair out next to me and slumps himself into it.

"You two," Buck grumbles before he reaches for his paper and begins to read.

"I know right," Pacey smirks as he eyes Austin.

We fall back into easy conversation and Austin sits next to us, Blue potters making lunch and Buck just joins in every now and again with his opinion on the matter when he feels it is needed.

The hours slip by and we're back in the truck and driving towards home. Pacey made the call to get the nurses there and deep down, I am grateful that he made that decision for me.

"When are you getting your horse?" I ask Pacey as I gaze over to him, his hair all thick and wavy as it blows in the wind from having the windows of the truck down.

"Oh shit yea," he grumbles, pulling his eyes from the road for the moment and looking at me. "I was supposed to get him today," he sighs.

"I can get him tomorrow? Dusty can help me if that helps," I suggest and give him a smile and he nods at me.

"Okay, that would work if that's okay with you?"

"Sure," I mumble as we pull into the driveway of the ranch and my heart begins to beat quickly.

"You okay?" he asks as he cuts the engine, his eyes scoping my face.

I nod.

"It's just..." I pause for a moment as I look up at the house. "I have had such a lovely day with your family and the Warrens and now reality has hit me in the face at what is going on," I drop my head, looking at my bit to fuck nails.

But his hand is there, scooping mine up into his.

"I know," he says softly and he could have said so much more and tried to give an explanation about what is going on, but I am grateful that he doesn't.

"Come, let's go and sit with him. I'll make the tea," his thumb brushes back and forth across the back of my hand and I bob my head.

"Will you come with me to see him?" my voice is quiet.

"Of course," his smile widens before he drops my hand into my lap. Opening the door, I step down and walk side by side with him as we enter the house.

He takes my hand in his as we climb the stairs and the nurse is just walking back into his room.

She gives a soft smile and then steps aside so me and Pacey can enter the room.

I pause for a moment, my legs suddenly feeling heavy as I take a deep inhale, holding it for five then releasing as we walk through the door.

He stays right beside me.

My pops' eyes find mine and a small smile spills onto my lips as I walk cautiously into the room.

"Hey," I say softly, looking down at him and pushing his hair away from his face, my brows furrow when his hot skin molds into my cold hand. He has tubes up his nose and a drip running into the crease of his elbow, a bag full of liquid and I know it's the strong stuff to make him comfortable.

"Hey sweetheart," his voice grumbles and his hand trembles as he reaches for my hand that is resting on the bed.

"You doing okay?" I ask but his eyes have drifted over

my shoulder to Pacey, a hint of a smile pulling at the corner of his lips before his main attention is on me.

He gives a soft nod.

The sound of the bedroom door closing has me looking over my shoulder, the nurse walking towards us.

"He has had his meds, we're going to head off now if that's okay and we will be back in a couple of hours." She asks and she looks so cautious.

"Of course," I turn fully and place my hand on the top of her arm. "Thank you," I whisper.

"He is comfortable, but if there are any changes then please do give us a call," she glances over at Gerry and gives a warm smile. He holds his hand up at an attempt of a wave before she is walking out of the door and it's just the three of us.

"Are you hungry?" I ask, sitting on the edge of my pops' bed and he nods. "Let me go..." I pause when Pacey's hand is on my shoulder.

He continues, "Let me go out and grab something... will you be okay for like..." his voice trails off as he looks at his watch and then his eyes are back on me, "twenty minutes, thirty max?" and I am a little hesitant, but I give him a nod anyway.

"I'll make sure Dusty is close by, I'm going to pop into Sunny's, what would you like?" he asks the both of us and I look at my pops before I twist my upper body to him.

"I'll have a meatball sub," I lick my lips and my pops grumbles then holds his thumb up. "Make that two," I smile at my husband and his eyes glisten when they find mine.

"I won't be long," he whispers and for a moment, I feel like he is going to step towards me and place a kiss on my forehead, but he doesn't. He turns slowly and walks out the room, pulling the door two.

Sighing, I watch my grandad like a hawk, plucking conversation from the air to try and keep him awake until Pacey comes back.

I am terrified of something happening whilst I am alone.

I hear the front door close and the sound of Dusty's voice drifting up the stairs as he calls my name.

"All okay?" he asks and the sound of his footsteps hit the landing, his head pokes around the door, cowboy hat in hand.

"Yup," my chest aches as I look at him lying in bed.

How the hell did he deteriorate this quickly.

"Do you need anything?" Dusty asks as he steps into the room, and I shake my head.

"Pacey will be back soon, I'm sorry to call you in on a Sunday," and guilt eats away at me.

"Ma'am," he steps a little closer. "I live in the cabin at the bottom of the ranch, this is my home, my life... you call, I come. Marsha knows that. I am home for supper every night and there for breakfast because my boss takes the early shift so I can eat with my children..." he pauses for a moment as his eyes narrow on mine. "So please don't feel sorry for asking me here, Pops is so much more than the big boss," he winks at me, and I laugh softly at his playfulness. "I owe him everything," his fingers fiddle with the trim of his hat and my breath catches at the back of my throat.

Dusty was convicted of a crime when he was a teen, wrong place, wrong time. He was set up by his own flesh and blood, someone he trusted with every fibre of him. Everyone knew what really happened, even the old sheriff but they told him if he took the fall, he would be out in twenty years. He went away, did his time and came out ready to make something of himself.

I still think he deserved more than the life he has, but he is happy.

And isn't that what we all want in reality?

Happiness.

Whether that be with someone or without... a happy life was what I always dreamt of.

"He loves you like you were his own Dusty," I whisper and smile through glassy eyes, my pops softly snoring.

It was the truth.

When Dusty came out of prison, he had nowhere to go. His dad fled, he had no siblings and his mom was nowhere to be seen.

He turned up on my pops' door, wet and cold, clothes ripped and soaked through.

He asked to stay for one night, he never left until he met Marsha. My pops cleared out the cabin at the bottom of the ranch and made it up for him and his wife.

He never let him go after that.

Pops said Dusty always felt bad and promised to pay him back everything, but my pops would never take the money from him.

Told him to put it into the kid's trust funds.

Dusty tried to argue it.

Pops shut him down.

"I know ma'am," he stammers over his words when we hear the front door close. "That must be Pacey, I'll catch you tomorrow," and before I can tell him he doesn't have to leave, he walks out the door.

I'm not alone with my thoughts long when Pacey walks into the room with two large brown bags and a cup holder.

"I didn't know what you wanted to drink..." he pauses

as I look at the four cups then back at him with a giddy smile on my face. "So I went for soda, coffee, shake and some weird energy drink thing," he shrugs his shoulders up as he places it on the side unit and then places the bag on the bedside table and that's when my pops opens his eyes, squinting slightly.

"Meatball sub for the boss," he licks his lips as he places it on my pops' lap and his eyes light up. "Another sub for my wife," he tilts his head as he hands it to me and the warmth feels good against my hands. I have no idea why I feel so cold.

"What did you get?" I ask, looking over the bag as he fists his hand in there.

"Tuna and pickles," he licks his lips, and I turn my nose up.

"Tuna and pickles," I gag.

"Have you tried it?" he asks, holding it out to me and I shake my head. "Then how can you judge?" he shrugs his shoulder up as he walks around the other side of the bed and perches himself on there.

"I can't," I smirk, placing my own sub down and unwrapping my pops'. I had no idea if he was going to eat, but I would like him to just try and have a mouthful or two.

Standing from the bed, I move next to him and he takes the sub from me and takes a mouthful, groaning in appreciation.

"I do love a meatball sub," he says as he looks at Pacey, "good shout about going to Sunny's," he winks, and I feel a little content as I sit back at the foot of the bed and unwrap my own sub.

"What drink do you want?"

"I'll have the milkshake," Pops pipes up and I laugh.

"Hey, that's what I was going to go for."

"You can't deny a dying man..." he smirks, his eyes flitting between mine as playfulness dances around in them.

"He has a point," Pacey says as he stands and grabs the shake from the cup holder and pops the straw in.

"What flavor?" he asks as Pacey puts it into his hand.

"Strawberry," I hear the hesitance to Pacey's answer.

"My favorite," he takes a sip, and I see how happy a little milkshake has made him.

"What do you want babe?" Pacey says then freezes, his eyes widening at the name that just left his mouth, and I stare at him.

Babe.

"Soda," I squeak, suddenly my throat is dry.

Pacey walks over to the other side of the room and reaches for the soda and pinches a straw up before he is back beside me, handing it to me.

"Thank you..." I trail off, looking up at him, "*babe,*" and he smirks, eyeing the floor as he laughs softly and joins us back on the bed with a coffee and we fall into an easy conversation with pops.

We spent most of our afternoon in there and by the time he had fallen asleep, the nurses are back and it is just us two.

"You all set for work tomorrow?" I find myself asking as Pacey ties the trash bag up and pulls it from the bin.

"I am never set for work tomorrow," he grumbles as he walks past me and out of the front door, but within what feels like seconds he is back in the house.

"Did you always want to be sheriff?" I find myself asking as I put a new trash bag into the bin.

"Nope," he sticks his hand under the warm faucet and washes them with soap.

"What did you want to do?" he shakes his hands off then reaches for the hand towel, patting his hands dry.

"No idea. When I was a kid, I wanted to be a cowboy," he scoffs a laugh and his eyes trail to me. "But then I grew up, I finished school, worked on the ranch for a bit, then went into being livestock agent... and well, Tripp stepped down and gave me the badge."

"You must have felt proud."

He shakes his head.

"I wouldn't say proud..." he sighs, "it's more a burden... I'm not sure how long I will do it for. But at the minute, I have no other option but be the sheriff of Lovelock Bay," he shrugs a shoulder up.

"You must have a dream?" I ask him, pushing for more and I know I should probably back down, but I don't.

"Never had a dream, Sunflower. I've always been one of those that just go with the flow..."

"And look where that got you," I snort a laugh.

He looks at me as if I have said something wrong, his hands fisted into his pockets as he steps towards me slowly.

"It got me married to a sunshine cowgirl... wouldn't say that was a bad thing."

My cheeks pinch a rose pink and I cast my eyes down.

"How about you... dream?" he asks, and my fingers find my hair as I twirl it around.

"Not really, never left Blossom Cove, never wanted to either... but I never really had a dream to become more than what it is here. I love the ranch, love my life here... just sad that my pops won't be around much longer."

I sigh, letting my eyes drift to him.

"But now there is you as well, and I know I am not

alone." I nod, pushing my hands into my back pocket of my denim jeans.

"Babe," the pet name slips off his lips as he closes the gap between us, and I am desperate to feel his fingers on my skin. "You'll never be alone again."

The breath catches at the back of my throat, and I don't know why but his words make me feel safe and terrified at the same time.

I have never been the type to need a man's help, and yet here I am seeking out his.

I don't want to do this alone.

And now I didn't have to because I had him.

The door catching has me jumping back, eyes cast over my shoulder as I look towards the hallway and see two new nurses.

"Evening," I smile as they give me a nod and I find myself following.

"How is he?" the male asks as we reach the top of the stairs.

"Sleeping, he ate a bit and had some water and a milkshake but he seems to be comfortable," the words slip from my lips as I walk into my pops' room.

He is awake, humming *you are my sunshine* and my heart hurts a little more.

He used to sing me that song when he tried to get me to nap.

Always been *our* song.

"Hey Gerry," the male says, walking over and checking the machine that is next to him and then his drip.

"Evening," he sweeps his eyes over the both of them and I give him a smile.

"Do you need anything pops?" I ask as I hold onto the bedroom door, waiting for him to answer.

"No sweetheart, go and chill out. If I need you the nurses will come grab you," he places his fingers to his lips and blows me a kiss. I catch it, holding it to my heart and blowing one back before I slip out of the room and back downstairs towards where Pacey is still in the kitchen pottering around.

"What do you need for your horse?" I ask as I drag a chair out and sit at the table.

"Just his saddle and bridle. I'll grab everything else tomorrow in the truck. Need to get his food and rug so just worry about the horse," he smiles at me, and I watch as his eyes glisten.

I give a nod.

"Just so I am clear and know where my husband duties lie..." he pauses as he drags his own seat out, swinging it around and sitting on it so the back is in front of me, legs either side.

"Go on," I lick my lips.

"Am I going to have any jealous exes coming out the woodwork to try and win you back?" his eyes darken ever so slightly as he lowers his sights on me.

A nervous laugh bubbles out of me.

"Not at all," I whisper because the nerves cripple me.

"No?" he raises a brow at me, a boyish smirk on his lips.

"There is no..." I pause for a moment, rolling my lips then nibbling on the inside of my cheek.

"No?" he waits for me to answer.

"No ex."

His brows furrow tightly.

"No ex?" and he looks confused.

"No," I shake my head from side to side.

He pauses.

"I've never been in a relationship with anyone... so no

boyfriends," I whisper because for some reason I feel ashamed of the words I speak.

Pacey sits a little taller in his chair, his eyes widening ever so slightly before they soften on mine.

"Never?" he repeats, and I am not sure if it is just a reaction but I find myself nodding, but his lips turn into a smile. "So I'll be all your firsts then..." he trails off when my eyes widen slightly, "hypothetically obviously?" he teases the words and butterflies flutter inside of me.

"Hypothetically... yes." My cheeks turn pink. "I just never seemed to find someone I liked enough to want to have them as a boyfriend... I was so busy with this place that dating was just not on the cards for me. Sure, I liked a little flirt down at Randy's but that's as far as it went. I knew I would find someone eventually, but I wasn't really looking I suppose..." I pause and lick my lips, "but then you came along."

A hint of a smile dusts across my lips.

"Like a wrecking ball," he winks, and my cheeks burn a little warmer.

"The same could be said about me," I sigh, crossing one of my legs over the other.

He shakes his head.

"Believe it or not..." he trails off for a moment and lowers himself, leaning forward so his top half is over the back of the chair slightly, his lips pursing and I find myself placing my elbows on the wooden table, leaning myself in, hanging on his words. "You were the sunshine I had been so desperately craving in the darkest time of my life..." he pauses, and his words floor me. "Sure, this isn't conventional, but here we are. This wasn't in my own plan, but after the last few months I have had... well, you were like a breath of fresh air," his truths seep out of him, and I find my heart weeping inside my chest.

In these five minutes he has shown me a slice of vulnerability and I am forever grateful.

"I will answer everything you want to know, I know our name leaves a bad taste in some of the towns mouths, but I promise, it'll be fabricated. You had every right to be cautious and keep me at arm's length, but I am asking you to trust me. Asking you to talk to me if you want to... I'll answer everything truthfully."

I find myself swallowing, a lump so present in the column of my throat that I can't even get the words to pass if I wanted to. My lips part then close, but my eyes burn into his and after what feels like hours, he breaks away.

"You don't have to say anything. I am just laying my truths out to you, laying my soul bare for you to see. But my heart," he sits back, placing his hand over his chest and I imagine his heart is beating steadily beneath his palm. "I can't show you that yet. It's battered and bruised, and I don't know if it is capable of beating for another girl. But I want to try... I just need you to be patient with me. Because honestly, Sunflower, I can see this between us blossoming into something beautiful."

My sharp intake of breath catches at the back of my throat and all I can do is nod, my insides tingling, my fingertips numb.

He gives me a slow smile before he stands up and walks over to me, looking down at me and I feel the way my heart stutters in my chest.

"But right now, we need to focus on the here and now, your pops, the ranch, the suits..." he cups my cheek, his callous thumb pad brushing against the softness of my skin. "We need to focus on our future... but we can't do that until all of this is sorted."

I nod but then find myself leaning into his palm and a warmth radiates through my chest.

He steps back before he turns and walks out of the room, and I am left sitting with feelings I can't decipher.

Sighing, I slump back against the chair and let his words repeat over me.

He wanted to give this a shot.

But I just couldn't see this working out.

He has demons.

I have my own issues.

I have no idea how to be around someone like him.

How can I be his wife when I don't even know how to be a girlfriend.

Shaking my head from side to side, I push from the chair and make my way up to my bedroom.

I needed a moment.

Or two.

CHAPTER ELEVEN
PACEY

Never had a boyfriend.

Never been in a relationship.

My blood rushes around my body, I feel it burning through my veins.

I love the fact that she has never had a boyfriend, that she will be mine and only mine.

I have no idea if this marriage will work. I have no idea if she wants to make it work.

But, I didn't tell one lie downstairs.

I did want to be honest with her, wanted to try and make this work.

Sure, this is not what I wanted out of my life, and I swore off women and just would have focused on myself but then she happened.

A bright ball of sunshine pulling me in.

She caught my attention at the wedding when she rode in on her horse, and then again in Randy's.

I wouldn't say there was an instant attraction but there was enough to keep me interested.

She gave off a certain air about her. Confidence seeped

out of her, but yet here, with me in her home, she isn't like that at all.

She's pure.

Sweet.

Caring.

But it seems she needs me maybe more than she wants to admit.

Inhaling heavily, I shut the faucet off to the shower and step out, wrapping my towel around my waist and rough drying my hair with a spare towel.

I take time brushing and drying it then clean my teeth.

Tiredness pricked behind my eyes and I knew I needed to get an early night. I had a lot to deal with and I needed to make a start on looking into what caused the explosion. I kind of buried it at the back of my mind.

Didn't want to deal with it after the wedding, and then the weeks slipped past and now, here we are, over a month away and I still haven't looked into it.

I needed to.

But I think it runs deeper than just the explosion.

Things with my dad are still so raw, I am mad at him, but so in awe of him at the same time.

Anger coats my skin in a shiver but I shake it off.

He didn't leave any of us alone, us Riveras stick together and my mom has her three boys around her at her beck and call.

I needed to put my focus on finding out who did it, needed to find these suits and shut them down once and for all.

There was no way they were going to continue trying to buy Lovelock Bay. There is no way in hell that I will let them close to Rivera Ranch or Cottonwheel.

They can declare a war and I will gladly suit up and go to fucking war.

I will not have them threaten to take away my family's legacy.

We've had enough hurt between all of us, I will not be the reason for more.

Pacing back into my room, I push the door slightly and dress in cotton pyjama pants and a tee.

Hanging my towels to dry, I lay on my bed, arm behind my head as I cross my feet at my ankles.

I let my mind wander back to the last six months.

Austin getting framed for Clay's death.

That one plummeted me into a darkness that I never thought I would climb out of.

To see your best friend be thrown to the wolves for something he didn't do and watching him slowly crumble into nothing was hard.

But of course, we proved his innocence. It was a little too late, the depression sunk in and I turned to drink.

My mom and dad were worried about me, but at that point, I didn't care about anyone else apart from myself.

And that was so fucking selfish of me.

Riggs tried. Tripp tried.

Fuck, even Aspen tried.

I just couldn't get a grip on it.

The day I walked through the door drunk, telling Riggs it was all his fault with Austin, well, that was a new low.

I never meant a word of it, but it was easier to hurl my anger at him than it was at anyone else.

We were all involved that night.

We were all there and knew that we put him in the back of the truck.

But then it seems a few others ended up having a hand in his death.

No one wanted him to die.

He wasn't a bad guy in truth, just a greedy businessman who wanted to take what was ours.

But I think what gutted us all the most when we found out was that Lainey now didn't have her dad.

Sure, she has Tripp, she will never know different, but half of her is gone.

She'll never get that chance to meet the man whose blood pumps through her veins.

And that is on all of us in a way. But it was also on Kelcie, Lucian and Clay's brother. They murdered him instead of getting him help.

They're rotting away behind bars now.

We just had to find the rest of the fuckers.

My mind is filled with the day of Clay's funeral. It was a stupid idea to think that nothing was going to happen.

We were the gasoline to an already out of control fire, yet we didn't stop.

The screams still haunt me.

My screams still haunt me.

I was so consumed with making sure my brothers were okay that when I saw Harlow fall to the floor, I took my eye off them for a split second and that's when the bullet seared into my skin, sinking into my stomach and I swear I thought I was going to die next to Harlow.

I remember when I looked around, Austin was on his knees. Tripp was on the floor, leg crushed by his dead horse.

I screamed for my dad.

In that moment, I was transported back to being just a

boy who needed his dad. I remember watching through tear filled eyes as he had to decide between me or Tripp.

Dixie switched out with my dad, cradling my brother's head as my dad rushed over to me and did all he could to help.

I swear I saw my life flash before my eyes, the piercing ringing in my ears was deafening and anything my dad was saying was silent.

I couldn't focus on anything but the sound of my heart racing in my chest, pounding against my ribcage.

Fear was not something that ever paralysed me, but on that day, I was trapped in a body and I couldn't do anything about it.

It felt like hours had passed when in fact it was seconds before I blacked out.

Next thing I knew, I was in hospital, bandage wrapped around my torso then told all over again that Harlow had died, Tripp had sustained injuries and the men that murdered our friend in broad daylight got away.

I always vowed I would hunt them down and torture them.

But that revenge plan soon settled down, and I put my energy into fixing myself back up.

I'm getting there, I know I am.

Some nights I fall into a peaceful slumber and for those hours, my mind is quiet, and I don't dream. Others, I am waking in sweat, heart thrashing, throat dry waking up from a nightmare.

It's always the same.

Back at the funeral.

But everyone dies.

And just when the gun is lifted and locked on me, they

shoot, the bullet hits my skin and just as the searing pain rots through my skin, I wake up.

It doesn't matter how much I try and keep a positive mind, the dreams still come and they haunt me. I am just praying that one day they'll stop and I can move on from that part of my life, but not forgetting a single detail.

My chest vibrates as I exhale a heavy breath and then I feel the ache radiate through it. Turning on my side, my eyes pin to the door and I am silently willing for her to walk past.

No idea why.

I know there could be something between us, but I don't know if I can let myself fall.

I know I shouldn't compare her to Aspen, but I do.

And it's so fucking annoying because I don't feel for Aspen in that way at all.

She was another piece of my life from the past, but maybe it's because I haven't found anyone like her.

Then again, she still broke my heart the same time she broke Riggs'.

I gave her every part of me and she dangled me until I was of no use, yet I still craved something from her, but I didn't know what.

I had her friendship, I always had it.

She was finally with the man she loved, the man it has always been and I couldn't even be mad. Her and Riggs were soulmates.

I knew that. Damn, everyone knew that.

My stomach knots.

I hear the sound of footsteps in the hallway and I find myself holding my breath.

They stop for a moment and disappointment settles in

my stomach but then I hear them again, and this time they get closer.

I see her shadow on the floor, and I find myself sitting up and waiting.

Her head pops around and I give her a lopsided smile.

"I just wanted to..." she trails off for a moment, hovering in the doorway.

I wait for her to speak the words. I didn't want to interrupt her.

"Well," she knots her fingers. "I just wanted to thank you for opening up a little... it was nice to hear."

I nod softly.

I could say so much more, but then again, I didn't want to burden her with the shit that was going on in my life.

Silence creeps around the room and I have to stop myself from pushing to my feet and scooping her pretty face into my hands, dust my lips over hers and make her mine.

But she isn't there.

Neither am I.

She would just be a rebound maybe? A little fun before I got bored and moved onto the next girl.

I suppose I had a bit of a reputation, picking girls up then never contacting them again.

I was always a sucker for a blonde.

I didn't want to have that with Morgan. I wanted to get to know her, develop our friendship and see what this could become.

We could fizzle out into nothing, just stay platonic until we both agreed that the ranch was safe and so was she.

Or we could have a whirlwind romance and fall head over heels.

I don't see it being the latter, even though there is a

slither of hope in me that this could become more... but I don't want to get my hopes up.

I don't want to hold onto something that is a complete fabrication of my mind.

"Well, goodnight," she says softly, and I wish her a goodnight before she closes my door and I am alone again.

My ALARM SCREAMS at me and I groan as I hit the snooze button.

I didn't sleep great.

Took me ages to drift off, and when I did, my mind was plagued with nightmares.

Hated it.

Forcing my eyes open, I let them pin to the ceiling and I am already wanting to be back in bed.

After five minutes, I find myself pushing from the bed. Walking quietly over to the bathroom, I wash my face, brush my teeth then move back to my room to get dressed.

Pulling my jeans up, I buckle the belt and then slip my badge onto the holder. I reach for a light brown checkered shirt and a plain white tee that I pull on first. Slipping my feet into my boots, I run my hand through my hair and rough it up slightly before I reach for my cowboy hat.

Swiping my phone from the side table, I slip it into the back of my jeans and make my way down stairs, careful not to wake Morgan if she is still sleeping and even more mindful not to disturb Gerry.

Tiptoeing down the stairs, my eyes fall on the back of a man. Skinny, long brown hair that curls at the base of his neck, worn out shirt, dirty jeans and muddied boots.

I clear my throat, and he turns to look at me, giving a sweep over.

Teeth a little crooked, cheeks rosy and eyes dark as mud.

"Morning sir," he tilts the rim of his cowboy hat in my direction. He steps towards me and holds his hand out for me to take, which I do, giving it a firm shake.

"Morning," I smile, and he gives a knowing nod.

"You all good?" his accent is thick as he turns around and walks back to grab his coffee mug. I nod, but he doesn't see it.

His eyes find mine over his shoulder, my hands pushed deep inside my pockets and I nod again.

"Want one?"

"Please," I smile and the heels of my boots skate across the floor.

"How do you take it?" he asks, the rasp in his voice evident as he reaches for a mug.

"However it comes, not fussy, coffee is coffee," I admit as I sit at the small table.

"As long as it touches the soul right?" he smirks and glances back at me and I give him a knowing nod.

"Right."

We fall into a comfortable silence whilst he makes my coffee then places it down on the table and drags his own chair out.

"I'm glad she has you," he admits, lifting his chin.

I curl my fingers around my mug and drag it towards me.

"Me and Marsha," and I cock a brow. "My wife," he smiles, "we knew that Gerry was unwell..." he pauses and takes a mouthful of his coffee, wincing as he does. "We were worried about how Morgan would cope in this house, the ranch... the looming dread of a sale."

I keep quiet.

"Damn, if I had the money I would snap this place up in a heartbeat," he shakes his head softly from side to side. "But this just isn't my workplace, it's my home," he swallows, and I watch the way his throat bobs.

"Gerry took me in back when I was a teen, got me out of trouble more times than I can count," he chuckles softly, his eyes drifting to the small window that overlooks the rolling green. He looks lost in thought but I just sit and drink my coffee. "So yeah, I care a lot about this place, about Morgan... about the future." His eyes are back on mine.

"I get it," I roll my lips before licking the coffee remnants from them.

"You're going to make her happy yeah? You're going to try and keep the land from those greedy suits, right?" and I can hear the desperation in his voice.

"Yeah," is all I say because how can I promise something that I don't know is achievable.

"Good," he gives a nod then pushes back on his chair. The sound of boots fills the room and a knowing smile pulls at my lips as I look over my shoulder and see her standing in the doorway.

Cream tee, low rise jeans and tanned cowboy boots. Her blonde hair is pulled into a low pony, cowboy hat pinched between her fingers.

"Morgan," Dusty says as he walks past her and leaves it just me and her.

She hovers for a moment before stepping into the kitchen and standing by me.

"Morning," she smiles down at me and I feel the air shift between us.

"Morning," I reply and take a sip of my coffee.

"Sleep okay?" she asks as she begins to move towards the coffee pot, letting her fingers brush ever so slightly on the pot to make sure it's still warm. Reaching for a cup, I let my eyes roam over her back, slipping down to her rounded ass and shuffle in my seat.

I don't want her to know I am checking her out.

Crossing that line is not on my agenda.

Sure, our sex would be explosive, but I am not sure if we should.

It then goes from a marriage of convenience to an actual marriage and an annulment will be out the window.

"Yeah," I admit, I didn't need to tell her that I slept awful and I was plagued by nightmares. "You?"

"So so," she sighs as she fills her cup and comes to sit with me.

"Wanna talk about it?" I ask as my eyes settle on her. She twists her lips and drops her gaze for a moment.

"Nope, because if I talk about it, I'll cry and I don't need that today when I have to move the heifers to the lower field."

I wait for her to look at me as I sit and drink my coffee. Seconds pass and her watery green eyes connect with mine.

"Okay," I say softly and give her a smile.

She nods and we sit in silence as we drink our coffee.

Once we're finished, we put our mugs in the sink and I hover by the doorway.

"How's your pops?" I find myself using the name she does and my heart warms.

"Yeah, he is good, nurses said he was stable through the night, levels are good and all that," she waves her hand in front of her.

"Well, that's good," my lips turn up and she smiles back at me.

"Yeah," she nods and walks towards me.

"You ready for the day?" I ask, a little hopeful.

"Think so, my first job when the sun comes up is to go and get your horse," she hovers a hand over my chest and for the first time I want her hand on my chest, I want her to feel the way my heart beats so she knows I'm not a complete lost cause; that I can love, but I just have no idea if it would be with her.

"Thank you for doing that for me," I say softly just as her hand retracts back beside her.

"You don't have to thank me," she whispers.

"I know I don't have to, but I want to…" I tilt my head just as I lift my hat and run my fingers through my hair.

Her cheeks turn pink and I fucking love that. She gives me a soft nod and walks past me and towards the door.

"I've got to go into my office, have a few things to look into and then I'll be back around lunch time. I'll check on pops and sort lunch, let me know what you fancy and I'll grab it on my way in."

Her eyes trail over her shoulder and she gives me a smile.

"Surprise me," she flutters a wink towards me before she opens the door and walks away.

CHAPTER TWELVE
MORGAN

The fresh air hits my face and I didn't know how much I needed to feel that. I look back at the house and then let my eyes hover towards the bedroom where my pops lays.

Nerves settle in my chest.

I wish I could stop the thoughts, but I can't. Always sitting there thinking is this the day he is going to die.

I know it's coming.

But it's the thought of not knowing.

Inhaling heavily, I feel my lungs expand as I move towards the stable and get my horse ready. Placing a kiss on her nuzzle, my fingers find her cheek as I scratch softly before letting my hand glide down to her neck.

Placing my head against her nose, I stand for a moment and try and let my heart slow slightly.

I felt anxious.

"Morning love," I whisper to her as I step back and her ears prick forward when the sound of boots fill the small stable block.

I spin and see Dusty walking towards me, and I smile.

"Morning boss," he tilts his head then strokes down Barley's neck, his eyes bouncing between mine.

"Morning," I smile.

"What's the plan for today?" he steps aside, hands in his front pockets.

"I've got to go and get Pacey's horse at some point; we need to move the heifers down the front field and tag the calves."

"Busy day then," he chuckles.

"You could say that."

"Marsha is sorting us lunch today, she said she'll bring it up the house for one."

"Oh," I stammer and look past Dusty when I see Pacey walk towards his truck. "One second," I say to Dusty as I run out of the stable and towards where Pacey is. "Pacey!" I call out, my boots gliding across the gravel.

His eyes find mine and I see the moment of panic that glazes his face.

"What's wrong?" he stops and turns fully to face me.

"Don't worry about lunch," I pant, a soft smile tugging at my lips.

"No?" his brows furrow.

"Marsha is making food, bringing it up the house for one. You're welcome of course to eat with us unless you wanted to grab something else."

"I'll be home for one," he gives me a wink and turns his back on me as he climbs into his truck, closing the door behind him.

I watch as the engine of his truck kicks in and with one last smile, he drives out of the ranch. I find myself waiting until he is on the main road before I move back towards where I have left Dusty.

"Sorry," I half laugh when I am back in front of him.

"What was that about?" he asks, looking behind me then letting his eyes settle on mine.

"Pacey was going to bring lunch in for us, but then you mentioned Marsha so I told him that she is cooking and bringing lunch up for one."

"Fair," he nods then turns his attention to my horse.

"So, we know the plan yeah?" I ask as I reach for the saddle off the stand.

"Yup," he nods and gives Barley one final stroke.

"Cool, let's start moving the heifers, then just before lunch I'll go grab Pacey's horse, then we can have lunch before tagging the calves."

"Okay boss," he salutes me off the tip of his cowboy hat before he walks down the stables to his own horse.

A bay American Quarterback called Soldier.

We rescued him a few years back. I wanted him for myself at first, but he and Dusty bonded and I didn't want to take him away from him, so, he became his horse.

Tightening the saddle, I reach for her bridle and slip it on, making sure her mane is out and over the brow strap.

"You're so pretty," I beam, lowering my lips and giving her nose another kiss.

Footing her stirrups, I pull myself up and settle myself into the saddle. Kicking her on, I move her forward and wait for Dusty to join me.

Whilst I am waiting, I look over the land that is ours, and pride blooms in my chest.

Me and my pops built this. Changed so much to make it work. But doubt settles and I am unsure if cow farming is the right path for us now.

We're a small ranch compared to Rivera Ranch who do most of the work around here, they're always first choice.

Sure, having Pacey here would help but I think we need

to move back to what we did before or go into something completely different.

Once pops goes, I have no idea if I would be able to keep doing what I do without him.

Shaking my head softly, I try and push my thoughts away.

I couldn't think about that now.

I had to focus on just working towards the end goal which is to keep the ranch turning over money so we're not at a loss and to stop the suits from bullying us out.

Without Pacey I would have fought them off for a while, but I would have crumbled and given in.

I knew I would have.

Then I would have beat myself up for the rest of my life that I rolled over and gave in.

Would have let them take everything from me, from my pops.

It's our legacy.

Sighing, I watch as the sun rises a little higher in the clear morning sky when I hear the sound of Soldier's hooves crunching.

"You ready ma'am," he asks, the reins loose in his hands.

I give a heavy nod and kick on as we move into the paddock. Dusty closes the gate behind us and we walk slowly up towards the top field.

"Do you think we need another cowboy?" I ask, glancing over at him and he shrugs a shoulder up.

"I mean, it wouldn't hurt. It's long days for just the two of us. But if we're going to move some of the heifers off...." he turns his head to look at me and I know where he is going with this conversation.

We have both aired our concerns, both spoken about

what we think should happen once pops passes on... and now we're here and neither of us want to let go.

"I know," I say quietly as I swallow down the lump that is in my throat.

"We will work something out, there is so much we can do here," I can hear the optimism in his voice.

"I know," I repeat my words.

Our chatter falls quiet as I glance over at our neighboring ranch and my brows lift.

"We have new neighbors," I say quietly to Dusty as I halt my horse.

"Oh yeah, so we do," he pauses.

"Shall we go and say hi?" I ask, nosiness getting the better of me.

"I mean..." he pauses as he glances at his watch. "It's eight a.m. I'm not sure they would be happy to have some strangers knocking on the door and waking them up."

"How do you know they'll be asleep?" I furrow my brows.

"Morgan..." he laughs, shaking his head from side to side. "How about we go and move the heifers and then we can go and introduce ourselves before lunch."

I roll my eyes in an over-exaggerated manner which gets a low chuckle from my friend.

"Fine, let's go," and just as the words slip past my lips, I am kicking my horse into a gallop as we move down the fields and towards where the cows are happily grazing.

The move takes longer than we planned and I feel mentally and physically worn out. Dusty closes the gate and he dusts his hands.

"Please tell me it wasn't just me that struggled with that?" he sighs, climbing back onto his horse and turning him around.

"Nope, not just you," I wipe the sweat from my forehead with the back of my hand. "I felt like they were feeling rebellious today," I smirk as I turn my own horse.

"They were," he smirks back at me and he begins to walk away.

"Where are you going?" I call out then begin to move forward.

"To meet the new neighbors!" and I kick my horse on to catch up with him.

"Wonder what they're going to be like..." I trail off as we approach their driveway.

"We'll find out soon enough," he gives me a wink as we approach.

A few horses are grazing in the fields. The house is cute, tucked away with the mountains behind.

I wait for a moment to see what Dusty is doing but he is already off his horse, so I follow his lead, swinging my leg off Barley and holding onto her reins as we walk forward.

"Let me knock," I whisper as I climb the steps and hover my hand over the door, inhaling heavily I knock.

I side eye Dusty and within seconds it swings open and a young, pretty red head opens the door, her eyes volleying between mine.

"Hey," I tuck my spare, sweaty palm into the back of my jeans. "I'm Morgan, this is Dusty," I nod my head towards him. "I own Cottonwheel Ranch, next door," I continue, "we were riding up the field to the cows and saw we had new neighbours." I pause for a moment, and she smiles wider. "Well, we just wanted to welcome you to Blossom Cove."

"Hey back," she says and she has a New York accent, "I'm James..." and before she can carry on, a little blond haired boy runs up behind her, his arms wrapping around her leg and she glances down at him, her hand on the top of his head. "This is Tanner," she smiles, "we have moved here from New York, my grandparents used to live here, but then I moved to the city as a teen and well, I decided I wanted to come back," a warm laughter surrounds her and the sound of footsteps have me lifting my eyes from hers and over her shoulder.

Dirty blond hair, black rimmed glasses and dressed in a loose tee and jeans, he wraps his arm around her waist and nuzzles his chin into her shoulder.

"These are our neighbors," James says softly, looking at him then her eyes are back on me as he stands a little taller and swoops the blond haired boy into his arms. "Morgan and Dusty..." she trails off and I give her a nod. "They live up at Cottonwheel Ranch," and he extends his arm for Dusty to shake, then moves it to me.

"I'm Nate, nice to meet you," he says with a smile.

"We have friends who have moved over to Lovelock Bay, followed us from New York," she pauses. "So even though we're far away from home, we have some friends here, but it would be nice to make some new ones," she gives me a lopsided smile.

"Sure, we can sort out a coffee or a lunch..." I trail off for a moment.

"Cool, I'll get your number?" she pats herself down for her phone and I nibble on my bottom lip.

"I actually don't have a phone," I shrug a shoulder up and she blinks at me.

"How do you communicate?" she laughs softly.

"I just head to where I need to go, if the person I need to speak to is there, great... if not, well, I'll go back. I've never been out of this town; everyone I need is here."

Silence crackles.

"What about your husband... does he have a phone?"

My eyes widen.

"Dusty isn't my husband," I laugh, looking at the man who is like my brother and he laughs back.

"No?"

"No, my husband owns Rivera Ranch," not exactly the truth but also not technically a lie.

"Riggs?" Nate eyes me and I roll my lips.

"Pacey, the youngest brother."

"Ohhh, the Sheriff," James nods a knowing nod.

"Yes, the Sheriff," my cheeks turn pink.

"Riggs popped up a couple of days ago, think he has met my friend Titus," his lips twitch into a smirk

"Yeah, I am sure Riggs made himself well known when he saw the moving trucks roll in," I laugh, Barley lifting her head, ears turned forward. "This is a nice place you have here, glad it's finally got a family living in it, it's been empty for so long," I sigh and glance over my shoulder.

"I had my eye on it for a while, and like I said, my grandparents used to live in Blossom Cove way back when, and when it finally came up on the market I knew I wanted to make it into a horse rescue and well, it seemed like the perfect spot."

A blissful sigh leaves her as she smiles into the distance.

"I think you made the right choice." I admit, finally letting my eyes drift back to her.

"Me too," Nate steps close and Tanner throws his arms around his mom's neck, kissing her on the cheek.

"Anyway." I falter back and foot my stirrup to climb into the saddle and Dusty follows. "It was nice to meet y'all," I tilt my head down at her, fingers pinching the cowboy hat.

"Right back at you," she winks. "And about that coffee, how does Friday work?"

"Friday, one, Sunny's?" I ask.

"Sounds perfect, can I bring my friend?" her head tilts and her eyes glisten in the sunshine.

"The more the merrier," I lower my chin before turning Barley and kicking her on, a soft trot forming as Dusty catches me up.

"They seem nice," he says as we approach the top of the drive.

"Yeah, they do, don't they," I smile, looking at him as we make our way back home for lunch.

My heart flutters in my chest when I see Pacey's truck parked up front. I know it's only been a few hours, but those hours feel like days.

Slowing Barley I lead her to the stable and untack her before putting her into her stall. She makes a move for the fresh hay, and I stand and watch her for just a moment longer.

Turning, I make my way towards the house. Letting myself through the door, I kick my boots off and sigh in relief. It's been a long morning, and I am so ready to have a hot bath and climb into bed.

But I still have more work to do.

Walking into the kitchen, I see Pacey facing me, back to the work surface, arms crossed in front of his chest. His eyes trace up and down my body and my cheeks burn and I internally roll my eyes.

How can he affect me from just a look.

Sighing, I cross my own arms over my chest and step a little further into the room.

"How's your day been?" I ask, kicking my toe to the floor.

"Busy," he sighs, "had something come up, ranch across town has had its cows moved across the border."

"What?" I know what he said but I am shocked.

"Yup," he puffs his cheeks out. "Never a dull moment," he winks, and I nod. "How about you?"

"Cows were a nightmare," I admit, "but I met the new neighbors,"

"Yeah?" his brows raise.

"Yeah, they're from New York," I bob my head.

"Nice, Riggs said we have new neighbors too," he admits, and I watch the heavy sigh that leaves him.

"Yeah, they're James and Nate's friends," I step a little closer, "I'm going for lunch with James and her friend Friday."

"Very nice, look at you making friends," he smirks. "Your pops..." he trails off just as his phone begins to buzz. He looks down, then back at me as if he is asking my permission silently if he can answer it.

I smile.

He takes that as a yes.

I take that as my cue to leave and check on pops.

Climbing the stairs, the nurse slips out just as I slip in.

"All okay?" I whisper as I look over at him sleeping.

She gives a nod.

"Doctor Carlos is popping in today, your grandad is complaining of pain in his stomach, he shouldn't be feeling it due to his meds so we just want to get him checked out."

My heart stills for a beat before I am nodding at her.

The smile she gives me is tight. She moves past me and heads downstairs. I look at my pops and suddenly he looks so small tucked into his bed.

Walking slowly towards him, my heart drops a little at his coloring. He is turning more gray as the days go by.

Sighing, my breathing rattles and I hold in the sob that blooms in my chest. I reach my hand forward and cup his, brushing my thumb back and forth over the back of his hand.

"Hey pops," I whisper to him, my eyes searching his face willing for him to open his eyes.

There is so much I want to speak about but at the same time, I want to sit here in silence and just watch him sleep.

The creaking floorboard has me lifting my teary eyes to the door to see Pacey standing there.

He gives me a sad smile as he leans against the doorframe.

"Lunch is here," he says softly and I palm away a tear that has run down my cheek.

I nod, looking back to my pops before I lean in and place a kiss on his forehead, lingering for a moment then push to my feet.

I sweep past Pacey and don't look at him, my eyes brimming with the unshed tears. I couldn't crumble.

I needed to stay strong.

Reaching the bottom step, I make my way into the kitchen to see Marsha standing at the counter unpacking her basket. Fresh rolls, soup, fruit and pastries.

My stomach grumbles.

"Morgan," Marsha smiles at me as she begins to set the table and I feel bad because I should be doing it but I know if I lift a hand whilst she is serving she will tell me off.

"Hey Marsha," I push a fake smile onto my lips and hover waiting for her to finish. "Is there anything I can do to help?" and I know the answer before the words even pass her lips.

"No, sit down," she gives me a smile and I do as I am asked. Dragging a chair out, I sit softly in it when I hear the sound of boots approaching.

Glancing over my shoulder, I see Dusty and Pacey walking in, light chatter amongst the both of them.

"About time y'all showed up," she rolls her eyes and shakes her head at them and my lips twitch.

Pacey places a hand on my shoulder and gives me a gentle squeeze before he sits next to me.

"All smells amazing," he rumbles from beside me and Marsha gives him a smile.

"This is Pacey," Dusty announces as he places a kiss on his wife's cheek before he settles next to me.

"Figured," she twists her lips as she reaches for five bowls.

"Pacey, this is my beautiful wife, Marsha."

"Nice to meet you," he says, tilting his head and she gives him a warm smile and some kind of curtsey.

"Are you all happy if I dish up?" she asks, eyes bouncing between the three of us and we all nod.

I feel bad sitting here but there is no chance of me even being able to sweep in and help. She reaches for her ladle and scoops three big spoonful's up and places them in the shallow bowl.

The smells fill the room and I am only just realising how hungry I am.

"Leek and potato soup," she smiles, placing the bowls down in front of us and then grabs the spoons and places them in the center of the table.

"Smells amazing," Pacey grumbles and licks his lips. I twist my mouth and reach for my spoon.

Next are the fresh bread rolls that she places on a wooden block and then slips the butter next to it.

"Thank you," I whisper and stir my spoon through the thick and creamy soup.

"Shall I take this up to your pops?" she holds the bowl up and I shake my head.

"Come and eat Marsha, I'll take it up shortly. I want to check on him before I head back out to work."

"No problem," she places the hot soup back on the work surface and finally comes to join us.

"This is delicious," Pacey says as he spoons another mouthful past his lips.

I hum in agreement as I take my first mouthful, and it hits the spot just right.

Pacey reaches in for a bread roll at the same time as Dusty and dips it into the liquid.

I eat a few more spoonful's before I swipe my soft roll through and take a mouthful and the mixture of the soup and the butter with the warm bread is what I feel like I needed.

Silence fills the table as we all sit and enjoy the food that has been laid out in front of us, Marsha looking between the three of us then drops her head as she spoons her own soup into her mouth.

Once finished, I swoop the bowls up before Marsha can even get a chance. Placing them in the sink, I turn and plate up the pastries with the fresh fruit.

Melon, strawberries, cherries, pineapple and blood oranges.

I place them down and grab small plates as I lay them out.

"I could get used to this," Pacey licks his lips and reaches straight for the pastry and pinches a few pieces of the different fruit.

Dusty goes next, then Marsha and finally I help myself.

Once lunch is tidied away and the dishes are washed, I

say goodbye to Marsha and invite her, Dusty and the kids over for dinner on the weekend.

I would love to have Pops join us, but I know that won't happen.

Sadly, this is the way dinner times will be now.

Without pops.

Sighing, I move upstairs and slip into his room.

His eyes trace mine and I smile.

"You're awake," my heart warms in my chest as I step closer to him and sit on the edge of the bed.

"I am," he smiles, his eyes not as full of life as they once were, the sparkle slowly seeping from them.

"Hungry? Marsha made soup."

His ears must prick up because the smile that spreads across his lips is wide, baring his teeth.

"Let me go get it for you," I reach for his hand and give it a squeeze.

"Okay," he nods as I push from the bed and make my way downstairs to warm his soup and get his bread roll.

Dusty told me to take as long as I needed and to spend the time with my pops.

Guilt eats away at me.

I feel bad that he is doing all the work whilst I am sitting here with him.

Pacey left shortly after lunch. We spent some time together with pops before he was called back away.

Placing the now warmed soup on the tray with his fresh buttered roll, his pastry and fruit and a water, I climb the stairs, cautious not to spill anything.

Pushing the door with my foot, I press a smile on my face as I lift my eyes from the tray and to my pops.

My smile slips.

My heart stalls in my chest.

"Pops." I say, softness wrapped around my tone.

Nothing.

"Pops," I say a little louder, my fingers curled around the edge of the tray, tightening as the seconds slip pass.

He doesn't respond.

And that's when it hits me.

I scream, dropping the tray from my hands, a loud clatter fills the room as I fall to my knees and sob.

"No, no, no, no..." the choked words leave my lips, and my body begins to tremble.

"It's okay, I've got you... I've got you," arms wrap around my body and hold onto me as I fall apart in his embrace.

I didn't even need to look to see who it was.

It was Pacey.

My husband.

The one who would need to pick every single shard of myself from the floor and carefully piece me back together again.

Bit by bit.

CHAPTER THIRTEEN
PACEY

Pulling into the space outside my office, I reach for my phone and instantly groan. It's not there.

"Fuck," I sigh, lifting my hat from my head and running my hands through my hair, tugging at the root slightly.

Placing my hat back on, I exhale heavily then put the truck into reverse.

Swinging it around, I make my way out of Lovelock and within minutes I am pulling up the drive of my home.

Dust kicks up from the tyres as I wobble in my seat slightly from the bumps. My mind drifts to Morgan and the want to take her on a date overwhelms me.

It has been such a short time but yet it feels like a lifetime has passed.

Strange really.

Funny how things work out like that.

Rolling my lips, I push the truck into park and then cut the engine. Opening the door and jumping down, my boots crunch across the gravel.

The closer I get, my stomach knots.

Footing the step, I move forward and twist the handle

for the front door and see my phone sitting on the stool. I roll my eyes and reach for it, slipping it into my back pocket and that's when I hear it.

The sound of a smash and a blood curdling scream.

Fuck the rules.

I run up the stairs with my boots and hat still intact and rush to where I can hear her sobbing.

"No, no, no, no..." I see her, crumpled on the floor, soup spilled, bowl shattered, glass smashed around her.

Her eyes are forward, and it takes me a moment to lift my eyes and see why she is on the floor, breaking apart in front of me.

My heart stills and I realize he's gone.

I drop to my own knees, scooping my arms around her waist as I pull her into me, holding her tight as her choked sobs rattle through her body.

"It's okay, I've got you... I've got you..."

I have no idea how long we sit like this for before I am fumbling for my phone and searching for Dr Carlos' number.

He answers on the second ring.

I try and lift her from the floor, but she shakes her head, wanting to stay grounded and anchored to where her heart obliterated into a thousand pieces.

"Doctor Carlos," is how he answers the phone, and I roll my lips.

"It's Pacey," I mutter into the handset, my voice is thick with gravel, my throat burning.

"I'll be right there," the phone goes dead, and I toss my phone across the room as I am back behind her, holding her until she is ready to move.

I don't want to rush her, but I also don't think it's right that she is sitting in here.

But I will do whatever she wants and if it's this, then so be it.

We're not alone long when two of the nurses walk in and I hear the gasp that passes their lips.

Their eyes cast down to where Morgan sobs in my arms, my tee soaked with her tears and my own heart has shattered in my chest.

The noise around me blurs but I hear in the distance talk of calling Carlos.

"I've already done it," my voice flat as her body continues to tremble against mine.

The noise fades out again and a high pitch ring replaces it, ringing through my ears.

My mind falters back to earlier today. I sat with Gerry, we had a laugh and a joke but then things turned a little sombre.

He turned his face to me and told me how grateful he was that I had agreed to do what he asked. Agreed to marry his granddaughter and save the ranch. He then continued to tell me where everything that I would need is locked away in the back of his wardrobe in a makeshift safe and the key was under the innersole of his favorite sneakers. That Morgan will know which ones.

I think I knew then that he knew his time was coming to an end.

He was making sure everything was in place.

The deeds were signed.

I was the owner of this house along with Morgan.

His estate was solely in my hands.

And his last testament and will were also in the same makeshift safe.

He made me promise that I wouldn't do anything to

Dusty, Marsha and the kids and I placed my heart over my chest and swore to him right there and then.

Then he asked me to love *his* Morgan with all of my heart.

I nodded my head and silently promised.

He understood.

He wasn't a silly man.

He knew I couldn't just switch my feelings on for her.

But I was sure they would come in time, and I truly believed that.

The sound of Carlos' voice slips around the room and that's when Morgan's eyes lift to the doctor. She shuffles, and I take that as my cue to lift her. Her legs are trembling, but I don't let her go.

I hold onto her, so she knows that I am there and I won't let her go.

"Morgan," his voice is low, and I can hear the sincerity in his tone. "I am so sorry, I didn't expect it to be this soon," he says as he steps closer and places a hand on her shoulder and I feel my stomach knot.

She gives him a nod and then his eyes find mine.

Secret words are exchanged, and I give him a soft nod, turning her into me as I walk her out of the room. We move down the stairs slowly, her breath shudders on her soft intake of breath and all I want to do is wrap her up in my arms and never let her go.

Leading her to the living room, I sit her down on the sofa and her eyes drift to his chair before she is crying into her hands again.

I stay with her for a moment, just watching her and I know I need to let Dusty know that Gerry has passed away.

"Oh my god," her voice cracks as she looks at me. "I forgot

to get your horse," her bottom lip trembles, her chin wobbling and I am on my knees in front of her, cupping her face as I brush my thumb across her cheek and catch the tears.

"Don't you worry about Chase, I'll sort that out later," I give her a soft nod and she just bobs her head up and down continuously. "Do you want tea?" I ask her and she just sighs, letting her eyes drift over to her pops' chair and my chest caves.

Pushing to my feet, I roll my lips and walk out of the room and into the small kitchen where I fill up the kettle and pop it on the cooker top, turning on the gas and letting it heat.

Slipping my phone from my pocket, I ring my ma.

She answers before it has a chance to ring.

"Pacey? Are you okay?" and I can hear the concern in her voice. I wouldn't normally call her during the day.

"I'm okay," I say, fingers tightening around the phone as I look over my shoulder and towards where Morgan is sitting. "I just wanted to let you know that Gerry has passed away."

The line goes silent, I swallow down the lump and nod my head as if she is in front of me and I feel my own tears pricking my eyes.

I hardly knew this man yet the grief that consumes me is heavy. But maybe it's because I am still dealing with the loss of my own father.

Grief comes in waves.

In ebbs and flows.

You don't just switch your emotions off.

Just some days are better than others.

"I am so sorry," my mom says, and I twist my lips. "Please pass on my condolences to Morgan and let her know that we're all here for her if she needs us."

"Thanks ma," I say, "love you." I cut the phone off and slip it back into my pocket just as the kettle whistles.

Picking a herbal tea, I pop it in her mug and then fill it with boiling water before giving it a gentle stir. Rummaging through the cupboards, I grab the honey and drizzle it into the chamomile tea.

I give it another stir and then hook the tea bag string around the handle and then walk into the living room, placing the mug down on the side table so she can reach it if she wants it.

Pacing back into the hallway, my eyes dart up the stairs and I am in two minds whether I should go and see Carlos or go and break the news to Dusty.

I didn't want Carlos coming downstairs and then having to speak to Morgan whilst I am not here, but at the same time, Dusty deserves to know too.

My boots walk into the living room, and I am staring at her.

"Where would Dusty be, babe?" the pet name slips off the tongue and I find myself swallowing the words around the lump.

She slowly turns her head to face me, eyes red rimmed and full of fresh tears and she looks fucking heartbroken.

"Stables maybe?" she whispers. "Or the field with the calves..." her face screws up as an onslaught of tears roll down her cheeks.

I give a soft nod and step back out of the room and pace.

I hear the sound of tires crunching on the gravel and my heart bottoms out. The blacked-out van rolls to a halt and two men dressed smartly step out and make their way into the house, a bob of their heads as they pass me, grimace smudged all over their faces.

They hover by the bottom step, and I give a delicate chin lift and they disappear upstairs.

Moving back to where Morgan is, she is staring out the window, shoulders shaking gently as she cries silent tears.

I suppose it doesn't matter whether you are prepared for a death or not, it never makes it easier.

"Babe," there's that word again, "they're going to be taking your pops now..." I trail off and I feel my own throat thickening as I swallow down the burning lump that has formed there.

Her blotchy face turns to face me and her lip trembles.

Holding out my hand for her, she stands slowly and carefully as she makes her way towards me and once her hand is in mine, I tug her into my chest and hold her tightly when the sounds of footsteps approach.

Her head is turned away, my hand on the back of her head as I gently hold her in place. She didn't need to see this.

One of the smartly dressed men move outside and within minutes he is back, a steel gurney waiting at the bottom of the porch and folded up thick material hung over his arm.

I knew what that was and I felt sick to my stomach.

He is back upstairs but not for long, the bottoms of their soles hit the steps slowly and steadily as they bring her pops down.

Carlos is off the bottom step first, he gives me a knowing nod and then steps in front of us, almost shielding both of us.

I glance over the doctor's shoulder when I see them carrying Gerry's body with such carefulness and that's when she turns to look, a harrowing howl escaping her lungs as she crumbles in my arms, her legs buckling beneath her. I hold her up, not letting her fall and cocoon her in my arms. They move him outside before laying him on the gurney and strapping him down.

The sound of the heavy doors close and only then does she fall silent.

"It's okay, it's okay," I stroke her hair, pressing my lips to the top of her head, my eyes closing as everything else fades around us.

"Morgan," Carlos' voice slips through our moment and she turns to look at him, pushing from my arms.

Green eyes rimmed in redness, cheeks blotchy and pink, lips dry and cracked.

"He wasn't in any pain," his words are meant to give her comfort, but I can see the anguish on her face. "We didn't expect it to be this fast, we will carry out the post mortem and I will let you know when his body is released."

She just nods. Tears streaming down her cheeks, licking the odd one away.

"Maybe you can contact me for that?" I step forward, wrapping my arm around her waist and pulling her back into me.

"Of course, whatever is easiest," he rolls his lips, his eyes not lifting from my wife.

"That would be easiest," I confirm just as the nurses walk into the hallway.

"If you have any concerns, please do not hesitate to contact me," he gives a shallow nod to both of us before he turns away and walks out of the door, the nurses following, heads bowed.

I let out the deep exhale of breath just as she slips from my grasp, stepping away from me as she stands in the open doorway, eyes fixated on the van as it pulls out of the ranch.

"I need to go find Dusty..." I whisper as I step closer to her and my brows furrow when I see Riggs' truck passing the van and pulling to a halt.

Ma, Aspen, Riggs, Dixie and Tripp step out with plates of food, flowers and warm smiles. Lainey is hooked on Tripp's hip and I can't stop the smile that is pressed against my lips.

They showed up for her.

My ma walks through the door first, glancing at Morgan with soft eyes then passes me the warm dish. I take it, and as soon as it is out of her hands, my ma throws her arms around Morgan, pulling her in and holding onto her tightly.

"Don't ever feel alone, I know your pops was your family, but you have us too," she says in a whisper as she places a kiss to the side of Morgan's head and that's when Morgan wraps her arms around my ma and holds onto her as if she is her lifeline.

My heart blooms in my chest, but it's pain that radiates, not warmth and love.

Riggs steps up and gives her head a rub then pats me on the chest as he walks into the kitchen with fresh wildflowers that look just picked.

Aspen gives me a sad smile then glances over at Morgan who is still sobbing into my mom's shoulder.

Next is Dixie who is holding another bowl of something and follows Aspen into the kitchen.

Tripp sighs heavily and we know the heaviness that Morgan will be feeling because we still feel it now, deep in the crevices of our broken hearts.

My mom ushers her into the kitchen and I follow them, leaning against the door frame.

"Can you just keep an eye... I need to find Dusty." I

swallow down the bile and Morgan's lip trembles at my words.

"Sure," my ma smiles at me as she rubs Morgan's back, Aspen pulling a chair out for Morgan to sit.

I give a nod, turning on my heel and walking outside the house, the warm summer breeze knocking the air out of my lungs as I give my heart a moment to settle down.

It's racing beneath my skin.

My legs begin to move but I have no control, I feel numb. My boots crunch heavily as I head for the stables, praying he is in there, so I don't have far to go whilst feeling like I am going to throw up the contents of my lunch.

Time moves slow as I push the heavy doors and step into the large space.

"Dusty?" my voice is loud as it echoes around the large space.

I hear the sound of metal hitting the concrete floor and my heart thumps.

"Yeah?" his voice floats towards me before I see him.

His face instantly drops when he sees mine.

"I'm really sorry..." I stammer out as I lift my hat from my head and let it drop to my side.

"No," he shakes his head as his feet move a little quicker beneath him as he runs out of the stables.

I stand for a moment, grounded.

He is going to remember this moment for the rest of his life and it's my face and words that will scar his skin.

Blinking away a tear that lines my bottom lid, I turn and move back towards the house, heart a little heavier than five minutes ago.

Stepping back into the hallway, I drop my hat to the floor and move into the kitchen where my family are all gathered.

"You doing okay?" Riggs asks, stepping towards me and I half nod, half shrug.

He pulls me into him, patting me softly on the back and I didn't realise how much I needed this hug.

I almost feel guilty for feeling some form of grief, but at the same time, I think it hurts more because I know how she feels, I know just how much pain she is in at the loss of the man in her life.

I lost my dad.

I know how it feels to lose a huge piece of you.

Until you have lost a parent, I don't think you can comprehend the feelings.

He holds onto me, my eyes scrunching shut.

It has just been such a rollercoaster over the last few months and this I feel, was just the final blow.

I need closure, I needed to fix what had been broken.

But Morgan being broken is not something I can fix by myself.

He lets me go and I give him a small smile.

The sound of boots hit the wooden floor and I know who it is.

Morgan glances her eyes over her shoulder and sees Dusty standing there looking as broken as her.

She pushes from the chair and throws herself into his arms.

I feel like a spare part.

I don't know her enough to comfort her in the way she needs.

My ma senses my mood and steps towards me, placing a hand to my cheek and I give her a sad grin.

"Love you," she whispers as the kettle begins to whistle.

Dixie and Aspen move out of the kitchen and begin

pottering around the house, picking up the odd pieces that lay around.

I finally let my aching legs rest as I sit down.

The tension brews in my temples and I feel pent up.

I have no idea how to maneuver this situation.

My glassy eyes move to her and Dusty, and I can't help but feel slightly envious of the both of them.

My ma's hand is on my shoulder as she places a cup of tea in front of me, Riggs and Tripp sitting next to me as he bounces Lainey on his knee.

"You doing okay?" Tripp asks and again, I shrug a shoulder up.

"I don't know," I admit, letting my chin drop towards my chest.

Curling my fingers around the cup, I pull it towards me.

"Morgan, darling," my ma's voice floats across the room and warmth radiates through me.

She finally steps away from Dusty as she takes the cup from my ma and rests against the worksurface, just as my ma hands Dusty a hot cup of tea.

I stand instantly. "You want to sit down?" and she shakes her head at me.

"I don't think I'll be able to stand again if I sit," she admits, voice cracking.

My ma is cleaning the kitchen, occupying herself whilst Riggs and Tripp exchange looks then both avert their gaze to Dusty.

He is standing, haunted, legs anchored to the spot, fingers curled around his cup.

"Dusty," my voice breaks him from his trance. His red, bloodshot eyes find mine.

"You wanna sit, man?" I ask as I stand and he doesn't respond, just moves towards me and sinks into the seat.

Dusty's eyes lift to my two brothers, slicing between the both of them.

"I'm Riggs," his hand pushes forward, and Dusty takes it, "not the best circumstances to be meeting for the first time…" he rumbles and then Tripp gives a soft smile and introduces himself.

I know they met at the wedding, but they didn't really talk much.

"We're so sorry…" Riggs says for the both of them and he just nods.

"I know you probably don't understand why I am so upset." Dusty begins, his voice kind of muffled.

Riggs rolls his lips and shakes his head from side to side, his eyes closing softly for just a moment.

"Gerry was more than a boss," and I hear Morgan's whimpers. "He took me in when I came out of jail, when I had nowhere else to go… no one else would have me but he gave me the chance. Made me work my fingers to the bone, but he let me work here under the radar… he was like the father I never had."

Tripp sighs, putting a fussy Lainey up and over his shoulder as she babbles in Morgan's direction, a ghost of a smile haunting my lips.

"You don't have to explain your reasons for being upset," his voice is low, "take it from three men who buried their father not too long ago, the feelings you have are valid, whether he was your dad or not, whatever the reason, he was a big part of your life."

Dusty nods, his eyes casting to Morgan and she has more tears rolling down her cheeks.

Aspen approaches in the doorway and nods her head for me to follow her. Pushing away, I move to where she stands just outside the kitchen.

"Do you think Morgan would want me to strip the bed…" she eyes the kitchen then back to me. "I think it needs to be cleaned," and I know what she is saying in a round about way.

I sigh heavily and ask her to give me a moment.

Dixie is in the living room, just tidying around.

The house is lived in, there is clutter everywhere. My ma's house is spotless, always has been, even with a rancher of a husband and three kids who were always in dirty clothes and muddy boots.

Stepping into the kitchen, I walk towards Morgan and softly tug on her elbow to get her eyes on me.

"Aspen is going to wash your pops' sheets, is that okay?" I whisper softly and she takes a moment to let my words settle in.

She nods ever so slightly.

"Okay," I roll my lips, and I am desperate to pull her into me, holding her tightly.

I move away and within ten steps I am back in front of the one who shattered my heart.

"That's fine," my chest rattles. "Leave it on the floor upstairs, I'll take it to the laundry room," her brows pinch, furrowing.

"Where is it?" she looks around the small space.

"Small shed behind the house."

"Okay," she smiles at me then places her hand on the top of my arm and my skin burns from her touch. "You doing okay?" she asks, head tilting to the side and I reply with a nod.

Because what else am I meant to say?

No, I'm not okay. I still hurt from all those years ago when you split me in two. No, I'm not okay because I am married to someone I don't know, that I want to know, but I am so fucking terrified of feeling anything for her when I am still trying to pick up the pieces that *you* caused. No, I'm not okay because I am not only grieving my father, but I am grieving my friend, *our* friend. No, I'm not okay because I am filled with so much hate and rage towards everyone and anyone who tries to tear down my family and yet there is nothing I can do to stop it.

"I'm okay," I mask the lie well and she drops her hand from my arm.

"Always here for you, you know that right?" her hazel eyes draw me in and I shut the memories down in an instant.

"Always," I smile and my heart throbs in my chest before she turns and walks away.

And I stand there, watching her disappear upstairs and for some reason, a bit of that pent up rage is aimed at her too.

"You doing okay, Pace?" Dixie asks me and I snap my face around to look at her, pushing my hands into my front pockets and telling her that I am in fact fine.

Turning, I go back into the kitchen and sit silently whilst my family try and delicately put Morgan and Dusty back together with their unconditional love.

Because that's who we are.

We're the Riveras.

We love fiercely and protect what is ours to our last dying breath.

CHAPTER FOURTEEN
MORGAN

ONE MONTH LATER

Numbness fills my chest whenever I think of Pops. Time has moved so slowly but at the same time passed in the blink of an eye.

We had the funeral at home and buried him at the bottom of the field, under the apple tree where my grandma is buried.

Dusty has thrown himself into the ranch, working all the hours he can, and I have just been trying to keep my head above water.

The grief comes in ebbs and flows, and honestly, I don't think I would have got through the last month without the Riveras.

I never knew how much I needed them.

I always thought I would be alone forever and having to deal with this huge change all by myself, but they haven't let me be alone ever since.

Pacey has been incredible, I think I always knew that he would be, but I never wanted to give him the chance I suppose. Then this huge moment happened, and he has picked me up every single time.

My heart is still broken, a thousand pieces scattered around the floor that he still hasn't managed to find, but I know it will take time.

I will never be fully whole again, but he can fix me the best he can.

Sighing, I step onto the porch and place my cowboy hat on the top of my head. The sun is warm, beating down on my sensitive skin. The soft breeze dances through the trees and I know it's pops. I feel him everywhere.

Smiling softly, I step down and my heart beats a little faster in my chest as my boots glide across the dusty ground beneath me.

Dusty is in the distance, riding down to the bottom field and I find myself drifting towards my pops' work shed.

The door is ajar and my brows crinkle, panic pricks at the base of my neck as I sneak around the wooden door and see Pacey standing in there, hands pressed into the front of his pockets, eyes scanning the room.

The sound of my boots has him looking over his shoulder, a warm smile spreading across his lips as he eyes me up and down before holding his hand out for me to move closer to him.

Inhaling heavily, I step forward, placing my palm in his as he pulls me beside him.

"What you doing in here?" I whisper, the dust settled on a lot of my pops' things, the smell a little musty where it's been shut up, but the hint of gasoline wraps around us from the scent of his old, rusty tractor.

"Just found myself walking in here," he shrugs a shoulder up as his grip tightens around my fingers. His face turns to look at me, eyes dusting up and down me. "How about you?"

"Same," I sigh, and my chest rattles, my heart hollow and weeping.

"Feels weird around here, don't you think?" he asks me before he focuses on the tractor, head tilting slightly.

"Yeah," my voice comes out in a whisper and goosebumps scatter across my skin.

I feel his eyes on me, but I refuse to look at him because if I do, I'll crumble, and I don't want to keep crying.

"Do you have much work to do?" my voice cracks as I settle my eyes on the dust sheets in the corner of the room.

"Baby," he sighs, "I always have work to do," a soft chuckle following.

I give a knowing nod as I kick the toe of my boot into the concrete floor beneath me.

"Well…" and he pauses before I look up at him, "I better get going," he gives me a small smile as he turns his back on me. "I'll see you for supper."

Before I can respond, he is walking towards the exit, slipping through the heavy wooden door then disappearing into the warm summer day.

My chest aches when I am alone, and I hate it.

Spending a small moment more in here, I say goodbye to my pops and close the door behind me, pushing down the large wooden panel to lock it shut.

Walking towards the stable, I grab Barley and climb onto her back, kicking her on and towards where Dusty will be.

I am trying to stay positive, but I just don't feel like my heart is in it anymore. I have no idea what I want to do with my life.

Reality sinks in that this is my life.

I am a cowgirl.

That was my path.

To run the ranch for my pops.

That's my destiny.

To keep the ranch turning over, keep our land safe.

Whether I wanted it or not... it wasn't an option.

I made a promise.

I wasn't about to break it now.

Dusty is sitting at the bottom of the field just staring at the cows as they graze. We really needed to move them along, plus the calves were being sold in the next month, then it's time to get ready for the cycle to start again.

Aspen had planned a night out Friday to Randy's and as much as I didn't want to go, I think we all needed it. They've been amazing, been here whenever I have needed them.

I couldn't have asked for better people to surround myself with.

The whole gang is going minus Dixie; Lainey hadn't been sleeping well apparently, going through some kind of sleep regression. Orla did offer to watch her, but Dixie refused. Said she just wanted a soak in the bath and an early night. Tripp said he would stay back and look after Lainey whilst she rested but Dixie told him he needed a few hours out.

I did mention it to James and Amora, I have no idea if they'll take me up on my offer, but I thought it would be nice for them.

Riggs is working with Pacey in getting the Boot back built up after Riggs bought the land.

That was their hang out.

I had only been there a few times, but I preferred Randy's.

It's what I knew.

Me and pops would always pop in on a Friday night, have a root beer float and he would have a beer.

Sometimes we would have dinner if he was too tired, others it was just a couple of drinks.

It feels a little tarnished now, but I still enjoy going. It holds good memories, and that's all I am trying to hold onto right now.

The good.

My heart has been obliterated inside my chest, and I fear it'll never be pieced back together again.

I am hollow.

The only light I find is Pacey, and I'm terrified he will leave me too.

Walking through the door just past five, I see Pacey's boots and my heart flutters. Kicking my own boots off, I lift my hat and hang it on the stand before walking into the kitchen and expecting to see him sitting there, but he is nowhere to be seen.

"Pacey?" I call out, looking up the stairs when I hear the sound of the floorboards creaking above me.

Smiling, I foot the bottom step and make my way upstairs cautiously and round the newel post as I walk down towards his room, his voice becoming louder.

Freezing, I eavesdrop to try and listen to the words that leave his mouth.

"It has to be a mole," the words slip past his lips, and I find myself gasping. "They know too much, they know things that my dad spoke about that only *we* would know. I am telling you Riggs, there is a mole among us, and I will fucking smoke them out."

Closing my mouth, I tiptoe back towards the stairs

when his bedroom door flies open, and his eyes settle on me.

No words are said but I can see how tense he is. Shoulders raised a little higher, jaw wound tight, and eyes narrowed on mine that look slightly bloodshot.

"I was just coming to check to see if you were okay..." my voice is timid and I find myself shrinking back towards the stairs, fingers curled around the handrail.

I watch as he inhales heavily, breath shaky as his body trembles.

"I've been better," he admits, and I watch as his head rolls forward, phone still in his hands as the other slips into the front pocket of his jeans. Slowly uncurling my fingers, I let them hover in front of me for just a moment.

"Wanna talk about it?" and his hand slips from his pocket, reaching around the back of his neck, rubbing the tension from the base of it.

"You must have already heard some of it?" his eyes burn with a flicker of rage, but I know it's not aimed at me.

"Only about smoking a mole out." I whisper but he hears every word.

He sighs, turning his head to the side as he looks towards the stairwell.

I don't push him.

Just wait patiently to see if he spills the words.

"You remember the explosion?" he asks, and I nod.

How could I forget.

It was the first time I had met him; I was so bold and confident and damn I miss the girl I was back then.

Sadness blankets me for just a moment before he begins talking.

"The way it was orchestrated... my dad spoke about

things in front of people who work for us, and the entrance they went for was where we think the Montana Pearl is, but of course, we don't know, even my dad didn't know. My grandfather took it and placed it somewhere safe... but yet, we were never told. We made peace with it, understood that he no doubt hid it for this very reason, but we've been attacked and I fear they'll just keep coming back. My job is to find the person who started it all, I know they're working with the suits, know that they will know the ins and outs of this ranch, hence why they went for the entrance at the base of the mountains."

He shakes his head from side to side.

"What has Riggs said?" I ask, stepping closer to him and now crossing my arms across my chest.

"That I am being over the top."

I lick my lips.

"Do you think you are?" and I hate that I am even asking him this, but I am just trying to get him to maybe rationalize his thoughts. A lot has happened over the last few months, he is bound to feel betrayed in some way.

His eyes cast to mine.

He shrugs a shoulder up.

"What do you want to do Pacey, what is the outcome with all of this..." dropping my arms, I push them into my back pockets, my eyes volleying between his.

"I just want to make sure our land is safe, that no one can take it from us, that no one can take our legacy," his voice turns to a whisper and my heart throbs in my chest.

"Then how do we do that?" I ask.

"I need to end the want to buy the land, I need to make them realise that there is nothing here but land that means so much to so many of us."

"They don't care about that though, they are just focused on the money and how much they can bring into whatever they want to build."

"Ski slopes and holiday resort."

I blink at him.

"Ski slopes?" my brows furrow for a moment.

"Apparently so," he nods heavily.

"Okay, so that's the winter months sorted... then what?"

"Well, they'll turn it into just a tourist holiday destination."

I nod, swallowing the bile.

"How big are we talking?"

I watch the corners of his lips lift and a playfulness flames in his eyes, my cheeks turn in an instant.

"Wife..." one of his brows lift, the corner of his lip digging into his cheek and causing a boyish dimple to present itself.

Pressing my hands to my face, I try and hide the fire that creeps onto my cheeks and I feel the flames burn against my palms.

"I didn't mean that..." and he chuckles softly before I feel his fingers wrap around my wrist, softly pulling my hands away from my face and his eyes meet mine.

"I know you didn't," he whispers against my lips, and I find myself tilting my head back, my lips parting slightly as he consumes me whole.

Silence crackles between us and I feel the panic pinch the back of my neck before my skin breaks out in cold goosebumps, smothering me in an instant.

"Morgan..." he trails off as his fingers slip from my wrists, his arms around my waist as he pulls me towards him.

"Pacey," I whisper, my throat dry and I am desperate to swallow to coat it, my heart thrashing in my chest, blood pumping in my ears.

He leans in a little closer, lips slanting just above mine and I find myself placing my hands on his chest and pushing him away softly, but I drop my head as I look at my feet.

His fingers grip my chin as he lifts my face so I have no other option to look at him.

"I have never been kissed," I admit, and I feel a blush creep over the entirety of my body.

His eyes widen ever so slightly, and if I wasn't being forced to look at him I would have missed it.

"Never?" he whispers, repeating my words and I shake my head, his fingers still gripping my chin.

"Never," I repeat the word, and my heart quickens in my chest.

"Baby," there's that name again that does things to me I can't even begin to explain.

I roll my lips, eyes still on him and his smile only grows.

"I get to be your first..." he whispers, and I find myself nodding.

He nods softly with me. "Not like this though," he leans in but places his lips to my forehead and lingers there for a moment more, his hands are now cupping my face and I find myself closing my eyes and enjoying having his lips on my skin.

He steps back, then finally drops his hand from my face.

"Hungry?" my voice squeaks, and I hear the crack.

"Famished," his eyes hood slightly before he is walking towards me, and I turn as he follows me down the stairs.

"What is your plan then?" I try and change the subject

and ignore the way that the heat blossoms between my thighs.

"For your first kiss?" he says with a cocky smirk on his face as he leans against the kitchen door frame, his eyes dancing up and down my body and I slap my hand against the top of his arm before I am walking towards the refrigerator, sliding out steaks.

"For the mole... for the ski slopes... for everything?" I swallow. "Because I feel like the longer this goes on, the harder it is going to be to fight this battle between the suits."

"I have no idea yet. Me, Riggs and Tripp are going to sit down with Conrad, Buck, Marty and Austin to see if we can come up with anything, but also to make up something to see if it gets back to the guys who are trying to fuck us over," and I hum in agreement as I grab some fresh vegetables and produce that I need for dinner.

"Do you think that will work?" I ask, my voice a little higher.

"I hope so, if not I will have to line them all up and shoot them," he replies deadpan and I turn quickly on my heel, dizziness causing my head to spin for just a moment before my horrified look settles on him.

He holds his hands up, lips tugging into a smirk. "I'm joking..." he trails off and I am not sure if I believe him or not.

"There must be a better way," I say softly, slowly turning to face the work surface again but not before trailing my eyes across my shoulder and giving him the once over.

"Yeah... torture..." he wiggles his brows, and I find myself sighing heavily at his response.

"I'm joking," he says again but I am getting the impression he isn't.

"Okay, so being serious now…" I trail off when I hear the sound of his footsteps echoing behind me.

"Yes wife?" his front is to my back, and I find my breath hitching as his fingers curl around my hip.

"What if there isn't a mole?" I whisper, slicing into the vegetables.

"But there is…" his breath is on the back of my neck causing my skin to pebble.

"How certain are you?" I ignore the way my skin is burning under his soft touch.

"Very," his grip tightens, and my chest expands as I swallow down a mouthful of air, willing it to relieve the burning that is slowly torturing me inside out.

"Okay," I whisper, my knife trembling as I hover it over the peppers when his hand places over mine and I freeze.

"Why are you so interested?" he whispers, and I find myself turning slightly, my eyes cast down to where his hand is.

"Just so I know if you're going to be bringing danger to my doorstep."

"Never," he brushes his lips against the back of my neck ever so gently, like a feather tracing across my skin and my breath catches at the back of my throat. "I would never do that to you," he reassures me just as he presses my hand down gently so the knife is now on the work surface before he spins me around, so I have no other option than to look at him.

I give him a nod because I know deep down, he wouldn't, but it still brings worry to me.

"I just wish this would all go away," I whisper, dropping my eyes for a moment.

"There is no need to wish, it will go away, I promise."

His fingers are on my chin as he lifts me to look at him, his eyes volleying between mine.

"I am just trying to be open with you, you heard part of my conversation, I don't want to keep you in the dark. You're my wife, this will affect you too, so I want to tell you what my plans are."

I nibble the inside of my lip.

"But I promise you Morgan, this will all be over with soon."

Silence crackles between us for a moment or two before he is stepping back and disappearing upstairs.

Letting my breath slow, my heart is back to beating steadily in my chest, I turn and get back to cooking supper.

It's not long before I am walking the dishes into the dining room, Pacey has laid the table and is sitting waiting for me.

The head of the table is empty, and a sad smile finds itself on my lips.

Placing the dishes down in the center of the table, I pull my chair out and sit opposite my husband.

"This all looks amazing," he chimes, shuffling in his seat as he grabs the serving spoons and tongs and begins to dish mine and his food up.

It's a quick dinner, but also full of goodies too. Roasted veg, creamed potatoes, steaks and a homemade sauce. Once he is finished with my plate, he serves his own.

"How are you?" he asks, sliding his knife into the medium rare meat.

I pause for a moment, a blink passing between us. "Not too bad..." my brows furrow as I pop a forkful of food into my mouth, chewing slowly.

"I just wanted to check in, that's all... I know it's been a tough few weeks."

I swallow then reach for my water, bringing it to my lips and taking a mouthful.

"It has," I smile at him, "but I feel at peace knowing he is out of pain, not that it makes my pain any easier, but..." I trail off and place my drink back down.

"I get that," he nods, forking another mouthful of food past his lips. "This is really good," he gives me a boyish smile and I smile back.

"Is there any update on the Boot?" I ask, trying to get the conversation away from me.

"Riggs has put the plans in and has instructed a construction crew to be available, but nothing much yet. He wants to make it pretty much how it was before. There is something about that place..." he pauses.

"That's how I feel about Randy's," I admit, cutting into my steak and swiping it through the creamy mash.

"I'm looking forward to going with you... maybe we can have a dance... re-visit all those weeks ago when you came up to me so brazen..." My cheeks turn pink at his words.

"You're not shy Morgan, far from it..." he licks his lips as he places his knife and fork on the plate and reaches for his water.

"Maybe I'm not..." I trail off and my insides are twisting as the seconds go on. "But then again, I had some tequila flowing through my bloodstream... and well, you seemed like a challenge but now we're married well..." and I see the way his eyes darken in seconds.

"Are you trying to tease me?" his tongue is pushed into his cheek, and I pull my bottom lip behind my teeth.

"Me?" my hand moves to my chest, "never." I shake my head from side to side.

He chuckles softly before picking up his cutlery and eating.

I wait a beat or two before I finish my own dinner and for the first time in a month, a slither of happiness wraps around a bundle of sadness.

But it's momentary.

CHAPTER FIFTEEN
PACEY

Pacing the floor of the Sheriff's office, my hands in my pocket as I wait for Riggs to get here. Rage simmers deep inside of me at what I may have uncovered, but I need to keep a lid on it until I have had a fresh pair of eyes on the evidence.

The door catches as it closes and I find my eyes lifting to see Riggs walking in.

Signature black jacket, brown cowboy hat, aviator sunglasses, a dirty tee and jeans and heavy work boots.

"You okay?" he asks as he slips off his glasses and hooks them in his tee neck, hands on his hips as his eyes bounce between mine.

"Not really," I finally stop, staring at him, one of my hands reaching up and pushing through my hair.

Riggs rolls his lips then looks at the manilla envelope on my desk.

His brow raises.

"Is that it?" he points at the envelope, and I nod.

I hear the heavy rumble of a sigh escape him as he

walks across to my desk and swipes the envelope from the surface.

Silence fills the hostile room, and my heart is banging against my ribcage.

He slips the paperwork out and just by the way his shoulders sag and his deep intake of breath rattles inside of him, I know I was right.

"Shit," he rubs his hand over his beard and the sound of the bristle meeting his skin is loud over the anger that burns inside of me.

"Yeah..." I roll my lips, hands back fisted inside my pockets.

"I'll deal with this," he grumbles, and I shake my head.

"No, I'll deal with it," I step forward, but Riggs glares me down.

"Trust me," he grunts, "let me deal with it," and I know not to push him when he is in that mood.

I give a shit attempt of a nod, there is no point even trying to argue with him.

"What the fuck are we going to do?" I find myself whispering as the rage teeters at the edge of my reasoning.

"Going to end this war once and for all."

I swallow down the bile that threatens to creep up my throat and ignore the angry tears that prick behind my eyes.

"Pacey?" the softer side of Riggs shows himself as he tosses the envelope on the desk and pulls me into him. "It'll be okay," he comforts me like a dad would his son and I find myself molding into him.

My chest tightens as the hot tears roll down my cheeks. I hated showing the vulnerable side of me, but hearing those words leave his lips brings everything hurling back towards me.

The shooting.

Harlow.

My dad.

All the stuff that haunts me in the evening is rearing it's ugly head in the daytime and I am terrified of the outcome.

"What if someone dies, what if they get to mom?" the anxiety riddles me, and I can't stop the onslaught of questions even if I wanted to.

"Nothing is going to happen," Riggs pushes me away, his hands gripping tightly to the top of my arms. "Do you understand me?" he looks down at me, tilting his head to the side, "nothing will happen to anyone," and his words are cemented into me like a promise.

I have no idea if he is telling me the truth or pacifying me so I don't worry, but either way, it helps... if only for a moment.

"I will fucking burn the town to the ground if I need to, no one, and I mean *no one* will take what is ours. I don't care if they're family, friend or foe, whoever it is, they'll pay."

I nod, over and over.

Rage turns to tears, tears turn back to rage and I feel myself begin to tremble in front of my brother.

I knew something like this was going to happen, knew we were going to find out, but it still doesn't make it any easier to swallow.

"It'll be okay brother," he says softly, the rasp in his voice has me looking at him.

I nod, sniffling and palming the lone tear that escapes and runs down my cheek.

"It just brings it all back," I admit, swallowing down the lump.

"I know, and I swear it Pacey, no one will get close to our family."

"You swear?"

"I fucking swear it," he presses his forehead towards mine, his hand wrapping around the back of my neck and holds me there. "And you know I don't go back on those."

Walking into Sunny's, I give her a solemn nod as Riggs steps in behind me.

"Well, hello Rivera boys," she smiles at us from behind the counter, a few people sitting in and enjoying a coffee and cake. My eyes cast over to see a group of people sitting at the larger table and I see a familiar redhead. I tilt my head and focus my attention back to Sunny as we approach the counter.

"Hey," I smile at her, and lift my hat from my head as I hold onto it, Riggs mirroring my move.

"What can I get you?"

"Two flat whites and two club sandwiches," I roll off mine and Riggs' order and he lifts his brows, a playful smirk tugging at his lips.

"Take in or take out?"

"Out please," I sigh then glance back over at the table and realization settles in my stomach. It's our new neighbors.

"Excuse me a minute," I say just as Sunny rings up the total and I hear Riggs grumble something that I have let him pay.

Walking over to where they all sit, their eyes find mine one by one.

"James, right?" I ask, giving her a small smile.

"Yeah, you're Morgan's husband... Case..."

"Pacey," I correct her with a soft nod of my head. I had

only briefly met her and her husband when I was with Morgan a couple of weeks back.

"Apologies, you've met my husband Nate," she holds her hand out, "this is Titus and Amora," she smiles at the older man sitting opposite her and again to the redhead next to him, "and finally Xavier and Royal, Amora's parents."

"Nice to meet you," I say with a tilt of my head and Xavier looks me up and down like I am a piece of shit on the sole of his boot.

A grumble has him turning away and Royal, his wife, gives me a roll of her eyes aimed towards her husband.

"He can be a little..." Royal begins and I can see she is thinking how to explain her husband, her British accent strong.

"Bit of a dickhead," Titus chuckles softly and Amora slips her hand onto her husband's thigh which only gets another growl from Xavier.

"Anyway," I give them a polite smile, "I better be going, just wanted to pop over and say hi..." I trail off when I hear the sound of Riggs' boots behind me, the crunch of the paper bag with our sandwiches in.

"Titus," his eyes lift over my shoulder as he steps forward and shakes Titus' hand.

It takes me a moment to remember that Titus and Amora are his neighbors. They moved into Bluebeak Ranch, bittersweet for us really.

"This must be Nate and James," Riggs sweeps past me, nodding at James and shaking Nate's hand.

"You're coming to Randy's on Friday yeah?" Riggs asks Titus and he gives a half shrug,

"Maybe, I know the girls definitely are... me and Nate aren't sure yet," and Riggs gives him a soft snort of a laugh.

"Will be nice for you to come down if you can… then when I have the Boot rebuilt, we will relocate back to our local." I find myself looking at Riggs then drifting my eyes back to Nate and giving him a soft nod.

"Anyway," I repeat my earlier words. "We better be off." I give Riggs a little wink and he tilts his hat, saying goodbye to our new neighbors before we turn and walk out of Sunny's.

Sighing when we're out on the sidewalk, I find myself looking back into the window as we walk past their table and Xavier's eyes burn into mine.

One brown, one ice blue, a scar that runs down from his ear to under his nose.

A shiver dances up and down my spine.

"You okay?" I hear the humorous tone in my brother's voice.

"Yeah, just that Xavier…" I trail off and look behind me at the diner that is now in the distance.

"I think we could use him," and I snap my head around, my eyes widening as we approach my office.

"What?" I ask, unlocking the door and pushing into it.

"Do you know what he used to do?" Riggs furrows his brows.

"No idea, this was my first meeting with him," placing my keys on the desk, "and I don't think it was a very good first impression on his part."

Riggs chuckles a little louder now.

"He does soften."

I turn my lips down.

Riggs places his hat on the stand and then sits on the chair opposite my desk.

"Are you going to enlighten me?" I sit in my own chair, kicking my boots onto the hard surface as Riggs tosses my wrapped sandwich at me, catching it and shaking my head.

He looks at me through his lashes, a boyish smirk on his lips as he unwraps his sandwich then takes a bite.

He chews slowly and I swear I am about to throat punch him.

"Riggs," I snap, brows etched into my skin.

"He was a fixer," he takes another bite.

"A fixer?" I unwrap my own sandwich and my stomach grumbles.

"Yeah," he glances his eyes down into his lap.

"What's a fixer?" and I can feel the agitation pricking at my skin and I know this is why Riggs is doing it.

"So, for example..." he pauses and reaches for his coffee, taking a mouthful, "when all of this went down with Clay, we could have called him, if we knew where the body was for example, then he would have just kind of... fixed it?" he lifts a shoulder. "From what Titus has explained, he was kind of like the clean-up guy... made it go away... no repercussions."

Then it clicks.

"Ah," I nod, knowing exactly what he means, taking a bite of my sandwich.

We chew in silence, our eyes locked on each other, a thousand thoughts whizzing between us without us having to say a single word.

Rolling my empty paper up, I toss it into the trash can that sits in the corner of my office.

"Shot," Riggs nods, then winks as he rolls his own paper up and throws it blindly over his shoulder and sinking it in the trash can.

"Show off," I roll my eyes and kick my legs down as I reach for my coffee.

"So," I shuffle in my seat, "back to Xavier…"

"What about him?"

I roll my eyes.

"You think he can help with this?" I drum my fingers on the manilla folder on my desk.

"One hundred percent…" Riggs trails off his words then gives a heavy nod.

"Can you set up a meeting?" I ask quietly.

"Don't see why not," he winks at me then pushes from his seat, grabbing his coffee as he does. "Anyway, as much as I would love to stay here with you, I actually have work to do," he rolls his eyes in an exaggerated manner, and I flip him off.

"See you later?" he asks as he places his worn cowboy hat on his head then slips his aviators back on before tugging on the door.

"See you later," lifting my chin, he steps out and closes the door behind him.

I sit for a moment and my eyes burn through the manilla envelope.

My blood burns as it flows through my veins and the rage consumes me.

I need out.

Pushing from my chair, I groan as my phone dances across my desk.

Marty's name is flashing up.

"Yeah," I exhale into the speaker.

"We have a situation," my head rolls back, and my fingers find their way to the back of my neck as I rub into the muscles, tension threatening at the base of my spine.

"When don't we have a situation," I grit down the phone as I swipe my keys from the desk and I am already out the door before I even know where I am heading.

"Where are you?" I slam the door of the truck and start the engine.

"Other side of the mountains... entrance to the mines," and my eyes widen.

"The fuck?" I hiss down the speaker as it connects to the car.

"Looks like someone has tried to get in again," and I cut him off.

I'm in a blind rage as I boot it towards the ranch.

Punching the screen with my thumb over Riggs' name.

"Miss me already?"

"Meet me at the sweeping hollow entrance," that's all I say before I cut the phone.

Tapping my finger on the steering wheel, I try and calm my mind.

It is racing at a thousand miles an hour and the closer I get to the mountains, the more I am getting myself worked up.

Glancing at the time, my thoughts momentarily move to Morgan, my heart slows to a steadier beat and my blood cools.

And that's when I realized that Morgan was my calm.

Slipping down the red dirt road that leads us to the back of the ranch, the house tiny in the distance and I feel my heart rate pick up again.

Slowing when I see Marty's truck, Austin is sat next to him on his horse and his eyes trail to mine.

Cutting the engine, I jump from the seat and my boots crunch across the gravelled floor as I walk towards where Marty stands, Austin jumping from his horse and letting his reins loose.

Austin has his hat on, hands on his hip and his eyes don't leave mine.

Marty is in his cowboy hat, dirty jeans and checkered shirt, but his eyes have drifted behind me when I hear the sound of tires approaching.

A smile lifts the corner of my lips and when I finally reach them and narrow my gaze, I see he has Tripp with him too.

He doesn't even cut the engine.

Just rolls straight from the truck and Tripp is on his heels.

"What the fuck is going on?" I turn to face Marty and his eyes bounce between the three of us.

He sighs, eyes settle on Riggs', his boot heels digging into the ground.

Austin steps forward and kind of hovers between us and Marty.

"We got a call about some cattle that were stuck at the base of the mountain, given the amount of herds that have just disappeared, we decided to come and check it out."

"Didn't you rule that they may have gotten across the border?"

"I mean, I couldn't prove it, but..."

"But what?" Riggs growls.

"Well, I assumed that's where they went," and Riggs scrubs at his face.

Tripp stays silent and just listens.

Me and Riggs are too hot headed and sometimes lose the little details that we're told, but not Tripp, he is calm and collected and he won't let a single detail slip past.

"Anyway," Austin interjects.

"We came out here, but there was nothing... no herds..."

"Right?" Riggs taps the toe of his boot.

My hands slip into the front of my pockets.

"The mine was open."

"Forced?" I ask and Marty's eyes sweep to Austin.

"Just come and have a look," Austin says softly as he begins to move forward, unhooking the gate that fences the path off.

I look back at Riggs who gives me a soft nod.

I follow, Riggs behind me and then Tripp behind him. Uneasiness settles in my stomach and something feels off.

Turning my face over my shoulder, Riggs is tense.

Shoulders are up.

Jaw is locked.

Something is up.

What the fuck aren't they telling us?

Trudging up the slight hill through the fields, we reach the peak before we're walking down a narrow dirt track to get us to the entrance.

I don't trust anyone since that manilla envelope landed on my desk and now I feel like I am walking on eggshells with everyone I once trusted.

I catch the look Austin throws me and my heart stills for a moment as we approach the entrance and that's when Marty turns his gaze to mine, his lips rolled into a tight line, his eyes batted to the floor where they stay.

My brows knit and Riggs pushes his way past me and walks the small turn in the path.

"Fuck!" his voice echoes and I find myself running towards him, careful to mind my footing and that's when I see him.

Conrad.

Bloodied and beaten.

Lifeless.

A sign around his neck.

'*You were wrong.*'

"The fuck," I whisper, losing my footing as I step back but Tripp is there, catching me. My eyes lift from Conrad's body to Riggs.

His hand is over his face, rubbing it across his cheeks.

"Who the fuck did this?" his eyes burn into Marty and he knows Marty isn't going to have the answers but Riggs is clearly upset.

"We have no idea, we just got a call."

"Who called you?" Riggs is stepping towards Marty as he squares up to him.

"The fuck Riggs?" Marty shoves Riggs in the chest to stop him coming closer but it is pointless.

Riggs towers over Marty.

"Who called you Marty?" I ask now, stepping forward and trying to calm Riggs down by placing my hand on his shoulder, giving it a gentle squeeze.

Tripp is there, standing next to Riggs as I focus on Marty.

"It was an unknown number, Austin was there, he can vouch for me."

My eyes skate to Austin and he gives me a shallow nod.

My brow raises.

"Really?" I ask and turn my attention to Marty.

"Yes," Marty's tone is curt.

"Give me the phone," I hold my hand out and Marty's eyes bounce between the four of us.

"What the fuck? I'm on your side."

"Then give me the phone," I tilt my head, a smirk tugging at my lips and I feel Tripp's eyes on me.

He wants me to look at him.

But I don't.

I am too in my head.

We know there is a mole, and we were led to believe the mole was Conrad... but here we are.

Marty's eyes skate to Riggs.

"He is being a lot more patient than me Mart, give him the fucking phone."

That's when Tripp lets go of Riggs, silently giving him the green light to go towards Marty. His heavy boots crunch along the gravel and Marty's eyes widen.

"Fuck, alright," he holds his hands up in surrender before his trembling hand is slipping into his back pocket as he pulls his phone out, tossing it towards Riggs but he throws it straight to me.

"Passcode," I grunt.

"6969."

"Subtle," I roll my eyes.

Tripp lets out a soft laugh.

His phone unlocks and I find myself going through his call list.

"Private," I grunt until one number catches my eye. "There is a number on here from Wyoming."

Marty's eyes cross to me, then back to Riggs.

"I have family there..." he pauses and then looks at Austin.

I slip my own phone out and punch the number into my phone then toss it back to Marty.

"Get this cleaned up," Riggs shakes his head in disgust, "then board the fucking mine up," he barks his orders before walking away, Tripp following.

Now it's just me, Austin and Marty.

"I suggest you listen to him, I'll be by tomorrow to get a statement."

Turning on my heel, my stomach coils and nausea

swims through me. I was not expecting that when I got the call.

Footing the sidestep of the truck, I slam the door then toss my hat onto the passenger seat. My hands are in my hair as I tug on the root.

What the fuck is happening.

Everything around us is slowly unravelling and I can't stop it.

Putting the truck into drive, I wheelspin on the red dirt road, kicking up dust around me as I speed towards the house.

I needed to meet with my brothers.

We needed to speak this over and work out what was next.

Someone wanted us to get a message, and well, we got it.

CHAPTER SIXTEEN
MORGAN

It's just past four when I walk through the door and my body aches.

Dusty was sick so it was just me lugging bales of hay up onto the trailer before driving the tractor down the bottom of the fields.

Long day with not much work done.

I also needed new fence posts put in but that could wait until tomorrow.

I slump in my pops' chair and sigh, my heart a little heavy. I sit for a moment longer before I am up and moving towards the bathroom. I can't be in that room too long.

The memories flood me and I am left feeling haunted for the rest of the day.

Warm water cascades down my body and my aching muscles thank me. My mind races to Pacey and I find myself feeling excited to see him in a few hours.

I know this is business, but I am only human. I wouldn't say I have fallen for him, but I may have a little crush on my husband.

I mean, who wouldn't?

My mind wanders and I am thinking about his day, wondering how it has gone and if it has been good or bad, and can't help wondering whether he thinks of me during his, but then I have to remind myself quickly that of course he doesn't and he is in fact in the right mindset with this *just* being business.

This is the problem when you have never been in a relationship. I have no idea how to act. No idea what to think or do in these situations.

So I find myself coiling inwards and rebuilding my walls carefully so the next time it gets knocked, it may not fall so easily.

Lathering the soap into my aching scalp, I gently massage it into my roots before letting the warm water wash away the suds, slipping down my back like pure silk. My eyes are closed as I rinse my hair and all I see is him. How can he consume me wholly when it's been a matter of weeks.

Sighing, I twist and reach for the conditioner before smothering the ends of my hair. Exfoliating and shaving whilst that works it's magic, I finally rinse my hair and cut the shower.

Pulling back the shower curtain, I grab the warm towel and wrap it around my body.

Padding into the hallway, I step into my room and close the door softly behind me as I dry myself and dress in a comfy gray lounge suit. Roughly drying my hair, I then tie it into a low bun and tuck a couple of wispy strays behind my ears.

Making my way downstairs, I glance out the window and see the sun lowering slightly. Evening is drawing in and I lift my eyes to the clock on the wall. Pacey should be home soon.

My stomach knots and a slither of worry slips through me, but I push it down with the rest of my feelings, burying it deep inside a crevice.

I busy myself tidying the kitchen, not that it is overly messy, but I needed to keep my mind busy before I start preparing dinner.

Lemon chicken and pomegranate salad with baked potatoes.

Simple but yummy.

We have the Riveras coming over on Sunday for dinner and Friday we're down at Randy's with our new neighbors.

I'm not one for plans, but seeing as the Riveras and Dusty are all I have in terms of family... well... I didn't want to rock the boat.

Sighing, I pull the chicken from the refrigerator and place it on the side. Turning the stove on I wait for it to heat up before lowering myself to crouch down and place the chicken in to cook.

I slam the oven door just as the front door closes and I find myself jumping before looking over my shoulder, my eyes dusting over his body as he steps a little closer and leans against the doorframe.

Straightening myself up, I turn slowly and let my green eyes connect with his. My heart aches silently in my chest and I can feel a sadness deep inside of him that has my feet slipping across the floor to get to him.

"Pace?" my voice is quiet as I stand toe to toe with him, hand lifting and resting on his chest, the feel of his heart racing beneath my fingertips.

His head lowers, his eyes hollow as they drop and panic pricks at the base of my neck.

"What's happened?" and that's when I allow myself to really look at him. Red dirt dusted across his cheeks, lips cracked and dry and hair messy. His skin looks a little worn, a little more tired than usual and his eyes are dull, the normally glistening whiskey color looks a little darker, the spark nowhere to be found.

He says nothing, but I feel the deep inhale of breath he takes and before I can say another word, his arms are around my waist as he pulls me close to him, holding my body against his, his face buried between my head and shoulder as he trembles, tears seeping out of him and all I can do is hold him and try my best to comfort him.

"Talk to me," I whisper, trying to push his heavy body off my frame, my hands gripping onto his head as I lift his red rimmed eyes to mine, a lone tear rolls down his cheek and drops onto the sweater of my lounge suit, the gray material absorbing it in an instant.

"It's just been a day," he chokes, his dirty palm rubbing his eye and I watch as his throat bobs, my eyes volleying between his.

"This is not because of a shit day," my voice is still low but he won't look at me, his eyes are locked into the window that overlooks the front of the ranch.

He sighs and I am silently begging for him to look at me, silently begging that he will tell me what is haunting him, but I don't know him well enough to know whether I should push for him to spill all to me or take the hint and step away.

I choose the latter.

I drop my hands from the side of his face and step back, turning on my heel and walking back towards the stove.

"Supper is at six," I say nonchalant because I am terrified to break in front of him when he is clearly so vulnerable.

I know I shouldn't feel pushed out and bitter, but the truth is, I do.

He says nothing, but I hear the sound of his boots being kicked across the hallway and then heavy footsteps taking him upstairs before the bathroom door is slammed shut making me jump.

Once I know he is out of sight, I drop my head and sigh, shaking my head from side to side.

How the hell am I meant to help him when I don't know him.

Lifting my head, I glance out the same window he did and notice an American robin sitting on the fence line, it's wings flapping slightly before it sits still and my heart jack hammers in my chest.

I ignore the way my heart swells in my chest and my throat burns with a lump that lodges itself there.

And just as quickly as the bird came, it left without warning and a small smile curls at the corner of my mouth.

"Bye pops," I mutter then find myself walking towards the corded phone on the wall.

I look over my shoulder and make sure the coast is clear before dialling a number and twisting my finger in the cord.

Three rings and she answers.

"Rivera Ranch 895."

"Orla," I whisper talk into the speaker of the phone.

"Morgan, sweetie, is everything okay?" and I pause for a moment as I try and collect my thoughts, licking my upper lip and I have no idea whether I should have even made the call. "Morgan?" I hear her voice again and it snaps me out of my thoughts.

"Erm, hi..." I trail off and look over my shoulder to make sure he is still nowhere to be seen.

"You okay?"

I nod before answering her. "Yes... well, maybe... I don't know." I continue to twist the cord around my finger.

She stays silent.

"Pacey came home... looked broken." I whisper. "I tried to talk to him, but he just pulled me into him and cried." My lip trembles.

"I'll get someone over," and before I can even argue with her, she continues, "thank you sweetie, he'll only talk to two people... he will open up to you, just give him time."

I nod as if she can see me.

"You did the right thing Morgan," she says softly before hanging up the phone and my stomach knots.

I have no idea if I have done the right thing, but if my gut is anything to go by then I know it wasn't.

Sighing, I place the phone back in the holder and busy myself with supper.

Pacey will be down in a moment, and I have no idea who else will be joining us.

I hear the familiar bang on the pipes, and I know he is finished with the shower. Anticipation pricks at the base of my neck and my palms are clammy as I begin to prep the baked potatoes.

The sound of the bathroom door opening and closing echoes through the quiet house and I sigh.

A knock on the door has my eyes lifting out the window and I see the black Rivera Ranch truck sitting out front and I know Orla has sent Riggs.

Running my hand down the front of my thigh, I inhale heavily as I begin moving towards the front door and swing it open, my brows furrowing at who I see standing there.

It's not Riggs.

But his wife, Aspen.

"Morgan," her voice soft, her head tilting to the side as she steps forward and wraps her arms around me, her chin resting on my shoulder before she pulls away and her full lips break into a smile.

"Where is he?" she asks me, her eyes drifting towards the kitchen as I step aside and let her in.

"Shower," I mutter, nodding towards the stairs and I hear the floorboards creak. "But no doubt he will be down in the next..." and I stop talking when I see his feet appear as he walks down the stairs.

He pauses on the middle step, confusion lacing his handsome face.

Hair still damp and pushed away from his face, stubble a little more prominent and a light moustache that he seems to be growing. His eyes bounce between me and Aspen, and I know I overstepped the mark. My eyes are glued to him, and I know he can tell by my expression that this is my doing. His hand slips in the front of his jeans, his baggy white tee tucked into the waistband slightly.

"I thought I would just pop in..." Aspen begins and her eyes dart to me before they're on her brother-in-law.

"Why?" his voice is gravelly and my heart races a little faster in my chest.

"Because after today, I thought you could use a friend... I know what you're like Pace, I know you'll pull away and push against anyone that tries to get close," her eyes are on me again, but I bat them to the floor where I focus on my bare feet.

I swallow down the lump before turning my back on both of them and head back into the kitchen.

"I'm not pulling away, I just don't want to talk about it," I hear how defensive his tone is when he is talking to her, but she doesn't take any shit from him.

I steal a look over my shoulder as he steps in front of her, his eyes pinned to only hers and she knows she has him right where she needs him. She lifts his arm and tucks herself underneath it as she leads him away and my heart shatters inside my chest.

Why is this bothering me so much?

Placing the potatoes on the baking tray I open the stove door and place them above the chicken.

Closing it, I step towards the archway in the kitchen and loiter as I listen to the calming and quiet voice of Aspen as she speaks.

"This is not your fault; you know that right?" she says and I edge a little closer.

"I know, but I am sick of people dying on my watch," he admits, and I can hear the sadness in his voice.

"Pacey, this is not on you, he didn't die on just your watch, he also died on Riggs, Tripp's, Austin's and Marty's..." she trails off.

"It shouldn't have happened; he wasn't a bad guy... sure we had our assumptions but..." and I hear the crack in his voice.

Who has died?

"I know..." she pauses, and I creep into the hallway and stand behind the door frame. She wraps her arms around his shoulders, and he rests his head on her. "But it's happened, and now you and your brothers need to work together to find out who killed him, find out why they killed him."

"I haven't even told Sunny yet, not that they were a thing as such but..." he pauses and lifts his red rimmed eyes to Aspen.

"I know," she gives him a soft nod, her eyes lowering to him and he looks at her in a way he has never looked at me.

My stomach twists and I find myself gasping for air as my lungs burn.

"What's Riggs said about it all?" she asks and gently pushes him away from her, he allows her to as he sits a little further back but still leaning towards her.

"He is as bummed as me. I thought we were going to find another attempt of getting down into the mine, yet we found Conrad's battered body lying there instead."

Nausea rips through me and I find myself swallowing, trying to coat the dryness that has suddenly laced my throat.

"Unfortunately this was always going to happen, greed does terrible things to people when they can't get what they want..." she trails off and places her hand on his knee and I watch as he gives her a small smile.

"You're a good man Pacey Rivera, everyone can see it."

He bobs his head as he tears his eyes away from her and focuses them down.

"Hey," she coaxes him, "look at me," and he does, he listens to her command. "You are Pacey, you are a good man, you all are," she smiles a little wider at him and he gives her a half shrug of his shoulder. "Despite what people may say or think about you Rivera boys," she laughs softly before pushing from the sofa and I recoil back, tip toeing into the kitchen.

"Thanks kid," Pacey says, voice low, wrapped in gravel.

"And open up to that beautiful wife of yours, she's there through the dark days as well as the brighter ones."

He doesn't reply and I scamper away and tuck myself back into the kitchen, pottering around so he thinks I wasn't eavesdropping.

I know I shouldn't have been, but I wanted to know what had him so shaken up.

And now I know.

Conrad was dead.

Another life taken and all leads will point to the Rivera family.

That's two bodies that have been found on their land.

I hear the sound of footsteps behind me and Aspen's voice follows, wrapping around the room like a warm cashmere blanket.

"See ya tomorrow Morgan."

"Oh," I spin acting surprised, "see you later Aspen." I hold my hand up and give her a toothy grin. She holds her hand up and waves. Pacey sulks in behind her, hands fisted into his front pockets, head down.

She pulls him in for a hug and rubs between his shoulder blades.

"Everything will be okay, it'll all get fixed, you know that," her voice is low but still loud enough for me to hear.

He gives her a sad nod before she turns on her heel and sees herself out just as I begin to toss the salad.

Silence echoes around the house and as the seconds pass, my heart beats a little faster.

"Morgan..." his voice rips through me like wildfire, the way my name slips off his tongue licks against my skin like a flame.

I inhale deeply, dropping the wooden salad forks into the bowl and twist with it in my hands, head cocked to the side as I let my eyes sweep over him.

"Pacey?" I answer him with a question, walking into the dining room and placing the salad in the middle of the table and I hear the sound of him following me like a lost puppy.

"I'm sorry," he just about manages to squeeze out and I stop in my tracks.

"For what?" one hand sits on my hip, and I can feel the rage bubbling inside of me and I hate it.

Because I don't even think I am mad at him.

I am mad at myself for calling his mom the second it got a little tough for me because I didn't know what to do.

I should have pushed a bit harder, knocked into his walls and I know he would have told me eventually, but I didn't.

"For not talking to you," and the crack in his voice has the breath catching at the back of my throat.

Opening my mouth before slamming it shut again.

"I know you called my ma," and if I wasn't staring at him, I would have missed the ghost of a smirk that caused the corner of his lip to lift.

"I... I mean..." I wave my hand around in front of me and stammer over my words. He shakes his head from side to side and steps towards me, closing the gap in two strides.

We're body to body.

Nose to nose.

And I swear he can see my heart lurching out of my chest.

"I didn't know what to do," I whisper, all rage that once was a fuelled flame was now nothing but a simmer of ashes.

"I know and that's on me," his hand cups my face, thumb brushing across my cheek.

"You don't have to tell me anything," I just about manage, my eyes volleying with his.

"I know I don't, but do you know what Morgan..." his voice slips away into silence, and I find myself edging forward, lips parting slightly, desperate to feel his lips on mine.

"What?"

"The first person I wanted to see when I found him was you. You have invaded my every thought. All I wanted to do was climb into the truck and boot it here, to wrap you in my arms and hold you until you could no longer stand it."

I say nothing, the words that spill from him wrap my heart up safe and sound, tucking it away so no one can ever hurt it.

"I can't stand being away from you."

I nibble on my bottom lip and a silly ass grin slips onto my lips baring my teeth but he isn't smiling. His jaw is wound tight, clenched. His eyes burn into mine, scorching my soul and I never want him to leave.

"I'm sorry for not talking to you," he whispers against my lips.

"You don't have to apologize," I whisper back, eyes still on his. "You owe me nothing, Pacey Rivera."

Now he smiles, his lips lifting into a smirk.

"I owe you everything Morgan Rivera, you just don't know it yet."

"Kiss me," my fingers tiptoe to his chest, my hands flattening over his heart as I wait for him to respond but he says nothing. "Kiss me, please," my fingers pinch the soft cotton of his tee just as his other hand cups my cheek, lifting my lips to his and that's when the magic happens.

His lips slant over mine ever so softly, and my eyes flutter shut as he does, his tongue teasing mine and my body molds into him, my grip on his tee tightening as we lose ourselves, our kiss growing hungrier and as first kisses go, I am sure this is the best damn kiss I could have ever had.

Hands slip around the back of my head, fingers tangled in my hair as he drags my head back softly, his lips tracing a line down my jaw, my throat, my pulse point, my collar bone and panic claws at my throat.

I push back on his chest and his eyes lift to mine, worry etched onto his face and my cheeks turn blossom pink under his heated gaze and I notice he is panting.

"What's wrong?" he asks, eyes searching my face.

The pink turns deeper.

"I..." I lick my lips, dropping my eyes from his as I focus on a small pull on his tee, just where my hands are, my fingers gently playing with it. "Erm, I..." and I swear my throat is thickening the longer I am trying to get these words out.

"What is it, Morgan?" and there is no harshness to his tone, no, it's like being snuggled in the coziest and warmest blanket.

I sigh heavily, keeping my eyes on my fingers.

"I'm a virgin," I whisper the words as if they're sinned, shame flames against my skin and I squeeze my eyes shut as I try and calm my erratic heart.

Fingers grip my chin before my head is being tilted back, his eyes burning into mine.

"Are you mad?" I just about manage.

"Mad?" and I can see the shock that slaps across his face, eyes softening as he loses himself into mine and that's when I realize he is looking at me like he looked at Aspen.

And I have no idea if that's a good or bad thing.

"Baby," he rasps, his head tilted to the side. "I would never be mad," he shakes his head ever so slightly, "but do you know what it means?"

I shake my head, his fingers still clasping my chin.

"It means I get to experience it all with you, for the first time, and that to me that is something to not be mad about."

He leans into me and I find myself pushing onto my tiptoes and kissing him, letting my lips press against his and his fingers loosen before his hand is back on my cheek.

"We will take it slow, everything on your terms Sunflower, it's me and you... *forever*." His words break our kiss, and I know he will have me free falling, but I never have to worry about hitting the ground, because he will always be there to catch me.

"As much as I want to kiss you, so, *so* much more, I am also starving and I really do want to take you on a first date... do things the right way," and he lifts his lips to my forehead, placing a kiss there and lingering for a moment and my eyes close, my hands still firmly on his chest as his heartbeat finally begins to return to a steady beat.

He steps back and my hand slips from him and I instantly miss him. He gives me a slow wink and my heart gallops and a silly smile tugs at my lips before I twist them and replay the way he kissed me on repeat, and I really don't think I could have had a better first kiss than that.

Pacey lays the table, and I snap out of my daydream as I reach for the chicken and the baked potatoes from the stove and carry them to the table, placing them in the center next to the salad.

"Iced tea?" he calls out from the kitchen as I adjust the knives and forks.

"Please," I reply and he walks in with a fresh jug and two glasses, popping them down.

He pulls out my chair, placing a kiss on my cheek and I sit, before he takes his own seat opposite me.

"That's a pretty smile you're wearing," he compliments as he lays a napkin over his lap then reaches for my plate and begins to dish up my food before he plates his own up.

He hands it to me and I thank him as I place it down in

front of me and wait for him and once he is done, we both tuck in together.

We make small talk, and I try my hardest to not bring up the day he has had. Normally, we would talk about our days, but today, today I think we can swerve it and talk about anything else.

And that's what we do.

We make small talk and it was perfect.

CHAPTER SEVENTEEN
PACEY

I lay awake most of the night.

It isn't uncommon for me.

Normally only three things keep me awake.

My pa, Harlow, and getting shot.

But tonight, six things have kept me awake, but two have been for good reasons.

My pa, Harlow, getting shot; Conrad, kissing Morgan and finding out she was a virgin.

I wasn't shocked, I don't think. I kind of thought it anyway. She had never been kissed, so why would I assume she has done anything else.

Kissing her though... now I knew what people meant when they said the ground moved beneath their feet.

Fuck.

I was floating through the air.

Then she kissed me back.

She. Kissed. Me.

Then she thought I was mad.

Fuck.

My hand lifts to my chest and I find myself rubbing in small circles to try and alleviate the ache that resides there.

How the fuck could I be mad at her.

My heart twists.

She called my ma.

Ma sent Aspen.

She's a weakness I hate to admit.

She just *gets* me.

That's all there is to it.

But to Morgan... well, it could seem a little more than that.

I have a history with Aspen and fine, if I really dug into the depths of my soul there would be a minuscule cube of love there.

But I *loved* Aspen.

Way back when.

But not anymore.

I still cared for her, yes.

Loved, no.

Sighing, I twist in the sheets and roll on my side, eyes on the door.

Wonder if she's awake.

Staring at the ceiling.

Wondering what I am thinking and vice versa.

Is she thinking about the kiss?

Is she thinking about *more*?

I roll back over, eyes glued on to the white ceiling.

A heavy sigh leaves me, my chest rattling. We were down at Randy's tomorrow, and I cannot wait to be back in the Boot, where we belong. It's our stomping ground and it doesn't seem right sitting across the town line.

But this is Morgan's town. I respected that.

Plus, this is the first time we have all been out in so long.

The week has whizzed past us and to be honest, up until the shit show of today, my week was going pretty good.

Then Conrad happened.

Hand on heart, and I do, I place my hand over my heart, and I focus on the way it beats in a steady, slow, rhythm. It wasn't Conrad that is stirring the pot around here.

My head turns to the door once more when I hear the creak of the floorboard just before my room.

Either she's awake or we're being robbed.

Sitting up, I hold my breath as I listen.

It creaks again.

Looking around my room for something, anything to grab just in case we're under attack but there is nothing.

Shit.

Tossing the covers back, I spring from the bed, swiping my phone from the side table and slipping it into my pocket. Moving towards the door, my fingers curl around the handle as I slowly ease it open, eyes squinted as I try and focus on the dark, narrow hallway.

"Morgan?" I call out but my voice is quiet.

Nothing.

Inhaling heavily, I step out of my room and pace down the hallway towards where she sleeps and just as I do, she appears out of nowhere scaring the living daylights out of me.

I let out a scream, she shrieks and her wide eyes soften when they land on me.

"You scared me, why are you sneaking around!?" her voice is loud, and I swear she sounds a little mad at me.

"Why are *you* sneaking around?" I narrow my gaze on her and twist my lips.

"I thought someone had broken into the house," she admits, and I hear the exasperated sigh that leaves her.

"Same," I shrug a shoulder, and a silly smile graces my lips.

"So, it was just you?"

The smile fades.

"Was it me what?" confusion paints across my face and I watch as she face palms herself.

"Making the noise downstairs," her brows furrow and my blood runs cold.

"I heard a creak outside my door," my hands move out and I link my fingers through hers as I pull her into her room and then shut the door.

"Let me out," she hisses through the door.

"No," I turn away from her and then roll my eyes.

"Where is your pops' shotgun?" and fear pricks at the base of my neck.

"You're being dramatic."

"Am I?" sarcasm drips from my tone and I shake my head from side to side.

Silence for just a moment.

"Top of the closet, locked away, code is 8765."

I don't reply, I just rush towards Gerry's room and ignore the eerie feeling that creeps over me. I haven't been in here since before he died and I'm not sure how I feel about it.

Pacing towards the closet, I drag the doors open and then fumble with the code to reveal the shotgun. Grabbing it, I check it has bullets then load it.

I am hoping it's just an animal digging around under

the house, but then with everything going on, I couldn't be too safe.

Creeping out of his bedroom and down the stairs, I give Morgan's closed door one more glance before I disappear, taking my time on each step.

Once at the bottom I see the cracked glass in the front door and my skin smothers in goosebumps.

My heart is racing beneath my skin and all I can think about in this moment is keeping Morgan, my wife, safe.

It was all about her.

Rustling catches my attention coming from the living room and I stand with my back against the wall, holding the gun close to my chest. I inhale heavily, letting my eyes close for just a moment.

One.

Two.

Three.

I move around the door frame and point the gun at the blacked-out figure.

"Turn the fuck around," my voice booms through the small living room and I see the figure spin, holding their hands up.

"Don't shoot," he calls out and I step a little closer.

"The fuck you doing in my home?"

"I was sent here."

"I don't give a fuck," I growl, standing so close that if I was to pull the trigger, he would take the hit pretty hard... so would the wall.

"Look, I don't want no trouble," I can hear the tremble in his voice, his accent thick and well spoken.

He isn't from around here.

"You were in trouble from the moment you broke into my home."

"Please," his voice cracks as I push the barrel of the gun against his chest, and he quivers.

Keeping the gun where it is, I slip it forward, pressing harder into his skin.

Reaching into my pocket, I grab my phone and press Riggs' name.

He answers on the first ring.

"I need you."

I cut him off and pin my eyes to our masked stranger.

"Now, I am going to give you a friendly piece of advice."

He says nothing but I can feel how fast the shotgun handle is moving up and down against my shoulder from how quickly his chest is rising and falling.

"You can either tell me what the fuck you're doing here and who sent you," I look at him through my lashes, a stupid smirk on my lips. "Or," I turn my spare hand towards me and look at my nails as if not phased in the slightest. "You can stay mute, and when my brother gets here, he will beat the words out of you."

I shrug a shoulder up as if it really does not bother me when in fact, my blood is boiling beneath my skin that this no-good piece of shit is in my home.

He says nothing and I chuckle softly just as I hear the sound of tires crunching over the gravel.

"Wow, he made it over here in record time." I glance behind me but keep the barrel of the gun pressed into him so if he even thinks about moving, all I have to do is pull the trigger. "I'm the nice one," I click my tongue to the roof of my mouth.

Heavy boots crunch over the broken glass in the hallway, and I tilt my head to the side. The masked man turns his face to look at Riggs before his slits are back on me.

"I don't know nothing," his voice is rushed, and I roll my eyes.

"Man, give over, you obviously do otherwise you wouldn't be here."

"You're being far too kind brother," Riggs is beside me, his face turned towards me before he focuses his attention on our new friend.

Riggs takes the gun from my hand and lifts it from the guy's chest before pushing it back into him, using it to shove him against the wall.

"I'm pissed," he growls, his voice tight.

I exhale heavily and pray to Gerry that Morgan stays in her room.

"Not only have I been woken up from my peaceful slumber..." he leans in closer, the handle of the gun sliding under his arm, but the barrel is still on him, "but someone has taken it upon themselves to invade my brother and his wife's privacy... so yeah, I am pretty fucking pissed right now," he shunts the gun forward and the man groans, doubling over slightly.

"I don't think he is going to talk," I run my hand over my stubble, the short, coarse hair catching on my wedding band.

"Nah," Riggs' eyes meet mine across his shoulder just for a moment before they're back on our new friend, "I don't think he is either."

Riggs' drops the gun and, in an instant, his hand is around his throat, squeezing him against the wall, lifting him slightly so his feet are slightly off the floor. The man's hands are trying to pull Riggs' grip away but it's no use.

"I have a special place where we deal with people like you," Riggs grunts, dropping him to the floor like the worthless piece of trash he is.

The guy gasps for his breath, rolling around over the floor but Riggs doesn't give him a second more. He bends down, grabbing him around the back of the neck and drags him to his feet.

"I'll let you know once this piece of shit talks," and I nod as he passes me the gun, my fingers tighten around it, watching as Riggs walks him out the house and as soon as Riggs is gone, my heart drums deep inside my chest.

Exhaling deeply, I unload the gun, pulling the bullets and shoving them deep inside my pocket before I move to find Morgan. Taking the stairs two at a time, I barge into her room, and I see her curled up in the corner, arms around her knees that are wrapped into her chest. Turning the light on, her red rimmed eyes find mine and my heart aches when I see her tear-stained cheeks.

"Hey, hey," I whisper as I place the gun on the floor and rush to her side. I'm on my knees in front of her, my hands cupping her cheeks as I hold her eyes on mine. "It's okay, it's okay," I soothe her, pulling her into my chest as she quietly sobs.

My hand is on her head, fingers smoothing down her hair as I try and calm her down.

I was terrified, but I didn't want her to know that.

"Riggs has taken him," I kiss the top of her head, and she clings onto me like I am her lifeline.

"Where was he?"

"Rummaging through the cabinet in the living room."

She shudders.

"I hate that someone has been in our home," and my chest aches.

"Me too baby, me too," I whisper against her hair.

I have no idea how long we have sat on the floor for, but I needed to move. My ass was numb, my back ached.

Trying to push to my feet, she stops me by holding me close to her.

"Don't leave me."

I shake my head.

"I wasn't going to, I just need to get up," I give her a sad smile and she pushes away from me, eyes all wide and I could lose myself in her beautiful green eyes.

Standing, I hold my hand out for her to take which she does, and I smile a little wider at how her hand fits perfectly in my palm, her delicate wedding band catching my eye.

Pulling her to her feet, I lift her hand to my lips and kiss over her wedding band.

"Mine, wife." I whisper against her skin and lead her to the bed.

She sits on the edge, watching my every move. I reach for the blanket and tug it towards me.

"What are you doing?" she asks, and I can hear the fear that has wrapped itself around her voice.

"Making a bed on the floor, I need to clean the glass up downstairs and didn't want to wake you when I come back upstairs."

She shakes her head from side to side, hands buried in her lap of her frilled pink shorts and matching cropped tee and I can't stop my greedy eyes wandering over the small bit of skin that is on show.

"Sleep with me, I need you next to me," her voice tremors and I drop my head, looking down at my feet for a moment.

"Of course, Sunflower," I lick my lips, fingers still clutched to the blanket that I toss back onto the end of the bed.

Glancing back towards the door, I sigh, before stepping and closing it softly.

"The glass can wait until the morning," I whisper through a smile, and she still looks absolutely terrified.

Pulling back the covers, I usher her to get back into bed and my heart aches a little more when I look at her.

I climb onto the bed and lay myself behind her, one elbow propped up as my head rests on my hand, the other is resting on my side.

"No one would have hurt you," I whisper and she rolls to look at me, eyes all glassy and I fucking hate it.

"I wasn't worried about that," her bottom lip trembles and my brows soften, my eyes locked on hers

"Then why are you so upset?" Curiosity peaks and I find myself leaning a little closer to her.

"I was scared *you* were going to get hurt, I was scared *you* were going to die," and a fresh tear rolls down her cheek, but I swipe it away with my thumb pad.

"Nothing was going to happen to me," and her eyes fall to my scar that is on my stomach, and I sigh heavily, her eyes lift to my tattoo and her shaky fingers draw it out.

"But what if it did," her eyes flick to mine and I want to tell her over and over that it won't but how can you promise something you can't keep?

"Baby, none of us are promised tomorrow," my hand slips and I cup her face, the need to have her skin on mine overwhelms me.

"I don't want you to die," her chin wobbles and a light-hearted laugh slips from my lips.

"Sunflower, believe it or not..." I pause for a moment, rolling my lips before my tongue darts out and runs across my lower one. "I don't want to die, but these things are inevitable. We will all die, the question is when... no one knows that. You can't go through the whole of our lives worrying about me dying. I don't want you to die but do you know what..." I pause and let go of her face as I wrap my arm over her small waist and pull her towards me. "I'm not worried about it because right now, in the moment, we're both here, alive..." I curl my hand around her wrist and drag her hand down, placing it on my chest. "You feel that?"

Boom, boom, boom.

Her lips curl into a soft smile.

"That's my heart baby, it's beating."

Her eyes well again.

"Now, close your eyes and sleep. I promise I won't leave your side."

She nods, snuggling down and I finally lay my head on the pillow next to her, holding her close to me and not letting her go.

***

I WAKE, startled and it takes me a moment to realize where I am. There is a loud tapping that pulls me around a lot sooner than I would have liked. Blinking my heavy lids a couple of times, I finally come to.

Smiling proudly at her still laying in my arms warms my chest. Shuffling slightly, I try my hardest to get back to sleep but that tapping noise grows louder.

Sighing, I slip her from my arms and roll her away softly. Hate that I need to leave her lying here.

Glancing at the small alarm clock on her bedside table, it's just past six and panic claws inside of me.

Shit.

My alarm goes off at four a.m., so does hers, so how the fuck had we slept through both of them.

Moving from the bed, I stand before turning and

looking over my shoulder at her, her blonde hair fanned out behind her, full lips parted as soft breaths slip through them and I am instantly jealous of the air that passes.

Shaking my head, I sigh and move downstairs, the tapping continuing.

Once I am at the bottom, my eyes drop to the shards of broken glass and for just a moment I had forgotten about last night.

Then I see his boots.

"Wakey wakey, sunshine," Riggs beams at me, tapping on the outside of the door again.

"How long have you been here for?" I groan, running my hand around the back of my neck and giving it a squeeze.

"Ten minutes maybe," he looks at the hole in the glass then back up to me.

"Why didn't you let yourself in?" I yawn, nodding for him to follow me into the kitchen.

"Bit rude, isn't it?"

"Not really," I shrug a shoulder up as I go about putting the coffee pot on.

The sound of his boots crunching over the glass has my eyes tracing over my shoulder.

"Didn't think of cleaning this up?" he looks disgusted before his eyes find mine.

"Morgan was spooked, didn't want me coming back down."

"So, you just left it like this... all night?"

"Yeah," I say as if it isn't a big deal but in reality, I was really quite stupid.

"Idiot."

"Coffee?" I ask as the pot begins to warm. He doesn't

answer, just pulls the chair along the tiled floor and takes a seat.

I am assuming that is a yes.

Filling the cups, I twist and sit opposite my big brother, handing him his coffee.

"Have we found out who our little friend is?" I ask, bringing the cup to my lips and blowing softly.

"Oh yes," a wicked smirk tugs at his lips, his eyes cast down.

I wait for a moment when I hear Dusty's voice.

"Hello," his voice drawls through the hallway, "what in the hell happened?" his boots crunch.

"In here," I call out and he is in the doorway, eyes bouncing over me. "We had a little visitor last night," I grumble, and Riggs looks over his shoulder, greeting Dusty with a boyish grin on his face before he turns and takes a mouthful of coffee.

"The fuck, who?"

"Still waiting to find that out," I swing my leg forward and land a foot into my brother's shin.

"Ouch you fuck bag," he groans, and I chuckle.

Dusty walks in the kitchen, helping himself to a coffee as he stands, back to the work surface waiting for Riggs to spill.

"Morgan okay?" he glances at the time and I know he thinks something is off.

"Yeah, just what with the broken sleep last night, we both slept through our alarms. Sorry man," I wince as I catch his glare.

"It's cool, she covered for me all day yesterday, pulling a few hours for her really isn't a big deal," he smiles, placing his hat down beside him and taking a sip of his drink.

"Riggs," I tilt my head at my brother.

"Yeah?"

"Who was it?" I shuffle in my seat, both elbows on the table as I stretch my arms out, pushing my cup along the surface of the table.

"Luke," he says bluntly.

"Luke as in…"

"Luke as in," he sighs, nodding his head.

"Fuck, I thought he was dead."

"Unfortunately not," he smirks, "but he took a good beating, still none the wiser on who sent the little weasel."

"Was half expecting another word to round that sentence off."

"Little weasel cunt, better?" Riggs snorts a laugh, and I chuckle softly.

"What happened last night? Who's Luke?' Dusty asks, pulling his own chair out, the legs dragging across the tiles and echoing.

"We heard someone rummaging around down here, found him in the living room. No idea what he was looking for, called Riggs for backup, he still wouldn't talk so Riggs took him away…" I sigh, scrubbing my face with one of my hands, the cool metal from my ring on my skin.

"So, who is he? Who is Luke?" and even hearing his name is like fingernails on a chalk board; I find myself shuddering.

"Luke is Aspen—my wife's—dickhead ex who cheated on her."

"Right," Dusty looks confused as hell.

Poor Dusty.

He doesn't do drama.

Just gets up, kisses his wife and kids goodbye and works the ranch, a very simple, but happy and rich life.

"He got in with the wrong crowd... then he disappeared when Clay Attaway died."

"Ohhhh, the guy who was found on your land?"

"Who we didn't kill, might I add," thought I better get that in there, just to keep the record straight.

Dusty nods but edges closer, clearly enjoying this a little more than he thought he would.

"And well, he is back but not sure why," I let out an exasperated sigh when I hear the floorboards creak above us and my lips twitch.

Within a couple of minutes, she walks into the kitchen like a pure ray of sunshine. Hair wild and messy, eyes glistening as she looks at the full kitchen and a ghost of a smile creeps onto her lips.

"Morning, Sunflower," I raise a brow and a smile tugs at the corners of my mouth.

"Morning," her voice is soft and quiet and the most perfect sound on an early Friday morning.

"Morning sweetheart," Riggs chimes and she shakes her head, looking down at herself and tiptoeing past us.

Riggs and Dusty soon avert their gazes and fall into quiet chatter.

But me? I couldn't stop staring even if I wanted to.

Something had shifted but I was unsure what... but whatever it was, I counted my lucky stars because I never thought I would feel something other than an icy block where my heart once was, but slowly, ever so fucking slowly was she thawing it out.

My eyes trail over my shoulder and I get a teasing look at her legs, desperate to skim my fingers up the back of her thighs, tucking them under the hem of her shorts just to feel how she feels under my fingertips.

Dusty coughs and it has me spinning my head quickly, cheeks blushing softly at being caught.

"What's the plan with Luke then?"

"Luke?" her voice swarms around me, tucking me up safe.

"Yeah darlin', the coward who broke into your house last night."

"Who is he?" she asks as she stirs creamer into her coffee and she hasn't even noticed the time, or if she has, she clearly isn't bothered.

"Aspen's ex," Dusty fills her in and I smirk, eyes loitering on him slightly and I can see just how much he cares for her.

Best of friends those two.

My heart aches a little.

Bit like me and Aspen but I burned that bridge eleven years ago when I spilled truths that weren't only mine.

Sure, it's rebuilt, but it'll never be as strong as it once was.

"Oh," is all she says. She steps forward and perches herself on my knee at the table and I try my best to keep my cool, but inside I am like a lovesick teen who's ultimate crush has sat on his lap.

Riggs eyeballs me and I look away, not wanting him to make me a joke.

"Do we know what he was after?" she curls her fingers around her cup and my hand finds itself resting on her upper thigh, my fingers tracing slow circles on her skin without a second thought.

"Well, that's where I was hoping you could help us," and I watch as her eyes widen slightly as she looks at my brother, his eyes on hers. His hair thick and curly and unruly, eyes glisten slightly, his cheeks a little rosy.

"Me?" she stutters.

"Yes darlin', you."

She swallows and I feel the way her shoulders lift and sag.

"Do you know of anything that your pa would have had that would have been of interest? I am sure Luke is working with the suits, makes sense seeing as he was approached by them way back when," Riggs clenches his fist and then unclenches.

"No," she shakes her head softly.

I can see the disappointment that spreads across Riggs' face, he drops his head, and I sigh, my fingers still on her thigh and that's when I twist my head to see Dusty, his mind is ticking, his eyes locked on the mug that sits in the middle of the table.

"What is it Dust?" his reaction piques my interest.

Riggs' brows lift at my words and his narrowed gaze drifts to Dusty.

"He knows something," Riggs points his finger at him and Morgan twists her face so now we're all looking at him.

"Not necessarily," he screws his face up, rubbing his hand across his stubble. "But..." he pushes to his feet and after a beat or two Riggs is up. I slip my fingers from my mug then place both hands on her hips, gently lifting her from my lap as we both begin to walk towards where Dusty disappeared to.

He ducks into the living room, Riggs is hot on his heels and Morgan throws me a concerned look, worry etched into her eyes.

My fingers flex beside me before they trace her fingertips.

She freezes when Dusty unhooks a painting from the

wall and I hear the soft gasp that leaves her lips. Dusty looks over his shoulder but his eyes trail to her and only her.

"This was just between me and your pops," he gives her a frown, lips turning down.

She says nothing, just waits with bated breath.

Dusty twists the dial for the safe and it clicks open after four turns.

Riggs catches my gaze, and I am as confused as him.

I had no idea.

Gerry didn't mention any of this on his death bed, but then again, he rambled on about a few things and I still hadn't been through the paperwork. Guilt twists my gut, but I don't have a second more to think about it when Dusty says, "This."

My eyes widen and Riggs floats his gaze my way. Swallowing down the dryness that coats my throat.

"Is that what I think it is?" Riggs steps closer, his eyes narrowing on what Dusty is holding between his fingertips.

"No fucking way," my lips part, my eyes widening as I step closer, pulling Morgan behind me.

I glance at Riggs, his cheeks puffing out.

"How did they know?" I turn to Dusty who shrugs it off.

"No idea, the only two people who knew that it was hidden here was me and Gerry."

"What is it?" Morgan whispers from behind me, head popping over my shoulder as she looks at the glistening stone between Dusty's fingers.

"The Montana Pearl," myself and Riggs say in unison.

CHAPTER EIGHTEEN
PACEY

I pace in the hallway of our family home.

Mom is soothing Lainey, Tripp's knee is bobbing as he sits in the living area and Riggs is leaning against the door frame.

Aspen and Dixie look lost, Morgan has no clue what is going on, her eyes are bouncing around the room trying to gauge anything that she could maybe ask or suggest.

Dusty stands by the large fireplace, hands tucked into his pockets.

"Where is Luke now?" Tripp asks, and Aspen's nose scrunches in disgust.

"Basement," Riggs grunts, and I stop pacing.

"Has he spoke any more?"

"Not a word, thought I would try and scare him a bit, but he has stayed pretty tight lipped."

"Asshole," I hiss, walking into the room and I catch Morgan's gaze. She looks worried and I hate that. Wish I could scoop her in my arms and let her know that all will be okay.

But I didn't know how this was going to go.

We've had people trespassing and blowing up parts of our land looking for this diamond.

Honestly, we all thought it was a myth... but alas, our grandpa was telling us the truth.

He hid it well, I had no idea that Gerry and my Pa would have even been friends, but you learn something new each day.

"We all need to take a step back," ma says, standing with Lainey whose little arms are reaching out for Dixie.

Dixie smiles, giving a soft look as she strides towards where her daughter is, lifting her into her arms and Lainey snuggles into her chest, her little fingers playing with the delicate gold chain that sits around her neck.

"We don't have time to take a step back, we have some sneaky cunt sitting bound downstairs, suits are still sniffing around, and we have no idea what the fuck we're going to do," Tripp snaps, and Riggs bolts towards him, fists clenched.

I roll my eyes.

Moving across the floor, my hand is on Riggs' shoulder as I try and calm him down.

"Don't." I warn.

Not that I stand a chance when it comes to Riggs.

He would floor me.

"Don't speak to her like that," Riggs snarls.

Tripp's eyes widen, his hand pushing through his hair and he drops his head.

"I know you're stressed, but don't you fucking dare," his tone is a little softer now.

"Riggs," ma's voice floats around the room like a blanket, swaddling the three of us up and calming us in an instant.

Tripp pushes up, chest to chest with our big brother.

His eyes are soft, and I feel the way Riggs' shoulders drop in an instant.

"All I am saying is, we don't want to jump the gun with this. We need to move the diamond, get it hidden, so *if* they come back and look, they'll be wasting their time."

"Where do you suggest we hide it?" I step away from Riggs as he turns around and looks at ma.

"Leave that with me," she gives a nod as she walks out the room, and Dusty's eyes are pinned to Morgan.

"I need to go," Morgan whispers as her hand rests between my shoulder blades.

Glancing over my shoulder, my eyes fall to her lips, and I am so fucking desperate to kiss her again.

"Okay, I'll catch up with you in a bit," I smile softly and my heart bangs in my chest.

"Okay," she gives me a smile, "I'll see you in a bit, cowboy," her nose crinkles, her green eyes dancing with mine.

My cock twitches and I find myself clearing my throat as she steps away from me, her eyes dusting down my body and I know she has me right where she wants me.

She walks out and Dusty nods at the three of us before disappearing out the front door and no longer than a second after it is closed, Riggs is on me.

"Can we trust him?" his voice is gruff.

"Yes," I don't give him a second to make him doubt me, when in truth, that's what I hope.

"Something is off," Tripp says as he stands beside me.

Aspen sighs, pushing to her feet as she steps in front of Riggs, her small hands on his chest.

"You'll figure it out big man, I am sure of it," she winks then presses onto her tiptoes, kissing his cheek.

He growls in response.

My lips tug into a smile as she turns and walks down to find ma, I am assuming.

Dixie says nothing, just twists her lips at Tripp. He shrugs a shoulder up and she gives a small smile back.

"We need to sort out a plan, something doesn't sit right in my gut and the gut never lies," Riggs voice is low before he pushes forward and slams the front door behind him.

I sigh, shaking my head and tilt my head at Tripp and Dixie before I follow in the trail of my brother.

I had my own shit to sort out on top of this.

The drive into town was short and not enough time to let me decompress half the shit that was in my brain. But I knew my first stop had to be Sunny's.

Pulling into the parking spot outside, I lift my hat from the passenger side and place it on my head before I step out of my truck, closing the door behind me.

My chest aches and I find myself dragging in a deep breath as I walk towards the building.

It's quiet, which I was grateful for.

Pushing on the door, the small bell rings above my head and my heart constricts in my chest, a tightness spreading and I have to really try and focus on my breathing as I step closer.

Her eyes brighten when she sees me, her lips pressing into a smile but that soon fades when my lips turn down and I lift my hat from my head.

"Can we have a chat?"

She doesn't answer for a moment, her eyes just bounce between mine and finally, after what feels like a lifetime, she nods, ushering me out the back.

"What's wrong?"

I sigh.

"And don't tell me it's nothing to worry about because

you wouldn't be here, like this... waiting to implode my whole day."

I swallow.

"What is it?" she whispers, and I can't look at her. Her eyes are glassy.

"It's Conrad." and that's all I can squeeze out without the burning lump lodging itself there, making it near impossible for me to continue.

"No," she shakes her head, fresh tears roll down her cheeks as her hands cover her mouth.

"I'm so sorry Sunny," and I pull her into my chest as she silently weeps in my arms. "So, so, sorry."

***

I LEAVE Sunny's and decide to walk down to my office. My heart feels heavy in my chest, and with each step I take, it grows heavier.

This is not what I thought the end of my week would look like.

Another dead body on our land.

Another heart broken.

And there is nothing I can do to take the pain away because I have my own pain lodged in my chest.

Climbing the stairs to my office, I unlock the door and sit at my desk. Fingers curl around the drawer as I tug it open and pull out the manilla folder. I unhook the clasp and pull the paperwork out.

My finger and thumb brush down my moustache as I look at the paperwork and seeing Conrad's face there in color haunts me a little.

He was beaten black and blue.

I just hope that he didn't suffer.

A shiver breaks over my skin and I give myself a moment before I continue looking at the file.

We were sure it was him.

But this was just another dead end.

I don't see how we got it so fucking wrong.

All roads led to him.

Shaking my head, I lay the paperwork down on my desk and lift my eyes to the window, looking out at the quiet sidewalks of Lovelock Bay.

My mind drifts to Morgan and I cannot wait for tonight.

I wanted to date her, wanted to take her out and spend the night with just her.

But I had to pick my moment.

I wanted to kiss her under the stars, make out at the back of the movies and walk hand in hand along the sidewalks sipping coffee.

I wanted all the little things with her, but I also knew we had to take it slow and I wanted to make all of her firsts perfect.

Yes, I rushed the kiss... I knew that but it just felt like the right moment last night when she was in my arms.

We were both feeling vulnerable and she wanted it as much as me.

My phone buzzes on my desk and I see Riggs' name.

Sighing, I scoop it up and bring it to my ear.

"Yeah," I scrub my face before my eyes are lowered on the paperwork that sits on my keyboard.

"Have you looked into that number you took off Marty's phone yet?"

I sit up, eyes wide.

"Shit, I forgot about that, what with everything going on..." I pause just as I see Austin walking up the steps. "Austin is here," I whisper into the speaker just as he walks through.

"The fuck?" he hisses, twisting the lock on the sheriff door and sitting in front of me.

"Which *the fuck* moment are you referring to?" my eyes bounce between his and Riggs is still sitting in my ear.

"Conrad."

I push a breath out, then roll my lips.

"Look into that number and see if Austin can give anything away that might help, don't forget, he is on our side... *always.*"

The phone goes dead, and I toss it beside me.

"I know," I sigh, sitting back in my seat. "Not long broke the news to Sunny, broke my damn heart," I admit, and my throat thickens.

"I bet," he nods, lifting his cap from his head, running his fingers through his hair before placing it back and twisting it around. "I'll pop and see her after I am done here."

I roll my lips.

Austin sits forward, brows raised as he looks down his nose at the paperwork that sits on my desk.

"So, you thought Conrad was up to no good..." I catch his gaze and his lips roll into a tight line.

"I wasn't sure... just a tip off I got a couple of months back, then when he pulled away from everyone..." and guilt crashes through me.

"You had a hunch?" he sits back, head tilted to the side.

"Maybe?" I drop my face into my hands, elbows resting on the desk.

"Maybe was a big risk man," he says softly and there is nothing malicious in Austin's tone, but I feel like he has slipped a dagger between my shoulder blades as I gasp for air.

"What would you have done?" I pin my question to him, my eyes now burning into his.

"I have no fucking idea," he admits, and I lick my upper lip.

"What's Marty's stance on this? Who got the tip off about Conrad's body?" I ask, my fingers tapping on the paperwork beneath me.

"Marty got the call."

"It wasn't on his call log?" my brows scrunch and my eyes narrow. "The time of the unknown number and Wyoming didn't match up with what he has said."

"Then he deleted it," Austin says bluntly.

"That snake," I slam my hand down on the desk and Austin jumps.

"Calm it," Austin lowers his voice, his eyes drifting over his shoulder. "You could be jumping..." he trails off as he faces me.

"Really?" my brows raise and he nibbles on the inside of his lip.

"Or you're right on the money and you have every right to be suspicious."

I sigh, scrubbing at my face again, this time a little harder than before.

"Do you think he killed Conrad?" I ask him as bluntly as intended.

Austin sighs, waiting a moment before he answers. I feel like a shitty friend asking him things like this when he is going through his own grief.

But he worked closely with Marty. If it was a year ago, I would have been having this conversation with Riggs.

My question bounces around in his mind, but his eyes are steady as they pin to me.

"No," the response slips from his lips quickly, and I wonder if the word tasted bitter on his tongue.

"Out of towner?" and I get a shrug of a shoulder as he slips back into the chair, kicking his boots onto my desk.

"Maybe," hands in his lap, thumbs resting over the top of each.

"This is not helping me," I groan, sitting back in my own chair, tilting my head to the side.

"You're the sheriff, isn't it your job to work out who did what?" and I don't miss the slight venom that laced his tone, but I ignore it.

I chose not to respond, just give him a roll of the eyes.

"I didn't mean..."

I hold my hand up and shake my head

"You don't need to say a word more."

Guilt flashes across his eyes and I know better than to act out on his impulsive words.

He is bitter at everyone.

The world included.

He lost a great love, yet everyone else is moving on around him and finding the second half of themselves.

But not Austin.

He is stuck here, in this permanent hell.

Silence crackles around the hostile room and as the seconds slip past, the more the agitation is nipping at the base of my neck.

"Check that number," Austin says when he lets his boots drop from the desk then pushes away, standing.

His eyes cast down to me, my lips twitch and there is so much more that could be said, but neither of us breathe a word.

I give him a soft nod.

"See you tonight, yeah?"

Swallowing, I nod again.

Honestly, I was in no mood to go out drinking with anyone other than Morgan, but I'll smile and stay quiet and let my thoughts fade into the abyss whilst everyone around me enjoys themselves.

He doesn't say another word before he walks out and leaves me sitting in my own silence.

I only agreed to go out tonight because Morgan asked. She wanted to give our new neighbors a warm welcome, but after the week I have had, I could do with just nursing a whiskey at home by myself.

Sighing, I slip my phone across the desk and unlock it, opening it up and looking at the number I jotted down.

I debate whether I should call it or try and find Marty, to speak to him and find out whether I should push for a little more information. See if he trips himself up when it comes to Conrad.

He knows something.

The more I think about it, the more I realize he is yanking our chain.

He is—or was—the closest thing to Riggs until Riggs pushed him to become livestock commissioner.

He has the governor in his pocket, he knows who runs where and who's pushing what livestock.

But then so do we.

Marty is a good way in with the suits, he can tell them everything that is going on and we wouldn't even know it.

They say keep your friends close, your enemies closer, well this might be the case when it comes to Marty.

Glancing out the window, I let my mind drift for a moment.

I could have this all wrong, maybe it's just because I am so desperate to find who killed Conrad and who the mole could be that all roads lead to him.

Sure, I had my suspicions, and I thought it was Conrad but look how wrong I was there? Maybe I needed to take a step back and just let everything settle.

There is no point jumping the gun.

I could go for Marty and be blindsided by who was actually orchestrating.

Because let's be honest, Marty is probably the puppet.

Snapping away from my thoughts, I pick the papers up and slip them back into the manilla envelope, closing the tie and slipping it inside my drawer.

That's enough conspiracy for one day.

Waking my computer up, I check my admin and lose myself for an hour or two before I am packing up my desk and locking it for the weekend.

Driving my truck home, my mind drifts to Morgan. The way she lights up my world in a way I couldn't even explain, even if I wanted to I don't think I would have the words to describe it.

Aspen made me feel things, but she was my first, and your first love is always the one that makes you grow, helps you learn... Aspen definitely did that.

Soft country music fills the cab of the truck and my long finger drums against the steering wheel as my eyes cast over to Crooked Creek.

Memories flash in front of my eyes of our childhood, the way we spent hours outside, causing trouble but most importantly having fun, being kids, doing everything we shouldn't.

But then we grew and as teens, we thought we knew

everything. We thought we were adults and how stupid were we to think that.

My chest aches, and I suck in a deep breath as prom night flicks through my mind, playing out like a home movie.

SITTING IN MY ROOM, my fingers locked as I heard my dad shouting at Riggs. I had no idea why he treated him differently, but for whatever reason he did. We all knew it. We all could see it but none of us stood up and said something.

The sound of heavy footsteps float away and I sit, waiting for my bedroom door to open. Riggs always comes in here when it gets too much with Dad. Kind of like his escape I suppose.

The door handle goes, and I see the worn work boot and I know it's my dad.

"All okay?" I ask, eyes lifting slowly and I know that it's not okay. I just heard what had gone on and my dad had broken Riggs' heart in three seconds flat.

I knew how excited he was about tonight, we all did. Me and Tripp were laughing because he was so nervous and wanted it all to be perfect.

We knew that Riggs crushed on Aspen but would never act on it because she was Austin's kid sister, but once she admitted that she had feelings for him, well, all bets were off, lines were about to be crossed.

"Get your tuxedo on," my dad doesn't even look at me, just grunts and nods towards my closet.

"Why?" I act dumb because I am in disbelief that he would be so cruel.

"Because you're taking Aspen Warren to prom," he says bluntly, and I feel the air whoosh from my lungs.

"But," I don't have a chance to finish my sentence because he cuts me off.

"No buts, you're taking her."

"Dad..." I stand, not to protest but maybe to get him to reconsider his decision.

"Get dressed Pacey, this is happening. I will not have Riggs ruin what I have with Buck. I will not have him break her heart and jeopardize what I have worked so hard for..." he trails off for a moment and that's when his eyes skate to mine. "Get dressed."

He steps back, closing the door behind him and my chest aches.

I know how much he wanted this, and my dad has taken that away from him because he is fucking selfish.

My fists ball by my side and I squeeze my eyes shut as I try and calm my racing heart.

A soft knock on the door has me unclenching and I inhale heavily.

"Come in."

Sighing in soft relief when I see my ma.

"Pacey," her head tilts and I can see the anguish on her face.

I shake my head from side to side, dropping my eyes to the floor.

Her soft, warm hands are on the side of my face as she lifts me up to look at her.

"I feel awful," I whisper as a tear runs down my cheek and I feel like an asshole because I have always liked Aspen, but I love my brother and knowing that I am taking this night away from him doesn't sit right with me.

"He'll understand," she tries to make me feel better as I roll my lips.

"I don't think he will ma," I admit, sadness dropping from my tone.

She pats my cheek then thumbs a tear away.

"Now get dressed my sunshine boy, Aspen will be waiting," and I see her sad smile which crushes me even more.

Letting my face drop just as she steps back, I wait for her to leave the room and only when I know she is gone, do I pull myself together and get dressed for tonight.

I should be happy.

I get to take the girl of my dreams to prom.

And maybe, just maybe... she might realize that she likes me how I like her.

Once dressed, I walk cautiously down the hallway, passing Riggs' room and the urge to go in there and make sure he is okay has me opening his bedroom door.

He is sitting in the dark and I can just about make out his silhouette.

"Riggs," I call out, my voice timid and I have no idea why, but nerves are swirling in my stomach.

"Just go," he says exasperated.

"But I— "

"Pace, please," and I hear the crack in his voice.

I nod, fingers tightening around the doorknob.

"Just promise you give her the best night, do whatever she wants, give her a prom night to remember," he squeezes out and I find myself nodding.

"I will," I whisper and wait for a response, but he says nothing. "I'm sorry Riggs."

He stays silent.

So, I step back and close the door softly behind me. Turning, I walk downstairs and see my ma standing at the bottom, looking proud and my heart throbs.

Tripp doesn't look at me, just scoffs in disgust as he sits in the living room, back to me.

"Ignore him," my dad says as he grabs the lapels of my jacket and tugs down. "Have fun, be safe."

He pats my cheek, and I reply with a nod.

Mom places a small flower in my boutonniere, before handing me a corsage for Aspen. My eyes fall and I look at the pretty flower that matches my boutonniere and my heart thrums a little faster in my chest. She kisses me on the cheek, and I return it with a smile.

"Have fun," she chimes in after as she opens the door and I swallow down the nerves, my dad following behind me as he unlocks the truck, the lights flooding the front of the drive and I can't help but look over my shoulder at Riggs' room and that's when I see him, sitting in the large sash window, staring down at me.

But when he sees me looking, he disappears, and I fight with myself if he was ever really there or just my mind playing tricks on me.

Glaring at the truck, my heart constricts when I see the fairy lights that are looped around the roof racks. He gave her fairy lights because she is scared of the dark.

This is so wrong.

I shouldn't be going with her.

Slamming the door closed, rage simmers dangerously close to the surface.

The engine starts and the need to bite my tongue overwhelms me.

I know I should be saying something to my dad, but I don't, because I am a coward. Easier to keep my mouth shut and do as he says.

The drive is short, and my dad leads me to the Warren's house. A soft knock on the door and within seconds, Blue is opening the door, and I see the look of confusion on her face when she sees it's me standing there and not Riggs.

"Pacey," she breathes out as she forces a smile onto her face.

"Mrs Warren," I smile back, ducking inside the house and I

can hear my dad speaking quietly and I know he is spinning her a web of lies to cover his ass.

"Pace?" Austin says from the kitchen, and I hold my hand up. "What happened?"

"Riggs couldn't make it," the lie falls a little too easy from my tongue, "so I offered, I didn't want Aspen to not have a date, and well, I am still a Rivera," I smirk but Austin just glares over me.

"Right," he lifts his chin, and I know he doesn't buy my bullshit story.

Tucking myself in the kitchen, nerves nip at the base of my neck, and I just want this night over with already.

Blue was disappointed to see me; fuck, Aspen is going to be heartbroken that it is me and not Riggs.

But what was I meant to do?

Austin disappears out into the hallway when the sound of Blue's voice floats down the stairs, footsteps approaching and my heart jack hammers in my chest.

I can hear Harlow talking to Austin and I know I need to walk out there. Closing my eyes for a moment, I inhale deeply and try and calm myself down.

One, two, three and my legs are moving me to the hallway and I see her face and how devastated she is as I appear around the doorframe.

"Pacey," she presses her hand to her heavy rising chest, and I know this is not how she planned her night to go.

"I'll be taking you this evening now, I hope you don't mind?"

She hesitated and I know she is trying to piece this all together.

"Of course not," she smiles her wide and beautiful smile at me, but I don't miss the way her tears threaten to spill.

I push the corsage box towards her, her eyes dropping to the *three delicate white flowers that sit inside, my fingers tapping on the box. She finally steps off the bottom step and closer to me.*

"You look stunning Pen," my fingers tease forward as they curl around her wrist, tugging her gently towards me and I kiss her softly on her cheek.

My blood burning, my heart racing that my breath catches to the back of my throat.

We take photos outside and I know the smile she wears is fake, but she still puts on the prettiest show.

My arm snakes around her waist as I lead her to the waiting truck and that's when she glances up and notices the fairy lights that decorate it.

Her dad is chattering but I zone out because all I can do is focus on her, in this moment and the range of emotions that slips across her face.

"After you Pen," I whisper, pulling her out of her head as I usher her into the truck. She foots the bar of the truck but freezes. The soft breeze dances around her and I see her head turn slightly as she looks down towards the paddock.

There he was.

My brother.

Watching as I take the girl we both love to prom.

He should be here.

He should be the one giving her this night.

But it isn't him.

It's me.

She finally climbs into the truck, and I let out my bated breath. Closing the door behind me, Harlow calls out excitedly and I know Aspen will do everything in her power to give herself the best prom night, the one she deserves.

.   .   .

I AM BACK, my eyes darting as I focus on where I am. I was so lost in thought that I went into autopilot. Turning on my blinker as I pull into Cottonwheel Ranch, I flit back to that night, a small smile tugging at my lips.

She had the best prom night, she got what she deserved.

She got it all and for just one night, I got her.

Wholly.

But in doing that, I pushed her away.

If I could go back to that night I would, I would re write it all and drag Riggs there myself.

I know when I was asked a while back if I would do it again, I said yes.

Ask me again and the answer would be the same, but I would do everything differently.

I would have fought for Riggs.

Because it was always him and Aspen.

It'll always be him and her.

And that truth finally settles deep inside of me.

She was never meant to be mine.

But the pretty blonde cowgirl who is waiting at home, wearing my ring and my last name with pride... that's the girl who has my heart.

Morgan Rivera.

Never thought I would see the day that I would move on from Aspen, but here we are.

Slowing the truck, I gaze across the wild flowered fields and that's when I see her.

The wind dancing in her hair, flecks of gold reflecting from the sun. Her cowboy hat slightly tilted back, seated in the saddle as she rides her horse down the paddock and towards the house.

Time moves in slow motion, if only for a minute and I find myself watching her in awe.

She looks so beautiful.

The car rolls to a halt and I hadn't even realized I had stopped. Full blown stopped in the middle of the winding drive.

It's not long before she pulls her horse to a halt, turning to face me and I have no idea why, but I find myself blushing.

Full on blushing at being caught by her.

She trots towards me, and I slip down the window of the truck, arm hanging out, a boyish grin on my face.

"Well hello wife," she crinkles her nose at me, her lips fighting the smile.

"Hey," she turns her horse slightly and I let my eyes sweep over her.

"You finishing up?"

She sighs, looking over her shoulder before she is back focused on me.

Her shirt is cream, two buttons undone and I tease a gaze at what is underneath, but she gives nothing away. The front of the loose shirt is tucked into the waist band of her high waisted jeans and my eyes continue until they land on her tanned boots.

Fuck.

What I would do to see her in just those fucking boots and her matching cowboy hat.

Long golden hair cascading down her back, and I am hard just fantasizing about it.

"I still have some small things to do, Dusty had to leave early, something happened at the school with his daughter so..."

"Give me five, I'll take Chase up and meet you."

"Honestly—"

"I didn't ask, wife."

She sighs, eyes dropping for a moment.

"I'll always show up for you Morgan, whenever and wherever I can."

Her sparkling greens catch mine and I swear I feel my heart skip a beat.

"Give me five," I say again and push the truck into drive, the tires kicking up dirt and I am desperate to get near to her.

The thought of spending time with her tonight consumes me whole and I am counting down the hours.

I know I said I wasn't looking forward to it, but now, well, now I was foaming at the mouth at being sat next to her, in a dimly lit bar.

Chucking the truck into park, I cut the engine and climb out before I am moving towards the stables. The sound of my boots echoing down the stalls is the only thing I can hear over my erratic heart.

I have no idea why I am so nervous.

I feel like a teen again with his first crush. But this time, it wasn't just a crush. I fancied the bones off my wife.

What started out as a business arrangement has quickly turned into more.

I never thought it would but here I am.

Rushing towards my horse to help the girl I crush on so she can finish her chores just so I can date the fuck out of her tonight.

Tacking him up, it doesn't take me long and I am on his back and trotting to the large iron paddock gate. Letting myself in, I close it behind me and kick Chase on, moving into a soft canter as I make my way down the fields to where she waits for me.

"Took you long enough..." she pauses for a moment, "cowboy," she winks at me and my heart thrums in my chest.

"Wish I was just a cowboy," I think out loud as we move to the bottom of the field.

"Bad day?" she turns to look at me, her eyes flitting across my face.

"Suppose you could say that," and I sigh. I forgot what it feels like to just sit on the back of a horse. I know Tripp swore me in to be sheriff but I kind of wish he didn't. I was happy as the livestock agent, happy with my days, happy sitting on the back of the horse. Best of both worlds.

Now, now I am tied behind a desk dealing with shit that people dump in my lap.

I'm tired.

"I miss this," I admit when we reach the small mount, overlooking rolling green fields, cows scattered down the bottom by the creek.

"Would you give it up?" she asks me on a whisper, I can feel her eyes burning into the side of my head. Dragging the fresh air into my lungs, waiting for them to fill before I turn and look at her, my eyes softening, my lips twitching and tugging into a smile.

"In a heartbeat."

"Then what's stopping you?" she asks me as she turns to look forward and I watch the way her eyes soften at the sights in front of her.

"I have no idea," and I am being truthful, but maybe if she was to ask me on a deeper level, I would tell her that I was terrified of moving into something new. Terrified of getting hurt again. Terrified that I would get killed for protecting the ranch.

"You only live once…" she begins to speak but I shake my head.

"You're wrong, Sunflower," my lips turn into a small smile.

Her perfect brows furrow as my statement confuses her.

"You live everyday… you only die once."

Her throat bobs as she swallows, tears threaten to spill over her tear line, but she manages to hold them back.

"I have never thought about it that way…"

I nod softly, tilting the rim of my cowboy hat towards her.

"Now, what are we doing cowgirl?"

CHAPTER NINETEEN
MORGAN

Not that I wanted to ask for his help, but I was so grateful that Pacey offered. I would have been working well into the evening if I didn't have him with me.

But, we got it all done.

Riding in silence back to the ranch, I can't help but steal a glance at him every now and then. He looks so perfect sitting on the back of his horse, like that's where he belongs.

He looks so free. Shoulders sat back a little more, his body moving softly, like he is one with the horse. A small smile slips onto his lips as he looks towards where his ranch sits, tucked behind the mountains. My eyes fall to his mouth, and I am desperate to have his lips back on mine, but this time I want him to *really* kiss me. A small laugh catches at the back of my throat at his little moustache that he is growing. Since I have known him, he has always had a light dusting of stubble, he caught my eye the first time I met him, but with his moustache, I don't know, it takes him to a solid one hundred.

How could I be obsessed with a man I haven't known

for long, how could I be obsessed with a man when I have no idea how I should be feeling.

Sure, I've had crushes, but nothing like this.

This blows anything I once felt for any man out of the water.

Every one of my nerve endings singed as I imagined what it would be like when we finally crossed the line.

We were married.

I found myself thinking about how it would feel, what he would do.

"You good?" he finds me staring at him and I laugh it off, cheeks blushing at being caught.

"Yeah," I rush the word off my tongue as if it burned.

"Sure?" he asks.

"Sure," I swallow, tightening my grip on Barley's reins and kicking her on, a slow canter and I can't help the giggle that leaves me. Glancing over my shoulder, I watch as Pacey kicks on his horse, clicking his tongue to the roof of his mouth before making a loud noise as he canters behind me. Facing forward, I push my hands up her neck and lift my ass out of the seat.

"You won't beat me wife," he calls out and a smug smirk spreads across my lips. He knew I was going to beat him, but he still gave it a good go, bless him.

Slowing when I get to the paddock gate, my chest is rising and falling as I cast a look over my shoulder at him. His tongue swipes across his bottom lip, eyes wild as they sweep over me and I blush, internally grateful that I have my hat to shield my cheeks.

"Told ya," I wink then unhook the gate, pushing Barley forward as I walk towards the stalls, Pacey follows me and I can hear the soft laugh that vibrates through him.

Comfortable silence consumes us and as much as we were working, I have loved having him with me today.

Swinging my leg over the back of my horse, I jump down and lead her to her stall and finish untacking her in there. Pacey walks past and I don't miss the fire that simmers inside his beautiful whiskey eyes as he looks at me.

He walks into the stall next to me and he begins whistling a soft tune, I recognize it but can't quite put my finger on it.

Placing her saddle on the side, I hook her bridal over as I fill her hay bag then slip out, saddle on my forearm, bridal thrown over my shoulder as I walk towards the small tack room.

I'm not in there alone long when I hear the sound of his boots scuffing across the concrete floor.

Inhaling heavily as I lift the saddle onto its stand, then hang the bridal on its hook.

"Thanks for today," I whisper out to him as his footsteps stop.

"You never have to thank me, this is our home, our ranch... I will always be here when you need me wife, *always.*"

My breath catches at the back of my throat, my eyes dusting closed for a moment.

I find myself jumping when the sound of his saddle hits the stand, dust kicking up.

Letting my eyes open softly, I feel him behind me and my skin pebbles. His warm breath teases the base of my neck.

Desperate to have his fingers trail up my arms, across my shoulders, up my collar bone...

"We better get ready soon," he whispers and my skin blankets with goosebumps.

"Yes," I just about manage to whisper.

"Please tell me you feel something more than just friends... please tell me it's not in my head... because Morgan," and the back of his fingers dust down my arm, trailing off at my wrist and slipping against my hip. His hand curls, before he spins me around to look at him.

His lips are parted, his gaze catches mine and I am transfixed on him.

"I fear I am falling for you," he ushers the words out quietly as if too scared to say them out loud, his head pressing against mine as his spare hand moves up, fingers gripping my chin as he tilts my face up to look at him.

"Please don't tell me I am imagining that there is something more between us... that something has changed... it feels as if the ground has shifted beneath me, the chemicals in my brain altered somehow," he pauses and his eyes fall to my lips, "tell me I'm not the only one."

My mouth opens and closes, eyes glazing over ever so slightly and I feel the thickness coating my throat.

"You're not the only one," my voice cracks and I see the relief wash over his handsome face, eyes misting over as his hand cups my cheek, holding me there as his smile widens, his lips hovering over mine.

"I know we said your first kiss would be perfect... and let's be honest, it wasn't quite what I planned when I kissed you in the kitchen but—"

I silence him by placing my finger over his lips, shaking my head from side to side.

"You were everything and more Pacey Rivera," and I can just about finish my sentence.

His head tilts ever so slightly as he covers my mouth with his and my body sags.

"I love that I am getting all your firsts," he whispers against my lips, and I am still floating through the abyss from his kiss. "I just wish you were getting mine."

His lips are back on mine, his body pressing up against me and heat flames across my skin, his tongue strokes mine, his mouth moving slowly as our kiss deepens. I was always nervous thinking I wouldn't know what to do, but I find myself following his lead, him building me up and my body reacting.

I let my hands slip against his chest, his heartbeat dancing under my fingertips.

He pulls away and I find myself whimpering at the loss.

"Not here, not like this, I've stolen enough kisses, I'm not about to steal anything else until you ask for it. Until you give me everything," his voice is soft, hand still cupping my cheek and I find myself leaning into his palm.

"I want all of your firsts to be perfect Sunflower, and to me, this isn't perfect," his lips twitch into a smile as he steps back and looks around at the dark, damp, tiny tack room.

I nod, lifting my fingertips from his sweat coated tee and bringing them to my lips, dusting them across as I embrace the burn from his kiss.

"Come," he whispers, linking his fingers through mine and pulling me towards the large door of the stables and I follow him, all giddy and woozy from just having him, if only for a moment.

I am showered and sitting at my dressing table wrapped in a towel, my hair damp and resting down my back. I am normally in Randy's every Friday, but since pops,

I've not been near there. Just couldn't quite bring myself to go.

But tonight is different. I have invited my new friends out and I am hoping to have a great night. The Rivera family are coming and of course my Pacey.

My.

He is mine.

My chest aches as my inner thoughts settle.

I never thought I would have someone to call mine.

I never thought I would have a boyfriend, let alone a husband.

Sure, we were put together by my pops. All to keep the ranch safe and keep me out of harm's way.

Neither of us thought we would fall for each other.

A few years maybe then we would walk away...

But here we are, not even a month in and somehow, we've tripped and ended up entangled.

Not that I am complaining.

But still... this was not on my agenda.

Marriage. Kids. Forever.

None of it.

A heavy sigh expands my lungs as I look at myself in the mirror.

Guilt echoes around my chest and my stomach twists.

How can I feel happiness but then grief bulldozes me? Should I even be feeling anything other than earth shattering grief, it had only been a couple of weeks and somehow, I have made room in my heart for Pacey Rivera.

Fear pricks behind my ears, tears loitering but I push them down, swallowing them whole.

The sound of the bathroom door has me jumping slightly as I peak a sneaky look through the crack in my door.

He walks out, towel hugging his waist, a smaller towel in his hand as he rubs it back and forth over his hair.

My eyes slip down his wet skin, his tattoo over his heart *live by the ranch, die by the ranch.* My chest rises and falls, and I want to know what his silky skin would feel like beneath my fingertips, tracing them down his toned stomach, but instead, my eyes trail where I am desperate to run my fingers.

The raised scar tissue makes my heart throb in my chest, a prominent ache radiating through me.

He was shot.

He nearly died.

And I find myself blinking a couple of times to make sure that he is in fact, actually in front of me.

His head turns in my direction, and I slip back in my seat, sitting taller and my cheeks flame at the thought of being caught.

Nibbling the inside of my bottom lip, I twist my mouth and try and stifle my giggle.

Shaking my head, I reach for my hairbrush and drag it through my ends before I dry and style into loose waves.

I do my make-up and smudge a soft pink into my eyelids, finishing with mascara and winged liner. A tanned bronzer dusts across my cheeks, and I match my lips with my eye shadow.

Dressed in bellbottom jeans and a pink cropped tee, I slip my feet into my tanned cowboy boots and press gold hoops through my ears.

Spraying my perfume, I grab a white cardigan as I walk for the door.

Walking towards the stairs, I pause for a second outside his room and wonder if he is still in there.

I debate knocking but decide against it as I make my way down the stairs and that's when I see him.

Standing at the bottom, his whiskey eyes on me and a silly smile slips against my lips.

"Baby," he rasps, and I give him the once over.

Eyes all hazy, hair pushed back away from his face and his little moustache cuddling his top lip.

I was really digging it.

He wears a white tee that clings around his muscly arms and light wash jeans, finished off with his boots.

"You look…" he pauses, his eyes dragging up and down my body. "You look so god damn beautiful, Sunflower."

My cheeks blossom pink, matching the color of my makeup.

"You don't look too bad yourself, stud," I mutter, and I shock myself by the little nickname that slips off my tongue.

A boyish grin passes his lips, and I duck my head as I slip off the bottom step and reach for my purse but he grabs it for me, holding it out for me to take.

I thank him and slip the strap up my arm.

My eyes cast to the living room and a wave of feelings cascade over me.

His fingers brush against mine.

"You okay?" he asks me, pulling me from my head and the tidal wave now laps against the shore.

I just nod.

I didn't want to be bearing all to him tonight, not when we were going out. I needed this more than he knew, I didn't want to bring myself or anyone else down for that matter.

"Let's go cowgirl," his hand slips over mine as he softly tugs me towards the boarded up door and I follow. Closing and locking it up behind us, he leads me towards his truck. I miss the way my hand feels in his when he drops it. Opening my door, he steps back and lets me climb in.

Nerves swirl in my stomach but I have no idea why.

Maybe it's the pressure of tonight? Maybe I am expecting something more to come of this... maybe deep down I want tonight to be the night that I give myself to him. Mind. Body. Soul.

The sound of his door closing snaps me from my thoughts and I press a small smile onto my lips.

His hand reaches across and slips between my thighs as he gives my leg a gentle squeeze.

"I am looking forward to tonight," he admits as he pushes the truck into drive as we pull down the dusty dirt track.

"Me too," I admit, swallowing down the lump that presents itself there.

"I still will die on the hill that it's not as good as the Boot," he chuckles softly and I roll my eyes.

"Po-tay-to, Po-tah-to," I shrug my shoulder and look out the window.

The sky a mix of pink and violet as the evening draws in. A few stars scattered through the colors and the sky has always amazed me.

"How are the renovations to the Boot coming along?" I find myself asking, face still turned out of my window.

"Yeah okay, bit of a halt this week because of the issues we've had..."

I nod, face slowly turning to face him.

"How did Sunny take the news?" and I wince as the words leave my mouth.

"As expected."

I nod, licking my lips.

"I have no idea if they were a thing as such, but they still had history and after it all they were friends, we all were," he sighs, and I watch as his fingers tighten around the steering wheel.

"Any idea who killed him?" and the words leave me in a whoosh, the air suddenly feels thicker.

"Nope," his tone is curt, and I roll my lips.

"I'm sorry," I say after a beat or two, just as he turns his blinker on and we roll down the red dirt track.

"For?" he glances over to me, his eyes bouncing between mine.

"Bringing all this up, the last thing you want tonight is to relive this week," I feel the heaviness settling into my chest. I didn't want to talk about my feelings and yet here I am trying to coax his out of him.

He gives me a lopsided smile, his arm back across the center of the truck as he scoops my hand into his and pulls it ever so softly over his side, his lips dusting across the back of my hand and I swear he is trailing the number eight.

"Sunflower," he murmurs against my skin, his lips feather soft.

I blink at him, letting my body turn in his direction and rest my head on the truck seat.

"Never apologize, you can always ask me anything and I will tell you the truth." A kiss to the back of my hand has my skin tingling. "But for tonight, can we just enjoy spending time together with no talk of work?" his brow lifts as we pull into a parking space.

"Of course," A wide grin spreads across my top set of teeth and he gives me a flirty wink.

Tension crackles between us and I know how much I

want this night to end a certain way, but I need to know that he is on board with it too.

"Ready?" he asks as he cuts the engine and lowers my hand gently into his lap and I drag it back across, fingers linking.

"Think so," I whisper and reach for my purse that has fallen into the footwell of the truck.

I twist around and look out the window, my eyes pinching to see if I can make out any of the trucks.

Rivera Trucks line up to my left in the distance and my lips tug into a smile.

"They'll always show up for you," Pacey's voice breaks through and I turn to look at him, eyes all adoring as I soak up every minute of this moment.

"I am beginning to realize that," I whisper, my eyes suddenly becoming glassy.

He scoffs a gentle laugh as he leans across the middle, elbow resting on the arm rest, his left hand reaches forward to cup my face and my heart races beneath my skin.

The coolness of his wedding band on my flushed cheeks feels nice against the warmth.

His lips edge closer to mine and I find myself holding my breath as they slant across my mouth, his tongue slowly pushing past my lips and I melt into him, his grip tightening around my cheek and a soft moan passes my lips and I feel my face flame red.

I feel his smile press against his lips, our teeth inches from touching and I feel so embarrassed.

"Oh my god," I whisper, dropping my head but he doesn't give me a second to hide, his fingers are gripping my chin and he tilts my face so I have no other choice but to look at him.

"Don't you dare hide yourself from me Sunflower, don't

ever feel embarrassed about how your body reacts..." he trails off and I see a wicked glint flash across his whiskey eyes. "Turned me on," he rasps as his lips brush against mine and my stomach coils, heat blooms between my thighs and I know I needed to get out of this truck now before I am dry humping his lap.

I pull back and open my door, letting the warm summer breeze dance over my skin as I find myself dragging the same air into my lungs.

I hear his boots hit the ground, crunching across the gravel as he walks towards me.

"No running, baby," his voice wraps around me like a cashmere blanket and all I want to do is snuggle into him and ask him to never let me go.

"I didn't mean to..." and his strong arms are tucking behind my back as he pulls me into him, our bodies close, our noses touching and his lips are gravitating towards mine.

"I want to kiss you again, but I know if I start now, I won't want to stop," he whispers and brushes them across my lips ever so slightly, like a feather touch and my eyes flutter shut, my breath catching at the back of my throat and I have no idea how he can make this so sensual without doing anything to me.

What baffles me more is that I have no experience, but my body is reacting in a way like she knows what to do, what to expect and how to act.

His smile grows and his lips trail to my cheek where he places the softest kiss.

I smile back and that's when his fingers find mine, walking me into Randy's.

Walking into the familiar bar, memories flood me, and I promised I wouldn't get into my feelings tonight.

Pacey leads me to the large booth in the back and I see Riggs, Aspen, Tripp, Dixie and Austin sitting there. I had only met him a few times, but I knew of him, heck most of Montana probably knew about him.

Nerves tickle the base of my neck, but I ignore them, swatting them away as Pacey pulls me in front of him, kisses me on the cheek and then lets me slip into my seat.

"Hey," I smile, my eyes bouncing between the Riveras and they all give me a smile, a wave or a hat tilt until Aspen knocks Riggs' off his head, shaking her head in a disapproving manner.

"Where are your friends?" Riggs asks, looking over my shoulder and I give a shrug.

"No idea, told them seven..." I pause for a moment and turn my wrist to face me, my delicate gold watch showing just past seven. "Still time."

Riggs smiles, reaching for his beer bottle and bringing it to his lips.

"How's your week been?" Dixie asks me, her warm voice floating across the table as she sips on her coke.

"Bit up and down really, but seems everyone has had a bit of an off week."

They all nod or hum in agreement.

"What do you want to drink baby?" and I watch as Riggs smiles, Aspen's eyes trail to Pacey as she sips her wine and Dixie and Tripp giggle to each other.

"What?" Pacey stands a little taller, clearly riled up by them.

Aspen looks to Riggs then back to Pacey.

"Just feels so weird... like... you both were so different back at the wedding... and now, well, it's clear as day."

Pacey rolls his eyes and turns his back fully on his family.

"What would you like to drink?" his brows raise, and I twist my lips just as he places his hand on his hip.

Hushed voice echoes behind us and I know he is going to be getting wound up as the seconds pass.

"Wine," I make a quick decision and instantly regret it but it's fine, I'll move onto something else after.

He nods and walks away, not looking back.

"Are we invisible?" Tripp grunts and Riggs lets out a deep, throaty laugh.

Aspen winks at me and I feel so out of the loop.

Dixie side eyes her and gives her a knowing nod.

"What?" I look between the four of them, "What is as clear as day?" I find myself lowering my voice even though he wouldn't be able to hear me. The bar is over the other side and there is music playing in the background.

"Pacey is head over heels in love with you."

I scrunch my nose and shake my head from side to side, lifting my hat from my head and tossing it down beside me.

"No, you have that all wrong," I giggle, and I am not sure whether it is nerves or what but now I have started, I can't stop.

"Oh, trust us, we know Pace and that boy has it baaaaad," Aspen nods and Riggs follows with a heavy dip of his head.

My heart stutters in my chest and I know he said he was starting to fall but starting to fall and being head over heels... that's a big difference and quite a big statement to make.

All their eyes trail over my shoulder and Dixie's smile is wide like the cat who got the cream.

I finally allow my eyes to glance over where they're looking and that's when I see his eyes on me.

Soft and hazy, a small smile lifting the corner of his mouth and my heart bangs against my rib cage.

I twist around quickly, my chest rising and falling as I look at Aspen.

"Told you," she winks playfully, "we know him all too well."

And for some reason, them saying that has me feeling giddy like a schoolgirl with a crush.

CHAPTER TWENTY
PACEY

Sitting at the table, my arm is thrown around the back of her chair and my fingers up and over her shoulder, but with each stroke, the tingling intensifies.

I watch her with intent, the way her eyes light up as she listens to Amora's stories from back home in England, her lips pressing into a smile as she soaks up every word that leaves her lips.

Titus is sitting proudly next to his wife, his arm hooked around her shoulder. Nate and his wife James sit the other side of Titus and they're in quiet conversation with Tripp and Dixie.

Riggs and Aspen shuffled around next to me and Aspen seems to be bouncing between the two conversations that are going on. Trailing my eyes over my shoulder, I look at my friend and my chest feels heavy for just a moment. Austin is standing at the bar with Sunny, both sitting with sombre looks on their faces as they talk amongst themselves. It must feel weird for both of them to be sat at a 'couples' table and not feel like they belong.

Which is silly, because of course they belong, but I also get why they would think that.

Sighing softly, my spare hand reaches for my chilled beer bottle as I bring it to my lips and take a mouthful.

"So how long have you two been married?" Amora's British accent sweeps across me and I let my eyes land on her. Red hair, ivory skin with a dusting of freckles and indifferent eyes. One brown. One blue.

"Few months," Morgan answers and I smile, placing the bottle back on the table.

"Ah, still in the honeymoon period," she smiles back at me and leans into Titus.

My nose scrunches and I bite my tongue.

"No such thing as a honeymoon period," Riggs grunts beside me, a cocky smile on his lips. Aspen rolls her eyes and shakes her head from side to side.

"For you," Aspen twists her lips, "but we have good and bad days don't we."

Riggs raises his brows as if this is new information to him.

"You may darlin' but everyday with you is a good day," and I laugh softly beside him.

"I didn't mean that," Amora smiles, looking up at Titus then back to Riggs. "I just meant right now, everything is so new and exciting. You soon fall back into the routine of life, just with an extra person by your side." her hand moves to her stomach, "or an extra two," she crinkles her nose.

"How exciting," Morgan claps her hands, "when are you due?" a giddy smile on her face and I watch as her eyes light up.

"Still got another six months to go," she smiles down at her bump, hand dipping beneath it.

"Ah, so not long after Dix," Aspen flutters her eyes over

to Dixie and tilts her head to the side. Dixie sighs, her hand rubbing her bump.

"I am so ready to have this baby out of me though," she admits then shuffles in her seat.

Riggs tears his eyes away for a moment and I watch as his large hand covers Aspen's.

"Do you have kids?" James asks and I see the way Aspen's smile drops and sadness floats through me.

Aspen just about manages to shake her head and Riggs clears his throat as he scoops her small hand in his, bringing it to his lips and dusting soft kisses on her skin.

"We haven't been blessed with children," she looks up at my brother and my heart breaks.

I can see the way Amora, Titus, Nate and James' faces fall at her sad tone.

"We will be though, it's just not the right time for us yet Wildflower, that's all," Riggs pulls her towards him and lets her slip under his arm. "Plus, what with your book signing... they're in our path baby, just not yet," and she sniffles a little and Amora's lips turn down.

"I'm so sorry," her hand reaches across the table and rests over Aspen's.

"Please don't be sorry," she smiles across the table. James sits a little awkward and Nate gives her a reassuring thigh squeeze.

"It's one of those things; we're blessed with health and a good life. A child would be a bonus, and like Riggs said, we will get our time," she sits up and reaches for the stem of her wine glass, dragging it towards her.

"Who fancies a tequila?" Morgan says her voice a little chirpy and Aspen's eyes light up.

"Yes please!" she happy dances in the booth and Riggs

lets out a heavy sigh, scrubbing his face and I chuckle softly beside him, Tripp joining in.

Drunk Aspen is the best Aspen.

Morgan shuffles out which in turn has me moving out my seat. I wrap my arm around Morgan's waist and pull her towards me.

"Don't drink too much *wife*, I have plans for us after tonight," and I hear her breath catching at the back of her throat, her face slowly turning to look at me.

And I know she is probably thinking I am talking about me sleeping with her, but that isn't what I have in mind at all.

In fact, I am taking her to see the stars, get to know her a bit more... and as much as I am desperate to be between her legs, my lips on hers, my fingers tangled in her hair... this means so much more.

Just me and her.

Placing a kiss on her cheek, I give her a slow wink then slip towards the table as Aspen shimmies past me. I roll my eyes, and she swats me in the top of the arm but I chuckle.

"God help me," Riggs grumbles as he watches his wife's every move.

"You'll be in for a fun night," I smirk, hand fisting into my pocket.

"Don't I know it," Riggs smirks, licking his lips and I hover at the end of the table, Nate staring at me.

"You don't even realize who I am do you?" he laughs, and I look at him dumbfounded.

"Errr, Nate? You live next door to me and Morgan," I look at Riggs, then to Tripp and they both shrug their shoulders.

"You called me last year.. asked me to put a tracker in someone's phone."

It takes a moment for the cent to drop but it does, and my mouth drops open.

"Ohhhhhh shit," I laugh, rubbing my chin, the stubble scratching at my palm.

Nate smirks, standing from his seat and giving me a pat on the back.

"I trust all was okay," he looks at me and I give him a nod.

"It was my wife's phone you tracked," Riggs pipes up and I nod.

"Was she in trouble?" Nate looks between me and my brother, and I roll my lips.

"No, she was going on a date and Mr possessive over here couldn't stand the thought of it."

Nate chuckles, running his hand through his messy hair.

"Sounds like something me and my friends would have done," he bobs his head, and I hear his wife James tut.

"Of course I wouldn't do that now," Nate spins, tracking back and placing a kiss on her forehead.

"I'm going to join the girls for a tequila," she announces, moving from her chair and disappearing towards where Morgan and Aspen are tucked up at the bar and I clock some random talking to her.

Spur boots. Aubergine crocodile skinned leather wrapped around them. Clean light denim jeans. Crisp white shirt. Matching aubergine cowboy hat, lowered so unable to see his face, but even if it wasn't, the bottom half of his face was covered with a bandana.

Riggs catches me staring, Nate is beside me and Riggs grunts.

"Who the fuck is that?"

And we hear Tripp murmur.

"Fucking hell, here we go," but we ignore him. Tripp is the peace maker, likes to be involved in the drama but doesn't like the confrontation.

But he would always be by our side if we needed him.

"You know him?" Nate asks.

I shake my head.

"Not a clue, but this isn't my stomping ground. We don't drift far from our town line but since our bar got burned down, and well, since I've been married to Morgan... this has become our local."

He lifts his chin.

All three of us stand and watch the guy at the bar, watch how he leans in slightly, but it seems he has his eyes on one girl in particular.

My fucking girl.

I step forward but Riggs' hand is on my shoulder, pulling me back in line.

"Calm it, you don't want to lose your head."

Glancing at him, I narrow my gaze on him.

"Are you shitting me? Who are you and what have you done to Riggs?" rage bubbles deep inside of me but after a minute, I realize he is right.

I don't want to go in all guns blazing when it could in fact be a harmless conversation.

Riggs' hand slips from my shoulder and that kind of feels like a go-ahead sign.

I look at him, he looks at me, but then his eyes drift to Nate who nods in the direction of the trio.

Glaring forward, that's when I see them.

Walking over with a tray full of tequila shooters and relief settles in my stomach, cooling the rage that was once consuming me deep inside.

"See, could have got messy for no reason," Riggs leans down and says quietly in my ear.

"I don't like this new Riggs," I groan as my lips purse into a smile when she stops in front of me.

"I knew you were watching me *cowboy*."

"Did you?" I look down at her, eyes darkening for a moment.

"Mmhm," her soft voice floats over my skin and goosebumps prick at the base of my neck.

Time stands still for just a moment and we're not in Randy's. We're standing in a meadow. The sun is low in the sky, warm on my skin. Her hair blows in the soft summer breeze and the smell of wildflowers consume me whole. I want to slow dance with her right here, right now, but not here in Randy's. I want to dance privately so I am consumed wholly.

With. Her.

I snap out of my thoughts when I feel her hand on my chest.

"Move over cowboy," she winks, tilting her head back as she looks at me.

I do as she asks.

I step aside but my eyes follow her as I do, landing on her ass for just a minute and I feel like I am about to be caught sneaking a look at her.

She places the tray on the table, and I see James' eyes light up.

"Tequila is the best shooter, convince me otherwise," Morgan murmurs as she takes a glass and holds it in front of her. James and Aspen take one too.

Nibbling on my bottom lip, I cross my arms across my chest and can't fight the smile even if I wanted to.

Aspen's eyes are bouncing between the girls and Riggs

is waiting with bated breath knowing that this is only going to go one way.

Aspen is going to get drunk.

She either cries or laughs.

I am hoping it's the latter.

Sunny moves over, head popping over Morgan's shoulder.

"Tequila?" her voice is high, and Aspen wiggles her brows. "Can I join in?" she asks, stepping beside Morgan and myself and Aspen nod eagerly.

Sunny moves forward, reaching for her own glass and holding it between her finger and thumb.

"Ready?" Morgan asks, her eyes slowly drifting to mine as she waits for the girls.

"Ready," James, Aspen and Sunny all say in unison.

Morgan beams her beautiful smile that lights up the whole room.

We watch as they shoot them back and Dixie groans, "Wish I was shooting back tequila."

"Not long Dreamcatcher, just think in a few months we're going to have a beautiful baby and once he or she is here, I will stay home, and you can go out with the girls like you deserve."

She leans into Tripp, and he lifts his arm and lets her snuggle into him, he presses a kiss to the top of her head and murmurs, "*I love you.*"

A small smile lifts the corners of my lips before I turn and look at my wife, who is now taking another tequila and shooting it back.

It's nice to see her relaxed, maybe even having fun. She's had such a good few days and it's nice seeing her letting her hair down.

"Woo!" Aspen shouts out, her eyes squeezed shut

before she shudders when the bitter tequila taints her tongue.

"More?" James asks, spinning her finger around the tray and I look at Riggs who lifts a shoulder in a nonchalant way.

Sighing, I tilt my head and look at Morgan.

She's giggling as James leans into her, and I have no idea what she is saying. Sunny is leaning onto Aspen, her arms locked around our friend, they're both smiling.

"They're happy," I mumble.

Riggs breathes a heavy sigh, "They are."

I give a soft nod then slip into the booth, Riggs beside me and we watch as Nate whispers something in James' ear, her cheeks turning pink in an instant.

Nate smirks then sits back opposite us. Titus gives him a knowing look and Nate's lips twitch as if he is trying to hold back his words.

"So," I say, picking the label of my beer and Titus points at my empty bottle, giving me a raised eyebrow. "Please," then he turns his attention to Riggs who shakes his head.

Riggs doesn't really drink when we're out.

The odd whiskey or beer here and there, but he'll drink more when we're at home.

Nate shuffles out the way and when he does Amora slips out and finds James, standing next to her, Dixie follows.

I watch for a moment as they talk amongst the group, Sunny away ordering more tequila, and after a couple of minutes Amora and Dixie perch up a small table, sitting on the stools and go back to a conversation between them.

It's nice watching Dixie open up a little. She is such a closed book when it comes to new people so to see her finding common ground with someone is great to see.

Nate sighs as he sits back down and slides closer to Tripp, giving him a soft nod before he is facing me and Riggs.

"You started a sentence I think," he pushes his glasses up his nose, waiting for me to speak again.

"I was going to say," I cough gently, clearing my throat, "how are you finding Blossom Cove?"

"We love it, we always knew we wanted to come back because James lived here for a while and her dream was to come back. I was a little hesitant at first, wasn't sure that I would ever leave New York, but then..." he pauses for a moment as his eyes graze over to his wife.

"You did it for her?" Riggs says, his fingers linked, hands resting on the oak table.

"Yeah," he nods slowly before his eyes are back on us.

I go to speak, but Nate continues.

"But do you know what?" he asks and we say nothing, "I am so glad I did because life just seems a little..." he trails off, looking at where Titus stands at the bar.

"Easier," I finish his sentence.

"Yeah," he scoffs a laugh and lets his head fall forward, "which I know probably sounds stupid to you both, seeing as you live here and work on the ranches and that."

We both nod.

"It's not all sunshine and rainbows," Riggs chuckles.

"I can imagine it's not, we've only got the horse rescue and I feel like that's hard enough," he sighs, casting his eyes to James and she catches it, giving him a wide smile.

"I suppose when you've come from somewhere like New York to rural living, it's a bit of a wakeup call," I say softly, not to be a dick, but just speaking the truth.

"Exactly, I worked behind a desk. That was my job.

Computers, security, hacking..." he rolls his eyes, "then to do manual work well..."

"It's hard work."

Nate laughs, hitting his palm on the table softly.

"Yes! It is," he admits before sitting back in the chair and rolling up the sleeves of his shirt. "But do you know what, I wouldn't change it. What with Tanner and James... I am honestly in such a happy place. I never thought I would find someone to spend the rest of my life with," he gets sappy just as Titus walks back and scoffs, placing the drinks down and then giving his shoulder a reassuring squeeze.

"Best decision we made," Titus agrees as he takes his seat.

"Yeah?" I ask as I thank him for my beer, slipping it towards me.

"Yeah," he nods, "I mean..." he pauses for a moment, "I miss my daughter, Arizona, but she has her husband and her kids... she doesn't need me anymore," he smiles but I look at him a little confused.

"You have another child?"

His throat bobs as his head dips.

"Yeah, Ari, she's twenty-two."

"Wow, so soon you'll have three kids."

He chuckles, taking a sip of his beer, "Yeah, three."

"Two girls and maybe a boy?" he smirks at my words.

"I have no idea but honestly, as long as they're healthy then I am happy."

"His daughter is married to our best friend," and Riggs' mouth drops open, and I sink my teeth into my bottom lip to try and not smirk.

"What!?" Riggs' thunderous tone echoes around the bar and Nate chuckles beside him, Tripp just sits and listens, his eyes on Austin at the bar.

I catch a look and see him talking to the croc man and I make a mental note to ask him who he is.

"Yeah," Titus sighs and then scrubs his face.

"How... I mean... how old... what?" Riggs' brows furrow and he scrubs his own face.

"Just happened I suppose," he shrugs and swigs another mouthful of beer.

"And that doesn't bother you?"

"It did," he admits as he spins his bottle on the table.

"What changed?"

Titus' ice blue eyes meet Riggs'.

"I saw how happy and in love they were... he treats her well, he respects her and honestly, as much as it was a kick in the teeth and bitter pill swallow, I couldn't be happier that she found someone who loves her as much as Keaton does."

"How did they feel when you left?"

"They were gutted," Nate nods along to Titus.

"So was Connie, Kaleb, Killian and Reese but they understood that we wanted to move."

I try and keep up, but just go along with the conversation, nodding and making noises when needed.

"This wasn't planned," Nate slips in, his finger passing between him and Titus.

"So, you're friends too, like from way back when?" Tripp decides to join the conversation, still nursing his beer from earlier.

"Yeah, all went to school together, then started our business."

"What happened with that?" Riggs asks and I know this sounds like twenty-one questions but we're just trying to get to know our new neighbours.

"Kaleb and Keaton are still running it, but it'll be scaled

back... I wanted out for a while and when we decided to move here it just felt like the right time," Nate admits and Titus nods.

"We've had such a hectic few years so walking away was needed," Titus slips in his version.

"How did the move between you happen?"

Nate smiles then looks over at James.

"We were at Amora's art gallery one evening, me and James decided to announce that we were moving to Montana, then Titus jumped on the bandwagon and told us he was moving to Lovelock Bay. As soon as he said it, I felt my heart warm as I knew it was the next town along." Nate finally looks back at us. "Even if they didn't come, I don't think I would have felt homesick, because as soon as my feet touched the soil, I knew this was home."

We all smile, and I knew exactly what he meant.

There was something special about where we lived, and I could never see myself leaving.

This was home.

The ranches.

The towns.

The people.

It would always be our home.

CHAPTER TWENTY-ONE
MORGAN

We say goodnight to our group of friends, Riggs holding onto Aspen as he leads her into the truck, Dixie and Tripp climbing in behind her.

Aspen pushes down the window and leans out, waving but Tripp pulls her back in.

I giggle as I cozy into Pacey's chest and under his arm as we stand and watch.

Riggs salutes us off his temple just as he begins to pull away and I hear Pacey snort a laugh.

"Thanks for tonight," I murmur as I look up at him and his eyes glisten putting the stars to shame.

"You don't have to thank me," he admits, leaning down and gives me a kiss on the top of my head.

My heart sings and my skin prickles with goosebumps.

Titus and Nate follow behind Riggs, then it's just me and him.

Alone. Sort of. In a parking lot.

He spins me out of his arm, his hand clutching mine before he pulls me close to him. Our bodies pressing together.

"Do you think you have a few more hours left in you Mrs Rivera?" he whispers against my lips and my heart races in my chest.

I nod, losing the ability to speak for just a moment.

"Or have you had too much tequila?" he teases, a beautiful smile on his face.

"No, not too much. Three shooters didn't even touch the side," and I'm not lying.

"Okay, only if you're sure," he says softly and I smile at him.

"Totally," and he presses his lips to mine, his arms around my back as his kiss deepens, his tongue sweeping against mine and I melt into him.

His lips press into a smile, and I never want him to stop kissing me.

"Come on, we need to move otherwise I am never going to want to stop," he murmurs and reluctantly pulls away.

Sighing, he leads me towards his truck, and I wait for him to open the passenger door. Stepping up, I lift my hat from my head and place it down by my feet. Running my hands through the root of my hair, I let it graze through the ends.

I wait patiently for him to get in the car and my heartbeat is steady as he sits next to me, hand slipping over the middle of the truck as he gives my thigh a squeeze. I have no idea why but that lights something deep inside of me, my innocence shining through like a mirror ball.

Nerves swirl in my lower stomach but excitement soon lashes against them like a tidal wave, turning them from a whirlpool to a soft crash against the quiet beach.

His hand moves from my skin and he locks them around the steering wheel, the loud roar of the engine as he turns the key and I smile hazily over at him, eyes a little heavier.

"You tired?" he asks as he pulls down the dirt road and I shake my head.

"Just cozy and content," I admit, a lazy smile dragging onto my lips.

"We won't be out late," he says quietly as we begin to move, "I just really want to date you, Sunflower," and his words warm my skin.

"Why sunflower?" I mutter, trying to keep the excitement that is growing deep inside of me.

"Because you remind me of one," he says softly and my nose crinkles at the bridge.

"I do?" confusion laces my voice and he can see it in my expression.

His eyes widen for just a moment before they soften, a hint of happiness shines in them.

"Yeah," he nods as we pull into Lovelock Bay, my body twisted towards him as I curl myself on the passenger seat. "When I look at you, the first thing I notice is your golden blonde hair and your sapphire green eyes..." he pauses for a moment and lets his tongue trail over his top lip as he turns his blinker on and pulls into Crooked Creek.

"But if you asked me on a deeper level, I would tell you it was because you radiate happiness and good feelings, you remind me of a warm summer day, an ice cold whiskey, the warm glistening creek as it runs through the rocks that sit at the bottom of the creek bed." He sighs. "You're loyal babe, so fucking loyal," he scrubs his hand over his face, "you remind me of everything good in my life Morgan..." he pauses as he slows the car to a halt in front of a wooden paddock gate.

My eyes lift to look at him, my lips parting ever so slightly as I wait with bated breath for the next words to tumble from his lips.

"And then it sinks in," he reaches his hand across to mine, cupping it and bringing the back of it to his lips. "You are the good in my life Morgan, you're my sunflower."

A small gasp leaves me as I feel a tear trail down my cheek, but I don't have a chance to catch it, he is there, wiping it away from the pad of his thumb before bringing it to his lips and kissing it away.

"I'm not worth your tears baby," he hushes, and I roll my lips. "Never will I be worth your tears," he lets my hand go and then opens the car door before jumping down and opening the paddock gate.

He points to me and asks me through the windshield to pull the truck forward.

I nod, unbuckling myself and climbing over the center.

Pushing the truck into drive, I let it roll forward until I am far enough past the gate for him to be able to shut it.

He is at the door, pulling it open and climbing into the passenger side, a boyish grin on his face.

"Good girl," he mutters, and my cheeks flame red as I continue to pull forward, the truck bumping down the dirt road.

"Where am I stopping?" I ask, my voice quiet as I see the glistening creek just ahead.

"Just pull up here," he points over to the right and I do as he says, pulling it to a halt and pushing it into park.

Silence crackles around the cab of the truck and my heart stammers in my chest.

"It's peaceful up here," I admit, looking out to the creek.

"Isn't it just," his voice smothers me and I am desperate to crawl onto his lap and snuggle into his chest just so I could listen to the sound of his heartbeat.

Was it steady? Was it racing beneath his skin? Was it skipping beats the way mine was?

"So, what's your plan for our date?" I ask twisting towards him.

"Well, I thought we could lay in the bed of the truck and look at the stars," he snorts a laugh, and I watch as he blushes, his fingers picking at his nails. "I know that is cheesy and cliché, but..."

I have no idea what comes over me.

Maybe it was the wine.

Or maybe it was the three shooters of tequila, but I am climbing over the middle of the car and nestling myself on his lap.

My chest rises and falls and nerves pinch at the base of my neck.

Swallowing the thickness down, my hands clasp his cheeks and I find myself lowering my lips to his as I cover them.

I find myself intoxicated with him, the way he makes me feel and the way his lips feel on mine.

Everything about him feels like an addiction.

One that I know I will never get enough of.

One that will no doubt, eventually become too much of a craving.

"What are you doing?" he rasps, my legs either side of his lap, my hands still firmly cupping his face.

"I have no idea," I whisper because it is the truth. I have no idea what I am doing, just know that I want whatever this is with him.

A soft laugh bubbles from him, and it has my insides tingling.

"Baby," he whispers against my lips, a soft kiss planting itself there before he is curling his fingers around my wrists and dragging them from his face. "Take it slow, we have all night..." his whiskey eyes burn into mine and I swear he shows me his soul.

"Let me just do this one thing, let me take you on a date," his plea is almost desperate, and I find myself sighing but I know he is right.

As much as I want him, I want him to date me too.

Sure, we're married, but this is all so new to both of us.

Sitting for a moment more, he had a boyish grin on his face, and I wish I could capture this moment.

The way the moonlight dances across his skin, the way his eyes twinkle under the stars. He looks every bit handsome, and I know I am falling harder and faster as the seconds slip past.

His fingers fumble and hook around the door handle as he opens the door, and the warm summer air blows through the cab of the truck.

One of his legs kick out and his arm wraps around my waist as he lifts me off him, my legs locking around him as he does.

A shrill laugh escapes me as he spins me around, closing the door as he does, then he walks me to the truck bed and places me down, my feet touching the dusty ground for just a moment. Pulling back the cover that is over the back of the truck, deep dimples present themselves in my cheeks when I see the picnic basket and the blankets.

"I wanted to do something cute," he admits, locking the truck cover and I smile.

"It's really cute," I admit and before I can even catch my breath, his arms are wrapped around my waist again as he lifts me onto the truck bed, and I panic, thinking he is going to drop me.

But he doesn't.

He carries me effortlessly, then placing me down on the soft blankets. Leaning into me, he presses a kiss to my forehead, lingering for just a moment before he reaches behind me and drags the picnic basket towards us.

I glance a look over my shoulder as he grabs a punnet of strawberries and my stomach rumbles gently.

"I went for a non alcoholic champagne," he raises a brow and twists the metal clasp before popping the cork, the loud bang echoing around our quiet surroundings.

The cork hits the blanket and my eyes drift to where it lands and I pinch it between my finger and thumb, holding it up.

Pacey looks at me, brows knitted, and I nibble on the inside of my lip.

"I want to keep it," I whisper and his eyes lock on mine, "keep it as a souvenir," I admit and I feel the way my heart jolts in my chest.

I have no idea what the look that flashes across Pacey's eyes is but it makes my heart drop for just a moment.

"Is that okay?" and he nods, reaching for two glasses and pouring mine out first, handing it to me just as I slip the cork into my front pocket. My fingers curl around the stem of the delicate glass and bring to my lips.

Pacey mirrors me and he places the punnet of strawberries in the middle of us and I pinch one, pursing it at my lips as I sink my teeth into the juicy fruit and a soft moan escapes, the flavors bursting on my tongue.

"Fuck," I watch as his throat bob, his mouth slightly open.

"What?" I blink at him, letting my hand drop, the strawberry still pinched between my finger and thumb.

"Nothing," he rushes out and he blushes.

"There is clearly something..."

He swallows and I watch as his jaw tightens for a moment, his eyes darting beside him and my stomach knots. His amber eyes lock on mine and I feel the air shift between us, my heart throbbing in my chest.

"You want to know the truth?" he asks, and I nod, hesitation biting my skin.

He sighs, placing the glass on a flat part of the truck bed and I wait for him to tell me.

"You. That moan. The way your full fucking lips locked around that strawberry," his voice is constricted, it's raspy and delicious and full of gravel. "I know I said I wanted us to take it slow, I know I wanted to date, but the way that sound floated over my skin, every inch of me tingling with a want for you wife," he pauses for a moment and shuffles towards me. "I want to feel every piece of your skin under my fingertips, mapping it out, following a trail that only I can see, that only I can feel, that only I get to tease..." he sinks his teeth into his bottom lip, his sights falling to my lips and I hadn't even realised but the strawberry has fallen from my fingertips.

"Pacey," I whisper as his lips hover over mine.

"I want to see the stars, but I want to see the way I make them sparkle in your eyes."

Swallowing, my eyes bounce between his.

He takes my glass from my fingers and reaches behind him, placing it down before he is back on me.

Lips hovering over mine before he knocks my legs open.

He is knelt between them, finger and thumb gripping my chin.

"But only if you're ready," his eyes hollow into mine, his teeth sinking into his bottom lip. My eyes volley, one of my hands slipping up to his chest as I press softly.

"I am," I swallow down the thickness and I know I probably don't sound very convincing but I really do want this.

A slow sexy smirk pulls at his lips and I let my eyes finally fall from his as I focus on his mouth.

"Then let's look at the stars and then I'll take you home," he leans into me and kisses me softly, his fingers still gripping my chin and I can feel the way his heart jolts beneath my fingertips.

"Okay," I whisper and his mouth widens as he smiles, teeth baring.

He pulls back and I instantly miss him.

Miss the way his body fit between my legs, miss the way his lips singed mine, miss the way the swarm of butterflies break free in my stomach.

I miss it all.

He leans behind him and passes me my glass and I give a soft nod as I thank him.

Twisting, I rest against the back of the truck and he joins me, shuffling back. His hand drops to my leg and he gives it a squeeze.

Silence consumes us and I have never felt so at peace than I do now.

All grief and anxiety slips away for just a moment.

"Are you happy?" his question catches me off guard. I lick my lips then turn to look at him and find that his eyes are already on me, watching my every expression.

"I am," I admit, and it's not a lie. Maybe not if you asked me a couple of weeks ago, but right here, right now, I have never felt happier.

"I know this is not what either of us had planned... but," he gives me a lop sided smile and my heart jumps in my chest.

"I know," I nod, a smile slips across my lips as I focus on him.

"But I am glad I am doing this with you," he sucks in a breath before his eyes turn forward and he is watching the blanket of stars above us.

"Me too," I admit, reaching for a strawberry and pressing it to my lips before I take a bite.

Silence consumes me for a moment and a thousand questions bounce around my head at getting to know him a little better because lets be honest, we really don't know each other at all.

Sighing, I bite the bullet.

"What was your childhood like?" and he looks at me in utter confusion.

"My childhood?" he puffs his cheeks out and looks forward once more.

"Yeah," my words echo quietly around the two of us, lingering for a moment.

"It was okay, not the easiest, not the hardest..." he pauses for a moment and looks down at his now empty glass.

"Sorry I shouldn't have asked," I rush the words out as if they've burned my tongue and I feel stupid for even asking that question.

"Please don't be sorry." he smiles at me but I see the sadness that sits behind his whiskey eyes.

"We don't have to talk about it," I bite the inside of my lip and wish I could rewind back.

"No we can, I just think where everything is still so raw with my dad and everything that happened in between," and I know he is referring to when he was shot.

"I get that," I whisper. "I really do," I suck in a breath and try and slow my racing heart.

"But I was grateful at having the childhood I did... grateful that we had Austin, Aspen and Harlow too," he slips away from me a moment as if he is replaying a memory.

"I bet," my voice cracks. "I always wanted siblings, the closest thing I got to that was Dusty."

"Love Dusty," he scoffs a laugh, "good man."

I nod, "He really is."

"Austin was like a brother to me, *is* like a brother to me," he laughs shaking his head, "not sure why I am talking about him in past tense." I don't interrupt him, just let him talk. "Aspen was always around, Austin's annoying kid sister. But we never left her out, she was more part of our gang then Harlow. She came later," he looks up at the stars and sighs heavily. "Aspen had a crush on Riggs, she was always watching him or trying to sneak around with him, but he was oblivious at the time."

"So, they always had a thing then?"

"Not really, she liked him, he liked her, but they never really got it off the ground until a couple of years ago when she came back to Lovelock Bay," he nibbles the inside of his cheeks, eyes back down to his glass. "But they found their way back to each other in the end, that's the main thing... they were always meant to be. They just had a bit of a bumpy road to get there," he trails off then moves forward, taking my glass from my hands and placing it into the picnic basket.

I sit up a little taller, legs crossed beneath me, watching his every move. I watch as the boyish grin slips onto his face and my stomach coils with excitement and nerves.

"Can I take you home, *wife*?"

CHAPTER TWENTY-TWO
MORGAN

Pulling up to the darkened house, he cuts the lights on the truck and turns it off. Neither of us move for a moment and I know he is trying to work out if I am okay or not. He slips from the truck and closes the door softly and I count in my head how long it takes him to get to me, my eyes watching him the whole time he is on the move.

One.

Two.

Three.

Four.

Five.

Six.

Sev—

He is at my door, opening it and holding his hand out for me to take.

"Wife," his gravelly voice slips over my skin like silk, and I love the way it pebbles.

I smile at him as he leads me towards the house. Slipping my hand from his for a moment as he unlocks the door then steps aside. I frown at the boarded up glass and hate that someone did that to us.

The door closes softly and my head dips, eyes cast down to the floor as I lift my hat from my head and hang it on the hooks beside me.

The sound of his boots fill the small entrance hall, his breath on the back of my neck as he dusts his fingertips over the nape and tucks my hair over my shoulder before his lips press where his fingers once were.

His large hand slips around my waist as he pulls me against him and my head tilts back as I rest it on his chest.

"Baby," he whispers against my sensitive skin and I find myself nodding slowly. "Can I take you to bed?" and his words send a shiver across my skin.

"Yes," I breathe, and I feel the way his lips part into a smile on the base of my neck.

He reluctantly lets me go and steps around me, his hands cupping my face.

"If you don't want this..." but I don't let him finish the words that are about to leave his mouth.

I get too in my head at the best of times, I do not want to get into it now.

My lips crash into his and he moans, his tongue slipping past my lips as I let him take control. My hands are hooked around his neck, my fingers twirling in the hair at the nape of his neck.

Fingers trail down my body as our kiss deepens, his arms around my waist before he lifts me, my legs locking around his back and I can feel how hard he is through his jeans.

My emotions are all over the place, but I know I want this. I know that I am going to give all of myself to him tonight. He slowly turns and begins to walk up the stairs.

A giggle bubbles out of me, and I think it's a bit of fear that he will drop me.

"I've got you," he whispers against my lips as if he could read my mind.

I whimper into his mouth when we reach the top and he begins to walk to his room. Kicking the door, it bangs against the wall, and he winces.

"I'll fix that," he rasps before he gently drops me to the bed, and I gasp.

His eyes are wild and hungry and I know he is going to devour every inch of me.

Lifting his hat from his head, he leans down over my trembling body and places it on my head.

"You wear the hat..." he trails off and my eyes widen. "You become mine forever Sunflower, I am claiming you as mine," his voice vibrates through me as his lips are on mine, harder than before and I feel the heat blossom between my legs.

"This is all about you baby," he whispers, pushing up and stepping away from me. My chest rises and falls as I watch him, watch as he looks at me like I am his entirety. Looks at me like he adores every piece of me.

He falls to his knees as his fingers lock around the back of my boot but his eyes don't leave mine.

Slipping it off, he places it down next to him and does the same with the other.

"When we've done this a few hundred times, I want you wearing nothing but those boots and my hat," he teases and my heart slams. "You're so beautiful and sexy Morgan, and you're all mine," he growls as his fingers tease up the inside of my jean covered thigh and he unbuttons my jeans. He moves forward, wrapping his fingers in the waistband

and tugs them down and off my ankles, discarding them with my boots.

"Fuck," he groans, pushing to his feet as he looks down at me.

Wearing his hat, my pink cropped tee and white silk panties... I feel every bit brazen.

Dragging his bottom lip behind his teeth, a low rumble of a growl presents itself in his throat. Leaning forward, his body over mine as he dusts a loose strand of hair from my face, my breath hitches.

"I need to know," he says softly, his breath warm and wrapped in the bitter taste of beer. "Have you ever been touched..." his fingers trail down my jaw, my neck, my collar bone, a soft gasp slipping past my lips.

My head tosses to the side softly and his lips press against my sternum, "Fuck," he mutters against my skin and my body flames with heat.

"Have you ever been tasted..." and he knows the answer, I don't even have to shake my head. "Oh baby," he sighs as his kisses drag down past the hem of my tee and dust over my sensitive skin.

"Pacey," I whisper as his lips break on my pantie line, his whiskey eyes flicking up to look at me and my chest dips and rises.

"I'll be patient, we will go as slow as you need... this is all about you Sunflower," he rasps before his lips dust over to my hip bone, licking and sucking at my skin before giving the other side the same attention.

"I want to work you up, have you trembling beneath me. I want to try and make your first time as perfect as I can," he mutters, his fingertips teasing just inside my panties. "Do you trust me, Morgan?" his eyes are back on me as I rest onto my elbows so I am looking down at him.

"Wholly," my voice is soft, and I watch as his face lights up, a wide smile spreading across his lips before his eyes fall between my legs.

Nerves spread at the base of my neck and a hurricane of anxiety kicks up in my stomach. His large hand sweeps up and rests just at the base of my ribs, resting it in the center of my stomach.

"Don't be nervous baby," his lips brush across the front of my panties and a shiver blankets me as his spare hand cups under my ass, pushing my leg up and wider. My greedy eyes fall to him as I watch him skim his fingertips up and down my inner leg, teasing at the side of my silk panties.

"So fucking desperate to feel you on my fingers, taste you on my tongue..." he trails off just as his finger slips inside and dusts across my pussy. Dragging in a breath, I hold it a little longer as he lets a finger rub against my clit, my mouth popping open and there is something so hot about watching what he is doing to me.

"Does that feel good?" he asks, the pressure of his finger slightly harder as he circles his finger and I nod as a breathy moan slips past my lips.

A smirk tugs at the corner of his mouth as his hand that was once on my stomach now glides down and hooks around my panties and I whimper at the loss of his fingers as he curls them around the other side and pulls them slowly down my legs.

His large hand swoops between my legs as he widens them once more, his eyes on my pussy, my eyes on him.

Fingers are back on my clit, soft circles rubbing, a bubbling feeling placing itself in my lower stomach, a soft moan passing my lips which spurs him on to tease a finger at my opening, gently pressing where no man has ever been before.

"Pacey," I pant, eyes widen and his warm gaze catches mine.

"I've got you," he reassures me, placing a kiss on my inner thigh as he edges closer. "You're wet baby, so wet," his gravelly voice pulls the nerves from me, his fingers still on my clit, working me up to a whole new experience, his other finger teasing at my pussy.

Pleasure courses through my veins, my breaths fastening and that's when I feel it.

A sting pulling me from the moment as his finger slips into me, teasing me, stretching me.

"Oh god," I pant, watching him as he focuses on my pussy, focuses on the way his finger fills me with ease. His teeth are on his bottom lip, his finger buried to the knuckle but he doesn't move it, just keeps his fingers on my clit, rubbing and circling.

"You're doing so well," he praises me just as he pulls his finger out to the tip, circling then presses a second against me, edging and I tense. "Relax baby, I've got you," just as he pushes them both into me, and before I can even come to terms with the feeling that is currently paralyzing me, his mouth is on me, tongue rubbing my clit.

My eyes roll in the back of my head as it falls backwards. He moans, his tongue pressed against my clit and his fingers slipping in and out of my pussy with ease as he pulls them to the tip then plunges them to his knuckles.

"Oh, god, Pacey," my moany words echo around the room as I finally lift my head and allow myself to look at the way he is making me come undone second by second.

Pleasure consumes me, my legs widening as I find myself lifting my hips.

"Grab onto my hair," he lifts his mouth for just a moment, and I see a string attached to his lips from me and I look horrified.

He chuckles softly, his mouth centimetres from my clit.

"That's your arousal baby, look how turned on you are," wetness coating his fingers as he continues pumping them in and out.

Whimpering, his strokes become rougher but it doesn't hurt. I feel a burn coursing through me, my skin tingling and my stomach knotting.

His mouth is back on me and I do as he asks, I reach my trembling hand forward and grab the root of his hair tightly and he moans, as his tongue glides back and forth over my clit, his fingers buried inside of me as they curl up and rub softly.

"Oh," I moan, my eyes not lifting from watching him pleasuring me.

"That's it, let it go baby," he whispers, looking at me for a second and I see the smirk that pulls at his lips, his fingers in and out, his thumb brushing over my clit before his tongue is on my clit, sucking before he rubs harder, letting his tongue glide up and down.

"I'm going... fuck, oh my god," I don't even have the words as this feeling crashes over me like a tidal wave, heat flaming against my skin as it starts at my toes and travels up to my neck. My back arches and in doing so, I press his head further into my pussy, his finger slipping from me as he grips my hips and buries his tongue inside of me and I am pretty sure this is what an orgasm is, my skin is covered in goosebumps, pleasure rips me inside out and I am in pure fucking ecstasy.

"That's a good girl, fuck, you taste euphoric," he groans, his tight grip pinching my skin but I don't even care.

I release my fingers from his hair then fall back on the bed, panting as my skin tingles.

I feel his lips dusting up the inside of my thigh, kissing wet kisses against my skin before he is laying between my thighs and my cheeks blush a burning ember.

"You okay?" he asks, his hands cupping my face, his thumb brushing against my cheek and I nod, because words are too much for me to even try and form.

He smiles.

"Are you sore?" he asks and I shake my head from side to side.

"Good," he mutters, a goofy smile on his face as he lowers his lips over mine and kisses me, his tongue invading my mouth and I let him. I let him kiss me like I am the only form of oxygen, like if he doesn't kiss me, he'll die.

He breaks away and his eyes darken.

"I need you baby," he breathes against my lips, and I edge closer to him, pulling his lips to mine as I let my tongue dance with his.

"Then take me," I whisper against him and a growl buries itself in his throat.

He pulls away and pushes to his feet, his eyes trailing down my body but I don't feel self conscious around him, I feel confident and ready to lay myself bare beneath him.

Kicking his boots off, his arms cross in front of him as he curls his fingers around the hem of his tee and drags it over his head before he tosses it to the floor and I let my greedy eyes roam over his body.

Muscles ripple under his skin as his fingers play with the button of his jeans. They trail over his tattoo on his chest then dip down to his scar and my heart stops for just a moment.

"Eyes on me," he catches me, and I do as he orders, letting my eyes settle on him.

Pushing his jeans down, my eyes fall and my lips part.

"Eyes," his voice is soft, and I find my eyes obeying. "Let me finish undressing you," he rasps as he stands at the edge of the bed and reaches forward and takes my hand, pulling me up. Lifting his hat from my head, he drops it to the floor. His fingertips brush against my rib cage before he grips the hem of my tee, lifting it over my head and discarding it to the pile. I am sitting in just my bra and his eyes fall, watching as my full breasts rise up and down.

His hand grips my cheeks as he tilts my head back and leans down, swiping his tongue through my lips and my eyes flutter shut. His spare hand trails around my back, unhooking my bra and letting it fall down my arms.

I slip it down and let it fall to the bed.

Here I am.

Sitting on his bed.

Naked.

In front of my husband ready to give him every piece of me.

"You're so fucking beautiful," he whispers against my lips. "I am besotted with you."

My cheeks pinch and I squirm on the bed, desperate to feel his fingers over my skin.

He stands in front of me, head tilted to the side as he looks at me and I finally let my eyes fall to his boxers, then widening at his evident erection.

I swallow, my throat dry.

He moves forward, laying me down gently on the bed but not before pushing me up towards the headboard.

"You still want to do this?" he whispers, and I nod.

"Yes, I do," I lick my lips as he smiles and lowers his

mouth to mine, his fingers teasing down my side and roll my nipples between his fingertips as his kiss deepens.

"Good," he murmurs as he presses his hips forward, his boxers rubbing against my pussy.

His fingers continue gliding down my body and slip between my legs as he teases them at my wet opening.

"I want to taste you," I whisper as I watch him work my body up, two fingers slipping into me with ease and my lips pop a perfect 'o'.

"Not yet... tonight is all about you."

I tremble beneath his touch, his eyes falling between our bodies.

"So desperate to taste you again," his voice tight, "but I am even more desperate to fuck you," and his crass words have me moaning, my cheeks turning red.

Pulling his fingers from me, he brings them to his mouth and slips them in as he sucks on them, groaning. Clenching my pussy, he smirks.

"Does that turn you on baby," he asks, and I find myself nodding, blushing once again. "Don't blush Sunflower, it's such a turn on," he admits as he kneels back and fists his hand into his boxers, pushing them down his thick thighs and my eyes bug from my head.

Thick.

So thick.

And big.

My mouth dries and I try to close my legs, but he shakes his head from side to side.

"It won't fit," I look down at myself then back at him and he chuckles softly.

"I'll make it fit," his voice is low, and my nipples harden, my skin dusting in goosebumps.

His boxers are being tossed from the bed, his hands on my knees as he pushes my legs wide and his fingers are slipping into my pussy. My moans vibrate through me, as his other hand wraps around his cock, pumping up and down.

Fuck. That's hot.

Rocking his hips forward, he rubs the thick head of his cock over my clit, my lips parting as my breaths fall heavier, my chest rising and falling as I watch.

"Fuck, you're so perfect," he groans, head tilting back and I watch as his throat bobs.

The familiar feeling builds inside of me, and I know that an orgasm is building.

"I'm getting close," I managed to squeeze out, my eyes transfixed on watching him pleasure himself and me at the same time, the head of his cock still rubbing my clit.

"Me too baby, I am so turned on," he admits, his lazy stare finding mine and this feels intimate. I want to tear my eyes away but I can't.

His fingers slip out of me, and I find myself wincing slightly. Gripping onto my hips, he pulls me down closer to him and repositions himself, his fingers locked around his cock as he edges forward. My heart drums in my chest and as much as anxiety swirls deep inside of me, excitement licks the feeling away.

He freezes in an instant.

"Fuck," he falls back to his knees, and I panic, pushing up onto my elbows.

"What? Have I done something wrong?"

"Oh god, no baby, no no no," he soothes but he looks defeated. He sighs looking away. "I don't have a condom," and my brows furrow, disappointment surging through me.

"We don't need one..." I finally say after moments of silence.

"Baby..." he cocks his head as he looks at me. "You're not on the pill..."

"I don't care." I admit, and I know I sound needy but I don't care.

At all.

"Baby," he says again... trailing off and I can see he is fighting with himself.

"Please," my voice cracks and my chest is rising and falling as hot tears threaten to fall. I have no idea why I am even being like this but I think we have got so close that I don't want to lose what I am about to experience.

The heavy sigh fills the room and a small smirk slips onto his lips.

"I'm clean... I've never not worn a..." and I stop him from talking as I reach forward and drag his mouth on mine, kissing him with all I have.

I don't want to think about anything other than right here right now, other than me and him.

He pulls away and I am panting, gasping trying to drag clean air into my lungs. I am resting back on my elbows, my legs wide as he lays between them. Pressing his forehead against mine, he glances down between our bodies as he lines himself up at my opening.

"We'll take it slow," he whispers as he rocks himself forward and I feel the head of him stretching my pussy, a burning feeling blooming between my legs. Squeezing my eyes shut, his hand curls around my hip as he pushes into me a little further.

"Breathe baby, fuck... breathe," he whispers, and I nod, his fingers pinching my skin as he holds onto me tight, his jaw locked as he slowly fills me.

I hiss as the sting grows, the burn radiating across my skin.

"You're doing so well," he praises me, his voice tight.

"It hurts," I admit, eyes still closed, and he grunts.

"I know baby, but you're taking every inch of me perfectly," he whispers just as he rolls forward and I feel the pressure that was once there disappear and he moans as he slips deeper.

"Fuck," he groans, and that's when I open my eyes and let my gaze flutter between my legs to see him buried inside of me.

He doesn't move, just gives me as long as I need to adjust to him.

I am panting, my eyes bouncing between his and between our bodies.

"Are you okay?' he asks, pushing up slightly, his hand still firmly curled around my hip.

I nod. I mean. It hurts, but I think I'm okay.

"This will be uncomfortable for a while, but I promise it gets better each time," he teases and before I can answer, he pulls back slightly then rolls forward, filling me again.

Shit.

It still hurts.

"Want me to stop?"

"No, please no," I beg.

He continues gently, slipping in and out and with each roll of his hips, he pulls out further and the sting is finally easing.

"You feel so good, I want to fuck you so bad," he chuckles, his gaze down between us.

"You are..." I whisper.

"Oh baby, this isn't fucking," he winks at me as he holds

the head of his cock just inside my pussy then teases me with gentle pulses.

A moan slips out and he smirks.

"You like that?" he asks me and I nod.

"Yes," a breathy pant fills the room.

"Watch me baby, watch as I fuck your virgin cunt," and his dirty mouth does something to me, my pussy clenching and his smile only widens.

Rolling forward, his cock fills me and that's when he begins to move. Each stroke becomes harder, faster and I am losing my mind.

"Touch yourself wife, I want to make you come over my cock," he groans, his head tipping back.

My fingers skim down my body, my one arm holding my weight and I do as he asks, I rub my clit in soft circles and pleasure bubbles inside of me, an ache evident in my pussy.

"So tight, you feel so fucking good," he moans as he slips in and out with ease now, his cock stretching me out and I watch with how he works my body up, pushing me to my orgasm.

"You look so pretty like this, at my mercy, fingers on your clit, your cunt full of my cock," his words blanket me and cause a shiver to dance over my skin. "Mark my words Sunflower, you're mine, always and forever. No man will ever touch you, kiss you, fuck you like I do," and my eyes roll in the back of my head, the pressure building and I know I am going to come.

"Pacey," I whimper as his cock fills me.

"Let it go baby, I'll be right behind you," he whispers, and he is back to watching between our bodies, my fingers still dancing over my clit. My pussy tightens around his cock, and he smiles down at me. "There we go, come for me baby, come all over your husband's cock and I promise to fill your pretty cunt full of me, is that what you want?" and I hadn't realised but I have tears rolling down my cheeks as I nod, a whimpering mess as he fucks me.

"You're such a good girl," he praises as he leans into me, his lips pressing against my forehead and I come undone, my moans filling the room before I call out his name and he follows behind me, slamming himself in and out as he chases his own orgasm and as promised, fills me full of him.

We're panting, sweaty and blissfully lost in our orgasmic high.

I collapse beneath him, his body pressed against mine as his lips find mine.

"I love you Morgan," his whispers fill my aching heart. "I fucking love the bones off you, worship the ground you walk on... you're my forever Morgan, my wildest forever."

Tears stream down my cheeks and my tongue finds his as I kiss him back.

"I love you," I whisper through our kiss, "I love you."

"Fuck say that again," he smiles, pushing my damp hair from my face as he smiles down at me, his cock still inside of me, our bodies moulded as one.

"I love you Pacey Rivera," my lips curl into a smile, his lips dusting over mine.

"Say it one more time."

"I love you," I choke, the air snatching from my lungs at the realization of the power those three little words hold. "I'll love you forever Pacey."

He kisses me, holding me so I can't move and I never want him to let me go.

After what feels like hours, he slips from me and I wince

and feel a small gush between my legs. He looks down and then back at me.

"Let me draw you a bath, clean you up... then, if you're feeling okay... I am going to fuck you again." He smirks, rubbing his nose against mine.

"I look forward to it," I say as he pulls me up and I squeeze my eyes shut as I move and fuck I feel so sore.

"You sore baby?"

"Mmhm," I hum as I shuffle off the bed and notice the blood.

"It's normal," he reassures me as he stands from the bed then swoops me into his arms, carrying me towards the bathroom. "I'm going to clean you up, make you feel good then fuck you to sleep Sunflower."

"I can't wait," I hum as he walks me into the bathroom and closes the door behind us and for just that moment I am so blissfully happy. I never want this night to end.

Ever.

CHAPTER TWENTY-THREE
PACEY

I wish I could tell you what my brothers were talking about, but being honest, I had no clue.

My mind was on tonight and finally teaching Morgan how to pleasure me.

She asked.

I agreed.

"Pacey," Riggs' deep voice pulls me from my thoughts.

"Yeah?" my tone higher than normal and Tripp's eyes burn into the side of my head.

"What are your thoughts?" he asks, tapping his fingers on the large oak table of our dining room.

"About?" and there is no point lying. My mind was elsewhere.

"Fuck's sake," Riggs sighs and I watch as Tripp scrubbed his face.

"Did you hear anything?"

Again, no point.

"No." I shrug a shoulder up which gets an eye roll from Riggs.

"Luke... what shall we do with him? He still stands that

he had no idea who sent him, just that he was sent to find the diamond."

"I don't believe him, do you?" Tripp looks at Riggs and Riggs shakes his head from side to side.

"Do I fuck," he sits back in his seat, hands now clasped in front of him.

"Then we don't let him go," I say as my eyes bounce between my brothers. "I can throw him in the cell, I don't think it's right you have him chained up in the basement," I side eye Tripp who gives a subtle nod. "We can toss him in the back of the truck and take him to my place... or," my lips turn down as I look at Riggs, "we can put a bullet through the middle of his eyes and make him disappear."

"Not an option," he says, lips rolled into a tight line.

"Why?" Tripp asks, elbows on the table.

"We have enough shit on our plates at the moment, do you really think we need another dead man under our belt?"

"Technically, we didn't kill any of those men."

"Don't be a smart-ass Pacey," he growls and Tripp laughs.

"You sure you don't mind him being in the cell?" Riggs changes the subject rather rapidly and stares me down.

"Nope, no skin off my teeth," I shrug and then let out a deep, exasperated sigh.

"Cool, I'll get him moved later on." I nod. Tripp nods and then Riggs nods.

"Okay, moving on," Tripp says, sitting back, his head swinging between me and Riggs. "The suits..."

"We need to rid them once and for all. First they blew the mine entrance, then they cornered me and Buck and now Conrad."

"We don't know if it was them who killed Conrad," Riggs reminds me softly.

"I still think it was Marty," and as soon as the words leave my lips their eyes are on me.

"What?" they both say in unison.

Sighing, I lick my lips.

"I called the number that he said was his family's number from out of town…" I trail off and then fish my phone out my pocket. "It wasn't. It went through to some bar and as soon as I mentioned Marty's name, they cut the line off. Not been able to get back through since." I twist my lips and slide my phone across to Riggs.

"Have you searched it up?" Tripp asks the question and I roll my eyes.

"Duh," and he swats me around the back of the head, knocking my cap off as it lands on the table.

"You shouldn't even have that on anyway," Riggs makes a point of saying as he brings my phone to his ear then furrows his brow when he gets the same tone I did.

"Where is Marty now?" his pushes from the table.

"With Austin I guess."

"Does he know anything?" he asks, and I blink a couple of times.

"Who? Marty?"

"No, Austin," Riggs tone is growing more agitated as the seconds pass.

"Not really, just told me to check the number out," I take my phone from Riggs and glance down at the number.

"This is a shit show," Tripp mumbles and runs his hand around the back of his neck as he gives it a tight squeeze.

"That it is," I nod as I push away from the table and follow Riggs out.

"We really need to end this…" I look over my shoulder

just as Dixie walks into the room, leaning down and kissing Tripp.

"Before it ends us," Riggs finishes and I swallow down the bile that threatens to spill up my throat, burning as it does. "Let me speak to Austin, you still got the suits business card?" he asks as he lifts his hat from the stand and places it on his head.

"Buck took it," I mumble, and Riggs gives a nod.

"You sort a meeting with the suits, I'll speak to Austin."

"What about me?" Tripp calls out and I chuckle softly.

"You just worry about Dixie, we don't need you getting hurt now do we," he lifts a brow and doesn't give Tripp a chance to respond before he is out the door.

I hover for a moment, and I see Dixie give him a sad smile.

"Everything will be okay Dix, we're not going to let it get to a full-blown war," I try and reassure her just as mom walks around the corner.

"You hope," my ma says and I sigh.

"Ma, I am trying to make her feel better, not panic. She'll go into early labor," and mom rolls her eyes.

"We need to be realistic. This has been going on for a lot longer than us Pacey, our family have been dealing with this for generations. Sure, you might stop it for a few years, but before we know it, your kids will be dealing with exactly the same thing," and that sentence makes my blood run cold because she is right.

We're not stopping what's inevitable. We're just delaying it.

The first-born son will become heir.

If they choose to sell the land... then so be it.

She sighs as she sits down, and Tripp reaches his hand across the table and covers hers with his.

A fire burns in my stomach, and I find myself storming from the room and out of the front door.

Climbing into the truck, I glance the time. Four p.m.

Not too late for an unannounced visit to the new neighbours.

Pulling out of my family's ranch, I drive towards Blossom Cove. Slowing when I see their sign, I turn my blinker on and drive down the red dirt road before cutting the engine just before the car port.

Blood thrashes through my veins and I have no idea why, but my mom's words haunt me. Maybe because it is the truth. We can fight to save our little corner of earth, but we can only save it for so long.

Greed wins most of the time.

But not now.

Sure, years down the line our kids may decide to sell, but until then, I'll be fighting to my last dying breath to make sure no one gets their hands on my legacy.

On my families legacy.

On *their* legacy.

Climbing the three steps, my boots hit the wooden porch, and I knock softly on the door.

I wait for what feels like hours before Nate opens the door.

"Pacey, all okay?" he asks and I can hear the chatter of company.

"I need a minute," I step forward and Nate looks over his shoulder before stepping aside and letting me in. I give him a nod and take my cap off, holding it in my hands.

"You okay?" he asks quietly, his hands fisting into his pockets.

"Can you look into a couple of people for me?" and Nate smirks.

"Sure thing."

"Luke Montgomery, Marty Styles, and Dixie Walker."

He blinks at me.

"Dixie as in..."

"Dixie as in..." I repeat and roll my lips. "It's not about her man, but I need to know what comes up when you search her, can you do that for me?"

Nate nods and slips his phone out as he makes a note.

"Nate," a loud British accent booms around the large entrance hall and I see a greying blond man stop in the archway of I am assuming the dining room.

"Xavi, this is Pacey."

"The other Rivera boy, we have met before," his lips twitch before he steps forward and holds his hand out for me to shake, which I do, gladly.

"That's me," he drops my hand and then looks to Nate. "Really sorry to just show up unannounced but I needed someone like Nate to help me."

"You in trouble?" his odd color eyes burn into mine.

"I've been in trouble since the moment I was born," I admit on a sigh and try and have a chuckle.

He laughs and Nate gives the smallest smile.

"Just some issues with suits... won't bore you with the details," I run my hand over my hair and Xavier looks to Nate then to me.

"We can help, I used to work in a similar sector to Nates," and I see Nate raise a brow then look at Xavier and back to me.

"Wouldn't say they were similar Xavi, you helped clean up messes when things went to shit."

"Pretty much what you did was it not?" Xavier smirks and rocks into the ball of his feet, hands still tucked into his suit pant pockets.

"Now, now children," Titus' deep voice booms around the room and Nate rolls his eyes.

"Ah, Titty."

"Xavi," he grunts as he stands beside him.

"Would you like a drink?" Titus asks, stepping towards me and shaking my hand.

"No thank you," I decline politely. "I just needed Nate's help with something."

"Oh yeah?" Titus looks from me to Nate to Xavi.

"Yeah," I sigh, "got suits on my back, random guys breaking into my house and sniffing around for shit that doesn't belong to them. Getting a little tired of it all now and just want this all dead and buried."

The three men all exchange looks.

"We'll help," they say in unison and a nervous laugh bubbles out of me.

"Honestly, I really don't want to have to drag you guys into this, I just needed Nate to look into a few people for me."

"The bigger the army," Xavi whistles.

"That's the problem though, I am not sure if we need an army. We just need to cut this off from the source, but that's the problem, I am not sure who or where the source is."

"Leave it with us," Nate nods then leads me to the door. "If you have any information or something that might help..." and I pause him, reaching for my phone and showing him this number.

"I need to know what this is. When I called it, it went through to a bar. I mentioned the name Marty and then they cut the phone off. Not been able to get back through since."

Xavier raises a brow.

"I think Marty is up to no good."

"I think you're right," I give Xavier a nod. "Only problem is, I think he knows we're onto him. We thought it was someone else in our circle, but he wound up dead at one of the entrances of our mines. But then again, it could have all just been a cover up. I feel like I am walking around and not sure who to trust anymore."

"We get it, we've all been in situations like this," Titus speaks up from behind Nate and for some reason that kind of fills me with reassurance.

"Thanks Nate," I say as he opens the front door. I wave bye to the other two and then make my way out the door.

"I'll be in touch," he says as he shakes my hand.

"Not a word of this to Morgan, I don't want to stress her out any more than I already have," I give a tight lipped smile before turning and walking towards my truck.

Climbing in, I start the engine and pull out of the dirt road and drive towards home.

Riggs would call when he needed me, but right now, I just wanted to get home to my wife.

Cuffed to the bed, her sheen covered body lay beneath me.

I know I said I would teach her to pleasure me, but I needed her more than I wanted her.

"Pacey," she moans as three of my fingers stretch her out, slowly fucking her.

"I know baby, I know," my voice is featherlike against her skin as my lips drag down her body and dip between her thighs. "But I need to taste you Sunflower, I need you to come on my tongue," my cock is throbbing, cum seeping from the tip as I hover my warm mouth over her cunt, teasing her before my tongue swipes through her folds, rolling and rubbing against her swollen clit, fingers buried to the knuckle in her tight pussy.

"Oh god," she moans, her back arching as she pulls on the silver metal cuffs.

"There's no god baby, only me," I lift my mouth for only a moment and her sage green eyes meet mine.

"Don't pull too hard Sunflower, the cuffs will nip at that beautiful skin of yours," her breathy pants turn me on as I focus on her clit, my fingers quickly bringing her to her impending release.

"Pacey, oh, like that, yes, yes," she moans, her hips gyrating over my fingers, her greedy pussy wanting more.

It had only been a week since our first night together and we have been inseparable ever since.

Any given moment I am on her, she is on me. I am drunk on her.

"I'm going to…" she struggles to get her words out as her orgasm slams through her, her body trembling, back arching and I use my hand to press on her lower stomach and pelvis, holding her as I enjoy every ounce of her.

Standing, my lips glisten with her arousal and her cheeks are pretty and pink.

"Fuck you look so pretty when you cum," smirking down at her, I kneel on the bed and grip her knees, pushing them into her chest as I slip my hard cock inside of her in one, swift thrust.

"Oh god," she cries out as I pound against her.

"Do you have another one in you baby; can I coax another orgasm from you?" I tease as I slip in and out of her, rolling my hips deeper.

"Yes," she whispers, her eyes closing and I know it's not going to be long before I fill her full of me, my orgasm is teetering.

"Give it to me baby."

I drill into her, my cock throbbing.

My fingers are on her clit as I help bring her towards another orgasm, and it's not long before she is free falling with me as I fill her pretty pussy full of me.

LAYING IN BED, Morgan's head on my chest and my fingers tangle in the ends of her golden hair. My left-hand curls around my whiskey glass, as I stare at the empty wall ahead of me.

We always seem to sleep in my room, not sure why but I am also not complaining.

My mind ticks over with the shit that is brewing, and I know it's not going to be long before the suits are back and demanding the land.

I needed this squashed with Marty.

We said there was a mole, but I didn't think it would have been him.

Especially as he was so close to my dad and Riggs.

But people do things for strange reasons, and I am sure there will be some cock and ball story he will spurt when we finally confront him.

Then there was Conrad.

The guy who we thought was the mole.

Also our friend.

Would Marty kill him? Maybe.

Why though? Unless Marty *is* the mole, and Conrad was going to out him.

Only way to shut him up was to beat him to death.

Sighing, I tap my finger on the glass before taking a mouthful and wincing at the burn that laces my throat.

I just wanted to live out my life on the ranch, watching

the sunsets and sunrises whilst listening to the birds sing. I want to sit on my porch and watch the winter snow melt and the meadows bloom.

I'm a simple man, wanting a simple life.

Honestly though, I didn't even want the badge.

Put me on the back of a horse alongside my wife and let me herd cows.

My phone buzzes and I try to move without waking Morgan. Placing my whiskey glass down, I reach for my phone and see Riggs' name.

"Bunkhouse. Now."

It's past midnight and my eyes are sore, my body tired but when he calls a meeting at the bunkhouse, you know it's serious.

Sliding her from me, she stirs and a soft moan passes her lips.

Her eyes flutter at me, blinking a few times.

"I'll be back soon baby, I've got to go meet Riggs," she pouts and her brows furrow. "Don't leave the house," and she rambles something incoherent before rolling and dragging the bedsheet with her, wrapping it around her naked body.

Dragging my dirty jeans from the floor, I tug them up then pull my tee over my head. I bring it to my nose and do the sniff test. Not great, but not rotten either.

Running my hand through my hair, I pick my hat from the back of the door and slip it onto my head. I catch my reflection in the mirror and I give myself a smile.

Proud of the man I am becoming.

Never thought I would feel this whole, and yet here I am.

Wanting nothing more than an easy life with my wife.

My eyes glisten a little, my lips curled into a smile and my stubble neat and my moustache growing nicely.

Glancing over my shoulder again, I watch her for just a moment, and I would love nothing more than to be back in bed with her.

Pulling in a deep breath, I step outside the room and close the door softly behind me and leave her behind.

Hated it the second I stepped out that door.

Walking down the stairs, I dodge the creaky board that I still haven't fixed and make a mental note to make sure I get that done as soon as I have a free half an hour.

Swiping the truck keys from the side, I unlock the front door and step out on the porch before locking it behind me. I check it three times to make sure she is safely tucked away.

I really wish she would get a phone, but apparently, she doesn't need one.

Scoffing a laugh at the way she crossed her arms in front of her chest and stomped her little foot like a bratty teenager when I brought the conversation up will always be one of my favorites.

That and the day I watched her walk down the aisle.

Up there in my top memories.

Climbing in the truck, I yawn before scrubbing my face then turn the engine on. Driving slowly out the drive, the skies are violet, the stars shining brightly and I would do anything to be stargazing with her on the back of my truck right about now.

The drive is short to Rivera Ranch and I can see the dimly lit light of the bunkhouse glowing.

Slowing to a halt, I cut the engine and drop out of the truck. Tiredness bites behind my eyes causing them to sting but I shrug it off. My heavy legs lead me to the front door and I knock three times.

I don't wait to be called in and I don't wait for the door to be opened for me, I push the handle down and step up and over the threshold.

Riggs and Tripp's eyes are on me, they both give a heavy nod as I close the metal door behind me.

"Evening," my gruff voice fills the room and Tripp holds his whiskey up. "That bad?" I lift my hat from my head and rub my hand around the back of my neck and try to rub the tension out.

Riggs lets out a drawn out, heavy sigh as he stands from his chair and begins to pace.

"What's happened?" and his dark eyes find mine, his hand running over his beard.

"I think I've worked out who is behind everything..." he trails off, eyes bouncing to Tripp before they're back on me.

"Who?"

Riggs takes a mouthful of his whiskey and then winces as the burn hits the back of his throat.

"I can't say..." his eyes lift to mine, silence burning through the room like wildfire, tension growing by the moment, "not yet anyway, I just need to check a few things out."

"Do you know?" I point to Tripp, but he rolls his lips and shakes his head softly. "Right," I take four steps forward and drag the chair out. "Where are the cowboys?" I look around and furrow my brows.

"Sent them down the fields."

I nod.

"Are we still sure on the mole?" I find myself asking, looking around the bunk house.

"Pretty."

"Pretty sure doesn't fill me with confidence."

"I just need a bit more time," Riggs tone doesn't change, it's flat and monotone.

"Everyone is too quiet which makes me nervous," I admit. "I don't trust Marty, not after what happened with Conrad."

"Luke is going over to the cell tomorrow, Austin is keeping watch on Marty, we know his loyalty is with us. What happened to Conrad was shit, yes, but it helped..." he trails off and my stomach twists with anxiety.

"Do you think it was Marty?" Tripp asks and he looks at both of us.

"I don't think so..." and the hesitation in his voice has my mind ticking.

I hum at his response.

"We need to start moving in now, we need to maybe get the suits back here, see if we can get a reaction from them... someone is behind them and like I said, I think I know who is orchestrating it but I just need to do a bit more digging to be sure." He drags a chair out and slumps himself in it.

"How long do you think you'll need?" I ask, tapping my fingers on the table.

"A week, maybe two."

Me and Tripp nod.

"Right, well let's focus on that then. Bring Luke by tomorrow, today... I don't even know what the time is," I sigh, rubbing my hand over my face.

"It's all connected, I know that much... just need to work out if Marty is working with them or solo... did you try that number again?" Riggs asks as he downs the rest of his whiskey and slams it on the wooden table.

"I passed it onto Nate, he is going to look into it," Riggs nods.

"Good, good… this is good," Riggs stands and places his hands on his hips.

"Xavier offered to stand behind us if we need it."

"It's always good having people on our side," Tripp agrees and Riggs mutters what sounds like *yes I agree.*

"I said we will let them know if we need them."

"No problem." Riggs sighs. "Okay, so, leave it with me, I just need a bit longer and then we can move in when I have it confirmed."

"Sounds good," I push up from my own seat at the same time as Tripp. "Meet me at the office, eight a.m. tomorrow." I tell Riggs as I lift my hat and place it back on my head and he gives a shallow nod.

"Has he spoken yet?"

"Not a fucking word. Should have just put a bullet in his head."

"Too easy," Tripp reminds Riggs and he chuckles softly.

"He will talk, we just need to get it out of him," I admit, turning on my heel and grabbing my keys from my front pocket.

"Hmm, I'm not so sure," Riggs says as he follows behind me and I tug the door open, holding it for Riggs, Riggs holding it for Tripp.

"Have faith, brother. He'll break eventually." I smile as I step over the threshold and out into the cool summer night.

"You could always use Aspen," Tripp rushes out which gets a shove in his shoulder from Riggs.

"No fucking way."

"I mean…" I stop in my tracks and turn to face him, "that isn't a bad shout," and Riggs shakes his head violently from side to side.

"No." his voice is harsh, and tone is quipped.

"I bet he would talk," Tripp says nonchalant and Riggs throws him a dagger glare as he walks back towards the house. "Just saying," Tripp hold his hands up but a soft laugh escapes him as he does.

"Idiot," Riggs grumbles and follows me to my truck.

"Think about it," I say with a little hesitation.

"I don't need to think about it," he shuts me down in an instant as he tugs on the door of his truck.

"Fine," I roll my eyes and climb into my own truck and slam the door.

He glares at me, and I give him a cocky smile before flipping him off. Pushing the truck into reverse, my wheels spin on the dirt and I am pulling out of the driveway and going home to my girl.

Freshly out the shower, I walk into my bedroom and just stand at the side of the bed, watching her.

She's on her front; her golden hair is spread behind her and her lips are parted as soft breaths escape.

Is it normal to be as infatuated with her as I am?

How the hell do you fall that quickly?

Stepping forward, I pull the covers back and I slip in beside her.

She murmurs as she shifts and rolls on her side.

"Only me baby," I whisper against her ear and place a soft kiss on her cheek as I wrap my arm over her body and slide her close to me, my face buried in her neck as I inhale her scent and within seconds, I am asleep.

CHAPTER TWENTY-FOUR
PACEY

Pulling into a space outside my office, I climb out the truck and move towards my office, locking it behind me. Twisting the lock on the door, I let myself in and walk to my desk, waking my computer up before I am back hitting the sidewalk and moving to Sunny's.

I hadn't checked in on her and the guilt nipped away at me, but I know her and Austin have been speaking.

They have something in common.

Someone they loved both died.

Under our watch.

Again.

And I am so ready to have this damn cycle broken.

I really do feel like someone is out to test us as a family, but they need to know that they won't break us.

Ever.

The bell chimes as I walk into Sunny's. She isn't technically open yet, but for me, she comes in a little early.

She appears from the back, dark hair tucked behind her ears, eyes a little watery and I know instantly she has been crying.

"Sun," I sigh, as she rounds the counter and into my arms. "It's okay," my voice is quiet as I tighten my grip around her small frame and let her cry.

She trembles in my embrace and I have no idea how long we stand here for, but I don't care, she is part of our family, I am not leaving her when she clearly needs us.

"I'm sorry," she sniffles as her small hands press against my chest, stepping back and running her fingers under her eyes.

"Please don't say sorry," I mumble, head tilting as I look at her.

She nods, bottom lip trembling.

"Aspen and Dixie are coming over later on."

"That'll be nice," I nod, as she turns her back on me and moves back behind the counter.

"Normal order?" her voice heightens.

"Hmm," I look at the board, pushing my hands in the front of my pockets. "Make it a double shot flat white, and I'll have a breakfast wrap," I nod as she touches the till and places the order through.

"No problem, give me a minute." She prints the ticket and hangs it in the small kitchen behind the counter.

Sammi works the kitchen, she helps Sunny out on certain days.

"You know we're always here for you if you need us," and she looks at me through her lashes, blinking a few times.

"I know," she nods.

"And I hate to do this..." I pause for a moment as she preps my coffee. "But I need you to come down the station when you have five... just need to ask a few questions," and I watch as her shoulders rise and fall.

"Of course," she whispers, and I know deep in my gut

that she had nothing to do with it, but even if she saw Conrad leading up to his murder, at least she might be able to give some clue who could have done it. "I can come down after this?" she offers, and I glance at the time. It's ten to eight.

"Yeah, that works, Riggs is bringing someone in, but apart from that it's a day of admin," I sigh, her eyes dropping to the gold badge that sits on my belt loop.

"Sounds tedious," a small smirk slips onto her lips, and I smile back.

"It really is, it was nothing like I imagined." I admit, sighing and following her down the counter as she finishes my coffee.

"How did you imagine it?" and I can hear the soft laughter that is teasing her tone.

"Like the old black and white western movies," I admit, my brows furrowed.

"Oh," she twists her lips.

"It's fine, you can laugh," I roll my eyes in an over exaggerated manner.

"No, I wouldn't dare," she turns her back on me just as the bell rings from the kitchen.

She passes me my wrapped-up breakfast wrap and my coffee.

"Sorry to be a pain," I wince, "can you make one for Riggs too... I forgot about him."

"Not a problem," she laughs, ringing it up and I pay.

"So, how's the wife?" she asks, waiting for the breakfast wrap as she makes his coffee.

"Amazing," I sigh, admitting that out loud has my heart fluttering in my chest.

"She seems real nice," Sunny nods.

"She is," a giddy smile plays against my lips just as the

bell rings and she passes me the other breakfast wrap and coffee. "Thanks, Sunny," I give her a wink and begin to move towards the door when I hear her footsteps behind me.

She grabs the door, and I walk out. "Won't be a minute!" she calls out to Sammi before she follows me towards the office.

Riggs isn't there yet and I am kind of grateful.

I just feel like once Luke is put in the cell, shit is going to come down on us.

There is a niggle in my gut that I know how it is going to go, but I am also not sure if it is anxiety.

Pushing my office door open, Sunny walks past me and I follow before placing our coffees and wraps down on my desk.

I quickly check my computer and make sure nothing urgent is sitting on there.

I have a meeting with the judge in a couple of weeks, just to go through a few things on his list.

Mostly nothing to do with me.

Marty is due there too.

But if this is going the way I think it is, a new livestock commissioner will be sitting in his place.

Locking my computer, I nod for Sunny to follow me to my side room, and I text Riggs telling him what is going on just so if he turns up and sees my office empty, he knows where I am.

Closing the door behind me, we sit down, and I reach across for my notebook and my recorder. Turning it on, I look down at it to make sure it's got battery.

"Okay, this is just a quick five-minute interview if that's okay?" I say softly, trying to reassure her and she nods.

I give her a nod then press record.

"Please state your name," I grab a pen out the pot and get ready to jot it down.

"Sunny Olivia DeLuca."

I continue with the normal questions, place of birth, date of birth, where she lives etc. It's all routine and I don't really want to be doing it but you can never be too careful.

"When did you last see Conrad Fisk?"

"Last Tuesday," she says loud and clear.

Perfect. Conrad was found a couple of days after.

"And how was your meeting?"

"Fine, we arranged to go for drinks on Friday down Randy's..." she pauses and her bottom lip trembles.

"Take your time Sunny."

She nods, knotting her fingers in front of her and I fucking hate this.

"He had a phone call just before we said goodbye. He stepped away and spoke quietly. He didn't seem panicked, more excited maybe. Who knows. Conrad was always a happy go lucky kind of guy."

And I nod, knowing exactly what she meant.

He was a wind up but nice with it, he liked to spark a reaction but more for amusement.

I honestly don't think he had a malicious or vicious bone in his body.

"Do you know who it was?" I press her but she shakes her head.

"Words Sunny," I point to the recorder.

"No, no idea," she speaks loudly, and I smile. "There was someone I saw him with on the Wednesday evening when I locked up though..."

"Yeah?"

"Yeah, looked like an out of towner," and the base of my neck prickles, "but then Marty rolled up not long after. They were all talking, hanging just outside your office."

I swallow down the lump that has formed in my throat.

"I thought it was a bit strange but then again... I didn't think much more of it at the time," and I see the remorse that flashes across her eyes. "I should have told you, I'm sorry..." she trails off and I shake my head.

"Please don't be sorry, why would you think to tell me? Marty is a good friend of the family." I pause, *lie*. "And Conrad is loyal to us isn't he," I try and see if anything changes in her expression but nothing.

"If I can get Conrad's phone from evidence, would you be able to go through his call log and tell me what sort of time the call came in?"

"Of course," she steadies her gaze on me.

"End of interview," I pause for a moment and glance up at the clock, "eight oh five a.m." and I press the stop button.

"Was he in trouble Pacey?" she whispers, and I can see the fear that creeps onto her face.

"I think so," I admit. Whether he was in the midst of planning it or whether he was just on the sidelines, either way, he was caught up in something he shouldn't have been.

I push away from the table, and she follows my lead.

"Thanks for doing that for me Sunny," I stretch my arm out for her to exit the room.

"Not a problem, not sure if I was helpful or not," a nervous laugh bubbles out of her.

"You were helpful," I smile as I close the door to my side room and usher her through my office just as Riggs walks in with Luke.

Sunny freezes and my front hits her back.

Riggs looks between me and Sunny, and I nod to the door that leads to the cell block.

Riggs grunts as he shoves Luke forward and punches the pin into the keypad, the door clicks and they disappear.

"Pacey," she whispers, her voice shaking as she turns to face me.

"Yeah," I look at her, brows furrowed as I hang on her silence for the words to leave her lips.

"That was the out of towner," and a single tear rolls down her cheek.

"Okay," my voice is quiet but inside I am reeling.

Of course it was fucking Luke.

"It's fine, everything is okay," I say softly and try and reassure her before I lead her to the front of the office and walk her back to her cafe.

"I'm scared," she admits, and I can see the way her body is trembling.

"You have nothing to be scared of, I promise. He isn't getting out that cell anytime soon. We are already dealing with Marty... we will figure this out. But if you remember anything, call me. I'll let you know about the phone," I give her a curt nod and wait until she is the other side of the door.

"Shit," I lift my hat and run my hand through my hair as I run back towards my office.

Pushing through the door, Riggs is sitting at my desk, and I am panting.

"What?" he asks, mouthful of food in his mouth.

"Sunny said Conrad and Marty were outside my office Wednesday evening," I puff out my cheeks as I sit on the edge of my desk, looking at my brother. "With an out of towner."

"Right?" his brows furrow.

"The out of towner was Luke."

Riggs' eyes widen and I nod.

"I know," I whisper.

"Fuck."

ONCE RIGGS HAS LEFT, I settle myself down and dial my old mate Tyler in evidence.

He answers in three rings.

"Yo, Pacey," his tone is light as his voice floats down the line.

"Hey Tyler, you okay?" I start the conversation off with a little chatter, didn't want to get straight to the point.

"Yeah, all good my end man, how about you?" Tyler is a couple of years younger than me, always a good kid, good family.

"Yeah, not too bad," I let my tone trail off for a moment.

"What can I do ya for?" he asks, and I hear the sound of his pen tapping on the desk.

"Well, I need a favor... and I know it is a lot to ask but if it wasn't important..."

"Sure thing dude, what do you need?"

"I need Conrad's phone."

The line falls silent for a moment, my heart bangs in my chest.

"Be at the office for five o'clock."

"You got it."

"See ya, Pace!" and before I can respond, he puts the phone down.

I turn my attention to the cell door and fight with my inner thoughts. I shouldn't go down there but at the same time I feel the rage simmering deep inside of me that I'm not sure I can keep contained.

Riggs is meant to be coming back this afternoon and we're going to question him together, but time is ticking and the longer I sit, the more antsy I get.

Agitation nips at the base of my neck and my fingers drum on my desk.

My email pinging has me turning my head as I see a new email sitting there. Scooting over I narrow my gaze and look at the sender's address.

It is random numbers and letters.

It piques my interest but still puts me on edge.

The subject reads:

I THINK YOU SHOULD SEE THIS

"The fuck," I mutter under my breath. I hover the mouse over the email and inhale sharply, dragging the air into my lungs and then I hold it as I open it.

It's a video attachment.

I don't hesitate and click onto it within a split second.

It takes a moment to load and it's grainy as fuck but I think I can make out what it is.

There are four people.

No one is speaking and after a moment or two, the camera focuses, and the image becomes clearer.

"So, we agree, we hit the ranches and once we've run them out, your guys will move in and take the land?"

I know that voice in an instant.

Marty.

Fucking snake.

"Yeah, that's right," now that voice, I have no idea. He is tall, a little rounded and his voice sounds like he is from out of town. A soft orange glow from his fingers and I realise he is smoking.

"I don't think this is a good idea, the Riveras are not going to be run off their ranch." Conrad's voice is the next one I hear and my blood boils.

"Fuck the Riveras," Luke snarls and Marty chuckles.

"They'll kill you," Conrad's voice is hard like stone and a sense of pride blooms in my chest.

"They can give it a go, I've got an army ready to take down the Riveras, don't you worry about that Conrad." The man I don't know says and my fist balls.

"Remember Conrad, I will kill Sunny then pick your family off one by one if you do not get us in there like we asked."

Get them in where?

"We've already done the The Old Dusty Boot, next it's the ranch, then I'll pluck their houses and finish off with the sheriff and then finally, that badge will be mine."

"Fuckers," I growl.

"It was easy enough to wipe Jorge out, he was the glue that held that family together, next will be Orla, then Riggs..."

"Let me put the bullet between his eyes," Luke bounces on the spot and I see Conrad look across to where the video is being recorded, the camera zooms in, and I see Conrad give him a soft nod. If you weren't looking for it, you would have missed it.

"I want out," Conrad says with a trembling voice.

"You want out?" Marty toes him and Luke is behind Marty in seconds.

"Yeah, I won't let you get near Sunny, my family or the Riveras. You want the land? They won't give it to you, so you think it is acceptable to take it from them, murdering them…"

My blood runs cold and that's when I see Marty snap, his fists pummel into Conrad's face and he falls to the ground, shielding his head and face. Bile creeps up my throat, my closed fist in front of my lips as I watch it all unfold.

Luke and Marty beat him with their fists and feet till he barely has a pulse. He doesn't put up a fight, just takes it and my fucking heart breaks. Marty and Luke step back, glancing at each other as Conrad just lays there.

"We stick to the plan, first the ranch, then we will take the rest out one by one…" the stranger says as he walks over to where Conrad is and tosses his cigarette onto him. "Finish him," he orders Luke, giving him a squeeze on the shoulder before he and Marty begin to walk away.

And that's when I watch our friend die.

Another one strikes off the list.

All because they want the land.

What a fucked up and sad existence I have found myself in.

Where greed takes precedence over a life.

I close out of the email and reach for the trash can next to my desk and before I can try and stop it, I throw the contents of my stomach up.

Once I have calmed myself down, my trembling hand reaches for my phone and I dial Riggs' number.

"Yeah," he sighs down the phone.

"I need you at the office, just been sent something," I swallow down the thickness that coats my throat as I cut the phone off and toss it to the side.

Riggs is storming through the door ten minutes later.

All it took was one look and he knew just how bad this must be.

"Show me," he walks around the back of my desk, placing his hand on the surface and leans down so his eyes are level with the screen.

I inhale heavily and my shaky hands move the cursor back over the video link but this time, I don't look. I can't go through that again.

"Well fuck..." Riggs stands slowly and casts his eyes to the floor and I know he has seen my sick filled trash can. His eyes burn into the side of my head. "You good?" and I nod, closing my eyes for a second.

"It was just a lot," I admit, and I feel Riggs' hand on my shoulder as he gives it a gentle squeeze.

"I know," Riggs' voice is low and I find myself looking up to my big brother for just a moment. "We've got that asshole now though," he turns to look at the cell. "Weasel," he hisses, and I scoff a laugh.

"Weasel?"

"First thing I could think of," he smirks, looking down at me.

I sigh.

"Shall we?" I glance over at the door that leads you to where Luke is.

"Yes," Riggs gives me one last squeeze on my shoulder before he steps back and waits for me to join him.

"No point in questioning him now, right?" I ask and I see the wicked glint in his eye.

"Nope, get that video over to the judge, we need to move in before they do. Only problem is we have no idea when they're planning to storm the ranch."

I sigh.

"It won't be long, I need to get the suits business card from Buck, give those cunts a call," I shake my head.

"One step at a time baby bro, come," he nods as he pushes the code into the lock and the door clicks. "And honestly," he says with a heavy sigh, "I think the call will be pointless."

I know he is right, my chest heavy.

I follow him down to the cell and see Luke sitting there looking a little worse for wear, half asleep, head hanging.

"Wakey wakey," Riggs' loud, deep voice booms around the cell block, echoing from the walls and his hands bang against the window which causes Luke to jump, eyes bloodshot and wide.

"Fuck you," Luke growls, pushing to his feet and walking up towards the window.

"The gigs up my friend," I say with venom lacing my tone, my upper lip curling.

"How's that?" Luke's eyes bounce between mine and Riggs.

"We know *everything*."

He blinks a couple of times and then laughs.

"Bullshit."

"That's the difference with our small town and where you have lived in la la land," Riggs licks his lip, fisting his hands into his pockets. "We're respected around here, people know who we are, people know how our family have been wronged..." he pauses and scoffs a laugh, "but you? No one knows who you are here, no one respects you and they certainly didn't from what I hear from people back in LA." Luke's smile slips for just a second. "That's the problem Luke, you wanted to be somebody, wanted to make a name for yourself..." Riggs swings his head slowly to look at me.

"And the only name you're going to make for yourself is

the one that will be ringing around our town..." I inhale heavily as his eyes lock on mine.

"Oh yeah, and what's that?" Cockiness coats his tone and I am so desperate to punch him.

"Murderer."

Luke's face pales and I watch the way his throat bobs.

"The video has been sent to the judge, you won't be leaving here anytime soon so I would get comfortable if I was you."

Riggs salutes him off his temple as we begin to walk away.

"Hey, wait! Riggs, please..." and Riggs steps falter and I raise my brow. He whistles through his teeth and then walks back towards Luke.

"What?" his tone is curt.

"They're coming for you all... I never wanted to get involved in this but I did because I was desperate for something other than what I had... but don't let them win..."

Riggs looks at me as I begin to walk down to stand by his side.

"When are they coming?"

Luke is hesitant for a moment, his eyes trailing between me and Riggs.

"Sunday, dusk."

Riggs gives a heavy nod and begins to march away and I know I didn't have to, but I tilt my head and thank Luke.

He didn't have to say anything.

But he did.

And he'll never know how much he has just helped us.

CHAPTER TWENTY-FIVE
MORGAN

The evening draws in and I have laid the table but Pacey isn't home. Fear pricks at my skin but I try and push the invasive thoughts down.

I know he is okay, I also know he is really busy and what with Conrad winding up dead, well, his work load is even more strenuous than it was before.

Walking into the kitchen, I duck my head down and look down the driveway. It's just past six and he is normally home a lot earlier than this.

My heart rumbles in my chest and I know I need to call Orla.

Moving towards the phone, I dial her number and wait for her to answer.

"Rivera Ranch 895."

"Orla, it's Morgan."

"Hey darling, all okay?"

"Yeah, I think so, just confirming lunch Saturday? I am so sorry I had to cancel last week," I pause for a moment and relive the way I spent my weekend, tangled in the sheets with her son.

"Oh, please don't be sorry, it's fine, these things happen but yes, we're all looking forward to Saturday," and I smile.

"Good, okay," I twirl my finger in the cord of the phone, "erm, also, have you heard from Pacey?" and that's when I hear the sound of tires crunching across the dirt and gravel outside the front of our house. "Oh, he is here. He has just pulled up," I smile down the phone before we say our goodbyes.

I place the phone back in its cradle and the front door opens and closes. I move towards him as he paces towards me and his arms are around me, holding me tight as he lifts me, my legs wrapping around his waist.

"Are you okay?" I whisper as he buries his face between my neck and shoulder.

"I am now," he admits, his breath warm on my skin.

Silence coats both of us for a while and just as I go to speak he looks at me, his eyes bloodshot and watery and my heart drops.

"Not tonight, I just need you. To be wrapped in your arms, to love you all night long. I need out of my head baby and you're the only one that can help me."

My eyes volley between his.

"I just want you, Morgan."

I nod, scooping his heavy head in my hands as I flutter kisses across his eyes, his temples, his nose, his cheeks, his jaw and finally I am on his lips.

Slow and torturous but in the best way.

Every emotion that tenses his body slowly slips away as our kiss deepens, our tongues dancing to a song that only we can hear.

"I love you," he whispers against my lips and a wetness dampens our kiss.

Letting my eyes open, I notice a streak of a tear that stains his cheek and my heart throbs in my chest.

He walks me up the stairs slowly, his grip tightening around my body, my legs still looped around his waist, our lips are locked once more as he continues forward to his bedroom and drops me to the bed.

We break away for just a moment, my eyes wide and hazy as I focus on him.

He looks broken and I wish I knew what was wrong.

I know he will tell me, but right now I need to give him what he needs, and that's me.

Grabbing the hem of his tee, he tugs it over his head and discards it to the floor. His knee presses into the mattress between my legs, his hands either side of my head and I find myself holding my breath.

"I love you Morgan," his voice cracks as he lowers his lips to mine.

I want to scream it back, scream it from the rooftops that I love him too but now is not the moment.

My hands stretch around his toned back as I gently tease my fingers up and down his skin, our kiss deepening and I hear the soft rumble of a moan in his throat.

Pushing to his feet, he unbuckles his jeans and pushes them down in one swift move along with his boxers and normally I would admire him for a moment or two but I don't get a chance to.

His fingers curl around my pants as he drags them down and tosses them behind him. Sitting up I lift my tee over my head and his needy hands skim around my back as he unhooks my bra and lets it fall from my body.

"You're so beautiful," he rasps before he is back over me, our bodies as one as he slips between my legs.

His large hand reaches underneath me as he spreads my

thigh a little wider, rolling his hips forward as his cock slides deep inside of me and I gasp for air, my lungs burning as he begins to move, each thrust slow and hard.

Fingers brush my hair from my face, his hazel eyes piercing into mine as he loves me how he needs.

"I don't deserve you," he chokes, his lips pressing to my forehead.

"You are the most deserving man I know Pacey Rivera," I whisper as his lips dust across my temple before they brush over my lips, and this is how we spend the remainder of the night.

Him loving me, him fucking away whatever is causing him anguish, him filling me with all of him.

He needed me and I didn't realize just how much I needed him right back.

***

MY LIPS CURL when I see him push through the door with two cups of tea. It's past two in the morning and we should be sleeping, but instead we are sitting in bed, it's a wonderful life playing on mute in the background and snacks layered between us.

"Thank you," I say as he passes me my mug and I bring it closer so I can inhale the warm liquid.

Turning to watch Pacey as he climbs back into bed and tugs the covers up his chest, his back towards the headboard as his mug buries into the duvet on his lap.

"I love you," my lips pull into a bigger smile and his eyes glisten but his brows furrow. "What?" Panic hits me in the chest, my eyes volleying between his.

"I will never tire of hearing those three words, those eight letters, fall from your lips," and all panic that once set up camp in my chest slowly packs itself up and buries itself back into the deepest crevices.

A pink, crimson slips against my cheeks, a soft laugh bubbling out for me as I drop my eyes to my lap, focusing on my tea.

"Are you okay?" my hand slips from my side and moves over to him as I scoop his hand in mine.

"I am," he gives a soft nod, but he doesn't fill me with confidence.

"What happened today?" I push for a little more and I have no idea how he will react, my heart pounds in my chest, my palms feeling a little clammy.

"I want to tell you…" he drags my hand to his lips and dusts a kiss across the back of it, "but not now… I just need to forget about everything that happened."

"And I respect your choice," I lean back into the headboard and let my eyes linger for a second more before I drag them away and settle them on the television and this is how we spend the next few hours before exhaustion takes us both into a deep slumber.

The vibration of a phone pulls me from a dreamless sleep and slowly I turn to where Pacey should be.

My eyes shoot open as I sit up, panic entwining through my blood but that's when I see him, standing by the window with his phone next to his ear.

The choppy waves settle to a calmness, and I hate that I feel like I am on edge and the worst bit is I have no reason to be.

"Okay, I'll be in soon," he says quietly before cutting the call.

I watch as his shoulders lift and drop with a heavy sigh before his eyes trail over his shoulder and lock with mine.

Lips curling into a slow smirk as he turns his body and steps towards the bed.

"Morning wife," he crawls onto the bed and lays his body over mine, his head on my stomach, arms either side of me.

"Morning handsome," my voice is soft as my fingers brush through his hair, trailing back and forth and twisting the odd lock around them.

"Sleep okay?" he asks, not lifting his head from my chest.

"I did, did you?"

I drag my fingers up and down over his scalp and I hear a deep breath leave him.

"Mmhm," he manages.

"Good."

Silence creeps around the room but it's peaceful.

Soft snores soon replace that silence, and I glance down at the man who is laying on me and a warmth radiates through my whole body.

I should wake him, but I make a promise to myself to let him have ten minutes more and then I'll wake him, but right now, I am enjoying this too much and I wanted to be a little selfish, soaking this all up.

BOTH DRESSED, he walks towards me and snakes his arm around my waist as he drags me towards him, a boyish grin on his face as he kisses me goodbye.

"Have a good day," his voice rumbles against my lips.

"I'll try," I smirk and place my hand on his chest. "Have a good day too," I kiss him back.

"I'll try," he nods, stepping back and taking the lunch I

packed him. He told me he had a lot to go through today and wouldn't be home until supper.

"I'll see you soon then," I follow him to the front door as he pulls it open and steps onto the porch.

"I'll see you soon then," he tilts his hat down and my heart somersaults in my chest.

With one last smile and a flirty wink, he turns his back on me and I watch until his truck is driving out of the ranch and I instantly miss him.

Sighing heavily, I let my eyes fall to the floor as I begin to push the door shut but the sound of boots hitting the wooden porch floor has me snapping my head up.

"Morning," Dusty smiles as he walks, with two empty mugs in my direction.

"Morning," I smile, taking a step back as he walks in and lifts his hat from his head and dropping it onto the hook beside the door.

I follow him into the kitchen as he places them in the sink.

"All okay?" I ask, leaning up against the archway that leads from the hallway and into the kitchen.

"Yeah," he washes his dirty hands and shakes them off before running them down the front of his jeans to dry them.

"I am sorry I've not been much help," I admit and dart my eyes away from him as guilt riddles me.

"It's fine Morgan," and the heavy sigh that leaves those three words has me knowing that it isn't fine. "But if you're going to pull back, we either need to get another hand in or sell half the cattle."

I don't respond, just nod and swallow the burning lump that has lodged itself in my throat.

I know what he is saying is the truth, but I don't want to.

"I'll be down the back field when you're ready to join me," and I take the dig as he intended it.

Dusty isn't a malicious man.

But he can be bitter.

And right now, he is very fucking bitter.

I nod again as I follow him out to the door and see him out.

He doesn't say goodbye and neither do I.

Instead, I slam the door as my temper simmers deep in my core and once I know he is far enough away, I drag myself into the living room, fall into my pops' chair and curl up into a ball, my arms wrapped around my knees before I let the tears fall.

I knew I needed to make a choice.

The ranch is haemorrhaging money, and I don't have much more to give.

We promised we would keep the ranch, keep his legacy... I never promised to be a cowgirl for the rest of my life.

And for the first time since my pops passed, I had no idea what to do.

CHAPTER TWENTY-SIX
PACEY

Riggs is already waiting at my office and nerves ripple through me.

"Morning," I chirp, and Riggs' raises a thick brow before glancing at the clock on the wall.

"This is not morning," he grumbles and rolls his eyes. He is sitting at my desk, his hands in his lap, fingers locked together.

I follow his gaze and look at the time. It's ten thirty.

I shake my head.

"I didn't sleep well last night," I kind of lie, but kind of not a lie either.

It took me ages to fall asleep last night and even though I had Morgan curled under my arm, her head on my chest, my fingers trailing down her spine, I just couldn't get Conrad out of my mind. I just couldn't get what those assholes did to him.

I kept thinking of how scared he must have been, how alone and betrayed he felt.

My stomach twists and Riggs clocks my expression.

"You good?" and I nod, swallowing the bile that is threatening to pass my lips.

Swiping the coffee from the desk, I bring it to my lips and try and wash away the nerves when in truth, the coffee will only make it worse.

"Pace," Riggs pushes from the chair and steps towards me. He doesn't have to say another word, just pulls me into him and holds me tightly and I didn't know how much I needed that from him. With everything going on, he has been there every step of the way and by my side.

Tripp's voice breaks through the moment as he clears his throat.

"Am I interrupting?" I hear the humor that laces his voice.

Sniffling, I step back from Riggs and see the concern on his face when he looks at me.

"I just had a moment," I admit, shrugging a shoulder up.

"We all have them brother," Riggs says as his hand presses against my back and Tripp nods, moving closer.

"Right," he claps his hands together as I sit at my desk, Riggs and Tripp next to me. "What time do you have to take Luke to the courthouse?" and I sigh.

"He forgot," Tripp chuckles and I roll my eyes.

"I didn't forget," I lied.

I did forget.

Scrubbing my face and try to rack my brain.

"Four," I mutter.

"Is he going in front of the judge then?" Tripp asks and I shake my head.

"Nope, he will be detained until Friday and then he will face him in the afternoon."

Tripp nods.

"He won't get off, we have the evidence. We just need to get Marty too because let's be honest, he wasn't innocent in it." I look at Riggs and I watch as his jaw clenches.

"I still cannot believe that fucking snake," he growls and his fists ball.

"I know but we will deal with it."

"He has been by my side for years and as soon as I push him away into something he has always aspired to become he shafts me."

"No one has been shafted, we will get to him before Sunday."

Riggs' nostrils flare and I know this is winding him up the longer it goes on.

"Have you seen the video?" I ask Tripp and he tells me no. "Want to see it? I think you should... and I know that sounds wrong, but it would be ideal for you to see what actually happened."

"Shall I call Austin?" Riggs pipes up and that's not a bad shout. He needs to be kept in the loop with what his boss is up to. Austin is always on our side, there is no doubt about that. His loyalties will always lay with us.

"Yeah," I nod as I find the email and wait for Riggs.

"Aust," his voice is low, "I need you down to Pacey's office."

He goes quiet for a moment and I look at Tripp.

"Now," Riggs nods. "Okay cool, I'll see you in five," his voice is tight as he cuts the phone and slides it into his back pocket.

"He's coming."

"Figured," Tripp smirks and Riggs punches him in the top of the arm. "Dickhead," Tripp growls and punches him back and Riggs chuckles and I face palm myself.

"You seem uptight Pace," Riggs points out the fucking

obvious which has me turning in my chair and looking up at him.

"The fuck?" My brows knit, "why would I not be uptight? We've had someone else murdered; we have assholes gearing up to attack our homes and a fucking mole who has been working against us the whole time?!" My voice heightens, "So yeah, *brother* I would say I am a little uptight."

Riggs smiles down at me then a deep laugh escapes him.

"You're so easy to wind up," he mutters and squeezes my neck.

"It's a lot," I admit, turning around and stare at my computer screen.

"It is," Tripp admits on a sigh.

"But we will figure it out, we always do. It's not going to be easy, but we will do it," he nods, both of his arms stretching as one hand is on Tripp's shoulder, the other is on mine.

"Live by the ranch..." his voice a rumble.

"Die by the ranch," Tripp and I say in unison just as Austin walks through the door then glances over his shoulder.

"Sup?" he asks, and Tripp moves towards him, looking out the glass windows then locking the door behind him. "What's going on?" panic laces his voice and Tripp ushers him behind my desk and it's getting a little bit crowded. I shuffle in slightly and closer to my computer.

"Watch," Riggs growls and I drag a deep breath into my lungs, puffing my cheeks out as I press play and I can't watch again so I turn my head to the side but it doesn't help because I can visualise every single aspect of that video.

Just another thing to haunt me.

"What. The. Fuck," Austin's voice is loud and Riggs hums in agreement.

"Wait," Tripp says, leaning down and reaching for my mouse.

"What?" I look at him then back to the screen as he drags the video back.

"Him, I recognise him, and I don't know why," he admits and I pause it on the frame and try and zoom in and that's when I see it, ever so slightly.

"Aubergine boots?" I mutter and sit back, eyes wide and mouth a little laxed.

"From Randy's?" Riggs looks between me and Tripp.

"Yeah, he was talking to the girls, but he was hidden under his hat, couldn't see much of his face," I run my fingers over my moustache and Tripp shakes his head.

"I don't think that's why I recognise him," he stands up and then pulls his phone out before it's to his ear.

"Dreamcatcher," his voice is soft as he talks to Dixie, "can you come to Pacey's office, I just want you to confirm something."

We all wait with bated breath.

"Okay baby, we will see you soon. Love you more," he whispers then ends the call, slipping it in his pocket.

We all stare at him, waiting for him to explain.

"Just wait for Dixie."

Austin rolls his eyes.

"Marty is outside, what the fuck am I gonna do? I have to work with him," and I can hear the panic in his voice.

"Aust," Riggs places both hands on his shoulders and walks him backwards to the open lobby part of my office, his eyes levelling with Austin's. "We're dealing with it, trust me. Nothing is going to change. You're going to still work with Marty and I promise we will have eyes on you at all times. His war isn't with you, it's with us for whatever reason..." and I watch as Riggs drops his head, and I know he is struggling with this more than he lets on. Marty was a friend, is, I don't even know anymore. It's a blow for all of us but a lot more for Riggs.

Austin nods, dropping his head for a moment before Riggs places a hand on his cheek, lifting his eyes up to settle on his.

"I need you to trust me, have I ever given you a reason to doubt me before?" and I don't think I have seen this side of Riggs in a long time. He is fiercely loyal and protective over his family, especially when someone is threatening to rip us apart, leaving no trace of us ever walking this land.

Austin's head softly swings side to side.

"Then remember that. I need you to go out there and act normal, anything that passes his lips that you feel he is dropping in to test you, you let us know, do you understand?"

"Yes."

"Good boy," Riggs then pulls Austin into him and pats him on the back.

My eyes fall to my drawer, and I slip it open before I reach for the evidence bag Tyler gave me.

I haven't wanted to look through it because I don't think I need to, but maybe once I know things are settled, then I will go through it.

Nothing is going to change.

Luke and Marty killed Conrad.

We have the confession.

We also have the reason Conrad was wrapped up with them.

I am sure there is more to it, but I wasn't ready to dive into that.

Placing it back in the drawer and closing it, I spot Dixie standing on the other side of the door.

Tripp is already moving towards her, unlocking the door then dragging her in before he gives a look up both ends of the town. He closes the door and locks it back, his fingers lacing through hers as he pulls her softly towards my computer.

"What is going on?" her voice is panicked, one hand tucked under her bump.

"Nothing darlin'," Tripp says casually. "I just need your pretty eyes to tell me if I am seeing things…" he trails off as he tucks her behind my chair. I offer to stand but she shakes her head. I focus on Tripp, his hand skimming around her waist and resting on her neat bump and for a moment I find myself imagining that it was me and Morgan. Imagining a life where we have a sunshine blond boy running through the fields, giggling as we follow, chasing him down to the creek. But that's all it would be. My imagination. Morgan has made it clear that she doesn't want kids and I have made peace with that… I think.

"Oh my god," her eyes widen, her trembling hand lifting to her mouth.

"I'm right yeah?" Tripp looks at her side profile and her eyes fill with tears before she nods.

"What?" Riggs is now standing next to my desk, Austin mute.

"That's the guy with the aubergine cowboy boots from Randy's," Tripp confirms.

"Okay…" I trail off, confusion masking my face as I look between my brothers.

"That's my dad." Dixie drops the fucking bomb.

CHAPTER TWENTY-SEVEN
MORGAN

Cantering down the field, I stall at the gate and catch my breath. Dusty finished just after one so I have had the last few hours by myself, but I think I needed it. As much as I was busy, it gave me time to think about what I could do with the ranch. I needed to speak it out with Pacey, because it's not just my decision anymore. I had no idea if it was just going to be one money pit feeding into another, but I wanted to talk it out, float the idea and see what he thought.

This was a big old place to run, we needed money in, but being a cowgirl and raising cattle when you're going against the Riveras is not a money spinner.

Letting myself out the gate, I push it two and head for the stables. Dismounting off her back, I walk into the stalls and untack her before leading her back and hosing her down. She was sweaty and so was I.

Once she is cleaned, I throw her rug on her and turn her out into the paddock along with Pacey's horse, Chase. They frolic in the meadow, and I lean over the paddock gate as I watch them, my heart soars.

This is my happy place.

Here on my ranch, watching the horses, the livestock, nature... everything about this has always felt like home.

The sound of Pacey's truck approaching has my hand pressing over my eyes, blocking out the low afternoon sun and my brows furrow.

He jumps out the truck with a *baby I am here* look on his face, a smile that only widens as he steps closer to me.

"Welcome home sheriff," I mumble as he wraps his arm around me and pulls me close to him, his lips hovering over mine.

"Good to be home cowgirl," raspiness coats his tone.

"Wasn't expecting you just yet," I smirk, "I was just about to get showered because I am a sweaty mess," and he steps back, a look of confusion on his face, his eyes bounce over me, checking me out.

"You? A mess... never," he darts forward and places a kiss on my neck, teasing over my pulse point.

A giggle bubbles from me as I tilt my head back and let his lips trail across my throat.

"But, I do agree you're sweaty and you do need a shower," his voice vibrates against my skin, my breaths trembling and I smile.

"Is that so?" I lift my head up so my eyes are level with his and he nods. "Then we better go shower then," I tease, locking my fingers through his and lead him into the house and closing the door behind us.

Fumbling to get my boots off, he is already unbuttoning his jeans and kicking his boots off. I begin to climb the stairs but he catches me up, his arms circling my waist and I squeal as he carries me up the stairs and into the bathroom. He doesn't even shut the door, just places me down and turns on the shower. The loud banging of the pipes kicks in and while we wait for the water to heat, he is in front of me, undressing me with want.

My fingers tease under his tee as I run them across his muscly stomach before he is lifting his own tee over his head and kicking his jeans off.

His large hand cups my face as he tilts my lips up to his, slanting them across and I could kiss him forever. My feet are off the floor, my legs circling his waist as he walks us into the shower, the warm water cascading down over us as his lips dust down my neck, licking and sucking as he makes his way to my breasts, large hands kneading and squeezing, his hips pushed against me as he holds me in place.

"Pacey," I pant just as his hand slips between my legs, fingers rubbing my clit.

"Yes wife."

"I need you," my voice trembles, two fingers slipping into my soaked pussy.

"I know," his voice is tight, his lips back on my neck as he traces my pulse point with kisses, his fingers buried inside of me as he coaxes my orgasm, bringing me to the brink before pushing me straight back down into the depths, craving it.

"Please," I moan, my pussy grinding over his fingers so his palm rubs against my clit.

"You look pretty when you beg, wife," his voice trails off and my mouth pops open as he covers my nipple with his hot mouth and all my senses tingle as he submerges me in pleasure.

Fingers pull from me and his cock slides into my pussy, filling me slowly and my eyes roll in the back of my head. His teeth sink into his bottom lip, both hands cupped around my waist as he holds me in place, his hips pulling back and slamming forward.

"I will never get over how you feel, fucking you raw..." his head tips back as he pulls to the tip, edging me, pulsing the head of his cock at my opening and my stomach tightens, my skin burns and my pussy pulses, sucking him deeper but he shakes his head.

"I like teasing you," he admits and my eyes fall between our bodies and my moans fill the room.

"I can't hold off," I admit, my voice trembling, my teeth sinking into my bottom lip.

"Then let it all go baby," his eyes connect with mine as he slowly fills me, my mouth opening, eyes widening and it feels euphoric, my skin tingling and I know the burning swirl that is intensifying inside, my pussy aching and I know this orgasm is going to wreck me. Harder and faster with each roll of his hips, my arms hang around his neck, my back arching away and every ounce of emotion is being poured into this, poured into him fucking me until I am a trembling mess beneath him.

"Come for me wife."

His fingers graze over my hips, over my pelvis, my pubic bone and land on my clit as he rubs and I explode, my pussy tightening as my orgasm steams through me, knocking the air from my lungs as my moans fill the room.

"That's a good girl, fuck you're so sexy," he growls, his cock slipping in and out with ease as he fucks me until he is spilling into me, filling me.

We spend the next twenty minutes washing each other with the luffa, sudding up our skin as we clean every inch.

Wrapped up in a huge towel, we walk to my bedroom giggling, his lips pressing between my shoulder and neck.

"I'm glad you came home early," I hum as I lower myself to the bed.

"Me too," he smiles as he lays down next to me.

I turn slightly, looking down at him.

"We need to really start choosing a room to stay in..."

"Yeah?" he raises his brow, arm tucked behind his head.

"Yeah, we don't both need one..." I trail off and shuffle onto my knees then climb over his lap.

"Are you sure?" his eyes fall to where I am sitting before they're on me.

"Yes," I whisper, undoing my towel and letting it fall from my body.

"Fuuuuck," he drawls out as I push up, and wrap my hands around his cock and tease it at my opening. "You're a bad girl," he whispers as I slowly roll down the length of his thick cock and his eyes roll in the back of his head, his moans are erotic and I love that it is me making him feel like that.

"You make me bad, *Sheriff.*" I whisper as my hips begin to move and I lean down over him, my golden hair falling around our faces and I tease my lips over his, watching as he pants, his large hands skimming down my sides as his fingers dig into my ass cheeks, lifting me up and down over his cock.

"Fuck," he groans, trying to kiss me but I pull back every time his lips get close, my hips rolling over his cock. "I am going to fuck you so hard if you keep teasing me..." He trails off as a moan slips past my lips.

"Don't threaten me with a good time," my eyes flick up to his and that turns him feral. A hand lifts from my skin and cups the back of my head as he pulls my lips to his and his other hand is gripped firmly around my hip as his legs bend and I feel his thighs on my ass.

"I am going to ruin you," he whispers against my mouth as he tugs on my bottom lip with his teeth before his tongue swipes past them and I whimper a moan, his cock spearing in and out of my pussy and I couldn't even hold it back if I wanted to.

My body trembles under his touch, convulsing forward, pussy tightening as my second orgasm floors me and he follows, filling me again. Panting and sweaty again, I lay over his body and he wraps his arms over my back, his spare hand hovers as his fingers tease up and down my spine, shivers breaking against my skin.

"I love you, Pacey Rivera."

"Not as much as I love you, Sunflower."

I lift my head from his chest and furrow my brows.

"Not possible," I hum and try to turn away but he grips my chin and holds me so I have no other option but to stare at him.

"Possible," he growls and I smirk, "you're my wildest forever, my wildest dreams, my wildest love…"

My eyes soften as they bounce between his.

"You're it for me Sunflower, everything I never knew I wanted ended up being you. You fixed me, pieced the missing jigsaw puzzle back into place when I hadn't even noticed it was missing. You did that baby, *you*."

I blink back fresh tears, but I fail to hold them as they trickle over my tear line.

"I love you Morgan Rivera, if you asked me to lasso the moon and hook the stars, I would. I would do anything for you. Because this heart," he pauses and reaches for my hand, placing it over his chest so I can feel the way it beats under his skin, "has never beat the way it beats for you Sunflower… I will give you every inch of me, every piece of my soul, my mind, my body… all of me. I'm yours."

His thumb catches my tear, and I tremble against him.

"Forever Sunflower, it's me and you."

"Me and you," I repeat.

"Always."

"Forever," I whisper before he pulls my lips to his.

PACEY

ONE DAY UNTIL WAR.

I lean in the doorway as I watch Morgan potter around as she tries to get everything together for our supper. My family are over this evening and honestly, we could do without it but we, as in me, Tripp and Riggs agreed that we wouldn't tell the girls until we needed to, and we also agreed that we would give them this night.

We had the plan mapped out, but it didn't matter how much we went over it again and again, it still didn't feel like it was right.

Tilting my head to the side, my lips lift into a smirk as she lowers herself down, her top half leant over. My eyes scope the round of her ass in those light colored jeans and my dick throbs in my pants.

Gliding my feet across the floor, I stand behind her and curl my hand around her hip as she straightens herself up, her gaze catching mine across her shoulder.

"Do you need any help?" I whisper against her cheeks and I watch as her face lights up, her beautiful smile pulling me in.

"No thank you, but you can go get cleaned up for me,"

she pecks a kiss on my lips and shimmies herself from my grasp and I groan.

"Fine," I sulk off in a playful manner and climb the stairs.

Once showered, I am dressed in a loose tee and jeans. Roughing my hair up with product, I make my way downstairs, and the smell of the food warms my soul and makes my belly grumble.

"Done," I chime, and she spins on her heel and gives me the once over before her hips sashay my way, her small hand resting on my cheek as she leans in and kisses me.

"You look handsome," her nose scrunches and my cheeks blush. Not sure why, but there is something so hot when your wife calls you handsome. Gets me all giddy, heart races beneath my skin and goosebumps tease at the base of my neck causing the hairs to stand.

"How long until the Rivera gang are here?" I ask, my voice floating over to her.

"About twenty minutes," she shrugs a shoulder up as she begins clearing bits away.

"That'll be more like ten... us Riveras are always early," I wink and I watch as her eyes widen and the panic sets in.

"What!?" she shrieks as she looks around at the mess and I can see she is getting more and more overwhelmed as the seconds pass.

"Hey, hey," I mutter, closing the gap between us in five steps and cupping her cheek in my hand. "We've got this, tell me what to do and I'll do it."

She nods, but her eyes dart around the room.

"I'll tidy, you set the table," I whisper as I seal my words with a kiss before she can argue back. Spinning her away, I make quick work of clearing the countertops and wiping them down. I unload and load the dishwasher whilst she potters behind me, us moving in a dance that only we know, carefully moving around each other.

She disappears into the dining room and I know this is a big deal to her. She loves to cook, but she loves even more to cook for people.

The sound of a soft knock on our front door has my head spinning and her slender frame leaning around the doorframe.

"I'll get it," I tell her and move towards the door. Letting my fingers curl around the handle, I push it down before pulling the door to see my mom, Aspen, Riggs, Dixie, Lainey and Tripp.

"Hey ma," I say softly, she smiles and steps towards me and I place a kiss on her cheek. She is already searching for Morgan so I nod towards the kitchen. Aspen and Dixie walk past me, Lainey on Dixie's hip, her legs resting over her bump and she gives me a smile, Lainey gurgling as her little hands grab out. Tripp walks through next and gives me a shallow nod and closes the gap between himself and Dixie as he sweeps Lainey into his arms and she giggles as he blows a raspberry on her cheek.

Riggs is next over the threshold, and he places his hand on my chest, resting it where my tattoo is inked into my skin and after a moment, he pats it softly.

Closing the door behind him, I inhale heavily as we walk side by side and into the small kitchen.

"It's looking better in here," he admits as he looks around the newly decorated kitchen. The walls are a warm cream and new hardwood floor has been laid that runs through to the living room. We wrapped the cabinets in a sage green and up cycled some gold handles and you don't realise how much it makes the room. The counter is still the same, but it looks newer since the makeover.

"It is, isn't it?" and pride blooms in my chest. It's not much, but we're making the empty shell into a home. The small ranch house fell into disrepair when Gerry fell ill, and well, it never got any love or care. But now, now we had the time to give the home the love it deserved.

Dixie passes us and walks into the living room, and I glance over my shoulder as she places Lainey on the floor then unpacks her bag of toys.

Dixie sits in Gerry's chair and my heart aches.

I can hear mom talking to Morgan and my heart swells in my chest. She deserves to have a family like this. Her pops did everything for her, brought her up from a baby and turned her into the woman she is today. Fierce, strong, bold, beautiful, kind, empathetic... the list is endless.

Riggs walks past me and heads for Tripp and Aspen is carrying the plates through to the dining room.

"The house smells amazing Morgs," Aspen says before she tucks herself around the doorframe of the dining room and I hear her thank Aspen.

I turn and walk to Dixie, she watches her daughter with intent but her mind is elsewhere.

"You okay?" I ask, one hand fisting into my pocket. I know yesterday must have been a lot, finding out your dad has killed someone who was close to her husband and his family, but also, that he has been here, right under her nose and he hasn't even tried to reach out to her.

Madness.

She slowly tears her eyes away from Lainey and looks up towards me. She is hesitant for a moment before she nods.

"I know we're not overly close..." I trail off and a bubble of a laugh escapes from deep inside of her. "But I am always here for you."

Her head rolls forward, her brown wavy hair framing her face and my eyes move to her daughter who is babbling, a toy in her hand as she waves it up and down.

A sad smile crosses my lips as I look at her.

"We will fix this Dixie, you know that right," I crouch down in front of her and she looks at me and I don't miss the tear that glistens down her cheek.

"I know," she sniffles, "it was just a shock you know..." she nods then looks over her shoulder at her daughter.

"I know," I nod back at her.

Footsteps sound behind me and I push to my feet when I see Tripp in the doorway.

"Dix," I can hear the concern in his voice as he rushes over to her and falls to his knees as he scoops her face into his hands.

"I'm fine," she reassures my brother. Pushing to my feet, I take that as my cue to leave.

Rounding the kitchen doorway, I tuck myself into the kitchen and watch as everyone helps Morgan place the food on the table, well apart from Riggs. He just stands, his back against the countertop, eyes faced forward and his mind is a million miles away from here.

I walk past him and grab some glasses and place them on the coasters.

Morgan looks at me and gives me a soft smile and I know she is in her element.

For someone who never had a family, she sure is a family girl.

She calls for everyone to take their seats and Dixie, Tripp and Lainey join us. Tripp holds onto Lainey's booster seat and hooks it around the chair seat. Dixie places her in her booster and she kicks her legs with excitement.

"Someone's hungry, huh," my lips tug at the corner and Dixie gives me a warm smile.

"Loves her food," she lowers her lips to Lainey's head and dusts a kiss over her dark hair before her hand strokes across and twirls in her little curly lock at the nape of her neck.

I feel Morgan's eyes on me and I snap out of my gooey state and roll my shoulders back. Letting my eyes dust across the table, I furrow my brows at the missing wine.

"No wine?" I ask, eyes bouncing towards my wife.

"Oh, I forgot to grab it. Bottom cupboard..." she trails off and I am already walking towards the kitchen and lowering myself to grab one bottle of white and one bottle of red.

Walking back into the room, I pause for a moment and look across the table.

Everyone I care most about in this world is here, sitting with us.

Aspen is talking softly to Riggs, his lips locked into a smile, eyes glued to her as he admires every inch of her face. Dixie and Tripp are sitting either side of Lainey, their arms hooked behind her chair and their fingers intwined, loose smiles on their faces as Dixie talks softly, her hand rubbing over her bump. Mom is talking to Morgan but her gaze catches mine. I give her a soft nod before walking forward and placing the bottles of wine in the center.

"Who would like a glass?" I ask and the quiet chatter simmers down to silence.

Everyone raises their glasses, all but Dixie, and I fill glasses. Some with red, some with white.

Morgan has cooked up a whole roast chicken, creamed potatoes, vegetables, a red wine jus and bread rolls.

My stomach rumbles and I cannot wait to dive in.

"Who would like to say grace?" Morgan says sweetly, her eyes dancing around the room. Orla stares at Riggs and I know she is silently asking him to volunteer.

I clear my throat, ready to speak but Riggs raises his hand slightly.

"I'll do it," he shuffles in his seat and Aspen gives him a tight smile. He bows his head and everyone follows suit. I sneak a look, and his eyes are drifting between mine and Tripp. We're the only ones who don't have our eyes closed and we both wait until Riggs closes his eyes before we close ours.

"We're thankful for the food laid on the table, thankful that Morgan has spent the afternoon in the kitchen cooking and preparing to entertain us..." he trails off for a moment and I flutter my lashes open and see him shuffling in his seat.

"Lord, please protect my family, please keep us wrapped in your arms as we navigate through the next few days..." and my heart jack hammers in my chest, "please bless us as we prepare to fight one of the hardest wars of our life, to protect my family, to protect our land, to protect our legacy."

I side eye Tripp and he gives me an awkward shrug.

"I know I am asking a lot of you, and I know I am a man who doesn't pray and ask for your guidance, but I know you would never turn me away when I asked upon you." His voice trembles for just a moment but he styles it out with a light cough.

"Amen," and when his eyes open, everyone is looking at him.

"Riggs?" ma says, worry etched into her face and I inhale sharply, sitting tall in my chair as Morgan's eyes cast to mine.

"We're going to war ma," he says softly, and I watch as the girls faces turn to their partners, but not mom's. Her eyes are firmly on the oldest son.

She drops her head and begins to pray.

Morgan slips her hand across the table, and I dip my fingers between her thumb and index and give it a tight squeeze.

"I promise," I lean across and lower my gaze to hers, "we will end this war, once and for all."

CHAPTER TWENTY-EIGHT
MORGAN

We fall into light chatter and the tension is thick. I trust Pacey and I know him and his brothers wouldn't be doing this for fun... but he is right. The war needs to end. The war for land, the war for legacies that have been running for decades, the war to take something that isn't theirs.

Billionaires rock up to most remote places and want to tear down the nature around them just to replace it with a concrete city.

But for us, they want to build a ski slope and holiday village.

Orla is trying her best to put on a brave face, but every once in a while, I see her facade slip and the worry etches itself deep into her face.

My own worry teeters on the edge, pushing me that bit closer to be having a wobble but I remind myself he will be okay. They all will.

"I just want to say," Aspen speaks up and everyone turns in her direction, "this food is delicious," she licks her lips and reaches for her wine, holding it towards me. "To

Morgan," she chimes and everyone, including myself reaches for their glass and toasts the middle of the table.

"And..." Pacey sweeps in, his hand reaching for mine as he covers it, giving me a reassuring squeeze, "to family."

My smile grows as I look at him, holding my glass towards his before we all meet our glasses into the middle of the table.

"To family," everyone echoes.

Clearing dinner away, Aspen is on dish duty, Dixie is drying and I am scraping waste into the compost bin. Orla is tucked away in the back room with her sons, Lainey is napping in her travel crib and we're all trying to make conversation when in truth, all we want to know is what the hell is going on.

"It's going to be bad isn't it..." I trail off as I lean back and see if I can hear any movement.

"I am praying not..." Dixie sighs and places the dish cloth down as she rubs her bump.

"These Rivera boys are tough as nails... it'll probably all be resolved over a whiskey and a chat."

Dixie raises her brow and then shakes her head.

"This is the same group that killed your best friend," she averts her gaze to Aspen, "and shot your husband," she glowers at me, "not to mention shot *my* Tripp's horse and nearly crushed him to death."

We both stay silent and I roll my lips, glancing over at Aspen who lets out a heavy sigh.

"We can keep pretending that this isn't scary and that we aren't worried..." she trails off as she begins drying the dishes again, "but let's face facts... we're all fucking terrified."

My bottom lip trembles and I will not cry.

Pacey doesn't need me weak. Not now.

"I suggest we all spend the evening with them, reminding them how much they're loved and maybe we can all spare a thought for our mother-in-law. Her babies are putting themselves in the firing line to protect their homes... she has no one to turn to." Dixie's tone is assertive but not at all nasty. She's petrified. We all are. But she is pregnant and due to drop in the next couple of months, her worry is skyrocketing out of the world and it's mine and Aspen's job to be there for her like she is being there for us.

"We have to trust they have planned this out, none of them are stupid enough to make a rushed decision. I know Pacey would have delicately marked this out on paper, covering every possibility of something going wrong," and Aspen nods in agreement.

"Riggs will have sorted back up, they wouldn't go at this alone. Austin will be there too, Buck as well. Plus he has Marty," and Dixie twists her face towards Aspen too quickly which gives her away in an instant.

"Has he not told you?" Dixie blinks a few times and twists her body to face her.

"Told me what?" Aspen's voice is panicked, and it doesn't matter how much she tries to play it cool, her body betrays her.

"Marty is behind this... and the puppet master?" Dixie tosses the dish cloth over her shoulder and breaks her gaze away. "My dad."

My eyes widen and Aspen brings her hands to her mouth, her eyes widening as she lets Dixie's words sink in.

"What?" she whispers.

"Yeah, everything that happened, Harlow, Jorge..." she trails off, "it was all him," and Dixie struggles to get the last words out.

"Fuck," Aspen shakes her head in disbelief and I just stand a little awkward.

I heard what happened prior, but don't know enough to join into this conversation.

"I know," Dixie sighs and then she walks over to Aspen and gives her a hug. "I really do think everything will be okay, but we need to be realistic. Look how the wake went down after we were invited. It was all a play," she gives Aspen one last squeeze then steps back and my eyes bounce between the both of them. "But for what it is worth..." she trails off and looks over her shoulder, "Luke tipped them off about what's coming."

"Luke, as in my ex-Luke?"

"Yeah," she sighs, "he broke into Morgan and Pacey's looking for something..."

"That was your ex?" I stammer over my words and my throat thickens.

"Seems that way," Aspen mumbles and I don't know if she is shocked or annoyed. She lifts her eyes and lets them settle on Dixie. "Why wouldn't he tell me?" and I watch as her throat bobs.

"Probably just wanted to protect you..." she says softly, and I nod my head.

"Pacey kept it from me too, but I am a little different... I had no idea who these people were before I met him." Aspen sighs and Dixie gives her a sympathetic look.

"Don't be mad at him tonight... if anything," she pauses, "take it out on him tonight," her brows wiggle, "if you catch my drift, be mad at him tomorrow night when he is home and tucked up in your bed."

Aspen nods and then glances over her shoulder. "I need a wine, Morgs? Want one?"

"Abso-fucking-lutely," I throw my hands up and move across to where the bottle is and grab two fresh glasses.

"I'll just have a water," Dixie moans, rolling her eyes.

"Not long sweetie, and you can have a big ol' glass."

Dixie smiles, her hands cradling her bump.

"It's going so quick," she looks between me and Aspen, "can't believe Lainey is going to be a big sister soon."

"I can't believe I am going to have another baby to squish and love," Aspen goes soppy as I fill her glass up.

"You'll get your baby soon," Dixie says softly and Aspen just gives a heavy nod.

"It's just not our time yet."

"It will be, soon."

Aspen raises her hand, holding her glass up and we all move towards the living room and that's where we wait to be told what the plan of action is.

CHAPTER TWENTY-NINE
PACEY

Closing the sliding doors, I turn and look around the small room. Mom looks worried sick and I hate that we have made her feel like this.

"What's your plan?" she asks, her eyes passing over the three of us.

"We've been told—" Riggs says after an exasperated sigh.

"So, you don't know?" she cuts him off and he furrows his brows at her.

"Ma," I step in, and she glares at me and I back the fuck down.

"This is too big to not know everything."

"I agree ma, but we do know everything," Tripp backs us up and he is normally the quiet one.

She shakes her head from side to side and drops her gaze.

"We've been told that they'll attack at dusk," Riggs says, slightly rushed as he tries to get the words out.

"Where are they hitting first?"

"The ranch," I sweep in and run my hand around the back of my neck.

"Then where?"

"Then they'll take out mine and Pacey's homes, they admitted they torched the Boot," and I wish he had kept his mouth shut because the way my mom clutches at the thin material over her chest and silent sobs break through her has my heart obliterating in my chest.

"Ma," my voice cracks as I step forward and pull her into my arms, placing her head on my chest.

Tripp rolls his eyes and flips Riggs off who grunts in response.

He knows he fucked up because he has kept quiet.

"Ma," Tripp's voice floats through the room like the calm ocean. "Dixie's dad is behind this, so is Marty," and she lifts her head from my chest and looks at Tripp.

"What? Marty as in our Marty..."

"He is not *our* Marty," Riggs growls, his whole body tensing at our mom's words.

"How could he," a tear rolls down her cheek and I hate that she is crying over these worthless pieces of shits.

"Because he is a spineless cunt," Tripp answers her and Riggs nods in agreement.

"Exactly what he said," Riggs nods, pointing at our brother.

My lips twitch into a smile and it feels almost wrong to be smiling in a situation like this.

I comfort my ma until she is ready to push away from me. She paces the small room and me and my brothers exchange looks.

"So then boys..." her steps falter as she halts, "what's the plan and how can I help?"

We go through the plan another three times, letting

mum interject where she thinks we may need to be more cautious or where she thinks it may not work.

"Where do you want us?" she crosses her arms across her chest and stands a little taller.

"I have already agreed that you will all go to Nate and James', along with Titus and his family. They're our neighboring ranch," Riggs says, scrubbing his hand across his beard. "I don't want to risk them getting hurt."

"That's a smart plan."

"Nate told us they have a bunker that runs under their land. Not that I think it'll come to that but he is just being over cautious."

"Nothing wrong with that," she admits.

"Plus he is going to help us, getting us comms and he has pulled some strings to get some people here if needed."

"I like this Nate, make sure we invite him and his family for dinner," and Tripp chuckles.

"Let's just focus on the job in hand, ma," I scoff a laugh, and she nods, her own lips pressing into a smile.

"Fair," she winks, and Riggs claps his hands together.

"Right, so we go home, try and sleep and chill and whatever the fuck else you want to do..." his lips twitch, "we will meet tomorrow, ten a.m. at Sunny's. Then I've agreed she will go to Nate's too. Not getting her wrapped up in this shit show." I nod.

"Ma." He holds his hand out for our mom and she slips it into his palm as he pulls her in for a hug. "We've got this, I promise," he presses his lips to the top of her head. "It's time for us to end this war..." he murmurs before lifting his head. "Live by the ranch..."

"Die by the ranch," Tripp and I say together before we all huddle, protecting mom, if only for a moment.

"You boys are my purpose, my biggest blessing but also my biggest worry..."

"We will be safe ma," I say quietly.

"I know," her voice trembles. "But just in case I haven't said it in a while, I love you all."

And I don't know why, but that felt like the last time I would hear those words.

My chest aches but I ignore it.

I just needed to get through tonight.

CLOSING the door on my family and turning the lock, I let out a heavy exhale and it felt like I had been holding it for hours.

Morgan appears at the top of the stairs and I watch as she floats towards me. Silk pink nightdress, the lace trim sitting high on her thighs, her golden hair framed around her face.

"Fuck, you look like a god damn angel," raspiness wraps around my tone.

She hovers on the bottom step and I walk towards her, wrapping my arms around her waist as I pull her against my body.

"But I need you to ditch the wings and the halo tonight, Sunflower." I whisper as I lower my lips to hers and my heart jolts in my chest like a wild mustang galloping across the planes. Loving her was easy, thoughtless... like breathing.

"I can do that," she breaks the kiss and pulls my arms from her waist and lets her fingers trail to link through mine before she turns and leads me up the stairs.

My hand rounds the curve of her ass, my body laid over

her back as I tease my lips down her spine, tracing soft kisses.

"Oh god," her voice trembles as my cock slips in and out of her, her back arching as each stroke pushes her closer to the edge.

"I am besotted with you," I whisper my lips now dusting across her shoulder, her arousal coating my cock.

Her eyes meet mine over her shoulder and my heart slams against my chest.

"You close baby?" her pussy tightens around my cock, wetness gathering between our bodies and she moans a hum.

Pulling myself up, my fingers curl around her hips as I lift them a little higher and slide my cock to the tip, edging in and out of her.

"Pacey," her eyes roll in her head, her teeth sinking into her arm, her face still turned towards me.

Rolling forward, my cock slides deep inside of her and my once slow pace is now replaced with hard pounds into her.

"Yes," she moans, turning her face back around and my fingers tease up her back and wrap in the root of her hair as I tug her head back.

"Come for me wife, make a mess," I grit my teeth as I pump my own release inside of her just as her orgasm crashes through her.

I WISH I said I had slept, I was lucky if I managed an hour. Nerves were rip pooling in my stomach, anxiety laced my skin and my mouth was dry. I'm on my back, eyes pinned to the ceiling, hands resting on my stomach and a thin sheet over my legs. Slowly, I turn to look at my wife, to look at the love of my life who is still asleep next to me and I would do anything to stay here and sleep the day away but we both know that isn't an option.

Today was the day.

Rolling over, I wrap my arm over her body and drag her towards me as I bury my face in her neck and inhale her scent.

"I love you, Morgan Rivera," I whisper against her skin before I dust a kiss on her neck, trailing them to her ear, her cheek and finally pressing my lips against her temple. Her eyes flutter and all I can do is watch her with intent like it is the last time I will ever see her pretty face. My mind drifts and I find myself wondering what I would see in my last seven minutes and I know it's her.

"Hey," her voice croaks as she snuggles into me and I hold her tightly against my body.

"I didn't want to wake you," I admit placing kisses against her delicate skin, my fingers trailing up and down her bare skin.

"I'm glad you did," she murmurs, "I would have been really sad if you sneaked out of our bed Mr Rivera without saying a proper *see ya later*." Her ass rolls over my already hard dick and I moan in her ear, nipping at her lobe.

"You're a bad girl," I whisper against her ear, my fingers skating up the side of her thigh, teasing them under her silk nightie.

"You make me bad, Sheriff," she teases and my hand skims down and dips under her leg as I lift it, her back to my front.

"I suppose I can spare a few more minutes," I groan, a wicked smile crossing my lips, my hand tugging my boxers down and lining my cock up at her opening, I slip inside of her wet cunt in one roll of my hips and her erotic moans make my skin burst into goosebumps.

"Oh god," her arm lifts, her hand cupping behind my head as she pulls my lips towards her, our tongue dancing as I fuck her slow, pushing us both to our orgasm and suddenly, I am terrified of losing her.

SHE FOLLOWS me downstairs and out onto the decked porch, the sun sitting high in the dusty blue skies, the soft chirp of the birds in the distance, the sweet smell that surrounds the air and I welcome the warm breeze that wraps around our bodies.

I hate that I am leaving her.

"Okay, so you know the plan, yes?" I turn to look at her as I hold my hat between my fingertips and let it hang in front of me and she gives me a nod. She is dressed back in her pink silk nightie, her hair messy from this morning, the evidence of the night before surrounding her.

"Dressed and straight over to Nate's."

"That's the one baby," she steps towards me and places her hand on my chest, her spare hand reaching up as she places my hat on her head and my heart slams against my chest.

"Promise to come home to me," her voice is a whisper in the summer wind.

I swallow and my throat bobs as I try and rid the thickness that coats it.

"Promise you will be safe," her fingertips curl and pinch my dark gray tee as she clings onto me, my heart racing in my chest.

"I promise," my voice cracks and I hate that I have lied because I have no idea whether I will make it home.

We're going into this with no idea what is going to happen.

They're out for blood.

"I love you Pacey," she blinks and a tear escapes, trailing down her pretty face. My thumb catching her tear.

"I love you Sunflower," I tilt her face up, her lips parting as she waits for me to kiss her. Her breaths are short and tremble in her intake, another tear slips and my heart aches in my chest. "You're my wildest forever, my wildest dreams and my wildest love."

"Why does this feel like a goodbye?" she breathes against my lips.

"There are no such things as goodbyes," I dust my lips over hers, squeezing my eyes shut as my own tears escape, "only see you laters." My lips finally touch hers as I kiss her like it's the last time because honestly, it feels like I will never kiss her again.

Stepping back, she lifts my hat from her head and holds it out for me to take. I nod, gently pulling it from her fingertips as I place it on my head.

"See you later then," she whispers.

"See you later then," I choke and turn on my heel, taking one last look at the sky before I see Dusty walking out of the stables.

"Ready sheriff?" he asks as I walk down the steps and take my horse from him.

"Ready as I'll ever be," I admit, footing the stirrup as I climb onto the back of Chase.

He follows suit and kicks his horse on, and I look over my shoulder at my wife, the most beautiful smile on her face and my chest caves, aching as I reluctantly pull my eyes away and leave her behind on the porch, not knowing if that was the last time I would ever see her.

And that breaks my fucking heart.

CHAPTER THIRTY
PACEY

Once we knew Sunny and the wives were with mom at Nate's, we wait in my office for Nate, Titus, Austin, Xavier and Buck to meet us. I have no idea what the city boys will do but we're grateful that they stepped up to help.

I am antsy, my nerves are shot and my fingernails are bit to shit but we have this plan executed down to a tee. I have police sitting and waiting for my call, and I am hoping it will be dealt with cleanly.

This is nothing more than greed and it was all to do with Dixie's dad.

He was the number on Marty's phone, Nate confirmed that. He chose greed over his daughter and that's what guts us the most and I am sure Dixie feels the weight of his choices too, but, like we reminded her, and she reminded us, we're her family. She never needed anyone else.

Riggs' head spins when we hear the sound of a car approaching followed by two horses. Buck continues forward and tilts his head, Austin pulling his horse to a halt.

"Hello boys," his voice is low as his eyes trail between the four of us.

"You okay Aust?" I ask and he nods, but stays quiet.

"It'll be okay," Riggs tries to reassure him. The car door opens and closes and Nate, Xavier and Titus walk towards us.

"I have called a few people, I have them on standby. I don't think we'll need them but just in case..." Xavier nods.

"Also," Nate slips in, "I have managed to get into the suits computer systems," he coughs and raises a brow no doubt because he is what we would class as a suit, "and I have managed to remove any document that was ever signed for land in Lovelock Bay and Blossom Cove," he smiles, "plus I have completely fried their security so there is no more getting into that."

"Thank you, Nate," I say politely.

"No need to thank me, this is our home now too and we don't want to see it be sold off in pieces just to have the beauty taken away."

"We will be close, Riggs," Titus tosses up ear pieces and a phone, "keep that on you, and put them in, we can track you and you can call us if you need us."

"Thanks," he grumbles before slipping it into the saddle bag.

Their eyes fall to our horses, and I see the slow smirks that tease at their lips.

"They're some good guns," Xavier scoffs.

"Need to be prepared," I answer, my horse stomping his foot.

"We will let you boys get on, be safe," Xavier gives a firm nod and the three of them turn around and climb back into the car, slowly pulling off and disappearing.

Closing my eyes for a second, and all I see is her face.

The low sun feels warm on my skin and I know it's getting close.

"Are we ready?" Riggs asks and I roll my head forward and give a heavy nod. "Then let's ride," he kicks on his horse and leads us towards the ranch.

We need to be ready, and we know that's their first point of attack.

Our home.

My dad's final resting place.

Our legacy.

And we will not go down without a fight.

We're in place, tucked behind the bunk house.

"No sign as of yet," Nate says over the comms and I try and steady my breathing. Our guns are loaded and in our hands, and we know that is not going to be a simple hand shake and goodbyes.

They want what is ours.

Austin walks around and crouches down beside me.

"Horses are tied up around the back," his voice is low.

"Just to confirm Riggs, all the horses are away, and the cattle are in the top field."

"Yes," he nods, looking across to the glowing fences from the nightlights.

"Do you think we should have kept some of the cowboys back?" Tripp whispers and Riggs shakes his head.

"I made a call to keep them with the cattle. We have enough of us here to fight these assholes off."

"What if they have an army?" I whisper as my eyes are locked forward.

"Then we fight an army," Riggs admits.

Nerves cripple me inside out and my palms begin to sweat.

Memories flood me from the shoot-out at the wake and I am terrified of getting hurt.

But this is our home, and we will not let it go without a fight.

"Trucks approaching," we hear in our ears and Buck shuffles forward.

"Trucks?" Austin repeats. "Did he say trucks?"

"Calm it," Riggs snaps at Austin and he cowers down. "We're all stressed, I don't need you panicking now Aust."

Austin nods and slips behind his dad.

"Go into the stables Austin, keep your head down," Riggs orders and Austin does as he asks, moving to the back of where the horses are.

The sound of the engines soon fills the quiet void and my heart is banging in my chest, blood pumping in my ears and I let my eyes shut for just a moment and remember why we are doing this.

"Coming through the gate now," and it's not long before we can see the headlights in the distance pulling up the winding dirt road.

"Be ready boys," Riggs says quietly as he lifts the eye piece of his gun up, the handle resting against his shoulder.

I follow suit, and that's when Buck, Austin and Tripp move around the other side of the bunk house.

"They're in," is all we hear and my mind silences, shutting down every intrusive thought that comes in and all I care about is ending this tonight.

The engines cut, and the sound of boots hitting the gravel echo through the empty ranch.

We left the TV on, the radio humming and the lights turned down low so the ranch didn't look empty as such.

"Move out boys," I hear the same voice that was on the video and my blood boils. Leaning around the bunk house, I set eyes on him. Cigarette in hand, curly brown hair and tall. Marty is following behind him like a puppy dog and I hear the rumbling growl of Riggs beside me.

"Steady," I whisper, and I hear Tripp move slightly and watch as he slips back into the darkness only to give us a sign that he is tucked down the side of the house.

"Do you understand how hard it is to not pull this fucking trigger?" his voice is tight.

"Yes, because I feel exactly the same."

"Six on the ground, road is empty, no cars approaching," Nate says down the earpiece and relief swarms me.

I clock the two suited guys who walk around the large space in front of our home before they walk towards Dixie's dad and begin speaking.

"Those are the two that came up to me a few months back," I admit, my fingertip teasing the trigger.

"Don't," Riggs orders.

A laugh barrels through the night when I see Marty and some random guy light a clothed covered bottle and throw it through the windows of the ranch and the fire spreads quickly as another gets launched.

"Fuck," I swallow, sweat beading on my brow. "Why are we not shooting?"

"Because if we started shooting, they would know we knew what was coming. This way, they have no clue that we're here. Fucking hold it," Riggs talks into the comms so everyone can hear him.

Marty turns and looks in our direction and I swear I stop breathing.

I know he can't see us but still I am nervous as hell. Riggs holds his arm out in front of me as if trying to protect me.

Dixie's dad follows behind Marty, whispers something and Marty nods before he gives the firebomb to him. Marty wanders off slightly and then stumbles when he watches what he does.

"Light it up baby," a menacing laugh surrounds us as he throws the next bottle into the stables.

"What are you doing!?" Marty screams at Dixie's dad. "That wasn't part of the plan," he storms towards where the stables begin to light up and that's when he clocks us, his eyes widening but he doesn't have a chance to react.

"And neither was this," Dixie's dad draws his gun and shoots Marty between the eyes.

We watch as he falls to the floor and all Dixie's dad does is toss his cigarette onto his body as if he is nothing but trash.

"Fuck!" Riggs growls and that's when everything blurs.

The sound of the horses whinnying and neighing pulls my focus and as I go to move to the back of the stalls, the doors fly open and the horses stampede out and run for the fields.

Austin catches my attention as he appears from the stables and gives us a nod.

Dixie's dad whistles as he rounds up his minions before they load into the truck and begin to pull away.

"Now," Riggs bellows and we scramble around the back, pulling ourselves onto our horses as we kick on and follow their dirt tracks.

"Is this what you meant when you said you wanted to be an old school cowboy, Sheriff?" Riggs calls out as we track their trucks, Tripp catching us up and Buck and Austin behind us with Dusty snaking off to the left. My brows furrow but I trust he is sticking to the plan.

"Not quite," I snap, reaching for my gun as Riggs snaps

his shotgun up, aiming it towards the back of the truck before he pulls the trigger.

The bullet hits the back windscreen, shattering it which causes one of the trucks to veer off.

"Fire department are on their way," Nate's voice fills my ears and my heart drums in my chest as I take one last look at our home as it glows. Pulling my eyes forward, my heart races a little quicker matching the sound of Chase's hooves beating the ground.

The truck pulls onto the bank and Riggs goes for that one but tells me and Tripp to keep going. Buck falls back with Riggs but Austin keeps up beside us.

Gun shots echo and I just pray that it was Riggs that pulled the trigger. I daren't look back. I just silently pray that it wasn't one of ours.

We follow the other truck as it begins to slow at Crooked Creek.

Pulling the horses back, I hold my gun in place and so does Tripp and Austin.

I see the aubergine boots hit the sidestep before I see him and my stomach twists.

"Now, now, boys," he says, holding his hands up and stepping towards us. I hold my gun up, pointing it at him when another three men step out and my blood runs cold. There should only be six on the ground. Six!?

Lucian, Wallen and Kelcie.

"The fuck," and that has my attention slipping for just a moment as my eyes burn into them.

"Have you been keeping my sheriff badge warm Rivera?" Kelcie laughs and my skin crawls. I fucking hated him.

"Fuck off Kelcie."

"Ooo big man now," he rolls his eyes and then pulls a gun on me as I hold my gun on him.

"Drop it," I order, and he just laughs, Clay's brother shaking his head.

"How long did you cry baby Rivera when daddy died?" and I ignore him knowing he is only doing it to get a rise from me and I will not bite today.

Dixie's dad laughs, sparking another fag and taking a long drag.

"How about you big boy?" His attention turns to Austin, "How much did you weep when we shot your girlfriend?" and Austin has a harder time controlling his temper.

Dixie's dad walks towards me slowly but bypasses me and goes for Tripp.

"And you," his brows raise, "you're the one that took my daughter from Lucian," he snarls, dropping his gaze from Tripp for a moment and rolling his cigarette between his fingers, the orange glow catching my attention. "But don't worry, cos whilst you're here, chasing us... they're all in the back of a van, gagged and bound with that diamond you stole."

Tripp narrows his gaze.

But I am still stuck on what he said.

He is lying to you.

"Fuck you," Tripp spits on him and then presses the gun into his chest.

"Do it," her dad goads, hovering the cigarette dangerously close to his horse.

The sound of a gun being loaded has my eyes darting back to the three men, all three of their barrels are pointing on me.

The blood pumps around my body and I know if I move an inch, I'll have bullets sunk beneath my skin.

"Light it up," he shouts as two of the men drop their guns and move towards Aspen and Riggs' home.

It's now or never.

I needed to make a move or die trying.

Tripp whistles which gains the attention of Kelcie, who's gun is still pointed at me and I find myself pulling on Chase's reins and circling around the back of Tripp's horse as I go to hover my hand over his horse's rear.

Dixie's dad catches me, and he pulls a gun from his belt, shooting and grazing a bullet against my shoulder and I hiss as it burns.

I look at Austin and his eyes are wide as the bullet sinks beneath his skin and buries into his shoulder.

He screams and as he distracts everyone, I slap the horse's rear with my reins and yell, "C'mon" and Tripp's horse rears up just as I trot back to where he stands and aim the gun and fire.

Everything moves in slow motion as I watch the bullet spin towards Dixie's dad before it lodges itself in the back of his head just as Travis comes down, hooves hitting his face and head and he falls to the floor.

"Fuck," Tripp growls as he kicks his horse on to follow them down to Riggs' house and I turn my horse to Austin, my eyes scanning him.

"You okay?" my voice is laced with panic and he nods before smiling.

"Didn't even hurt," he winks as the blood seeps into his tee sleeve.

"Hmm, I think that might be shock," I laugh when I hear the sound of a gun being cocked and that's when those seven minutes flash before my eyes and end on the sound of a gunshot.

MORGAN

Between us all, we've paced every inch of this home. Glancing at the time, my heart is in my throat.

We have had no word from Nate to let us know that everything is okay and he said he would keep us updated.

Orla has prayed continuously; Dixie is trying her best to remain calm for Lainey's sake and Aspen hasn't moved from the window for the last hour.

The sound of tires crunching has me running for the front door.

"It's their trucks, they're all getting out," Aspen says as I pull the door open and that's when I see him.

Running towards me, ash on his face, sweat shimmering against his skin, dried blood on his hands and clothes, but in that moment, nothing matters.

I run for him, throwing myself against his body as he holds me.

Choked sobs make my body tremble, tears streaming down my face as he holds onto me. One hand around my back, the other around the back of my neck.

"You kept your promise."

"Always Sunflower, always," he rasps before I pull my head from his chest and kiss him, my hands holding his face.

"I love you, Pacey."

"I love you more," he whispers.

"Not possible," my words brush against his lips.

"I love you forever Sunflower, it's me and you."

"Me and you," I say back, his fingers dusting my hair from my face.

"Always," he smiles, his eyes falling to my lips.

"Forever," I whisper back before he kisses me one last time.

PACEY

We move into the living room, the sound of a fire crackling, our wives all sat near, ma in the corner with a whiskey and my eyes bounce around the room.

"It's over," I sigh, tapping my finger against my own whiskey glass, Morgan snuggling into my chest and my eyes skate over to my brothers, Austin included in that. Riggs fixed him up but we made him promise that once he had let his family know he was okay, that he would go to the hospital.

The gun shot that still echoes in my ears was the reason we walked away.

Kelcie and Wallen were ready to pull the trigger, Lucian holding his gun at Tripp but Riggs beat them to it and I still don't know how he did it.

He claims the police were there and I just didn't notice them but I didn't believe him. Distraction maybe? The sounds of gravel shifting and branches snapping and then the gun was fired, ending it once and for all.

He saved our lives.

He was right all those weeks ago in the bunkhouse when he thought he knew who was behind it. I never asked how he knew, just took his word.

"It's over," Riggs nods, bringing his glass to his lips and takes a mouthful.

"You won the war my boys," Ma says as she glances at the three of us.

"We won the war," I mutter as I curl my arm around Morgan and hold her tightly.

I didn't think we would come back alive from tonight, but here we are, and I am counting every single blessing.

Slicing my eyes to Riggs, he gives a heavy nod.

"Live by the ranch…" he trails off.

"Die by the ranch," the rest of us finished his sentence before we all raised a glass.

EPILOGUE
MORGAN

FIVE YEARS LATER

Peace radiates over Lovelock Bay and Blossom Cove; sure, there will always be threats, but the main one is diminished. Kelcie, Lucian and Wallen are buried in the ground.

The suits put behind bars and Dixie's dad and Marty, join the others six feet under.

The war was won and it was won by The Riveras.

All is fair in love and war, and that was the truth.

At least for all of us anyway.

Standing in the sunflower field, my fingers dust across the petals. A warmth radiates through my body and that's how I know I made the right choice.

A year after everything happened, we made the decision to sell the cattle. I knew I wanted more from the ranch and my pops' legacy, and I knew he deserved more than the cattle ranch. Pacey stood by my side every step of the way, and with the help of him and our family, Pops Ranch was born.

For a young girl who grew up here, in the beauty that is my home, I wanted to give children that same feeling.

I had tossed the idea around for a fair while and once I had my mind settled, I told Pacey my dreams and of course, he helped me soar with them.

Our summer camp had been running for a little over three years now and we were booked two years in advanced.

I truly thought me and kids would never work, but here I am, living proof that your dreams will always find you.

I believe my pops knew what I needed and that's why he was so against the ranch being sold.

"Mama," I hear her voice and spin to see her running towards me, curly blonde hair pinned back with a dusty blue bow, hazel eyes and apple cheeks, dressed in dirty denim overalls and a white tee.

"Hey baby girl," I crouch down and pick her up, holding her close to me.

"Me and daddy made lunch," she says sweetly, her hands on my cheeks.

"Did you now?" I smile warmly at her and she nods.

"Daddy said my grilled cheese is better than yours," and she giggles as she looks over her shoulder and teases her daddy.

"I don't think I did say that now did I, Jorgie?"

She shrugs her shoulders, a cheeky grin on her face.

"Come on, let's get inside, your cousins will be here soon," I place a kiss on her cheek and set her down.

She runs off towards the gate and I close the steps between me and him.

"We made it," I sigh on a blissful note.

"We did baby," his arms tucks over my shoulder as we

walk down to the house, my head on his shoulder and I have never felt more content than I do now.

PACEY

I watch on as the family all sit in the living room, the kids playing on the floor.

"Look how happy ma is," I say, leaning against the doorframe as Riggs swigs a mouthful of beer.

"I know," I nod as I look forward.

Ma is sitting on the floor, Megan—Dixie and Tripp's daughter—on her lap. Jorgie plays with Lainey and Aspen sits in Gerry's armchair, their son, Bodhi in her arms as she sings him a sweet lullaby and Tripp and Dixie sit on the sofa, his hand on her bump. Dusty and Marsha stand in the corner, their kids running out front and somehow we have become this perfect family.

Austin is in the kitchen talking to Buck and Blue and Sunny has just walked through the door with bags of shopping.

"We made it brother," Riggs says as he pats me on the back and hands me a beer.

"We made it," I nod, taking a mouthful and just appreciating for a second what we have right in front of us and I know dad would be looking down on us, proud as anything for us saving our legacy.

Our ranches still stand and when the time is right, all will be handed down to our children.

This will forever be our home, and our motto will be etched on our graves in years to come.

'Live by the ranch, die by the ranch.'

"Hey! Sorry we're late," Nate's voice sweeps through the room and I turn, smiling as I welcome them all into our home.

They all disperse into different rooms, and we spend the remainder of the day entertaining.

Sitting on the decked porch, the stars twinkle in the night sky and I feel at peace.

"How did we get so lucky?" her voice pulls at me as her hand slips over my shoulder as she sits beside me.

"No luck about it baby," I tease as I kiss her. "We were always going to get this life."

She smiles.

"I love you."

"I love you more."

"Sunflower..." I raise a brow, and she giggles.

"Always..."

"Forever."

And her lips finally find mine as I kiss her like the very first time, and I knew, I had finally found a home for my heart.

She was my wildest forever, my wildest dreams and my wildest love.

This right here was what life was about.

Don't waste a single second wanting more when everything you need is within reach.

Her head lands on my shoulder and we sit and stargaze, talking about our future and how all our dreams had come true.

I was the richest man alive.

The End

ACKNOWLEDGMENTS

And just like that, this is it... The end of the Lovelock Bay series.

Just over a year since I penned the first chapter and these characters consumed me wholly. I am sad to say goodbye to my cowboys, but it doesn't mean it's the end. I mean, with my books, is it ever the end?

I hope you all love Pacey and Morgan. They were so loud and once I started, I couldn't stop. I fell head over heels in love with them.

Firstly, thank you to you, my readers, without you, there would be no me.

Lea, my editor, once again, thank you for doing such an awesome job and being as amazing as always. Would be lost without you.

Robyn, my otter, thank you for everything you do. I am always so grateful for you and your friendship. I couldn't imagine not having you here. Thank you for letting me slide into your DM's all those years ago 🤍

Leanne, thank you for all of your help today and always. You will never know how much I appreciate you.

Leila and Lyndsey, thank you for being my emotional support through this book, the late-night sprints, the long day sprints and just being there when needed, I appreciate your friendship so much.

My husband, like I always say, there would be no Ashlee Rose without you, thank you for pushing me to continue, thank you for always being my shoulder to cry on, my biggest fan and my best friend. I love you, always & forever.

Lastly, again, my readers... Thank you... thank you.

www.ingramcontent.com/pod-product-compliance
Lightning Source LLC
Chambersburg PA
CBHW031737180726
48283CB00005B/1542